PRAISE FOR
Bernard Cornwell and his
Richard Sharpe series

"The direct heir to Patrick O'Brian."   —*The Economist*

"Cornwell's cinematically detailed battle pieces [are] literal tours de force."
—Michael Dirda, *Washington Post*

"Page-turners [that] fan clubs all over the world are devoted to."
—*Wall Street Journal*

"Tom Clancy could pick up a pointer or two from Bernard Cornwell. . . . Cornwell's blending of the fictional Sharpe with historical figures and actual battles gives the narrative a stunning sense of realism. . . . If only all history lessons could be as vibrant."
—*San Francisco Chronicle*

"Presents to the contemporary reader an important part of history that Americans know little about."   —*Los Angeles Times*

"Excellently entertaining. If you love historical drama . . . then look no further."
—*Boston Globe*

"Prepare to have your buckles swashed."   —*People* magazine

About the Author

MAJOR MARK ADKIN served in the British Army and is the author of several books on military history. He lives in Bedford, England.

THE SHARPE NOVELS (IN CHRONOLOGICAL ORDER)

* Published by HarperCollinsPublishers

THE SHARPE COMPANION

A historical and military guide
to Bernard Cornwell's
Sharpe novels 1777–1808

The Early Years

MARK ADKIN

Perennial
An Imprint of HarperCollins*Publishers*

Contents

List of Plates

List of Maps, Sketches and Diagrams

MAPS

SKETCHES

DIAGRAMS

Symbols used on Maps

Infantry		British Allies	Enemy
	Company	■	▭
	Batttalion	■	▭
	Skirmishers	●	
	Unspecified	▬	▭
Cavalry			
	Squadron	◨	▱
	Regiment	◨	▱
	Unspecified	◨	▱
Artillery			
	Battery (Guns)	╫	╫
	Battery (Mortars)	╫	
Ships		●	◗
Others			
	Camp	△△△	
	Site of Battle	✕	
	Sharpe	Ⓢ	

Why a Sharpe Companion?

The Sharpe Companion The Early Years covers the period from Sharpe's birth in 1777 until he transferred, as a disgruntled quartermaster, and still only a second lieutenant, from the 1st Battalion 95th Rifles to the 2nd Battalion based at Hythe in May 1808. (It was shortly after this that Sharpe went with the 2/95th to Portugal, the first of his Peninsular exploits. The first two chapters provide background on Sharpe's early life and the three regiments in which he served up to the age of thirty, while the five remaining chapters each relate to his activities in a specific novel. In focusing on Sharpe's first thirty years, I have been able to explore the details of his boyhood, the London in which he lived, and the conditions he endured as a recruit marching in the ranks of the 33rd Foot, as an ensign in the 74th and then, as a dispirited officer bent on quitting the army, in the 95th. The history of how each regiment developed, fought, expanded, contracted, changed its title until more modern times is also explored. Finally, a timeline has been included that sets out the dates of the highlights of Sharpe's life alongside some of the major historical events of the period. Throughout, the text is enhanced by maps, illustrations, boxes and margin notes, many anecdotal, which add interest and flavour to the main meal.

Richard Sharpe is a fascinating hero; his escapades are bewildering in their variety and always bloody in their execution – but they are not impossible. In writing this book

I have dissected the battles he fought in, pored over maps to plot his movements and locate the places he visited. Due to Bernard Cornwell's great skill at ensuring Sharpe's activities have accurate historical backgrounds I have never had any real difficulty in putting dates, even times, as well as locations to what Sharpe did.

This book can be used in a variety of ways. It can be read with equal enjoyment and value either before or after reading a Sharpe novel. If before, it will surely whet the reader's appetite for his adventures; if after, it will provide an understanding of the significance, in military terms, of what he did or achieved. It may also encourage the reader to dig more deeply into the immensely exciting world of Napoleonic naval and military history. *The Sharpe Companion – The Early Years* can be read from cover to cover, or dipped into at will; chapters can be read out of sequence, or it can be used as a work of reference for explanation or elaboration of what Sharpe was doing and why. This work, like the first book, is about 80 per cent fact and 20 per cent fiction. To enable the reader to tell one from the other, *fictional names of people, ships and places are written in italics*. The one exception to this rule is Sharpe himself.

Chapters 3 to 7 have the same title as the corresponding novels. Each commences with a brief synopsis of what the Sharpe book contained, a hint of what he did, what battles he may have participated in, what special missions he may have undertaken, and an indication of what was happening in the campaign or war at that time. This serves to remind those who may have forgotten what the story was about or to give those who have not read it a basic understanding of the events to be discussed. The main text explains the background to Sharpe's activities in the context of the campaign, describes their significance and introduces real people who influenced Sharpe directly or indirectly. In other words, it superimposes Sharpe's fictional undertakings, missions and tasks on what was really happening. Where a major battle takes place, the *Companion* gives an insight into the opposing commanders' plans and problems, highlights of the main events, and shows how Sharpe participated.

Maps play a key role in understanding what was happening – for real and for Sharpe. His movements, marches, battles and adventures are depicted on them. All chapters have at least two. The first is a campaign map that shows Sharpe's locations, movements and routes superimposed on what was happening in the real campaign. All his activities are highlighted with an 'S', together with suitable notes of explanation. The second is usually a battle map that depicts the actual fighting, and how Sharpe was involved.

Finally, there is the glossary, where abbreviations have been used extensively to save space. The glossary gives quick access to additional information on a person or place, event or military term. It includes nearly all the characters featured in the novels or the *Companion* (fictional and factual). In some cases only one line is needed, while in others a full biography is required. All entries covering fictional personalities also indicate the novel(s) in which they feature.

I want to reiterate my thanks to Bernard Cornwell for agreeing to my writing the *Companion* and for his support for a project that has been immensely rewarding for me. My hope is that Sharpe enthusiasts will find this book useful and stimulating. Continue reading Bernard's absorbing books – and at the same time reach for a *Companion*.

THE SHARPE
COMPANION

The Early Years

1

Sharpe

GENERAL

BY THE TIME HE WAS THIRTY in 1807 Richard Sharpe had, seemingly, done exceptionally well in the army. He had been brought up, literally, in the London gutters. When he enlisted he was a filthy, thin, half-starved, illiterate youth – still under sixteen. He was also a liar, a thief and on the run from the law for two murders; there would be no escaping the gibbet and the hangman's noose if caught. Fourteen years later, he was unrecognisable as the same person. Not only was he physically large – 6 feet 1 inch tall, lean, muscular and weighing twelve stone – but, most unbelievable of all, he was a commissioned army officer.

As a second lieutenant in the 95th Rifles, an elite fighting force, Sharpe wore their distinctive, stylish and much admired dark green uniform; he had a crimson sash around his waist and a sword hung at his belt. But on that sunny morning in late July 1807 Sharpe was a very, very unhappy man. He was back in London intent on selling his commission, quitting the army – in fact, as his regiment knew nothing of his doings, he was intent on deserting. For an officer to desert was unthinkable, virtually unique. But Sharpe hated the army. Still deeply depressed by the loss of his mistress, *Lady Grace*, and their baby son a year earlier, he hated his job as quartermaster and he faced being left behind as his battalion embarked for Denmark. He had no friends, his fellow officers despised him and he was disastrously in debt. The combination of circumstances had mentally crushed him.

Nevertheless, fourteen years in the army had made Sharpe into a professional killer of considerable experience and ruthlessness. As he walked down Eastcheap towards the Army Agent's office, he had already killed thirty-one men. Unable to sell his commission, he was fortuitously given another special operations mission in Denmark and, within the space of five weeks, was to put another nine men in their graves prematurely, including one civilian.

Forty was an impressive score even for a soldier who had participated in six battles (including one at sea – Trafalgar), four sieges, and been involved in four special operations. These were the known kills, the ones where it is certain his victim died at the time. There is no way of counting those he wounded who later died from their injuries. For example, at Trafalgar he had blasted the French crew of the *Revenant* with a seven-barrelled Nock gun as he led a boarding party of marines – how many died then is impossible to know. Sharpe had used the musket, the pistol, the knife, the bayonet, the spear and the sword to despatch his opponents. He had also bludgeoned men to death; he had drowned one, forced one into a raging fire and broken a man's neck with his bare hands. Of the forty, he had killed two as a youth of fifteen, seven while a private soldier, six on virtually his last day as a sergeant and twenty-five as an officer. In every case except one, they had met their death in hand-to-hand combat or at so close a range as to be almost in touching distance of their killer.

This brutal life had left its mark on the man. Mentally, it had given him a thick outer shell of callousness, immunity from conscience in killing. He had all the outward attributes and skills of a professional hit man. The only people who could seemingly penetrate the hard, unyielding exterior were beautiful women or small children. We will never know how many casual encounters Sharpe had, but we can be certain that by thirty he had been emotionally involved with seven women. When in love or infatuated, Sharpe became a much softer, caring, more human individual. Physically, he was scarred for life, having received seven wounds. He had been stabbed in the side, ribs, and hip, slashed on the left shoulder, while his left cheek had been sliced open, leaving a long dark scar. Twice he had escaped death by an inch when his head had been hit glancing blows. But it was his back that was the real mess. Two hundred and two lashes had flayed the flesh beyond recovery. The skin had grown again but it was twisted, taut, mangled, a livid mixture of raised mauve and dark brown weals that contrasted starkly with the white of his sides and buttocks. It was not an attractive sight.

Sharpe had been pulled back from the brink of certain personal disaster by his inability to sell his commission and General Baird giving him a mission that excused his un-authorised absence from his duties at Brabourne Lees. Never-theless, he was still seriously disgruntled when he stepped ashore at Yarmouth a few weeks later at the end of October 1807. As we now know, he still had at least another nine years of fighting ahead of him. They would take him to most battlefields in the Iberian Peninsula, and to history's famous fight at Waterloo, where the two military giants of the age, Napoleon and Wellington, met for the first and last time. As a middle-aged man he would take his sword as far afield as South America. But early 1808 is a suitable time to review this extraordinary soldier's career, to compare his experiences with others of his generation and to try to discover just how different – if indeed it was that different – his life had been from his contemporaries. His early life up to the age of thirty can be conveniently divided into four phases – as a boy, as a private, as a sergeant and as an officer.

THE BOY – A SQUALID LIFE (1777–93)

To be born of poor parents in London in the eighteenth century was to have drawn one of this life's particularly short straws. The city was overpopulated (at just under a million) and out-of-control house building, combined with a lack of

ATTACK ON A GIN
DISTILLERY
Many who joined the
rampaging mobs in
1780 were looking for
liquor rather than
papists; for them the
destruction of
Langdale's Distillery
was the highlight of
the Gordon Riots.
Hundreds descended
on the Catholic-
owned gin factory in
Holborn, which was
quickly broken open
and set alight. The
mob risked their lives
by dashing through
the inferno to the
cellars armed with
pails, jugs – even a
trough. They emerged
with blackened faces,
singed hair and red
eyes, carrying
overflowing containers
or untapped casks of
gin. Soon the heat
burst the stills and
fountains of raw spirit
gushed along the
gutters and over the
cobbles. People knelt to
gulp it down until they
collapsed. A
detachment of the
Northumberland
Militia arrived and
opened fire on
pickpockets rifling the
bodies strewn around
the street. Twenty
people, including
several women, never
got up – they had drunk
themselves to death.
One hopes that
Sharpe's mother did
not die in such
degrading
circumstances!

sanitation, provided a breeding ground for bacteria, disease and crime. Epidemics, infections, food shortages and violence led to an extraordinarily high death rate. In 1775, two years before Sharpe was born, more than eight hundred deaths recorded in the 'Bills of Mortality' were simply attributed to 'Teeth'. The connection between personal hygiene and good health was not understood. There was a fear of fresh air. It was thought to carry diseases like consumption, so windows were kept tightly shut at all times. As buildings were taxed on the number of windows, landlords tended to seal them off – with unpleasant results for the occupants.

There was a seasonal pattern to death. In summer the flies carried bacteria so diarrhoea and dysentery did most damage. In winter it was tuberculosis, influenza and typhus. Sanitation was unheard of; water was untreated and raw sewage ran in open drains. An amazing variety of filth slopped down the cobbled streets. London was filled with the smell of wet horses and their waste material. It was common practice for chamber pots to be emptied out on to the street, so that cesspools of human waste collected in puddles. Dead animals (dogs, cats, rats and even horses) lay where they fell and were left to decay in the open, along with the rest of the garbage. C. P. Moritz, a German visitor to England, wrote: 'Nothing in London makes a more detestable sight than the butcher's stalls, especially in the neighbourhood of the Tower. The guts and other refuse are all thrown on the street and set up an unbearable stink.' The frequent rain liquefied the dirt and animal manure. With the heavy wheels of carriages and horse-drawn carts constantly clattering through the streets it was a fortunate and agile man who managed to avoid being drenched by the putrid muck.

Such was the London into which Sharpe was born on 23 June 1777 in a house behind Howick Place, Westminster, near its junction with Artillery Row. If you drew a triangle between St James's Park tube station, Westminster Cathedral and the Channel 4 television studios, Sharpe's birthplace would be almost precisely in the centre. His mother, he freely admitted, was a whore. Neither she nor Sharpe had any idea who his father might have been. He was a backstreet bastard who, like thousands of other children born into similar circumstances, was almost certainly destined for a short, squalid life. He grew up engulfed by dirt, disease and drunkenness. As a young lad he would be compelled to depend for survival on his wits, on his ability to cheat, to lie and to steal. By accident of birth he had been condemned to a future that could be as short as a few weeks or, if lucky, perhaps a dozen or more years. The causes of his likely premature death were easily identifiable: malnutrition, sickness, violence or the gallows – singly or in combination.

In June 1780 mobs raged through the streets of London. 'Down with Popery! Death to Popery!' was the cry from thousands of throats. Lord George Gordon, a fanatical anti-papist, had whipped up sentiment to abolish the Toleration Act of 1778, which had removed some legal constraints imposed on Roman Catholics. When his petition to parliament was rejected, the outraged crowds ('upwards of 50,000 true Protestants') surged into Parliament Square to be confronted by a battalion of foot guards who, at the point of their bayonets, forced a passage for the Members to escape. Frustrated by the troops, the rioters began an orgy of destruction and violence. Catholic chapels belonging to foreign embassies were set on fire, as were the houses of several prominent politicians, magistrates, and even that of Lord Chief Justice Mansfield in Bloomsbury Square. Newgate Gaol was smashed open, releasing scores of bewildered but delighted thugs, vagabonds, thieves and murderers. The mob even managed to burn a Catholic-owned gin factory. The Bank of England, too, came under attack, but armed clerks and members of the London Military Association stationed on the roof drove the rioters off.

Reinforcements in the form of eleven thousand extra soldiers were rushed to central London. And then the shooting began in earnest. The disciplined crash of musketry soon dampened enthusiasm for mayhem. Some 285 rioters were

SURVIVING THE TYBURN JIG

The death throes of prisoners dangling from the hangman's noose were known as 'the Tyburn jig'. In 1447 5 men were cut down from the gallows still alive (as was the custom with those sentenced to be hung, drawn and quartered) and stripped. They were in the process of being marked up for dismemberment when a pardon arrived. The men were duly set free, but their clothes had become the property of the hangman – who refused to give them back. The released men were compelled to walk home naked.

Around that time it became customary for the crowd to surge forward after an execution to touch the body, which was believed to have medicinal properties. The hangman meanwhile would repair to a tavern in Fleet Street to sell off the rope at sixpence an inch.

Even death was no guarantee against hanging. In 1660 at the restoration of King Charles II Oliver Cromwell's body (along with several others) was dug up, hanged at Tyburn, beheaded and then buried in a deep pit at the foot of the gallows.

Newgate Gaol

——◦❧◦——

THE ORIGINAL PRISON, built in 1188, was so badly damaged in the Gordon Riots that it took two years to rebuild it. In the reconstructed gaol, completed in 1782 when Sharpe was a five-year-old in the Brewhouse Lane foundling home, the poor were confined to the 'common' area, while those who could afford it occupied more comfortable quarters in the 'state'. Further divisions separated debtors and felons, while up to 300 women and children were housed in a separate section. Newgate was notorious for its overcrowding, lack of air, lack of sanitation and frequent epidemics. While awaiting trial, detainees became so filthy that it was normal practice for them to be doused with vinegar before being brought before the court. Many never made it to trial, dying of 'gaol fever'.

On the eve of execution, condemned prisoners would assemble in the prison chapel. Seated round the edge of an enclosure called the 'dock', gazing upon an empty coffin placed on a table in the centre, they would be treated to a sermon on the need to repent, no doubt with vivid verbal pictures of the hell and damnation that awaited them on the morrow.

Despite the appalling conditions, a stay in Newgate did not come cheap. In addition to paying a fee upon admission, prisoners had to purchase all their clothing and bedding, together with any other basic comforts, from the keepers. And for those who were fortunate enough to be released, a final payment had to be made before the gates would open.

killed and 173 wounded by musket balls; many more perished in the fires and the general orgy of violence, and not a few from swilling neat alcohol while celebrating the destruction of the gin factory. The total body count was in the region of 850. Among them was Sharpe's mother. It is likely she died in one of the fires, possibly from a falling roof. By some twist of fortune her three-year-old boy survived, perhaps carried clear by one of the other occupants, or perhaps he was elsewhere at the time. He was too young to recall the details, or the fact that twenty-five ringleaders were publicly hanged on specially constructed gallows. Had he been a little older it might have registered that, of the men swinging by their necks, seventeen were eighteen-year-olds and three were under fifteen. Sharpe was now an orphan.

The Guillotine

In France, 'Madame' Guillotine was the preferred method of execution. Designed to make death more humane, the guillotine quickly became a symbol of tyranny during the French Revolution. Victims were positioned on a bench, face down, their necks between the uprights, with a basket strategically placed to catch the severed head. The actual beheading was very quick – the 88lb blade took only a split second to do its job – but some doctors have argued that it could take up to 30 seconds before the victim lost consciousness. In 1905, after experimenting with the head of one Languille, guillotined that year, Dr Beaurieux wrote a report that makes for ghoulish but incredible reading:

> The head fell on the severed surface of the neck and I did not therefore have to take it up in my hands . . . I was not obliged to touch it in order to set it upright . . . The eyelids and lips of the guillotined man worked in irregularly rhythmic contractions for about five or six seconds . . . I waited for several seconds. The spasmodic movements ceased. The face relaxed, the lids half closed on the eyeballs . . .

It was then that I called in a strong, sharp voice, 'Languille!' I saw the eyelids slowly lift up, without any spasmodic contractions . . . with an even movement, quite distinct and normal . . . Next Languille's eyes very definitely fixed themselves on mine and the pupils focused themselves . . . I was dealing with undeniably living eyes which were looking at me. After several seconds the eyelids closed again, slowly and evenly . . . I called out again and, once more, without any spasm, slowly the eyelids lifted and undeniably living eyes fixed themselves on mine . . . I attempted the effect of a third call: there was no further movement and the eyes took on the glazed look which they have in the dead . . . The whole thing lasted twenty-five to thirty seconds.

King Louis XVI of France was executed at what is now the Place de la Concorde three months before Sharpe enlisted. It is estimated that up to 40,000 people travelled on the tumbrils through Paris to die under Madame Guillotine. The last time the public watched her at work was in 1939.

Like countless infants in similar circumstances, Sharpe was deposited in a foundling home in Brewhouse Lane, Wapping, run by the brutal master, *Jem Hocking*. Some ten years earlier a parliamentary committee had reported that only seven out of ten children in such homes or workhouses survived for three years. He might have had a slightly less unpleasant nine years had he been admitted to the much larger Foundling Hospital, established in 1739 for the purpose of receiving 'foundlings' – children who had been abandoned for the public to find and rescue. This hospital was a charity, supposedly non-profit-making, whereas *Hocking*'s establishment, although funded by the parish, was run by the master as a moneymaking venture. The more children *Hocking* crammed in, the more miserly he was with food, fuel for heating and clothes; the harder he worked his charges, the richer he became – although we know the foundling home was by no means his only source of income.

Until he was twelve, Sharpe grew up in this cruel environment. He was beaten, bullied, semi-starved, clothed in shapeless cast-off rags, and put to work (slavery would better describe it) washing mountains of laundry and picking oakum. Oakum is old rope that has been unravelled or 'picked'; driven into crevices to render the planking watertight, it was used to caulk the seams of wooden ships. Such was the demand to supply both warships and merchantmen at that time, it was a labour often assigned to prison inmates. Sharpe would have found the work appallingly tedious (the phrase 'to pick oakum' fell into use as a colloquialism for any disagreeable, highly repetitive labour). It is likely he would have had to pick a pound a day.

During these early years Sharpe was pale and puny, frequently ill, forever sniffling. But although he looked sickly, his preparation for army life was, in some ways, unsurpassed. He lived hard, he expected no favours, he knew pain, and he understood hunger. Scrounging, lying, watching his back (and those of his fellow orphans), frequently fighting with fists and feet became second nature, his only means of survival.

In 1789 *Hocking* did a deal with a master chimney-sweep. Money changed hands and the 'ownership' of Sharpe transferred from the frying pan to the fire – almost literally. At

Water and waste

In Sharpe's London water was delivered to the city's residents through hollowed-out tree trunks running beneath the streets. Though it was possible to buy spring water from private companies, most people – and certainly Sharpe and his fellow orphans in the foundling home – relied on the sluggish, murky water of the Thames. The river was a busy thoroughfare for commercial shipping and the main repository for the city's sewage, yet no attempt was made to filter the water or protect it from pollution until the middle of the nineteenth century. In 1771 Tobias Smollet wrote:

If I would drink water, I must quash [the] mawkish contents of an open aqueduct, exposed to all manner of defilement, or swallow that which comes from the River Thames, impregnated with all the filth of London and Westminster. Human excrement is the least offensive part of the concrete, which contains all the drugs, minerals and poisons used in mechanics and manure enriched with the putrefying carcasses of beasts and men and the scourings of all the wash-tubs, kennels and common sewers . . .

twelve, he was rather old to start work for a chimney sweep, but it tells us that he was small for his age – *Hocking* had told the sweep he was not yet ten. It is uncertain whether the young Sharpe was actually sent up any chimneys before he took the opportunity to run away, though his ability as a grown man in 1807 to escape a house in Copenhagen by climbing out through the chimney would seem to indicate a degree of practical knowledge of their construction. And the very fact that he ran away might suggest a first-hand awareness of the hellishness of the job. Boys were often forced to work naked, which allowed them to slide and twist through the filthy blackness more easily, though in the confined space of a nine-inch chimney it was impossible to avoid constant scraping of knees and elbows. If the child was frightened of dark places or claustrophobic, the chimney-master would encourage progress by prodding him with a pole or pricking the soles of his feet with needles, perhaps even threatening to light a fire. Spines became twisted, kneecaps were misaligned, ankles deformed, respiratory ailments were unavoidable and eye infections commonplace. Falls or burns injured many children, while some died of suffocation when trapped. Until the use of children as chimney-sweeps was outlawed in 1870, it was normal for a six- or seven-year-old boy to serve a seven-year 'apprenticeship', at the end of which, if he survived, he would be too big to climb chimneys, left with no useable skills, and almost certainly crippled or sick from lung disease.

Sharpe did well to escape, ducking and weaving into the maze of sordid slums, brothels and taverns that made up St Giles Rookery (*see* MAP 12). There he ended up in the arms of *Maggie Joyce*, a prostitute who ran a gin-house in Goslitt Yard. This tiny back street can still be found off Charing Cross Road, close to Foyles bookshop, a stone's throw south of Tottenham Court Road underground station – although modern street maps have it spelt with an 'e'. *Maggie* sold both sex and gin – which went well together. As Charles Dickens (1812–70) wrote, 'Gin drinking is a great vice in England'. It was true, although he might have said 'one' of the great vices. In the 1730s and 1740s the gin craze had created an urban subculture not unlike that promoted by hard drugs in many inner-city ghettoes today. For thousands it was the only means to escape the miseries of poverty, the daily search for food, the squalor, the fight for survival. Gin was cheap, that was its joy – 'drunk for a penny, dead drunk for tuppence' as the saying went. It was consumed in staggering quantities: by the mid-1740s the average was two pints a week for every man, woman and child in London – around eight million gallons a year. To meet a demand of this magnitude required a monumental supply. Not only were there hundreds of taverns, but you could buy gin in workhouses, prisons, barber's shops, brothels (like *Maggie*'s) and from street hawkers. It has been estimated that every eighth house in London sold spirits. The bodies of the paralytically drunk littered the streets of Bethnal Green, Tothill Fields, Westminster and St Giles Rookery. An attempt to address the problem with the 1743 Gin Act provoked riots in support of the continuance of this endless availability of cheap liquor. The English novelist and playwright Henry Fielding wrote that gin was:

> the principal sustenance (if it may be called so) of more than a hundred thousand people in the metropolis ... The intoxicating draught itself disqualifies them from any honest means to acquire it, at the same time that it removes sense of fear and shame and emboldens them to commit every wicked and desperate enterprise.

By the time Sharpe was a boy the demand had fallen somewhat due to price rises, but not sufficiently to put *Maggie* and her like out of business. *Maggie* became a second mother to Sharpe (interestingly, in the same profession as his first), and later his first lover. She also taught him to live on his wits. Burglary became his speciality, but in later years he was strangely proud of the fact that he was never a pickpocket (they were regarded as the cream of criminal society, closely followed by highwaymen). However, he did indulge in some 'peter-laying', which involved cutting portmanteaus (leather suitcases) off the back of moving carriages. It required considerable agility, and not a little courage. Sharpe developed a deep and lasting affection for *Maggie*. He trusted her. He returned to see her in July 1813 to hand into her safekeeping the jewellery he had picked up after the Battle of Vitória.

At fifteen, after three years with *Maggie*, eating food of comparatively better quality and quantity, Sharpe was a tall, if still somewhat skinny, youth. He seemed destined for a life of crime in London – until, finding *Maggie* being beaten by one of her drunken male visitors, he intervened with a wooden stool and pounded the man's head to a pulp. The victim had been a notorious gang leader, and the threat of retaliation or revenge from the criminal fraternity forced Sharpe to flee London for Yorkshire. He had little to fear from the law, for policing was rudimentary at best. Each parish had its constables – mostly unpaid, frequently corrupt, invariably inept. Their most important and lucrative duty was to collect county taxes. As a body for deterring or detecting crime, their effectiveness was minimal. If Sharpe had picked a less notorious victim he could surely have avoided justice.

In Yorkshire he secured work at a coaching tavern. Within six months he had killed again – this time his employer. The reason for their fight was a pretty lass called *Elsie* to whom Sharpe and the inn-keeper had both taken more than a passing fancy. Luckily, his employer, a powerful man, picked the quarrel when he was besotted with his own beer. Nevertheless, there was a ferocious fight during which the boy's fingers were badly cut when he wrested the knife from his opponent's grasp. Sharpe slashed his throat and left him bleeding to death on the cobblestones of the tavern's yard. He was on the run again.

THE PRIVATE – A SOLDIER'S LIFE (1793–99)

Sharpe killed the tavern owner in March 1793. Within a month he had done what countless others in similar circumstances had done before and since – he took refuge by seeking sanctuary in a soldier's uniform. For the next six years he achieved anonymity, one among many thousands. Nobody was going to come looking for him in the army. Sharpe, however, did not really want to be a soldier. It had been forced upon him. He hated authority, resented discipline and valued his independence. But he needed shelter, he needed clothes, he needed food, and above all he needed invisibility from the law or vengeful relatives of his victims – and the army offered him all these things. Besides, once he felt secure, once some time had passed and his crimes had been forgotten, he could easily slip away – desert.

It was on 15 April 1793 that Sharpe heard a drummer outside an inn in the small market town of Sowerby Bridge in the West Riding of Yorkshire. For most of the previous three weeks he had been living rough, sleeping in barns and stealing food wherever he could, worrying that he had not put sufficient distance between himself and the scene of his recent killing (Skipton). And so he joined the throng of men grouped round the drummer, who was dressed in white uniform, white breeches, black gaiters and a black bearskin grenadier's cap. Alongside him stood a young-looking officer, addressing the small crowd in a raised voice. Clad in a red coat, crimson sash round his waist, a sword, and a black bicorne hat worn sideways, the officer was extolling the virtues of army life and prospects in the 33rd Regiment of Foot. What decided Sharpe to join – apart from the army offering an ideal, but hopefully temporary, hiding place – was the promise of beer and bounty: more than £7, cash in hand. He was, therefore, among the dozen or so who piled into the tavern for their free drink.

Once inside, he met the sergeant. Like the officer, he looked impressive. Indeed, had Sharpe not heard the officer tell people to go in and claim their drinks off the sergeant, he would not have known the difference in rank between the two. To the uninitiated, the uniforms looked almost identical. The sergeant, who had removed his hat, was wearing a sword and a crimson waist sash. Sharpe was not to know that the white stripe in the middle of the sash denoted a sergeant (chevrons were not introduced for NCOs until July 1802). But it was his face that fascinated Sharpe. It was unforgettable. Not only did it twitch uncontrollably, but there was heavy scarring around his neck and it seemed twisted, so that to look at you the sergeant had to hold his head slightly to the right. As he later discovered, the sergeant was then only about twenty-four, though he looked at least ten years older. The man in front of him was *Sergeant Obadiah Hakeswill*, the NCO who was to become his implacable enemy for the next twenty years. One day, in the distant future, Sharpe would put a rifle ball through this man's head after a firing party had failed to do the job properly.

Hakeswill was in full flow, shouting for beer for the lads – 'gentleman soldiers', he called them – and handing out pieces broken off from a large oatcake (it was from this

'HAVERCAKE LADS'

The 33rd Foot were nicknamed the 'Havercake Lads' or 'Havercakes' because, in addition to the usual inducement of free beer, their recruiting sergeants would hold out oatcakes on the end of their swords to persuade men to become one of 'the King's hard bargains'. *Haver* is Dutch for 'oats' and is usually used in conjunction with another word. Hence 'haversack' or, literally, 'oat sack', a bag in which British soldiers have carried their rations (and other things) for many generations.

practice that the 33rd Foot had become known as the 'Havercake Lads'). In taking his jug of beer, Sharpe was deemed to have agreed to enlist. Unbeknown to him, a shilling coin had been placed at the bottom of the glass by the innkeeper, and so he was considered to have accepted the 'King's shilling' or received his first day's pay – although until wages were raised in 1797, pay was in reality only eightpence a day. The landlord stood to make a handsome profit as the 'gentleman soldier' could buy a lot of beer for a shilling. Drunkenness often played a major part in the recruiting process. Sometimes the man was made drunk first and then the shilling was slipped into his pocket. A former recruiting sergeant has described a variation of the system:

> ... your last recourse was to get him drunk, and then slip a shilling in his pocket, get him home to your billet, and the next morning when he enlisted, bring all your party to prove it, get him persuaded to pass the doctor. Should he pass, you must try every means in your power to get him to drink [again], blow him up with a fine story, get him enveigled to the magistrates, in some shape or other, and get him attested; by no means let him out of your hands.

Sharpe's glib tongue and height got him through the perfunctory medical examination despite the fact that he was still under sixteen. But he was scared the next day when, along with eleven others, he was bundled in front of a magistrate for attestation. He had stupidly given his real name to *Hakeswill* the previous night so he was fearful that the law was about to catch up with him. Had he been a thief, vagabond, or even an escaped prisoner, he would surely have been allowed to enlist anyway. But a murderer, a double murderer, was different. His concern was unfounded. The magistrate was bored and in a hurry. Sharpe made his mark on 16 April 1793 and thus became a recruit, a private soldier in His Majesty's 33rd (Yorkshire West Riding) Regiment of Foot.

Within days of Sharpe's enlistment, an officer arrived in the regiment who would rise to be commander-in-chief in the Peninsula, defeat Napoleon at Waterloo and, ultimately,

Infantry pay rates 1797

UNTIL MAY 1797 the daily pay rate for Sharpe and his fellow privates was eight pence and one farthing a day. The pronouncement for raising the infantryman's pay on 25 May 1797 stated:

> From this day his pay shall be 1s daily, from which he is to pay the extra price of bread and meat, amounting to 1¾d a day. From this 1s a day a sum not exceeding 4s a week shall be applied to his messing; a sum not exceeding 1s 6d a week shall be stopped for necessaries, and the remainder, 1s 6d a week, shall be paid to the soldier subject to the usual deduction for washing and articles for cleaning his appointments. Thus, pay of a private:

	Infantry	Dragoons (cavalry)
	7s 0d a week	8s 9d a week
Stoppages as above	5s 6d a week	7s 1½d a week
Remains	1s 6d a week	1s 7½d a week

The daily pay of the foot . . . now stands as follows

Private	1s 0d
Drummer	1s 1¾d
Corporal	1s 2¼d
Sergeant	1s 6¾d

Although Sharpe was paid more than French soldiers of the same rank he earned less than the average farm labourer. One attraction of soldiering in India was that pay went much further; even privates could afford a daily shave from an Indian barber.

When he was commissioned, his pay rose, as an ensign, to 4s 6d a day. When appointed quartermaster it increased to 5s 8d (2d pay and 1s allowance).

become commander-in-chief of the British Army and Prime Minister. He would also shape Sharpe's entire career. Major Arthur Wesley (the family name was changed to Wellesley in 1798) was commissioned into the 33rd Foot on 30 April 1793. He was only eight years older than Sharpe, yet it was his sixth regiment in as many years, and within five months

'NECESSARIES'

A soldier's necessaries – paid for by deductions from his weekly pay – included: 2 pairs gaiters, a second pair of breeches, a leather (to secure hair), a spare pair of shoes and soles, 3 pairs of socks, 3 shirts, a forage cap, a knapsack (it was supposed to last six years), pipeclay, a clothes brush, 3 shoe brushes, a blackball (polish), a pair of worsted mittens, a black stock, a hair ribbon and 2 combs.

he was the 33rd's commanding officer – through purchase. Many years later, after his triumphs had earned him the title Duke of Wellington, this indisputable military giant of the age proclaimed that the army was recruited from the scum of the earth. Many at that time would have agreed. As one regimental officer remarked: 'The system of recruiting is so defective and so radically bad that in every regiment there are from 50 to 100 bad characters that neither punishment nor any kind of discipline can restrain.' He would certainly have thought Sharpe would turn out to be one of those hundred. Wellington was also to say, 'English soldiers are fellows who have enlisted for drink – that is the plain fact – they have all enlisted for drink.'

Sharpe had other motives, equally pressing. Nevertheless, within two days he realised that he, and most of the men who had joined with him, were in debt. Their bounty had disappeared down their throats and into the quartermaster sergeant's store. Sharpe had been credited with £7 12s 6d on the day he joined and from then on he was entitled to 8d a day. The army, however, was adept at ensuring a soldier would not see more than a fraction of his pay. For rations, normally two meals a day of stew and watery soup plus a quart of beer, he was charged 6d a day. Anything left of his bounty would be absorbed by annual deductions to cover his initial issue of 'necessaries' – expendable items such as pipeclay or blackball (shoe polish) – and contributions towards the cost of replacing large items of equipment that might be expected to wear out. For example, a knapsack was reckoned to last six years, so a sixth of its value would be deducted each year to finance its eventual replacement. A further shilling a year went towards the cost of maintaining the hospitals for old and incapacitated soldiers at Chelsea and Kilmainham. Fourpence a week was kept back to pay for his laundry – done mostly by 'wives on the strength'. Anything broken or lost would involve further stoppages – still a feature of army life today. The present writer recalls 'barrack damages' making a nasty hole in his pocket on a monthly basis. As a private, Sharpe was never going to be other than a debtor, which was why campaigning overseas with the prospect of 'winning' some loot was keenly anticipated by all, and not just private soldiers.

Sergeant Hakeswill did not feature in the weeks of drill, drunkenness and disillusionment that were the predominant features of Sharpe's early life in the army. *Hakeswill* was kept on the recruiting team, where the free beer and extra cash kept him happy (for each recruit enlisted, sixteen shillings were paid to the officer and fifteen shillings and sixpence divided among the team – we can be sure there was little left for the drummer). But Sharpe did learn of the sergeant's reputation as a bully, cheat and martinet disciplinarian – and the story of how he acquired his facial twitch. As a boy of twelve, *Hakeswill* had been sentenced to hang by the Sussex Assizes. He had been left dangling until cut down by his uncle, who was present to take away the body. To the uncle's astonishment, his young nephew was still alive, just. Slowly, miraculously, he recovered from his long dance with death. For ever afterwards *Hakeswill* was to regard himself as immortal and was firmly convinced that nobody could kill him. The experience had also left the scarring, twisted neck vertebrae and facial spasms – but his survival was not unique.

Executions were supposed to be a deterrent, so the public was encouraged to attend. Indeed, until 1783 when the location was switched from Tyburn to outside Newgate Gaol, execution days were called 'Tyburn Fair' holidays. Even apprentices were given the day off to go and gawp. It is likely that *Jem Hocking* would have taken Sharpe to see at least one as part of his 'education'. The procession from prison to the gallows, a distance of two miles, took a couple of hours, with the carts slowly making their way from the prison (now the site of the Old Bailey Central Criminal Courts in Newgate Street) along High Holborn, New Oxford Street, Oxford Street, past where Selfridges stands today to Tyburn (Marble Arch), where the multiple gallows had been set up. En route, the clattering cavalcade would stop at a number of taverns,

TYBURN FAIR HOLIDAYS

Executions were usually held on Mondays. During the morning large crowds would assemble to watch the proceedings. A seat overlooking the gallows cost up to £10 – a huge amount at that time. Not all condemned men (or women) were hanged. The alternative was beheading, but not always by an axeman. The last beheadings at Newgate took place in 1820, when the five Cato Street conspirators had their heads taken off with a surgeon's knife – what a sickening spectacle that must have been. Afterwards, fights would sometimes break out between surgeons (who were allowed ten bodies a year for dissection) and relatives of the deceased who considered 'anatomisation' a crime.

Public executions were abolished in 1868.

so that many condemned men were mercifully drunk by the time they reached their journey's end. Some even managed to keep their sense of humour, promising to pay for their drink 'when they came back'. At the gallows, the huge crowd was accommodated in a stand known as 'Mother Proctor's Pews'. A French observer, Henri Misson, has left a detailed account of the proceedings:

> The Executioner stops the Cart under one of the Cross Beams of the Gibbet and fastens to that ill-favour'd Beam one End of the Rope, while the other is round the Wretches Neck; This done he gives the Horse a Lash with his Whip, away goes the Cart, and there swing my Gentlemen kicking in the Air: The Hangman does not give himself the Trouble to put them out of their Pain, but some of their Friends or Relations do it for them: They pull the dying Person by the Legs, and beat his breast, to dispatch him as soon as possible.

Sometimes friends tried to support the hanging man in the hope of reviving him (as *Hakeswill*'s uncle must have succeeded in doing, for young *Obadiah* was a small, skinny lad). In 1709 a man called John 'Half-Hanged' Smith (what a nickname to have!) was cut down and lived to tell the tale.

Among the first things Sharpe and his fellow recruits had to learn was how to dress for parades. Initially this involved a demonstration by a corporal of how the various pieces of uniform must be cleaned, polished, whitened and worn. Great stress was placed on how immaculate everything must be, and how severe and swift the punishment would be if it was not. The basics of his uniform were the red coat with, in the case of the 33rd, red facings (collars, lapels and cuffs). The coat was of a cut-away pattern with long tails at the back. The lapels, cuffs and pockets had white buttons looped with white worsted lace. Under the coat, and visible from the front, was a white waistcoat with white buttons; invisible under that was his shirt. Over his chest were two white crossbelts, one over each shoulder, fastened together in the centre of his chest by a white metal belt plate. Around his

Soldier 33rd foot dressed for parade c.1793

neck, inside the upright collar of his coat, he had to wear a black leather stock, which forced him to keep his head up. He wore white breeches that fastened below the knee. His legs below the knee were enclosed in black linen gaiters with black buttons; these partially covered his black leather shoes. On his head was a black bicorne hat with a black cockade and white tape binding. It was worn horizontally across the head or, as the French would have said, '*en bataille*' (in line), as distinct from fore and aft or '*en colonne*' (in column).

As Sharpe quickly discovered, many hours of tedious washing, cleaning, pipeclaying and polishing were required in preparation for even a sergeant's drill, never mind anything grander involving a battalion parade with senior officers present. Every day there was an inspection, every day there was drill, every day uniforms got dirty, so every night the recruits toiled away in readiness for the following day. Mud, a shower of rain, oil from the musket after shouldering arms dozens of times – there was always something to ruin the previous night's drudgery. Even if your turnout was perfect, the NCOs made a habit of bawling you out for the sake of it; *Jem Hocking* was far from exceptional in this regard. Sharpe detested every minute.

Particularly time-consuming, messy and unhealthy was the attention the army paid to a soldier's hair. John Shipp, a man who joined the army at about the same time as Sharpe and who, like him, eventually became an officer, has recounted the painfully unforgettable first experience with the queue:

> I went into town to purchase a few things that I needed such as powder-bag, puff, soap, candles, grease and so on. As soon as I got back I had to undergo the operation of having my hair tied for the first time, to no small amusement of the other boys. A large piece of candle grease was applied first to the sides of my head, and then to the long hair behind. After this the same operation was gone through with nasty, stinking soap, the man who was dressing me applied his knuckles as often as the soap, to the delight of the surrounding boys who watched the tears roll down my cheeks. That part was bad enough, but the next was worse. A large pad, or bag, filled with sand, was poked into the back of my neck, the hair twisted tightly round it, and the whole tied with a leather thong. When thus dressed for parade, the skin of my face was pulled so tight by the bag at the back of my head, that it was impossible so much as to wink an eyelid. Add to this an enormous high stock, which was pushed under my chin, and I felt as stiff as if I had swallowed a ramrod or the Sergeant's halberd. Shortly after this we were called to dinner, but my poor jaws could hardly move, and at every attempt to do so the pad behind went up and down like a sledge-hammer.

In addition to the queue at the back, attention had to be given to the sides. The hair had to be grown long so that it could be combed to curl over the ears from under the hat.

Few men could cultivate the correct curl, so recourse was had to a hot curling iron. This was a fiddly task that often resulted in burnt ears and much cursing. Finally, the hair had to be powdered with baking flour to turn it white.

Though it could be said that Sharpe's queue saved his life at Assaye – the large ruby he had taken off the Tippoo at Seringapatam, hidden inside his queue, deflected a sword stroke – he found all this hairdressing a serious setback to the morning routine. Most men took to leaving their hair tied up for weeks on end, with only a touching up of the curls carried out on a daily basis, for once a queue was undone it required the assistance of an experienced comrade to tie it up again. Another short cut was to powder the hair the night before. This practice would soon be abandoned once a soldier discovered that during the night a rat, attracted by the flour, had made a meal out of his queue – much to the vindictive delight of his sergeant. Sweat, dirt, lice and baking powder, all cooked under a hat in the hot sun for several hours, were guaranteed to produce a revolting brew, leaving men demented by the itching and inability to scratch. We have a first-hand account of these problems from Captain James Trevor of the 55th Foot:

> . . . in order to avoid that inconvenience [loss of time] they frequently let their hair remain in [a queue] for some days together, giving it occasionally, without opening or combing it, a sort of outward slight dressing, by way of concealing their neglect from their officers; the ill consequence of which is that the man, by not daily combing his head, the skin contracts, and in a small space of time, not only stagnated humours, which break out into scabs and ulcers, but an accumulated mixture of filth, dirt and vermin, which proves as pernicious to the man himself, as it becomes infectious to others.

These were largely problems of the parade ground. No attempt was made to maintain this fixation with the hair (apart from keeping the queue) on campaign.

There were other aspects of his uniform that Sharpe found

QUEUES CUT OFF
Though the practice of powdering hair was abolished in 1795, the tedious trimming and knotting of the hair to form a queue continued for another thirteen years. When abolition eventually came it caused a row 'very little short of mutiny', in the words of Captain Thomas Browne, a staff officer during the Peninsular War. The loudest protests came from regimental wives, who had earned a tidy sum over the years acting as hairdressers. Browne describes how one commanding officer had each company parade in turn, the men sitting on benches outside the barrack accommodation to submit their queues to the barbers 'of which there are always plenty in every Regiment'. The wives, for fear of being struck 'off strength', looked on in grim silence. For the men it meant one less chore when preparing for parade. According to Browne, even the wives were soon 'reconciled to this great improvement'.

'GET ON PARADE!'

It would not have been uncommon for reveille to sound at 4 a.m. in order to allow Sharpe and his comrades time to prepare for an inspection or drill parade in peacetime. Sergeant Cooper of the 7th Foot describes the typical routine in the early 1800s: 'To be tolerably fit for parade required three hours' work. His pouch, magazine and bayonet scabbard were covered with heel-bore [blacking] like his cap. The barrel of his musket, the outside and inside of the lock, the bayonet and ramrod must be polished like a razor. In addition to the above he had to clean white leather gloves, cap and breast plate; his greatcoat must be neatly rolled up, and be exactly eighteen inches long. When blankets were issued, they had to be folded to suit the square of the knapsack. Many other things required polishing besides those already mentioned, such as the gun brasses, picker and brush, and the bayonet [scabbard] tip.'

inconvenient and annoying. The stock was hated for the discomfort it gave the wearer, especially in hot weather. During the Spanish campaigns many were conveniently 'lost' (despite the cost of compulsory replacement) or removed on the march or in action. Old soldiers sliced thin pieces off the top with a razor, thus reducing its height. Crossbelts tended to restrict breathing, which was hardly conducive to fitness, running or climbing hills. Gaiters took some twelve minutes to button up, more if wet, and there was always the chance that buttons would break off. This chore became intolerable in the field, so men tended to keep them on for long periods, which led to chafing of the leg, sores that went septic and eventually, if untreated, required hospitalisation. As for the headdress, neither the grenadier's cap nor the bicorne hat had chinstraps, with the obvious consequence that they were forever falling off. Again, Captain Trevor's comments are worth repeating:

> The height of it [the grenadier's cap] above the head is so enormous that any inclination or agile motion of the body will cause it immediately to tumble off. If the country ... happens to be either bushy or woody, off goes the cap at every branch, briar or twig, which comes in its way ... If the weather be windy, the cap is every now and then blown off; or if it be dusty and scorching, it affords no sort of shelter whatever to the face and eyes; or if the weather be rainy, it yields as little covering to the neck and shoulders.

And on the subject of the bicorne hat:

> ... which, though infinitely preferable to the cap, yet is not without some weighty objections; for by its projection over the shoulders, it is extremely incommodious to the man, when in the ranks or under arms, it being then liable, either by its own motions or by those of others, to be easily thrown off, which frequently happens. Nor is it that much less troublesome than the cap, in bushy or woody country, or in windy weather.

One wonders, on a blustery day, how many caps and hats were sent bowling across the parade ground to the fury of

THE BRITISH INFANTRYMAN'S
PERSONAL EQUIPMENT c.1803

(Sharpe would have been familiar with all these items in India)

FRONT

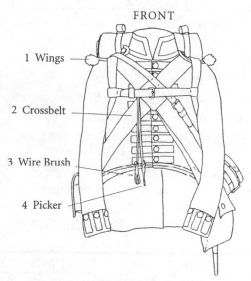

1 Wings

2 Crossbelt

3 Wire Brush

4 Picker

REAR

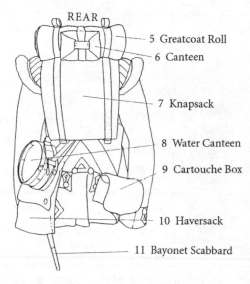

5 Greatcoat Roll

6 Canteen

7 Knapsack

8 Water Canteen

9 Cartouche Box

10 Haversack

11 Bayonet Scabbard

1 'Wings' on shoulder indicate a soldier in the grenadier or light company. They were useful in preventing the various shoulder straps from slipping off.

2 The British had two crossbelts, one for the bayonet, one for the cartouche box, with a belt plate holding them in the centre. The belts, which were white (pipeclayed), together with the three other straps that went over the chest, restricted breathing during a long march or when running.

3 Wire brush: part of musket-cleaning kit, used for cleaning the priming pan. Like the picker, often suspended on a string to avoid loss and facilitate quick use on the battlefield.

4 Picker: tool for cleaning touch-hole – essential during prolonged firing.

5 The greatcoat (or blanket) was usually carried as shown, but in India blanket and knapsack were often conveyed by bullock carts due to the heat.

6 Canteen: all-purpose individual mess tin.

7 Knapsacks were made of canvas, painted brown, usually with the regimental number or badge on the back. Used to carry spare shoes, shirts, trousers, stockings, cleaning brushes, pipe-clay and small personal items.

8 Official-issue water canteens were barrel-shaped and made of wood.

9 Made of leather, the cartouche held 60 cartridges in wood or tin compartments. Underneath the flap was a small pocket for spare flints and cleaning tools (although the latter were usually carried on strings, see 3 and 4 above). To prevent it being obstructed when speedy loading was of the essence, it was the only piece of equipment slung over the left shoulder.

10 Haversack: simple fabric bag slung over the right shoulder. Used primarily to carry rations.

11 Bayonet: only blade weapon carried by British infantrymen. Swords and pikes were a badge of rank for officers and sergeants.

FLINTS

All firearms handled by Sharpe were flintlocks. Without a good flint, a musket (or any other firearm) could only be used as a club or pike. Consequently the procurement and care of flints was of vital importance. The world's best flints came from the French village of Meusnes; prior to the Revolution they were widely exported. Flint-knapping was a skilled trade and the French artillery alone kept 168 such craftsmen fully employed.

A high-quality flint would continue to produce a spark for thirty to fifty shots (more than most men would fire in a major battle), but because they were easily dropped or lost each soldier had to carry several spares. During exercises or dry-run drills the French often replaced their flints with a piece of wood called the *pierre de bois* (wooden stone) in order to save the flints and absorb the shock on the lock mechanism.

the commanding officer. Experienced soldiers overcame the problem of keeping headgear on in a light breeze by securing it with a cord that ran round the back of the head, hidden under the long hair and queue.

These various discomforts were alleviated to some degree in 1808 with the abolition of pigtails, and the introduction of trousers to replace breeches and gaiters. Unfortunately the stock was retained.

Alongside having to cope with the intricacies and frustrations of dress, Sharpe, as a private soldier, had to learn the two indispensable skills of an infantryman: drill and musketry. Without drill a unit was an armed mob of individuals – no organised movement, no tactical manoeuvring was possible. Close-order drill filled the life of Sharpe and his fellow recruits from the moment they enlisted. For week after week, month after month, they drilled on the parade ground and then in the field. They had to wheel and turn, march and counter-march, advance and retire, form lines, columns and squares, all in accordance with the published regulations – commonly referred to as the 'Nineteen Movements'. Every man, every NCO, every officer (including the commanding officer) had to memorise the drill book. Sharpe had to understand, and instantly react to, the shouted orders of the sergeants. Later, officers would take command and put the unit through its drills. Good drill and steadiness under fire, combined with good musketry and fire control, won battles. Superiority in these areas made the British infantryman of the Napoleonic Wars virtually invincible. Other things being equal, he seldom came off second best.

Shooting the smooth-bore, India pattern, Brown Bess musket was also down to drills. Even a good shot would miss a man three times out of four at one hundred yards. Success in battle therefore depended on disciplined mass firing in controlled volleys, coupled with speedy reloading. The manual set out eleven separate drill movements required to fire a single shot. Each action had to be instinctive, requiring

Musket-loading procedure

ALL MUSKETS, rifles, carbines and pistols were muzzle-loading and fired a spherical lead ball, which varied in size according to the calibre of the weapon. The French musket ball was fractionally smaller than the British so it could, in an emergency, be used in the Brown Bess, whereas the reverse was not possible. The British ball weighed about an ounce and could inflict horrible injuries at close range when it flattened slightly on impact, smashing bones, ripping huge holes in muscles, causing massive bleeding and shock. A 'spent' ball could sometimes bruise, as both Wellington and Napoleon could testify. Cartridges, already made up with powder and ball wrapped in greased paper, were carried in a flapped leather pouch with a slotted wooden interior, each slot containing a cartridge.

To load, the soldier held his musket forward in his left hand, took a cartridge from his pouch with his right and bit the bullet end off the cartridge, retaining the ball in his mouth. This was an unpleasant procedure resulting in blackened lips, gritty teeth, and the taste of gunpowder and grease. He then pulled back the cock (hammer) one notch to the 'half-cock' position. If the trigger was pulled at this stage nothing would (supposedly) happen – although the expression 'going off at half-cock' should be remembered. The frizzen was pushed in the direction of the muzzle, opening the priming pan. A small amount of powder was poured from the open cartridge into the pan and the frizzen moved into the vertical position, thus sealing the powder. The musket butt was then grounded and the remaining powder poured down the barrel and the ball dropped (or spat) down it. The iron ramrod was taken from its channel underneath the barrel, reversed, and with the bulbous end the soldier rammed the empty paper cartridge down the barrel (awkward with a fixed bayonet). This compacted the 'wad', ball and powder firmly at the bottom of the barrel. The ramrod was then replaced in its channel and the musket returned to the horizontal, the cock pulled back another notch to 'full-cock', which made the trigger operational. When the musket was raised and fired, the cock flew forward, the flint struck the serrated frizzen, the sparks lit the powder in the pan and the flash travelled down the vent and exploded the powder under the ball.

no thought as to what had to be done or the sequence. The drill would have to be performed in battle when excitement, fear, shock, confusion, fatigue and pain would all combine to distract the soldier. Sharpe and his fellow recruits would have practised these movements over and over until they had mastered what to do; then they had to learn to do it quickly.

Musket-firing problems

THE FIRST SHOT fired by any soldier in battle was invariably the most accurate and reliable, because his weapon was clean and the loading procedures had been meticulously followed. Thereafter, the more he fired, the more inaccurate his shooting, the more unreliable his musket, and the greater the problems.

Misfires occurred on average once every nine shots. The most common causes were: damp powder (firing in heavy rain was impossible); the flint did not spark; there was a 'flash in the pan', but it failed to ignite the powder in the barrel; strong wind blew the powder from the pan when loading. A 'hang-fire' was when nothing happened for a second or two after the trigger was pulled because the powder burned too slowly; often the musket fired as the soldier began to examine the weapon.

The savage recoil got worse as the barrel fouled with prolonged firing, and ramming became increasingly difficult as fouling in the barrel accumulated. In addition to the physical discomfort of having your face peppered with grains of half-burnt powder from the pan every time you fired, dense clouds of white smoke often obscured the target, so that firing was frequently almost blind after the first volley.

Human error, as distinct from technical problems, was a major factor as fear and fatigue increased. Panic induced mistakes in loading, such as firing away ramrods left in the barrel, or forgetting the musket was loaded and so loading again – resulting in a burst barrel, eardrums or head. Men under intense pressure sometimes put the ball down the barrel before the powder, which meant it would not fire until they had extracted the ball – a fiddly, time-consuming process to be avoided in the heat of battle.

Sharpe took a liking to musketry training. In years to come he was, starting with a loaded musket, able to get off four shots in a minute quite comfortably. This was good shooting – the average in a battalion was about two. It was seldom much use firing even volleys at an enemy a hundred yards away. If you fired at that range and it took thirty seconds to reload, the enemy was likely to be thrusting his bayonet in your belly before you could fire again. There were ways of getting over this basic problem, such as firing by platoons (half-companies), firing by alternate ranks, waiting until your attackers were much closer – or a combination of these

Musket accuracy

A SOLDIER aiming and firing his musket at an enemy over 100 yards away in a battle situation would hit his target once in every thirty shots. If his target was 50–70 yards away the chances of a hit dramatically increased to one in three. At less than 50 yards, firing his shot as part of a volley from his company or battalion, the results were likely to be devastating. Controlled volleys of musketry fired at close range had great killing power.

The heavy bullet and considerable 'windage' (gap between the ball and the side of the barrel) led to low muzzle velocity, which limited the range and made for inconsistent and inaccurate shooting. Colonel Hanger, writing in 1814, said, '[the musket ball] will strike a figure of a man at 80 yards – it may even be at 100, but a soldier must be very unfortunate indeed who shall be wounded by a common musket at 150 yards provided his antagonist aims at him; and as to firing at a man at 200 . . . you may as well fire at the moon . . .'

During the heavy fighting at Talavera, in which Sharpe was to be engaged, Major-General Hughes (in his book *Firepower*) calculated that only three or four musket shots per hundred fired actually hit anybody. Another authority (R. Henegan, who was in charge of the field train) calculated that at the Battle of Vitória 3.675 million balls had been fired, causing around 8,000 casualties – one hit per 459 shots.

things. These, however, were officers' decisions and of no concern to a sixteen-year-old recruit. Nevertheless, even the dimmest of recruits could appreciate that soldiers who could load and fire four times a minute were going to beat an enemy who could only do so twice a minute.

Sharpe was to fight most of his battles in India and the Peninsula where, nine times out of ten, a single British infantryman saw off at least twice as many attackers. Historians have endlessly discussed the merits of the British line in generating more firepower than the assaulting column, but a key factor is often left out of the equation: morale. Sharpe and his comrades never expected to open fire at above one hundred yards. Much better to wait in silence with muskets shouldered, let the enemy see the long line and begin to anticipate how deadly the fire would be when it came. Let the attackers feel fear. During one such advance, a voice from

APPALLING STATE
OF SUPPLY
SERVICES 1794

'Lord Moira [bringing
reinforcements to
Flanders] had brought
with him guns but no
drivers; and there were
but two captains . . .
for the super-
intendence of a huge
mass of horses . . . The
Commissariat also . . .
was in a very bad
state. The men of the
new corps of Royal
Waggoners had been
recruited in London,
and were the worst
refuse of the popu-
lation. They were
known, in fact, as the
"Newgate Blues". "A
greater set of
scoundrels never
disgraced an army,"
wrote Craig, in his
usual pithy style. "I
believe it to be true
that half of them, if
not taken from the
hulks [prison ships],
have at times visited
them . . . They have
committed every
species of villainy, and
treat their horses
badly." But the worst
department of all was
that of the hospitals,
wherein the abuses
were so terrible that
men hardly liked to
speak of them. In
December 1793 the
inhabitants of one of
the English ports had
been dumbfounded
by the arrival of 100
invalid soldiers from
Ostend in
indescribable distress.

the attacking column cried, 'For what we are about to receive, Lord make us truly thankful.' At one hundred yards – nothing, muskets still shouldered; at eighty – the same; at fifty – the same; then, at between forty to thirty yards, the orders: 'Make Ready!' 'Present!' and 'Fire!' One long devastating volley, rolling from one end of the line and back again, would be followed by a wildly yelling bayonet charge. Fire control like that took a lot of withstanding.

It was essential that all orders for the basic movements of the battalion – to get it to advance or retire, change formation, make ready to fire, cease firing, halt, etc – were obeyed and acted upon instantly. In battle, a shouted command from an officer would all too easily be drowned out by the din of firing, yelling and screaming. To get round this problem, each of the ten companies had its own drummer, and there were four attached to battalion headquarters. The commanding officer's order would be relayed to his troops as a drum signal, repeated by the company drummers as necessary. A short roll to attract attention preceded most orders. It could take a while for new recruits such as Sharpe to distinguish one drum signal from another in the confusion of action, so NCOs in the ranks (or behind in the supernumerary rank) would assist by shouting the orders to the men around them.

Sharpe's career as a private was to last six years, all served in the 33rd Foot. This was far longer than he had ever intended to remain in the army. In common with many recruits – most of whom were drunk when they enlisted – on sobering up and finding himself subject to rigid discipline (not to mention penniless, having spent the bounty), his thoughts turned to desertion. Once inside the barracks, however, escape was far from easy. The best time for new recruits to disappear was before the barrack gates shut behind them – if they had sobered up in time. Some made a practice of 'bounty-jumping': taking the money, deserting, and then re-enlisting under another name in another regiment. Three years before Sharpe joined, a man was hanged in Ipswich after making the extraordinary confession that he had enlisted forty-nine times, netting himself 397 guineas in bounty money.

Prevented from immediate escape by the fact that he was still in Yorkshire and still on the run from the law, Sharpe was sent at the end of his basic training to join the battalion company in Cork. He was lucky not to have been drafted into the elite force made up of all flank companies (light and grenadier) of regiments in Ireland that was sent to the West Indies, where casualties from disease were horrendous – the two companies of the 33rd were 'totally destroyed', sixty dying in the grenadier company alone. Instead, Sharpe found himself among the main body of the 33rd, sent in June 1794 to Flanders (Holland) to participate in the Duke of York's campaign against the revolutionary French.

On 15 September 1794, at a town called Boxtel, Sharpe played his small part in a rearguard action. The 33rd was at the time commanded by the recently authorised second lieutenant-colonel, John Sherbrooke (not, as usually supposed, by Wesley, who was acting as the brigade commander). As a callow seventeen-year-old, Sharpe felt the sting of burning powder on his cheek when he fired his musket, saw blood on the ground, heard the screams of the wounded and the sobs of the dying. He had started to become a soldier.

The winter of 1794–95 was the worst in living memory. That Sharpe survived with only a minor case of frostbite to his feet was little short of miraculous. The River Waal at Arnhem froze to such a depth that troops could march across; sentries froze rigid at their posts – it was on sentry duty that Sharpe's feet were frostbitten. Throughout January the British–German force was in disastrous retreat. Discipline was collapsing, marauders from every regiment and nationality swarmed round the supply wagons. Fortescue, the British Army historian, has described the sort of scene Sharpe became familiar with:

... the Army that woke on the morning of 17th January [1795] saw about them such a sight as they never forgot. Far as

They had been on board ship for a week in the bitter wintry weather, without so much as straw to lie upon. Some of them were dead; others died on being carried ashore.'
A History of the British Army, J. W. Fortescue

THE WEST INDIES –
ISLANDS OF
SUNSHINE AND
SICKNESS

Postings to the
Caribbean, with its
reputation for lethal
diseases, were sought
only by young officers
desperate for pro-
motion. Commissions
in regiments destined
for the islands were
difficult to sell or
exchange out of, but
easy to purchase or
exchange into.
Fortescue estimates
35,000 men died in the
W. Indies 1794–96, the
majority killed by
malaria, sprue (an
intestinal disorder
characterised by
diarrhoea, fever,
malaise, cramps and
weakness) and yellow
fever (or 'yellow jack'),
a mosquito-borne viral
infection described by
one doctor of the day
as: 'Intense fever
coming on suddenly
and the symptoms
gradually becoming
worse, violent
delirium, yellow skin,
black vomit, collapse
and death. The vomit
was constant copious
and black.' There was
no vaccine or cure for
yellow fever at that
time. Scurvy, too, was a
killer until the means
of preventing it became
known and the
Admiralty mandated
lemon juice for all
sailors; in 1804 Nelson
procured 30,000
gallons for his fleet.

the eye could reach over the whitened plain were scattered
gun-limbers, wagons full of baggage, of stores, of sick men,
sutler's carts and private carriages. Beside them lay the horses,
dead; here a straggler who had staggered on to the bivouac
and dropped to sleep in the arms of the frost; there a group
of British and Germans round an empty rum cask; here forty
English guardsmen huddled together about a plundered
wagon; there a pack-horse with a woman [six wives per battalion were officially allowed on campaign] lying alongside it,
and a baby, swathed in rags, peeping out of the pack, with
its mother's milk turned to ice upon its lips – one and all
stark, frozen, dead.

In March the Government called a halt to the catastrophic
campaign and sent transports to Bremen to bring back the
survivors. On 13 April 1795, almost exactly two years after
enlisting, Sharpe sailed with what was left of the 33rd battalion
companies, destined for Warley in Essex. They left behind
206 corpses (only 6 of whom were killed by enemy action)
and 192 sick in hospital. *Sergeant Hakeswill* considered himself
fortunate to have been left behind, boozing, regaling and
enticing drunken recruits in the warmth of taverns during
these dreadful months. Now, with the regiment so weak, his
lucrative posting was extended.

If the cold had crippled the battalion companies in
Flanders, heat and 'Yellow Jack' (fever) had done much the
same to the grenadier and light companies in the West Indies.
The havoc wreaked by disease led to the urgent despatch of
another expedition to the Caribbean under the command of
Sir Ralf Abercromby. He was instructed to sail for Barbados,
where he was to deal with the situation in St Lucia and
Guadeloupe and then consider attacking the Dutch settle-
ments of Surinam, Berbice and Demerara. Some 18,500
officers and men in twenty-two battalions and one cavalry
regiment found themselves packed into the transports.
Among those battalions was the 33rd, and with his battalion
was Private Sharpe.

Due to contrary winds, the enormous convoy that had
assembled at Portsmouth was unable to sail until

16 November 1795. Two days later, the weather had worsened dramatically with a south-westerly gale driving the ships towards a lee shore. Below decks, in the wet and the dark, a hellish nightmare was taking place. Packed tightly together, the soldiers moaned and vomited as the ships pitched and rolled, flinging them first one way and then another so that they crashed into each other or fell in heaps. Many would probably have welcomed death; a fair number were not disappointed. The warships took shelter at Portland, other vessels at Weymouth; some, overladen or ill-handled, were driven ashore; several were lost with all hands.

On 3 December a second attempt was made to sail with 12,000 men. The 33rd were in a dreadful state. They were fortunate to be among the 6,500 men left behind, for there followed a repeat performance of the earlier attempt. A violent gale with mountainous waves caught the fleet in mid-Channel, dispersing them in every direction. The flagship Glory, with Admiral Christian and General Abercromby on board, battled for seven weeks to get clear of the Channel before staggering back to Portsmouth at the end of January. That this ship survived is a magnificent illustration of the sheer willpower, guts, strength, stamina and skill of British naval officers and seamen of the day. One wonders how any soldier on board that ship managed to endure such horrendous conditions twenty-four hours a day for almost two months.

Sharpe, along with the rest of the 33rd, was recuperating in Lymington. It seems likely that there was a shortage of junior NCOs at this time, for having shown, despite his youth and initial resentment of army life, signs of his latent strength of character and initiative, Sharpe was promoted acting corporal on 17 December 1795. His new rank was denoted by a white shoulder knot on his right epaulette. The promotion proved short-lived. During the Christmas and New Year celebrations, Sharpe was found in an alcoholic stupor. The fact he was the guard commander at the time compounded the problem. On 6 January he was reduced back to private. It was to be

FIRING RAMRODS

It was not uncommon for soldiers flustered in the heat of battle to forget to remove the ramrod after loading their musket. When fired, the ramrod would shoot out like an arrow, which was potentially lethal at short range. In 1808, at Valladolid, General Malher was exercising French army recruits with blank cartridges and made the mistake of standing in front of them; he was transfixed by one of eighteen ramrods shot away at a single volley (presumably all the soldiers were aiming at him). During a similar exercise at Leghorn in 1804 the 5th Ligne fired off a ramrod that killed a civilian spectator. An inspection revealed the culprit, but luckily for him the victim was found to be a notorious brigand taking the day off.

another three and a half years before he was promoted again.

By April 1796 the 33rd was back on board transports, this time destined for the East Indies (India). It was not until ten months later that Sharpe disembarked at Calcutta. The reason for the excessive time spent en route was a prolonged (and unexplained) stop at Cape Town, where the troops were disembarked and Colonel Arthur Wesley joined them – he had been sick when they left England and had caught them up in a fast frigate, HMS Caroline. The ship's commander, Captain Page, was horrified to discover that the colonel slept in his clothes (Wesley claimed he was getting accustomed to life on campaign), and was only mollified by the assurance that his guest washed his breeches before breakfast.

Within four months (August 1797) Sharpe was on the move again, heading for Manila with his regiment as part of the expeditionary force sent to capture it (the Philippines were Spanish possessions). However, on arrival at the island of Penang (north-west Malaya) the force was recalled to India where a far more serious threat was developing. There, Sharpe was pitched into his first serious soldiering in the Fourth Mysore War, his adventures in which are fully described in later chapters.

Sharpe's promotion to sergeant came on 5 May 1799, at the age of twenty-two. Six years as a private had turned him into a lean, hard, muscular young man who was fully entitled to call himself a veteran, having been on active service twice. He knew the horrors of the hold of a troop transport in a gale, the pain of frostbite, the terror and torment of the lash, and the searing, stabbing agony of a wounding. He had been, for a brief and ignominious time, a corporal. But above all he was a man of violence, a killer with nine confirmed kills (two as a boy, seven as a soldier), two more probables and a large number of possibles – the rockets and mine in Seringapatam must surely have accounted for many. Finally, most important of all for Sharpe, he was rich. The jewels and ruby he took from the Tippoo's corpse had made him, a mere private, as wealthy as most generals.

Enlisting in the Royal Artillery, 1801

A YOUNG MAN who was 'instantly seized' by military enthusiasm after encountering a regimental band in Glasgow wrote this description of his subsequent encounter with the recruiting sergeant:

I then walked with him to the rendezvous [a tavern], where he at once laid down a shilling which I took up, as an earnest that I was willing to serve king and country ... After drinking his Majesty's health, and success to his arms, the sergeant asked me to go to a surgeon ... I was afraid I would not pass, and felt a gleam of satisfaction when the surgeon pronounced me a fine, active healthy young man.

Next forenoon, I went cheerfully to David Dale, Esq., Charlotte Street and was attested, on Saturday the 25th April, 1801 ... The sergeant entered me as a day-labourer. At this I remonstrated, but he silenced me by saying that it was his instructions, for all those who had no trade, to be entered as labourers. I was forced to submit, but felt, for the first time, that I had suffered a severe degradation ...

I will give detail of the price I received for this disposal of myself. The bounty was eight guineas, and a crown to drink his Majesty's health. Now I, being an ignorant lad, was open to every imposition. I was to receive five guineas at present, and the other three, intended for regimental necessaries, as soon as I joined the regiment.

His protestations at deductions were unavailing.

My five guineas, therefore, I received under the following deductions, viz:

Bounty	£5 5s
King's health	5s
Surgical inspection	1s
Justice of peace attestation	1s
Enlistment money	1s
	8s
	£4 17s

This was the exact sum I received at this time. Whenever I objected to any thing, the sergeant's answer was, it was the rule of the service; and by this same rule he excused all his impositions, such as half-a-crown I had to pay the drummer, for beating the points of war, this was a constant rule, and could not be dispensed with. I must also buy a cockade from him, and a suit of ribbons for his wife; this was also a constant rule. In short, everything was the rule that tended to fleece the poor recruit. These same ribbons for the wife, for instance, were sold regularly to every recruit, as the sergeant always laid them aside for the next occasion. Perhaps they had been bought and sold a hundred times, for any thing I know.

THE SERGEANT – A DULL LIFE (1799–1803)

Sharpe was a sergeant in the 33rd Foot for over four years, from May 1799 until he was commissioned in September 1803 after the Battle of Assaye. Most of that time was spent in a backwater, away from all action or excitement, as the armourer sergeant at Seringapatam. It was dull, uneventful and a sinecure, though it had the advantage of keeping him well away from his fellow sergeant, *Hakeswill*. The 33rd spent those four years on line-of-communications duties, patrolling, picketing, guarding and escorting supply convoys well to the north of Seringapatam. While they marched and sweated, Sharpe led a lazy, easy life in the city. He became an accomplished armourer, able to maintain and repair any type of musket, pistol or sword. He knew the characteristics of each, their good points and weaknesses. He test-fired hundreds of weapons, he knew the ranges at which a hit was likely in varying circumstances, and he became a crack shot, able to reload a musket in fifteen seconds and a pistol in twelve. The weapon-handling and shooting skills that he perfected as an armourer sergeant would account for his survival in the years ahead.

As a private in a battalion company, Sharpe's first step up the promotion ladder should have taken him to acting corporal, then corporal, followed by acting sergeant and sergeant. The army tended to insist on acting rank before substantive because that way it got the duties performed but did not have to pay the extra. Sharpe's promotion, jumping the intervening rank of corporal, had been a reward for the successful completion of a special operation that few in his regiment knew anything about. Only days earlier he had been sentenced to 2,000 lashes for striking an NCO, so to many in the 33rd it was inexplicable, totally unacceptable that he should appear amongst them with a sergeant's sash and sword at his waist. It would have been bad for Sharpe and bad for

the morale of the battalion. The post of armourer sergeant
at the army's base was offered because it would keep him
well out of sight. It might have seemed a 'cushy' billet, perhaps with the prospect of making some cash on the side and
easy access to the fleshpots of Seringapatam, but it was not
a posting given to an NCO earmarked for rapid promotion.
Sharpe could see the logic behind the move, so raised no
objections.

If the object was to ensure that Sharpe was forgotten, it
succeeded. During those four years, Sergeant Sharpe remained an unknown within his battalion. This anonymity
had its drawbacks. He gained no experience of command, of
the regimental duties of a sergeant and, above all, he was
unable to make his name with any company officers or the
colonel. Few knew of him, nobody knew his real worth. Out
of sight, out of mind, he was never to make his name as a
competent NCO in the 33rd. If a slot became vacant, Sharpe's
name was unlikely to appear among the candidates for
advancement.

The next step up from sergeant would have been an
appointment as company pay sergeant, which involved handling cash and keeping the record books. For this a certain
degree of numeracy and literacy was essential, not to mention
honesty. The position carried no official increase in pay, but
the temptation to make something on the side was often
irresistible – and led to the speedy downfall of many an NCO.
Sir Charles Oman in his book *Wellington's Army* has this to
say about sergeants of the period:

> The responsibility of the non-commissioned officer cannot be
> exaggerated. It was easy to make sergeants, but not easy to
> secure them of the proper quality. Too often the man pro-
> moted for an act of courage or of quick cleverness had to be
> reduced to the ranks again, for some hopeless failing – he was
> prone to drink [Sharpe's brief rise to corporal comes to mind],
> or he was an over-harsh or an over-slack administrator of
> discipline. One of the commoner types of court martial was
> that of the non-commissioned officer who connived at and
> profited by the misdeeds of the men under his charge – whose

silence was bought by a percentage, when peasants were plundered, or convoys lightened of food, shoes or clothing. It was often to get at him – to prove he had known what was going on, and had contrived to see nothing. But the numbers of reductions to the ranks were notable, and lashes were often added when part of the *corpus delicti* was found in the sergeant's pack.

Sergeant Hakeswill is the archetypical example of the over-harsh, unscrupulous NCO whose dishonest dealings made him hated by those under him. In later years in the Peninsula he planted stolen property in a fellow sergeant's pack to get him broken.

There was no further promotion within the company for an NCO (colour-sergeants were not introduced until 1813), but there were two posts at regimental (battalion) head-quarters to which an ambitious sergeant could aspire. Both could lead to officer rank. The junior of the two was the quartermaster-sergeant, who might one day hope for com-missioned rank as a quartermaster. His duties lay with stores, rations, clothing and the maintenance of ledgers. It was a thoroughly responsible position demanding an educated man with administrative ability and initiative. The more senior position was that of sergeant-major – a rank that would one day be converted to that of regimental sergeant-major. 'Fortunate is the regiment which possesses a good sergeant-major.' He was, and still is, the commanding officer's right-hand man in all his dealings with the NCOs of the battalion. He had responsibility for discipline, duties and drill; he recommended NCOs for promotion; he organised the rou-tine parades, guards and duties of the battalion. Some had their eyes on the slim chance of commissioned status as an adjutant.

All these avenues to further promotion were closed to Sharpe for as long as he stayed stuck in the armoury at Seringapatam. For fifty months he led a dreary life repairing muskets, oiling muskets, counting muskets, issuing muskets and test-firing them. When not doing that he was making up cartridges and checking ammunition. Occasionally he would be given a task by *Major Stokes*, the engineer officer in overall charge of the armoury and workshops, that took him outside the city. It was on one such duty in early July 1803 that he was wounded in the head and left for dead when the post at *Chasalgaon* was overrun. He had been sent to bring back 80,000 rounds of ammunition that had temporarily been stored there. Little did he realise that his days as a sergeant were almost over. Plucked from obscurity for another special mission, he ended up three months later as a mounted orderly to his old commanding officer, General Wellesley, at one of his most famous Indian victories – Assaye. In the space of 'one crowded hour of glorious life' he was wounded, killed six enemy and saved his general's life. Two days later he was an officer.

THE OFFICER – AN UNHAPPY LIFE (1803–8)

Sharpe was twenty-six when he was commissioned ensign in the 74th Foot (Highlanders), ultimately the 2nd Battalion Highland Light Infantry on 25 September 1803. A battlefield commission for exceptional gallantry was something of a rarity at the start of the nineteenth century, though over the next twelve years, as the exigencies of the Peninsular War, the East and West Indies and then the American War of 1812 stacked up, so the demand for replacement officers soared. This led, among other things, to a noticeable increase in the number of senior NCOs being commissioned. That Wellesley had promoted Sharpe to officer status was certainly remarkable as he had an ingrained aristocratic prejudice against the practice. In later years he was to comment harshly upon ex-ranker officers, saying, 'their origin would come out, and you could never perfectly trust them.' Sharpe had saved Wellesley's life, so the debt had to be repaid, but there remained a huge gulf between them; mutual respect for professional ability, certainly, but mingled with a coolness that

GENERAL LAKE'S
GENEROSITY

Wellesley gave Sharpe
his commission for
gallantry, guts and
saving his life in
battle. He was never
known to buy one,
other than for himself.
While Wellesley was
respected for his
ability, Lord Lake,
who was operating
against the Mahrattas
to the north in 1803,
was also popular for
his kindliness and
generosity. John Shipp,
who served under
Lake, has given an
example: 'A very old
lieutenant had given
up all hope of getting
a company that was
vacant, knowing full
well that he could not
afford to buy it. I was
standing by him when
the orderly book,
showing his
promotion by
purchase, was put in
his hands. He looked
at it and said, "There
must be some mistake.
I have not a rupee to
call my own." Just
then Colonel Lake, his
Lordship's son, came
up and wished him joy
of his promotion.
"There must be some
mistake," the man
answered, "I cannot
purchase." "My father
knows you cannot,"
said the Colonel, "so
he has lent you the
money which he never
intends to take back." '

was not entirely due to the difference in rank. It was almost
as though Wellesley felt uncomfortable that he owed his life
to a sergeant. In 1836, when as Duke of Wellington he
addressed the Royal Commission on Military Punishment,
he was uncompromising in his general condemnation of ex-
ranker officers:

> [They] do not make good officers; it does not answer. They
> are brought into a society to the manners of which they are
> not accustomed; they cannot bear at all being heated in wine
> or liquor . . . they are quarrelsome, they are addicted to quarrel
> a little in their cups. And they are not persons that can be
> borne in the society of the officers of the Army; they are
> different men altogether.

The Duke's remarks in later life do not always reflect the
actions of the much younger general in the field. When a
regiment had distinguished itself in action it was not
unknown for him to call on the commanding officer to rec-
ommend a sergeant for a commission, as in the case of three
sergeants from the battalions of the Light Division on the
'blood-stained ridge' at Bussaco in 1810 who waited until the
enemy was a mere ten paces from them before firing, thus
knocking over a thousand Frenchmen in a few seconds and
smashing a divisional attack.

Serving in India at the same time as Sharpe was a soldier
named John Shipp whose career followed a remarkably similar path. Like Sharpe, he had been raised as an orphan by
his parish and then enlisted as a youth in 1797 into the 22nd
Foot (Cheshire). Whereas Shipp escaped a flogging by the
intervention of his commanding officer, the intervention of
the general merely reduced Sharpe's punishment from 2,000
lashes to 202. Both had a rough ride as private soldiers.
Eventually Shipp was made a sergeant and posted to India.
There he participated in Lord Lake's unsuccessful and costly
siege of Bhurtpore in 1805, leading several forlorn hope
storming parties. His daring and leadership as a sergeant
earned him an ensign's commission in the 65th Foot (2nd

A flogging

GENTLEMEN
VOLUNTEERS

It has been calculated
that during the
Napoleonic Wars
almost 5 per cent of
officers were
'gentlemen
volunteers' – young
men who, lacking the
money to purchase a
commission, were
willing to serve in the
ranks in the hope of
eventually getting a
free commission. With
the backing of the
regimental colonel,
while they waited for
battle or disease to
take its toll, these
volunteers shouldered
a musket, marched
and stood in the ranks
with the men (but ate
with the officers).
When a vacancy
occurred for an
ensign's commission
they were first in line.
If there was more than
one volunteer the
vacancy went
according to seniority.

Yorkshire, North Riding). Within three weeks he had secured
a lieutenant's position in the 76th Foot (Hindoostan) – a
regiment that would one day become the 2nd Battalion of
the Duke of Wellington's (West Riding) Regiment – Sharpe's
old 33rd Foot. Back in England, Shipp fell heavily into debt.
He partially blamed his sergeant (another *Hakeswill*?) for his
troubles:

> The routine of dissipation which was kept up at Wakefield,
> was not to be sustained by me without expense; and to meet
> these expenses I spent more than my income. This extrava-
> gance – with the loss of fifty pounds, of which I was robbed
> by my sergeant, who took advantage of my youth and inex-
> perience – soon involved me in debts, to liquidate which I
> was obliged to apply for permission to sell my commission.
> This, in consideration of my services was readily granted . . .
> with the residue of the money [I] repaired to London, where
> in about six months I found myself without a shilling, without
> a home, and without a friend.

Recruiting the Irish – a memorable undertaking

BENJAMIN HARRIS, who served mostly in the 95th Rifles from 1806–14 as a private, told his story in 1835 to Henry Curling and the result was published in 1848 as *The Recollections of Rifleman Harris*. Harris, stationed in Dublin, encountered a recruiting party from the 95th and immediately volunteered to join the second battalion:

This recruiting party, who were all Irishmen and had been sent over from England to collect men from the Irish Militia, were just about to return to England. They were the most reckless and devil-may-care set of men I ever beheld, before or since. Being joined by a sergeant of the 92nd Highlanders, and a Highland piper of the same regiment – a pair of rollicking blades – I thought we would all go mad together. We started our journey at the Royal Oak in Cashel. Early as it was, we were all three sheets in the wind. When we paraded before the door of the Royal Oak, the landlord and landlady of the inn, who were quite as lively, came reeling forth and thrust into the fists of the sergeants two decanters of whisky for them to carry along and refresh themselves on the march. The piper struck up, the sergeants flourished their decanters, the whole route commenced a terrific yell, and we all began to dance through the town, stopping every now and then for another pull at the whisky decanters. We kept this up until we had danced, drunk, shouted and piped thirteen Irish miles from Cashel to Clonmel.

After about ten days our sergeants had collected a good batch of recruits, and we started for England. However, a few days before we embarked . . . we were nearly pestered to death by a detachment of old Irish women. On hearing that their sons had enlisted, they came from different parts to try to get them away from us. They followed us down to the water's edge and clung to their offspring. When they were dragged away, they sent forth such dismal howls and moans that it was quite distracting to hear them. The lieutenant commanding the party ordered me – the only Englishman present – to endeavour to keep them back, but it was all I could do to keep them from tearing me to pieces.

From Pill, where we landed, we marched to Bristol and thence to Bath where our Irish recruits roamed about the town, staring at and admiring everything they saw, as if they had just been taken wild in the woods. They all carried immense shillelaghs in their fists, which they would not quit for a moment, seeming to think their very lives depended on possession of these bludgeons . . .

From Bath we marched to Andover, and when we came upon Salisbury Plain, our Irish friends got up a fresh row ... one of the Catholics gave a whoop, leapt in the air, and dealt his [dancing] partner – a Protestant – a tremendous blow with his shillelagh, which stretched him upon the sod ... This was quite enough. The bludgeons playing away at a tremendous rate, with the poor Protestants quickly disposed of. Then arose a cry of 'Huzza for the Wicklow boys! Huzza for the Connaught boys! Huzza for Munster! Huzza for Ulster!' and they recommenced the fight as if they were determined to make an end to their soldiering altogether on Salisbury Plain.

We had four officers with us ... Only when the recruits had tired themselves did they begin to slacken in their endeavours, and to feel the effect of the blows they dealt one another. They then suffered themselves to be pacified, and the officers got them into Andover where we obtained some refreshment. But we had only been there a couple of hours when these incorrigible blackguards again commenced quarrelling. Collecting together in the streets, they created so serious a disturbance that the officers got together a body of constables, seized some of the most violent, and succeeded in thrusting them into the town gaol. Their companions, collecting again, endeavoured to break open the prison gates. Baffled in this attempt, they rushed through the streets knocking down everybody they met. The drums now commenced beating up for a volunteer corps of the town, which quickly mustering, drew up in the street before the gaol. They were immediately ordered to load with ball. This pacified the rioters somewhat, and when our officers persuaded them to listen to a promise of pardon, peace was at last restored.

The next day we marched for Ashford, in Kent, where I joined the 95th Rifles.

Shipp re-enlisted into the 24th Dragoons and worked his way up to sergeant-major before being commissioned for a second time on the battlefield for a single combat with a Nepalese chief in the First Goorkha War of 1815. Forced by a court martial in 1823 on to half-pay, Shipp nevertheless ended his days as Chief Constable of Liverpool. Interestingly, although it was officially forbidden to sell a non-purchase commission, Shipp got permission to do so. He used the right channels, whereas Sharpe, equally indebted, planned to sell his commission directly to the Army Agents and dis-

Officers' expenses

THERE WAS NO WAY that Sharpe, or any other junior officer, could avoid mounting debts if forced to live on his pay. An officer of the 50th Foot at this time set out the daily, more or less unavoidable, deductions from his pay of 4s 6d a day as follows:

Dinner at the mess	2s 0d
Wine at ditto	1s 0d
Servant & sundries	0s 6d
Breakfast	0s 6d
Washing & mending	0s 6d
Balance left for pocket money & dress	£0 0s 0d

Out of this balance of nothing the officer had to provide and maintain his uniform and equipment. Sharpe was on active service overseas so was able to scrounge, adapt his soldier's jacket, 'borrow' items and purchase others cheaply at auctions of dead officers' belongings. Wellesley presented him with a telescope. In peacetime England, kitting himself out this way would not have been acceptable. Uniform, sword, and spy-glass (telescope) would have cost over £40 – an expense usually met by the young man's father. Had Sharpe been commissioned into the cavalry (a virtual impossibility) his pay would have been 8s a day, but his expenses would have included the maintenance of a horse and equipment. A regimental inquiry by the 15th Light Dragoons in 1804 revealed the cost of equipping a cornet (cavalry ensign) for active service was almost £460. The inquiry calculated that a cornet would need £381 a year in addition to his pay, even supposing that he drank only a pint of wine a day and did not have a civilian servant.

appear. Had he gone about it properly, he might have succeeded – but then he would never have gone to Copenhagen.

Unlike Shipp, who was well received in the 65th, Sharpe encountered hostility as an officer in the 74th Foot. He had been forced to change regiments because it would have been impossible for a soldier who had been flogged, then achieved promotion to sergeant by some covert activities in Seringapatam and spent several years in obscurity at the rear, suddenly to reappear as an officer in the 33rd. But as a Londoner he was never going to find it easy fitting into the 74th. Though they had abandoned their kilts for trousers in India, this was a Highland Regiment, intensely clannish and wary of outsiders. The officer cadre was almost entirely made up of

Scottish gentry and landowners; and even with the soldiers Sharpe was uncomfortable. He felt like a foreigner in their midst, and found it exceedingly hard to understand their broad Scottish accents. He lasted about two months as an officer in No. 6 Company before being shunted off as second-in-command of the bullock train – surely an appointment designed to humiliate. It was hinted to him that he might feel more at home in the new regiment, the 95th Rifles, which had recently formed in England. Unfortunately for Sharpe's morale there would be a long wait before he could leave India.

It was common for ex-rankers to be regarded as misfits – and not just by fellow officers. Soldiers, too, usually preferred to be commanded by gentlemen. After all, it was what they were accustomed to in civil life. A soldier in Sharpe's regiment, Rifleman Harris of the 95th, had this to say on the subject:

> I know from experience, that in our army the men like best to be officered by gentlemen, men whose education has rendered them more kind in manners than your coarse officer, sprung from obscure origin, and whose style is brutal and overbearing.

Percentage of infantry commissions purchased

BY THE TIME the Peninsular War was nearing its end in 1813 the percentage of infantry officers who had to purchase their commissions was quite small. The table below gives the numbers for line battalions (Foot Guards and garrison battalions omitted) compiled from the *London Gazette* for Sept. 1810 to Aug. 1811 and Mar. 1812 to Feb. 1813:

	Total promotions	% by purchase
Ensign to Lt	975	12.3
Lt to Capt.	407	22.3
Capt. to Maj.	126	30.9
Maj. to Lt-Col	50	18.0
Total	1558	17.7

SERGEANT'S PIKE

Except in Rifle
Regiments (where they
carried rifles) or light
companies (shortened
muskets), infantry
sergeants were not
issued with firearms –
depriving the battalion
of the fire of around 30
muskets. Instead they
carried a 7-foot pike –
also known as a
halberd or spontoon –
with a cross-piece
below the point to
prevent over-
penetration. Useful on
parade for dressing
ranks (the forerunner
of the sergeant-major's
pace-stick or sergeant's
cane), a pike required
the use of two hands.
Four halberd-wielding
sergeants protected the
King's and Regimental
Colours, carried by two
junior ensigns. Most
sergeants were content
with the pike as it was
easier to keep clean
than a musket and
served to advertise rank
and status. One
exception was the
sergeant of the 7th Foot
who, running with his
pike, tripped, caught
the point in the ground
and fell upon the metal
butt, which went right
through his body.

'Going to the
halberds' meant a
flogging. Unfortunate
offenders (like Sharpe)
would be tied to a
triangle of pikes to
receive their
punishment.

The promoted sergeant found himself in a difficult position, and it required a man of exceptional character to make good in his new role. As the wars progressed and more ex-rankers were commissioned, they tended to drift into appointments such as quartermasters, recruiting officers and barrack masters. A number also became adjutants. In command, they seldom seemed to shine. Sir Charles Oman in his research could only find one who had reached the rank of colonel and two who had become majors by 1815. So Sharpe's later promotions were well above average for men of his background.

Discounting veteran battalions (units of men, not fit enough for active service, employed to garrison fortresses around Britain, whose officers were mostly former NCOs), during the Napoleonic Wars just under 6 per cent of officers had risen from the ranks. That represents about one in twenty. In the 1780s the peacetime officer corps was largely a self-perpetuating body composed of the sons of officers plus a high proportion of the aristocracy (24 per cent) and landed gentry (16 per cent). Of these, the majority were in the Guards or fashionable Hussar Regiments; only 12 per cent were in the infantry of the line. The vast expansion of the army between 1793 and 1814 wholly changed the picture. In the year Sharpe joined there were 3,107 officers in the army (discounting foreign and veteran units); by 1814 there were 10,590 on full pay. During the Peninsular War the replacement rate for officers averaged about 1,000 a year. In 1813, for example, 426 died, 307 retired or resigned and 59 were thrown out for disciplinary reasons; 300 officers were required for new or expanded units. Demand had hugely outstripped the normal supply. It is a telling fact that by 1810 only around 19 per cent of new officers were buying their commissions.

Once commissioned, there were a number of ways Sharpe could, in theory, have secured further promotions. Having retrieved most of his booty of stolen jewels from *Hakeswill* in December 1803, he was a rich man who could afford to

Sharpe's rifle

SHARPE HAD BEEN a soldier for ten years before he was commissioned, and had spent much of that time marching with a musket or as an armourer sergeant at Seringapatam. He could perform all the musketry firing drills to perfection and, within the severe limitations of the weapon, was an excellent shot. Starting with a loaded musket he could get off five shots in a minute – the normal rate being three. When he joined the 95th as an officer, he made use of the five months before being made quarter-master to become proficient with the Baker rifle.

Designed by Ezekiel Baker, the rifle had a 30-inch barrel with seven grooves to spin the ball for greater accuracy, with a calibre varying from 0.615 to 0.70. A reasonable shot could hit a man at 200 yards under battle conditions. Trials at 100 and 200 yards with 36 and 24 shots respectively produced 100 per cent hits. It was an excellent weapon for sniping at officers or gunners, something that Sharpe drummed into his soldiers. The short barrel allowed for loading in the prone position, giving skirmishers a huge advantage. The barrel was 'browned' (rather than polished, like most muskets) for concealment. The Baker's main drawback was the slowness of loading (two shots a minute) due to the need to force the ball, wrapped in a patch for a tight fit, down the grooves. Initially a mallet was provided for this purpose because the early rifle balls were made from cavalry carbine moulds of virtually the same bore as the barrel, so there was no windage due to the very tight fit. Each rifleman carried a small tool bag, new flints and patches as well as cartridges, balls and powder. A 24-inch sword bay-onet was provided and to this day the command in Rifle Regiments is 'Fix swords' rather than 'Fix bayonets'. Some 30,000 Bakers were produced 1800–15 for issue not only to British Rifle Regiments but to allied units in the Peninsular War such as the Portuguese Cacadores.

buy promotion. The cost of one step up to lieutenant would have been £500 (had he purchased his ensign's commission for £400 rather than being awarded it free on the battlefield, he would only have had to pay the difference in value – £100). Even a captain's commission at about £1,500 would have been well within his means (though at least two years' service was required).

It was not lack of cash that prevented Sharpe obtaining promotion by purchase but lack of seniority and, far more important, lack of support from his commanding officer.

Any vacancy available for purchase had to be offered, for first refusal, to the next senior officer – Sharpe was initially at the absolute bottom of the seniority pile in the 74th. Applications to purchase then had to be submitted, along with recommendations from the colonel, via the Army Agents to Horse Guards in London. Sharpe's commanding officer would never have allowed his application to go forward. In any case, with the regiment in India, the application would have taken months, if not a year or more, to process.

Another route to promotion offered itself if an officer died in service or was dismissed, forfeiting his commission to the Crown – hence the popular toast to a 'sickly season or bloody war'. Free promotion into dead men's shoes became far more widespread as the wars in Europe gathered momentum. But even in these instances, seniority played a critical part. Thus, within a regiment, if a major died the senior captain was entitled to the promotion without payment. In turn, the senior lieutenant got the captain's vacancy, and so on until a free ensign's commission became available. Again, Sharpe would have missed out on this due to his being so junior and the general attitude of his superiors towards him.

As galling as his inability to secure promotion within the 74th was the fact that he could not secure recognition as a 'proper' officer. The junior ensign should have been given the honour of carrying the Regimental Colour on parade or in action, but Sharpe's background and status as an outsider precluded it. This knowledge sent him sliding into debt and decline; he became progressively more morose, introverted, and subject to bouts of sickness. For weeks at a time he was confined to his bed, alternately sweating and shivering or weakened by bouts of what is, perhaps impolitely, referred to as 'Bombay belly'. The only way, short of death, that Sharpe could be moved was to arrange an exchange. As far back as November 1803 it had been suggested that the recently formed 95th Rifles might suit his 'situation'. But the 95th were in England, correspondence took for ever to travel back and forth, making the arrangement of a transfer an intermi-

Sharpe's women

BY THE TIME he was thirty, Sharpe is known to have bedded seven women, all of whom he had become infatuated with. They were, in chronological order:

1 *Maggie Joyce*: In London between 1789 and 1792 (*SRegt*). He remained fond of and grateful to her throughout her life, and entrusted her with the sale of the jewels he picked up after the battle at Vitória.

2 A Yorkshire girl called *Elsie* (1793). He killed an innkeeper – the act that led him to enlist – over this girl.

3 *Mary Bickerstaff*: In India (*ST*). Anglo-Indian former wife of a deceased sergeant.

4 *Simone Joubert*: In India (*STr*). Wife of a French mercenary captain.

5 *Mrs Clare ('Brick') Wall* (*SF*). Widow of a British soldier and servant of *Captain Torrance*.

6 *Lady Grace Hale*: On ship coming home from India (*STraf*). Wife of *Lord William Hale*, she widowed herself during the Battle of Trafalgar. The first woman Sharpe was serious about. They lived together in England until she died giving birth to his son, who died a few hours later.

7 *Astrid Skovgaard*: In Copenhagen (*SP*). Daughter of a Danish businessman who also ran an intelligence-gathering operation.

---

nable process. Finally the regimental colonel of the 74th, with the Army Agents acting for him (certainly for a fee), managed to arrange an exchange with an officer in the 1/95th. It must have been a second lieutenant who was either disillusioned with life in the Rifles, wanted to avoid going overseas with them to Germany in October 1805, or had failed to impress his commanding officer, Lieutenant-Colonel Beckwith. Probably it was a combination of all three.

Having twice been prevented from leaving the country when sickness caused him to miss a sailing, Sharpe finally sailed at the end of June 1805, by which time he had spent fifteen months, since the end of the campaign against the Pindarris, in dull garrison duties at Poona. Ironically, the 74th also departed that year, three months after Sharpe.

*   *   *

On 16 November 1805, Sharpe arrived in England after an invigorating journey on the *Calliope* had raised his spirits considerably. He had killed at least six men and had gained, to use the modern word, 'a partner' in *Lady Grace Hale,* who had conveniently widowed herself with a pistol shot during the latter part of the voyage. The next ten weeks were the happiest Sharpe had experienced as an officer: he was on leave (the 1/95th was in Germany) and living with *Lady Grace,* who was pregnant with his child. It must have been with some reluctance that, in early March 1806, he reported to Lieutenant-Colonel Beckwith and the 1/95th at their barracks at Woodbridge, Suffolk.

Sharpe, now a second lieutenant, was initially posted to No. 3 Company, where he threw himself with considerable enthusiasm into learning the new tactics and drills of rifle-men. He became proficient at handling and firing the Baker rifle – it was to become, along with a heavy sword, a weapon from which he was seldom parted in the long years of soldier-ing that lay ahead. For the first time since he was com-missioned, Sharpe began to feel he could become a proficient officer. He enjoyed light infantry work, it suited his tempera-ment and, apart from some gossip about his relationship with *Lady Grace* among his seniors, the subalterns and soldiers seemed to accept him. For a little over three months he was content with his lot, training hard and slipping away whenever possible for a quick visit to *Lady Grace.* In June 1806, however, his life was shattered. *Lady Grace* died in childbirth and their baby son survived only a few hours.

Once again Sharpe lost interest in life, lost interest in sol-diering, became sullen and introverted, and renewed his interest in the bottle. His grief at the double bereavement was compounded by *Lady Grace*'s family, who claimed the boy was not Sharpe's son but her deceased husband's. Because the boy had died after the mother, everything had passed to him – and then to the family. Sharpe was frozen out.

In August 1806 he was sent for by his commanding officer, Beckwith. It was not a happy interview. Beckwith read the riot act, to which Sharpe responded with a surly silence. His commanding officer had other, more pressing worries on his mind apart from the personal problems of a moody second lieutenant. The battalion was preparing to move to join the 2/95th at Brabourne Lees in Kent, and there were indications that they could soon be required for active service in South America. On top of this, he had no quartermaster. Knowing Sharpe was an ex-ranker, Beckwith appointed him acting quartermaster.

Until 1779, when King George III forbade the practice, a quartermaster's commission could be bought and sold like any other. His Majesty, 'not thinking the office very fit for men of better extraction and consequently very improper for a Captain', had originated a custom, which continues to this day as a regulation, whereby quartermasters' commissions are given to ex-rankers. No wonder Colonel Beckwith thought Sharpe the best, probably the only man to fill his vacant post. In the modern army, quartermasters' commissions are given to senior warrant officers who have worked their way up the NCO promotion ladder. No officer with a combatant commission can be a quartermaster. Likewise, a quartermaster would never command troops in a combat role, except in dire emergency when no other officer was available. Although they hold identical ranks to other officers and can rise to lieutenant-colonel, they are listed separately in the Army List, always with the letters (QM) written after their rank.

That quartermasters should be officially regarded as second-rate officers irked Sharpe. He was above all a fighter, a combat soldier and leader who had considerable battlefield experience. A quartermaster's duties involved billeting, feeding, clothing, equipping and supplying ammunition within his battalion. He maintained stocks, kept records and, in peacetime, operated a central store from which issues were made. In effect, he was the commanding officer's supply officer. It was an administrative post of considerable importance, but a non-combatant one. As such, others looked down

Sharpe's wounds

DISCOUNTING MINOR INJURIES, flogging, torture, beatings-up, etc Sharpe had received seven wounds by the time he returned from Copenhagen in 1807:

1 Lance wound in side near Seringapatam, India – April 1799 (*ST*)

2 In head by musket shot at *Chasalgaon* – August 1803 (*STr*)

3 In left shoulder by *tulwar* (sword) at Battle of Assaye – September 1803 (*STr*)

4 In hip by bayonet thrust at Gawilghur – December 1803 (*SF*)

5 In ribs by sword thrust at Gawilghur – December 1803 (*SF*)

6 Deep cut to right cheek (scarred for life) by sword at Gawilghur – December 1803 (*SF*)

7 Side of head grazed by musket ball at Copenhagen – September 1807 (*SP*)

Interestingly, although he was involved in considerable fighting at close quarters at Trafalgar, Sharpe received not so much as a scratch.

on it. And in Sharpe's time it was a dead-end post with no possibility of promotion. Eventually the rank of 'lieutenant and quartermaster' was introduced, but, after the king's scathing comments, a captaincy was out of the question.

Sharpe was quartermaster at Brabourne Lees for almost a year. Within two months of his appointment half the 2/95th were sent to South America, followed shortly afterwards by half the 1st Battalion. Meanwhile he remained in England, bitter, frustrated and disillusioned with the army. During the first six months of 1807 his depression and debt deepened. He began to plan how best to quit the army and sell his commission. When the remaining companies of both the 1st and 2nd Battalions of the 95th were placed on standby for service in Denmark in July, Sharpe was told he would once again stay behind to look after the rear party as barrack master at Brabourne Lees. It seemed the ideal opportunity to put his plan into effect. Once the battalions were embarked, he would go to the Army Agents in London, sell his commission and disappear. It would have been an

Battles and sieges

BY EARLY 1808 Sharpe is known to have participated in the following battles and sieges:

— Boxtel, 15 September 1794 as Pte 33rd

— Mallavelly, 27 March 1799 as Pte 33rd

— Siege of Seringapatam, April 1799 as Pte 33rd (special mission)

— Siege of Ahmednuggur, 11 August 1803 as Sgt 33rd (special mission)

— Assaye, 23 September 1803 as Sgt 33rd (special duties)

— Argaum, 29 November 1803 as Ensign 74th

— Gawilghur, 15 December 1803 as Ensign 74th (temporary Lt Coy 33rd)

— Trafalgar, 23 October 1805 as Ensign 74th

— Køge, 29 August 1807 as 2/Lt 1/95th

— Siege of Copenhagen, August/September 1807 as 2/Lt 1/95th (special mission)

ignominious end to his military career and probably the start of a new one in crime, but a chance meeting led to another special mission, this time in Copenhagen.

When Sharpe returned at the end of October 1807 and reported back to his battalion at Hythe, Beckwith, who had been furious when the quartermaster he had left to supervise administration suddenly appeared in Denmark, put him straight back into his old duties. In April the following year, as his relationship with Beckwith continued to deteriorate, Sharpe heard rumours that the 2/95th might be destined for an expedition to oust the French General Junot from Lisbon. He applied to exchange with the quartermaster of the 2/95th who, for reasons of his own, wished to remain in England. Beckwith expedited the exchange. In May 1808 Sharpe became the quartermaster (still with the rank of second lieutenant) of the 2/95th. Many dramatic and dangerous years lay ahead.

2

Sharpe's Regiments

GENERAL

AS A FUGITIVE FROM JUSTICE, Sharpe had chosen a good year to seek obscurity by enlisting into His Majesty's 33rd Regiment of Foot. In 1793 the French Revolution was rocking Europe, a British military force on the Continent desperately needed reinforcement, and there was serious trouble in the West Indies, so the background of recruits, especially volunteers, was unlikely to be scrutinised. Some two months prior to Sharpe's enlistment, on the very day war had been declared, the navy had swallowed up two battalions of soldiers. When Parliament voted approval and money for a further 25,000 troops, frantic, ill-considered methods were resorted to in an effort to achieve this figure. Quantity was all-important, quality forgotten. One of the most unrewarding schemes was the offer of a free captain's commission to any man who could raise an independent company of about a hundred men. This incentive led to the recruitment of an inordinate number of useless wrecks and old men, who were sent to bolster weak existing regiments. The arrangement was roundly condemned.

The backbone of the army was the line – the infantry, or Regiments of Foot, that formed the main line of battle. The only infantry regiments not officially in the 'line' were the Guards Regiments,* whose primary duty as defenders of the Royal Household required their presence in England. Regi-

---

* 1st Regiment of Foot Guards (later Grenadier Guards), the Coldstream Regiment of Foot Guards (motto 'Second to None'; they were never referred to as the 2nd Foot Guards), and the 3rd Regiment of Foot Guards (later the Scots Guards).

ments were known by their number (titles came much later), the 1st Regiment of Foot (later the Royal Scots) being the first formed and therefore the most senior regiment in the line. In March 1793 only three regiments of the line were to be found south of the Scottish border, but by the end of the year eleven new regiments had been added: the 78th through to the 88th Foot – later to become the Connaught Rangers (The Devil's Own).

Unlike the French and most other European armies, a British infantry regiment was not a tactical formation. It was primarily an administrative unit, which never took the field; the tactical unit was the battalion. At the time Sharpe joined it was usual for regiments to raise only one battalion, but as the Revolutionary and Napoleonic Wars engulfed Europe and the West and East Indies, second or even third battalions became common. Of the regiments Sharpe served in, only the 95th had two battalions at that time, designated 1/95th and 2/95th (where only one battalion existed, as in the case of the 33rd, there would be no need to write 1/33rd). As the system developed and more second battalions were formed, it became common practice for the first battalion to have right of preference for active service, with the second battalion remaining at home, furnishing drafts to keep its senior partner up to strength. It was unusual for both battalions to serve overseas together, though this happened occasionally in the Peninsula, and the two battalions of the 95th Rifles both served in South America in 1806 and again at Copenhagen the following year.

THE STRUCTURE OF A BRITISH INFANTRY REGIMENT

Command and control

The commanding officer of a regiment was the colonel. In the case of new regiments, he would not only lead the troops

Officers' pay in 1685

OFFICERS' PAY SCALES had been laid down by a Royal Warrant of James II in 1685. They appear very low and, in comparison to other ranks' pay, remained low for almost a hundred years. King James and his successors never intended officers to live on their pay. Substantial sums were required to purchase a commission and considerable private wealth was essential for officers to maintain the standards of living demanded of a gentleman.

Colonel	12s per day, plus 8s as 'captain' of his company
Lieutenant-Colonel	7s, plus 8s for his company
Major	5s, plus 8s as above
Captain	8s
Lieutenant	4s
Ensign	3s

but raise them. Thus Sharpe's future regiment came into being in 1702 when the sovereign, Queen Anne, granted the Earl of Huntingdon a commission:

ANNE R

... to authorise you by Beat of Drumme or otherwise, to raise Voluntiers for a regiment of Foot under your command, which is to consist of twelve Companys of two Serjeants, Three Corporals, Two Drummers and Fifty-nine private soldiers, with the addition of one Serjeant more to the Company of Grenadiers ... And when the whole number ... shall be fully or near completed, they are to march to our city of Gloucester ... to receive arms for our said regiment out of the Stores of our Ordnance ...

The authorised establishment in 1702 was: 12 captains as company commanders; 2 commissioned staff officers (adjutant and quartermaster); 1 captain-lieutenant, 12 lieutenants and 11 ensigns – 38 officers. There were also 24 sergeants, 36 corporals, 24 drummers and 708 privates, making a total full establishment of 830 all ranks. Although called a regiment,

Junior officer training

TODAY'S YOUNG OFFICER, fresh from the Royal Military Academy, Sandhurst, is not considered sufficiently trained to be placed immediately in command of troops. No matter what branch of the army he is joining, he must attend (and pass) a further six months' specialist training. When Sharpe won his commission in India there was no officer training as his battalion was on active service and he was already an expert on weapon-handling and shooting, well versed in the intricacies of infantry drills. The same could not be said of newly commissioned officers straight from civil life in England. Many an ensign was totally ignorant of basic military skills and knew nothing of drill, musketry, swordsmanship or what words of command to give on the parade ground or battlefield. In other words, he was being put in command of men who knew far more than he did. In 1792 officer training was put on a formal footing with regulations. The extract below shows the extent of their detail:

> Every officer must be instructed in each individual circumstance required of a recruit, or a soldier; also in the exercise of the sword: and accustomed to give words of command, with that energy and precision that is so essential. Every officer, on first joining a regiment, is to be examined by the commanding officer; and, if he is found imperfect in the knowledge of the movements required from a soldier, he must be ordered to be exercised that he may learn their just execution. Till he is master of those points, and capable of instructing the men under his command, he is not to be permitted to take the command of a platoon in the battalion.
>
> Squads of officers must be formed, and exercised by a field officer; they must be marched in all directions, to the front, oblique, and to the flank; they must be marched in line, at platoon distance . . . [The present writer is reminded of similar subalterns' parades under the adjutant.]
>
> An officer must not only know the post, which he should occupy in all changes of situation, the commands which he should give, and the general intention of the required movement; but he should be master of the principles on which each is made; and of the faults that may be committed, in order to avoid them himself, and to instruct others . . .

in terms of active service in the field this was a battalion.

The officer structure needs some explanation. There appears to be no officer above the rank of captain in the regiment. In fact, there were three field officers – a colonel, lieutenant-colonel and a major. In 1702, and for several decades afterwards, the colonel was the actual commanding officer, with overall responsibility for all the day-to-day duties of clothing, arming, paying, disciplining and training his regiment (battalion), as well as leading it in battle. The lieutenant-colonel was his second-in-command, while the major had particular responsibility for drill and worked closely with the adjutant. In theory, each of the three field officers also commanded a company. In practice, those three companies were commanded by lieutenants (de facto captains), and the colonel's company by an officer holding the temporary rank of captain-lieutenant.

With the exception of the grenadiers, each of the remaining companies had a theoretical establishment of a captain, lieutenant and ensign. The grenadier company had a captain (usually the senior captain in the regiment) plus a first and second lieutenant. The surgeon and chaplain were, at this early stage, functionaries appointed by the colonel, not commissioned officers. Field officers did particularly well out of this arrangement as they drew pay for their actual rank as well as for being company commanders!

It was a rewarding honour to be the captain-lieutenant commanding the colonel's company. Not only was he the senior lieutenant in the regiment, and paid accordingly, but his status was equal to a junior captain, and he was entitled to be addressed as such. Moreover, when he was eventually promoted, his seniority as a fully-fledged captain was deemed to have commenced with his appointment as captain-lieutenant, allowing him to leapfrog captains who had previously been senior to him. This system lasted until 1803.

By the time Sharpe won his commission, the officer structure had been improved. In 1795 an additional lieutenant-colonel and major had been added to the establishment of every battalion. These officers did not have responsibility for a company. In May 1803 the Horse Guards issued instructions that 'in future each Troop [cavalry unit] and

Company [infantry unit] throughout the Army shall have an effective Captain, and therefore the Colonels, First [senior] Lieutenant-Colonels and First Majors, in the respective Regiments, shall no longer have Troops and Companies.' Three additional captains were added to the establishment and the rank of captain-lieutenant disappeared. Also added to the staff and ranking as commissioned officers were the surgeon, assistant surgeon and paymaster.

An essential element in the control of a regiment (battalion) in battle was its Colours – the King's Colour and the Regimental Colour. These formed the rallying point in battle; if things went wrong, they formed in the centre of the battalion line, column or square. Where the Colours were, there was the regiment. They represented the regiment's soul, its honour and its achievements. To lose them was the ultimate disgrace. Every man had to be able to recognise his regiment's Colours in the dust, smoke, noise and confusion of battle. Today's Trooping the Colour ceremony in London on the sovereign's official birthday has its origins in the need to recognise the Colours. Each year during the ceremony the Colour of one of the battalions of Foot Guards is borne slowly up and down the ranks of the guardsmen, showing it to the soldiers.

The King's (or Queen's) Colour was a Union flag with the regimental number/badge in its centre. The Regimental Colour was a flag of the colour of the regimental facings (cuffs, collars and lapels) with a small Union flag in the upper canton (top corner nearest the staff) and the regiment's number, badge, laurel wreath, etc in the centre. They were made of richly decorated silk and, from the early 1800s, had the regiment's most important battle honours embroidered on them. The dimensions of both were the same: 6' 6" x 6' tied to a 9' 10" pike. This made them extremely heavy. When unfurled in a strong wind, a young ensign in his teens (George Keppel, who carried the Regimental Colours of the 3/14th at Waterloo, was only just sixteen) holding the pike with both

In defence of the Colours

DUTY IN the Colour party in battle was an honour, but not always popular. In a battle such as Waterloo it was liable to be a death sentence – as Sergeant William Lawrence, who was ordered to the Colours during the afternoon of that battle, was all too aware:

> This . . . was a job I did not like at all; but still I went to work as boldly as I could. There had been before me that day fourteen sergeants already killed and wounded while in charge of these colours, with officers in proportion, and the staff and colours were almost cut to pieces.

A desperately bloody battle took place at Salamanca, Spain, in 1811 where the British/Spanish/Portuguese allies under General Beresford confronted the French under Marshal Soult. During the struggle (which cost Beresford 6,000 casualties, most of them British) the 1/3rd Foot temporarily lost their King's and Regimental Colours when caught by lancers while not formed in square. As the lancers crashed into the battalion, sixteen-year-old Ensign Edward Thomas held up the Regimental Colour after his company commander had fallen, yelling, 'Rally on me men, I will be your pivot.' A Frenchman shouted to him to yield, to which Thomas replied, 'Only with my life!'

Stabbed and slashed at from all sides, he fell and a lancer snatched up the precious Colour.

The King's Colour was carried by Ensign Charles Walsh, who was wounded by a roundshot that also smashed the pike. Lieutenant Matthew Latham seized the Colour. He was instantly surrounded by enemy horsemen determined to take the trophy. After receiving a brutal sabre blow across his face, half blinded by blood, Latham clung on until his left arm was severed from his body. Dropping his sword, he continued to cling to the Colour with his right hand until he was ridden down and speared many times by lance thrusts. With a last superhuman effort he ripped the Colour from the pike and stuffed it inside his coat.

After the battle the Regimental Colour was found by a sergeant from another regiment and returned. Miraculously, Latham, with the blood-soaked King's Colour still under his jacket, survived. He was later rewarded by promotion to captain and a gold medal from his regiment (that he was, uniquely, allowed to wear on his uniform). His appallingly disfigured face was repaired by a leading surgeon, the cost being borne by the Prince Regent. He retired in 1820 on a pension of £170 a year.

hands would be hard pressed not to be blown over. In practice, in such conditions, the silk was partly furled and held against the staff with one hand. A strong, buff leather shoulder belt supported the Colour when carried unfurled on parade or in the field. On the line of march or in camp the Colours were cased – that is, rolled up round the pike staff and covered by a black, brass-topped canvas case. Although today's Colours are smaller, taking them out of the colour belt, lowering them in salute while marching – all with one arm – requires, as the present writer can verify, a strong arm.

The honour of carrying the Colours on parade or in battle went to the two junior ensigns, the senior of the two having the King's (or Queen's) Colour. As junior ensign of the 74th in the attack at Argaum in late November 1803, Sharpe should have been permitted to carry the Regimental Colour. His posting to No. 6 Company was almost certainly a deliberate slight. Each officer had a protective escort of a pike-armed sergeant who, if his officer fell, would take up the Colour (until another officer could be found). This was an honourable, if not always popular, appointment for a senior NCO. Eventually 'Colour-Sergeant' became the next rank above sergeant in infantry regiments.

If it was an honourable job, it was also a deadly one. In a major battle the life expectancy of officers carrying Colours, and of the sergeants protecting them, was likely to be short. The Colours were in the centre of the battalion line, the companies had to keep their dressing (alignment) in an advance on them, officers and soldiers had continually to glance in towards the centre to see the Colours, so they had to be kept flying at all costs. The problem was they provided an obvious target. Knock down the Colours with gun or musketry fire and you created confusion, loss of control. Capture the Colours in hand-to-hand fighting and you won undying fame, as well as inflicting the ultimate disgrace on your enemy. So the Colour party was a magnet for enemy fire and, in a mêlée, for sustained and ferocious attacks. As one young ensign fell, so another had to be found to replace him (in the meantime a sergeant or anyone nearby grabbed the Colour). Finding replacements was normally the adjutant's task, so he would position himself, along with the sergeant-major, close behind the Colour party. Even in the press of battle, seniority played its part. Below is an account of an adjutant calling forward ensigns by seniority to replace those hit. It occurred in 1813 at the Battle of Vitória (at which Sharpe was to participate and get rich again).

> At this moment Mr Bridgeland's [the adjutant's] voice called for me to the Colours, and I proceeded there and found poor Delmar had been shot through the heart. In the confusion of the moment a mistake had been made and Mr Hill, being junior to me, should have been called. This, the adjutant discovered, and I returned to my company. But I had not been there long when a second call was made for me, and I found that Hill had been struck in the breast, similar to Delmar, and carried away . . . I now took the fatal colour and entered into conversation with Ensign Tatlow, bearing the other.

A lucky chance of seniority had, seemingly, saved Ensign William Keep's life.

The companies

The fighting strength of all infantry battalions was made up of company sub-units. By the time Sharpe joined the army the number of companies in a battalion had been reduced from twelve to ten, each under the command of a captain. These companies were divided into eight battalion (or centre) companies numbered from 1 to 8, one grenadier company and one light company.

The grenadiers originated in the eighteenth century when the tallest and strongest soldiers were picked to throw grenades – weapons that had fallen from use. Theirs was always the senior company, supposedly the elite sub-unit with the best soldiers. It formed on the extreme right flank of the battalion on parade or in battle. The soldiers could be distinguished by an all-white plume on their headdress – in Sharpe's case, when he was commissioned into the 74th, a bonnet. The battalion company men sported white over red plumes and the light company green.

The light company were the skirmishers. These were the regiment's best shots, its most agile men. The lights always formed on the left, and spent much of their time on the battlefield 100–200 yards out in front of the main position, opposing enemy skirmishers, or advancing ahead of the battalion. At this time (early 1800s) they were armed, like the others, with a musket and bayonet.

In between the grenadier and light companies were the eight battalion companies, formed up in the line with No. 1 Company on the left of the grenadiers and No. 8 on the right of the lights. Between No. 4 and No. 5 Company were the Colours.

When Sharpe joined the 74th at the end of September 1803 it was commanded by Lieutenant-Colonel William Wallace, who, as a favour to his friend *Colonel McCandless*, had accepted Sharpe into the battalion as an officer. He posted Sharpe to No. 6 Company under the command of *Captain Urquhart* (in reality possibly Captain Andrew Dyce). The establishment for the companies of a battalion of the 74th in 1803 was:

	Battalion Companies	Grenadier Company	Light Company
Capt.	1	1	1
Lts	2	3	3
Ensigns	1	–	–
Sgts	3	3	3
Cpls	4	4	4
Drms	2	2	2
Fifers	–	2	–
Ptes	71	71	71

At full strength, the companies would each have 4 officers, 3 sergeants and 77–9 other ranks, giving the battalion a total strength of 40 company officers and 802 other ranks. In practice, particularly in India on campaign, the actual numbers fell well below the establishment for both officers and soldiers. Drafts arriving from England made up some of the losses from disease and enemy action, but by no means all. The 74th had been in India since 1788 (fifteen years) when Sharpe joined them. The regiment had fought at Mallavelly, Seringapatam, Ahmednuggur and Assaye, where they had been cut to pieces (which was another reason why Wallace did not need much persuading to take Ensign Sharpe – he was desperately short of officers). We know that Sharpe was the only other officer in No. 6 Company and there were just two sergeants, *Colquhoun* and *Craig*. It seems reasonable to suppose that the men numbered no more than 60, which would mean an approximate total of 30 officers (including staff) and 600 soldiers in the 74th Regiment when they advanced to attack at Argaum on 29 November 1803.

Companies would advance to attack in a line two ranks deep. The regulations prescribed three ranks, but in practice two were preferred as they allowed greater firepower to the front. The frontage of No. 6 Company at Argaum would have been about 25 yards, with the men's elbows almost touching. This would have given the battalion a frontage of some 250 yards (the light company seems not to have formed a skirmish line ahead of the advance at this battle). The company commander (*Urquhart*) was on the right of the front rank with *Sergeant Colquhoun* immediately behind him as a file-closer in the rear rank. We know that *Urquhart* had a horse, but he would have sent it to the rear before the advance started – the only officers officially mounted in battle were the field officers and the adjutant. Corporals would have been on the left of both front and rear ranks, with Sharpe forming, much to his annoyance, a supernumerary rank on his own in the rear. It was the job of such individuals (usually junior officers or sergeants) to ensure that rear-rank men moved forward to fill gaps in the front rank, that nobody stopped to help the wounded and that, as casualties mounted, the soldiers closed in on the centre.

The companies, indeed the battalion as a whole, were trained to advance at a slow, steady rate of seventy-five paces to the minute. All ranks had to maintain the step and keep their dressing (alignment) by the centre of the battalion, i.e. from the Colour party. The Colours would be carried aloft using the shoulder belt to support them, the King's Colour on the right. Officers and NCOs in companies to the right of the Colours (grenadiers and 1–4 Companies) would glance left, while those in 5–8 Companies and the lights, if not skirmishing ahead, would look right. Before stepping off, the drummers would give a short cautionary roll, the commanding officer would shout the order and the drummers, marching in the rear of the companies, would beat 'The March' to signal the advance. This might continue if the advance was comparatively short or, if it was a long and difficult approach, the drummers might revert to just beating the time to assist with keeping step. If a halt was required, perhaps to deliver fire, the signal was the drummers ceasing to play. If the pace was to be speeded up, the 'Quick March' was played. If the line was to charge, the drummers beat the 'Point of War'.

Companies expected to take casualties as they closed the distance on the enemy. Officers and NCOs had to keep the advance moving regardless, with the line shrinking in on the centre as gaps were closed. Dead and wounded were left where they fell, the line became ragged, step was lost and the drummers continuously beat 'Point of War' as the distance closed to less than a hundred yards. At about thirty yards from the enemy the line would charge. It was, however, common practice for a British line to halt at about forty yards, fire one volley, and then charge with the bayonet.

Drill was paramount. Companies had practised their nineteen drill movements of the official regulations for countless hours on the parade ground and in the field. In action, following the familiar drill movements, listening to the company drummer and the shouts of the officers or NCOs, keeping in step, keeping dressing, all helped to take the soldier's mind, partially at any rate, from the horrors of what might be happening around him. An example of how fanatical some commanding officers could be about maintaining perfect drill during an actual advance was Lieutenant-Colonel Main-waring of the 51st Foot (later the King's Own Yorkshire Light Infantry) during a battle in the Peninsula. 'I shall never forget him,' wrote Private Wheeler, who witnessed the incident:

> He dismounted off his horse, faced us and frequently called the time 'right, left' as he was accustomed to when drilling the regiment. His eccentricity did not leave him, he would now and then call out 'that fellow is out of step, keep step and they cannot hurt us.' Another time he would observe one such a one, calling him by name, 'cannot march, mark him for drill, Sergeant Major.' 'I tell you again they cannot hurt us if you are steady, and if you get out of time you will be knocked down.' He was leading his horse and a shot passed under the horse's belly which made him rear up. 'You are a coward!' he said. 'I will stop your corn for three days.'

SHARPE TACTICS

The firing line

Infantry tactics were all about producing maximum musket fire at minimum range. Getting this right in battle was the job of the officers, particularly the commanding officer. Whether on the defensive or offensive, in order to produce maximum firepower to the front the battalion or company had to be deployed in a line; that much was common sense. There was, however, some argument as to whether the line should be in two or three ranks (a single rank was rightly rejected, for it was impossible to close gaps and too long and unwieldy to control). The French favoured three ranks; the British tended in practice to opt for two, having learned from experience that third-rank soldiers were often unable to fire for fear of injuring their comrades in front, making their usefulness highly questionable. So when Sharpe stood his ground at Boxtel or attacked at Mallavelly he did so in either the front or rear ranks of his company line.

The other vital element in getting the maximum number of musket balls into the enemy was speed of reloading. The first ball was always likely to be the most accurate, the least likely to misfire. This was due to the loading process being unhurried, the barrel cool and clean. The chance of a misfire increased the more shots fired – about one in eight or nine was the average. After the first shot, speed of reloading depended on not fumbling, not dropping anything. As with most things in the army, it came down to getting the drills right, doing things automatically; pausing to think could prove fatal. Starting with a loaded musket, any soldier worth his pay should have been able to get off three shots in a minute. If well trained, four was not uncommon even in the turmoil and terror of battle. When on form, Sharpe could manage five.

The maximum effective range of a musket was 100 yards, so well-led troops would hold their fire until they were less than that distance from their enemy. This applied to both attacking and defending units. As the enemy approached a defending battalion the overriding question for the commander was *When do I open fire?* The question of who should fire, or how, is dealt with below. At 100 yards, if the enemy were beginning to quicken their pace and had not suffered much during their advance, then he had about fifty seconds before bayonets were crossed. With a reasonably trained battalion, if he fired at 100 yards he might expect to get in three volleys – just. If he waited until they were about 75 yards away he would get in two. At less than 50 only one volley was possible – but it would be a devastating one with virtually all shots hitting home. If this was then followed immediately by a bayonet charge into the smoke, the chances of routing the attackers was high.

For the commanding officer of an attacking battalion, assuming it had deployed into line as it approached the enemy, the problem was somewhat different. The question was whether to halt and fire once, accepting the delay, or to press on as quickly as possible over the final 100 yards. The whole business was complicated if the battalion had advanced initially in column formation for ease of control (see below). Then the first decision was whether (and when) to deploy into line to get maximum muskets to bear, or to push on in column, forget about firing, and rely on the weight of the column to burst through the thin line ahead. If the commander left deployment too late there was likely to be an awful tangle, loss of control and confusion should the enemy fire effectively during this change of formation. In the Napoleonic Wars misjudging this moment cost the French dear on numerous battlefields, particularly when the British concealed their line behind a ridge so it was not until the French reached the crest that they realised what they faced. An attacking British line invariably halted at around 50 yards from the enemy, fired a volley and charged with the bayonet. To stand at close range and exchange musket volleys with an enemy line was a rare and bloody, though not unknown, tactic.

Having decided whether to fire and when, the next decision was how. For a battalion in line there were a number of options:

- One massive volley from both ranks. The obvious disadvantage being that nobody had a loaded musket for about 20–30 seconds, and unpleasant things could happen in that time. On the other hand, such a volley could devastate an enemy if delivered at close range, so it was certainly a good choice if it was to be followed by cold steel.

- Firing one rank at a time. Really a compromise on the first option. It could be extremely effective if the front rank fired at about 75 yards, the second rank at 40, so by the time the survivors had got to within 15–20 yards from the position the first rank could fire again.

- Firing by companies. Companies would fire volleys on the orders of their commanders. It could start on the right with the grenadiers, then No. 1, No. 2, No. 3 and so on.

By the time No. 8 or the light company had fired, the grenadiers would have reloaded and the whole process could start again. Either the left-hand company would fire first, or both flank companies could fire simultaneously with the firing working in towards the centre.

- Firing by alternate companies. In this case, every alternate company could fire simultaneously then, while they reloaded, the other companies would fire.

- Running fire. In reality this meant 'fire at will'. If a musketry duel lasted for more than two or three volleys it was likely that thereafter men would reload and fire as individuals. Unless control by company officers was rigid, casualties, confusion, dense smoke and a closing enemy would result in an erratic banging away along the whole line as each soldier frantically tried to get off one last shot to keep the nearest enemy off the end of their bayonet.

Such was the theory. Of course the battlefield bore little resemblance to a barrack square, or even field exercises on Clapham Common or Salisbury Plain. Discounting the problem of skirmishers often deployed by both sides, the enemy made things difficult by sheltering behind streams, hedges, ridges, or standing atop a steep slope. An advance might be hindered by having to go through or over obstacles, the ground might be uneven, parts of the line might be held up while others pressed ahead unless checked by the officers. And then there was enemy fire. At longer ranges roundshot came skimming and ricocheting through the ranks, decapitating, disembowelling and dismembering. One roundshot was quite capable of knocking over a dozen men if they happened to be aligned one behind the other. As the line closed the distance, howitzer shells would be mixed with the roundshot. If the length of fuse had been correctly judged (not an easy task) the shells would burst over the heads of the advancing troops, showering them with fragments of jagged iron. Finally, if the defenders were well disciplined, attackers would find themselves assailed by a hail of musket balls as soon as they were within range, and the enemy would disappear in clouds of white smoke. By this time the line would surely have shrunk substantially as gaps were filled to the yells of 'Close up, close up!' 'Watch your dressing!' It was at this stage that many attacks faltered, particularly if the final approach involved surmounting an obstacle or struggling up a sharp gradient – or both.

Columns (*see* DIAGRAM 1)

Most armies tried to fight in line and move in column. A column of troops marching along a road is easy to imagine. They could be in single file, or from two to six abreast, forming a long snake of men whose length was many times its width. This was not what a tactical battlefield column looked like. A ten-company battalion 800 strong, moving along a road four abreast, would stretch for about 300 yards (allowing for short gaps between the companies and for the Colour party). That same battalion in a close tactical column would be around 25–30 yards deep and 20 wide. In a quarter-distance column the width remained the same but the depth increased to about 50 yards.

These tactical columns were adopted to allow troops to be kept under the close control of their officers, thus facilitating ease of movement across a battlefield. Precise drill movements, constantly practised in peacetime, enabled a battalion to change quickly from column formation to either a line or a square and back again.

The disadvantages of the column were two-fold. Firstly, as their frontage was, at most, 30 yards wide (one company in line in two ranks) only a maximum of eighty muskets could fire. For this reason they were not intended as fighting (firing) formations. Secondly, these compact, dense formations made a target that was difficult to miss and were therefore very vulnerable to enemy fire, be it artillery or musketry.

DIAGRAM 1 shows how these columns were formed. The difference between the four types lies in the distance between

COLUMN FORMATIONS OF BRITISH (10-COMPANY) BATTALION

(Throughout his service as a soldier, NCO and officer Sharpe would have known the drills for forming, reforming and changing these formations blindfold)

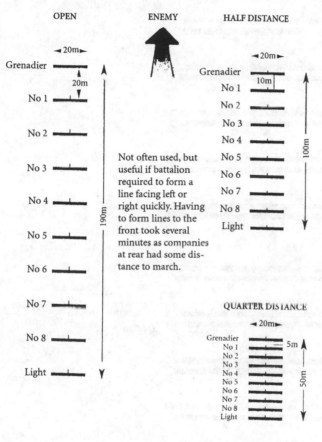

OPEN

◄20m►

Grenadier

20m

No 1

No 2

No 3

No 4

No 5

No 6

No 7

No 8

Light

190m

ENEMY

Not often used, but useful if battalion required to form a line facing left or right quickly. Having to form lines to the front took several minutes as companies at rear had some distance to march.

HALF DISTANCE

◄20m►

Grenadier
No 1   10m
No 2
No 3
No 4
No 5
No 6
No 7
No 8
Light

100m

QUARTER DISTANCE

◄20m►

Grenadier
No 1   5m
No 2
No 3
No 4
No 5
No 6
No 7
No 8
Light

50m

The most frequently adopted formation for initial deployment

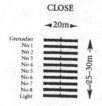

CLOSE

◄20m►

Grenadier
No 1
No 2
No 3
No 4
No 5
No 6
No 7
No 8
Light

25–30m

Formation used when manoeuvring when threatened by cavalry. Could quickly adopt 'closed column' and a closed square with soldiers turning outwards.

THE 74TH FOOT IN COLUMN OF COMPANIES AT QUARTER DISTANCE

DIAGRAM 2

(Ensign Sharpe and known officers and NCOs are named)

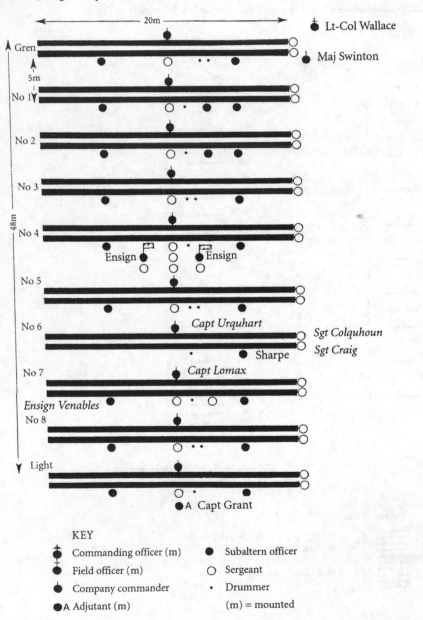

KEY

Commanding officer (m)

Field officer (m)

Company commander

A Adjutant (m)

Subaltern officer

○ Sergeant

· Drummer

(m) = mounted

the companies as they form one behind the other. The Colour party would form in the centre (as in a line) between Nos. 4 and 5 Companies. It was common practice to deploy the light company as skirmishers up to 200 yards in front of the battalion when advancing on an enemy position. DIAGRAM 2 shows the battalion of the 74th Foot formed in column of companies at quarter distance (i.e. a quarter of the frontage of a company between companies). As well as showing the position of the Colours, officers and sergeants, it names certain individuals, including Sharpe, and indicates where they would have been during the initial approach at the Battle of Argaum on 29 November 1803.

Squares

The price for infantry not being in squares when attacked by cavalry was invariably high. Cavalry, particularly heavy cavalry, could smash through a line of infantry, get round its flanks and cut it down from all sides — except the front, if it remained steady. For this reason skirmishers were never expected to face cavalry. A determined advance by mounted troops would scatter skirmishers with ease, sending them flying for sanctuary behind a nearby obstacle or into their own battalion square. If infantry was also caught on the move, and thus unable to fire effectively, the affair could be over in seconds rather than minutes. There were, however, times when it could be decidedly unhealthy to be in square. If the enemy brought up artillery and opened fire with canister or roundshot, the densely packed ranks would be torn apart. Prolonged and heavy skirmisher fire into a target so hard to miss could also be unpleasant.

Depending on the number of companies in a battalion (the French had six, the Prussians four rather than ten), the square was often, in practice, an oblong. Battalions (or regiments) of ten or six companies would normally form oblongs; those with eight or four, squares. The object was to present a hedge of bayonets and muskets with no gaps or

THE CAVALRYMAN CONFRONTS
THE INFANTRY SQUARE

(Although Sharpe knew the drills there is no evidence that he formed
in a square under attack by cavalry during his early life)

The third and fourth ranks are the main firing ranks. The most effective method was for one or both ranks to fire when approaching cavalry came within 30 yards.

The first two ranks are from the grenadier company, the rear two from No.1 Company.

The cavalryman is unable to reach the infantry with his sabre. A lancer might stab the front-rank man but probably not the second.

The horse-man is out-numbered here 4:1, but in reality it was usually nearer 8:1.

The second-rank soldier would be primarily a bayonet man reserving his fire.

The kneeling man in the front rank would not normally fire except in dire emergency.

Note the horse is rearing up, refusing to go into the bayonet hedge.

That the cavalryman has got this close to the square indi-cates that the infantry may have opened fire too soon.

flanks that could be exploited by horsemen. Faced with such a barrier, no horse could be persuaded, no matter how hard its rider dug in his spurs, to force a passage. Battalions that formed line in two ranks formed square in four, as the ranks were doubled up in the process. The outside (front) rank would kneel; those behind would stand. The Colours, the commander, the surgeon and the drummers would be in the centre of this hollow square (or oblong), and it was here that the dead, the dying and the wounded would be dragged. In his early service, Sharpe had no real experience of fighting in a square. It was not until the Peninsula and Waterloo that he saw how important it was for a battalion commander to exercise judgement in deciding when, or when not, to order his men into this formation.

BRITISH ARMY REGIMENTS THAT RETAIN THEIR OLD TITLES

The Royal Scots
The Black Watch
The Argyll and
  Sutherland
  Highlanders
The Duke of
  Wellington's
  Regiment
The Green Howards
The King's Own
  Scottish Borderers
The Royal Welch
  Fusiliers
The King's Regiment
The Cheshire
  Regiment
The King's Own Royal
  Border Regiment

SHARPE'S REGIMENTS

By the time Sharpe was thirty he had served in three regiments, although as an officer and sergeant most of the highlights of his career had been while detached on special missions. The only actions in which he had participated as a member of his regiment were Boxtel (33rd Foot, September 1794), Mallavelly (33rd Foot, March 1799), Argaum (74th Foot, November 1803) and Køge (1/95th Rifles, August 1807). During his four years as a sergeant in India he never served with his regiment in the field.

The 33rd Regiment of Foot

Now called the Duke of Wellington's Regiment (West Riding), the old 33rd Foot celebrated its three hundredth birthday in 2002, and is one of only ten infantry regiments in the British Army to have retained its name rather than disappear into the melting pot of disbandments and amalgamations that have all but destroyed the old regimental system of the infantry of the line. The 'Dukes', or 'the Dukes – Yorkshire Warriors' as they like to be known, are unique in being named after a non-royal personage. The title was bestowed by Queen Victoria in 1853, nine months after the death of the first Duke of Wellington, who had joined the 33rd Foot as a major in the same year as Sharpe. The date chosen was

PAY AND
PAYMASTERS

Regimental pay-
masters were
introduced in 1797.
Prior to this, money
from the public purse
had been given by the
paymaster-general to
the regimental agent,
who would transfer
the funds to an officer
selected by the colonel.
Having distributed the
money to the company
commanders who paid
the men, this officer
would account to the
agent, who would in
turn account to the
paymaster-general.
The appointment of an
additional officer
(with the rank of
captain) as paymaster,
corresponding direct
with the paymaster-
general, led to
confusion. The
paymaster (who could
obtain his commission
with or without
purchase), although
subordinate to his
colonel and bound to
obey him, was also
accountable to civil
court as a civil servant.
Thus he could plead
his colonel's
commands in evasion
of those of the
paymaster-general, and
vice versa. Agents were
delighted because their
workload was reduced
but their emoluments
were unaffected (they
still dealt with clothing
and purchase/sale of
commissions).

18 June, the first anniversary of Waterloo after the Duke's death. The present Duke of Wellington has been Colonel-in-Chief since 1974. He served throughout the Second World War and rose to the rank of brigadier.

When Sharpe joined as a raw recruit on 16 April 1793, the regiment had been in existence for just over ninety-one years. Raised in 1702 as a result of the need to rapidly expand the British Army to combat the French over who should rule Spain (the Wars of Spanish Succession), it was initially known as the Earl of Huntingdon's Regiment of Foot after its first commander. Over the next fifty years the regiment campaigned in Holland, Portugal, Austria, Northern France and Germany. Its first battle honour was Dettingen, 1743. During the American War of Independence (1777–83) it won the reputation of being the best-trained regiment in the army. Sharpe first saw action with it in the Low Countries (Boxtel) in 1794, but it was to be in India that the 33rd and 76th Foot (later to become the 2nd Battalion of the 33rd) won particular distinction. The 33rd gained the battle honour Seringapatam in 1799 (even though Private Sharpe, on a special mission inside the fortress, at one stage was forced to disrupt an attack by his own regiment). It was the regiment that had Sharpe flogged, but also the one in which he was promoted sergeant.

The Duke of Wellington had his old regiment under command again at Waterloo in 1815, where it combined with the 2/69th to form square to meet a two-hour onslaught by the French cavalry on the blood-soaked ridge of Mont St Jean. Sharpe was present as a staff officer and we may be sure he visited the regiment he had joined twenty-two years earlier. The Crimean War (1854–6) saw the Dukes in action at the Alma, Sevastopol and Inkerman. Then followed the Indian Mutiny in 1857 and the assault on Magdala in Abyssinia, which was the last time the Colours of the 33rd were carried into battle. With their amalgamation in 1881, the 33rd and 76th became, respectively, the 1st and 2nd Battalions of the Duke of Wellington's Regiment.

During the Great War 1914–18, twenty-one battalions were raised. Its service on the Western Front, in Italy and Gallipoli was recognised by the granting of 72 battle honours – won at the cost of over 8,000 lives. By a strange quirk of history the only battalion to escape the slaughter was Sharpe's old battalion, the 1st, which spent the war in India. After a particularly brutal and unsuccessful brigade attack in Gallipoli, the 8th Battalion was left with a single eighteen-year-old second lieutenant as commanding officer. One of the survivors, Sergeant Miles, wrote:

Poor quality of junior officers 1794

THE SCRABBLE to expand the army for the campaign in Flanders allowed large numbers of incompetent individuals to secure promotion and commissions:

> ... many of these young men [officers] were at once a disgrace and an encumbrance to the force. Hard drinking, which was the fashion then in all classes from highest to lowest, was, of course, sedulously cultivated by these aspirants to the rank of gentlemen; and it was no uncommon thing for regiments to start on the march under charge of the Adjutant and Sergeant-major only, while the officers stayed behind, to come galloping up several hours later, full of wine, careless where they rode, careless of the confusion into which they threw the columns, careless of everything but the place appointed for the end of the march, if by chance they were sober enough to have remembered it.

[In 1794] political interest rather than meritorious service was the road to promotion. While the shameful traffic of army-brokers [agents] and the raising of endless new regiments continued, every officer who could command money or interest [patronage] was sure of obtaining advancement ... Thus the men were very imperfectly disciplined; there were no efficient company officers; no efficient Colonels to look after the company officers ... [Major-General] Craig [chief-of-staff to the Duke of York] wrote that, 'The evil to the discipline of the army increases every day, and is likely to become very serious.'

A History of the British Army,
J. W. Fortescue

Sharpe was fortunate that the 33rd did not seem to have been adversely affected.

The recruiting shambles of 1794–5

FORTESCUE, in his *History of the British Army*, records:

On the 20th October 1794 the Government had suddenly sanctioned the raising of fifteen Fencible [militia-type units for service in Britain only] on a single day, and added to them twelve more battalions before the end of the year. Being then apparently at its wits' end to obtain recruits for the regulars, it had made in December a contract with an individual, bearing the rank of Captain, to supply four thousand recruits from Ireland at twenty guineas a head [about £200 in today's money]. This last measure [80,000 guineas – the equivalent of a modern National Lottery jackpot] was a climax of wickedness and folly, leading to deeds of atrocity and crime which old officers even sixty years later could not speak without shame and indignation. It was found too that fraudulent recruiting agents were abroad [active], and it was consequently necessary in March [1795] to cancel all beating-orders for the time. Then in May 1795 all recruiting for the army was practically suspended, owing to the demand for seamen. No fewer than four Acts were passed in the spring of that year to facilitate the manning of the Navy – one to raise men in the ports of England, another to levy them in the counties of Scotland, a third to sweep in all rogues and vagabonds and a fourth to draw seafaring men from the Militia.

It seems Sharpe would have been accepted with open arms no matter what his crimes, and if the army had not grabbed him the navy certainly would.

As soon as dawn broke we called the roll. What a lot of specimens we looked! There was roughly 250 of us out of a total of about 900. In my company alone we lost seven killed, 43 wounded, the majority of whom died of wounds, I expect, and 23 missing out of a total of 134. We had one officer left in the battalion out of a total of 29.

The Second World War saw another 23 battle honours gained, with battalions in action at Dunkirk, North Africa, Italy, Burma and across north-west Europe. But perhaps their most famous fight in more modern times was their defence of 'The Hook' in Korea in 1953. Under the inspiring leadership of Lieutenant-Colonel F. R. St P. Bunbury, while some 10,000

The disciplining of officers

COURT MARTIALS and dismissals created a number of non-purchase promotion vacancies that were invariably filled by officers from outside the regiment. In 1812 Wellington found the 1/85th Foot so useless he sent them home from the Peninsula. This did not solve the problems. Michael Glover in his book *Wellington's Army* has described what happened:

> Before the regiment went to Portugal in 1811 one captain had been cashiered and another shot in a duel ... Wellington sent the regiment home after eight months in the Peninsula, and once it reached England its condition deteriorated rapidly. The senior major was brought before a court martial on six charges fabricated by the regimental paymaster, and when they were dismissed, the paymaster brought two more charges alleging fraud. Since he could bring 'not a particle of evidence to support them', the major was again acquitted and the paymaster himself charged, found guilty and dismissed. Meanwhile a captain and a lieutenant were charged with 'conduct highly unbecoming an officer', including an assertion that the adjutant 'had had his nose pulled and

his posterior kicked, or words to that effect'. Both were found guilty and dismissed the service. No sooner had that case finished than another lieutenant was tried for 'entering into personal contest with Mr Henry Knight [then an ensign in the regiment] by repeatedly striking and receiving blows with a horse whip at the New Inn, Romsey'. He escaped with a plea of self-defence, and another subaltern was acquitted of two more of the paymaster's fraud charges. A captain was dismissed for asserting that the junior lieutenant-colonel was 'a coward and drunk on duty', and finally the adjutant was charged with describing one of the captains as 'a blackguard and damned insolent'. He admitted the charge, but since the captain concerned had already been dismissed for insulting him, the adjutant escaped with a reprimand.

At this stage the Duke of York (commander-in-chief of the army) intervened, the commanding officer was 'retired', new officers with Peninsular experience were appointed on promotion. The battalion returned to Spain and distinguished itself both there and subsequently in America.

Officers' 'ladies'

EVEN FOR OFFICERS, marriage below the age of 30 and the rank of captain was discouraged. The present writer recalls being unable to qualify for marriage allowance under 25 and having to obtain the commanding officer's permission before getting married. Marriage was, rightly, regarded as too much of a distraction and financial burden for a young officer, who should be devoting his undivided attention to his duties and his soldiers. The alternatives were mistresses and prostitutes. In India the former were commonplace, in England probably the latter. In his book, *The Colonel's Lady and Judy O'Grady*, Colonel Noel Williams gives the amusing example of Lord Alvaney who joined the Coldstream Guards at 15 in 1804 and was sent to Spain four years later, leaving behind an unpaid account with his regimental agent that included:

Lady	£5
Ditto a country girl	£2 2s
One night Mrs Dubois (grande blonde)	£5 5s
Modest Girl	£3 3s
An American Lady	£10 10s
Lately one night with Eliza Farquhar	£3 3s
All night Miss N from the Boarding School, Chelsea	£5 5s

Americans were, seemingly, in a class of their own, while country girls were at the lower end of the profession. Young Lord Alvaney's daily pay as a Guards ensign was 4s 6d, so the lady from across the Atlantic cost him about six weeks' pay and the country lass a mere eight days' worth! No doubt, being good business ladies, the charges were set according to the elevated social and private financial standing of their client.

There were, of course, unpleasant risks in these activities. As one lady who entertained officers wrote:

> The next I met a cornet was
> In a regiment of dragoons
> I gave him what he didn't like
> And stole his silver spoons.

In contrast to the high-class ladies of the night, a low-class 'scrubber' or 'brimstone girl' would permit a client to 'dip his machine in the canal' for 6d (about 15p of today's money). For 7d he could buy a meal of cold meat, bread, cheese and beer. However, a visit to the surgeon to treat his venereal disease would set him back £5 5s.

shells rained down on their position, they beat off a succession of massive Chinese assaults, inflicting over 1,000 casualties (including 250 dead) on the enemy at a cost of just over 100 of their own men killed or wounded. The brigade commander later remarked, 'My God those Dukes, they were marvellous. In the whole of the last war I never saw anything like that bombardment. But they held the Hook, as I knew they would.' From then on Headquarter Company of the 1st Battalion was called Hook Company.

If Sharpe could be resurrected today he would be immensely proud that his old 33rd Foot had achieved so much on so many battlefields since Seringapatam: 117 battle honours, 10 Victoria Crosses and a Conspicuous Gallantry Cross (instituted in 1993 as a decoration second only to the VC for battlefield bravery) won by Corporal Wayne Mills in the former Yugoslavia. The Regimental motto *Virtutis Fortuna Comes* – Fortune Favours the Brave – seems particularly appropriate.

The 74th (Highland) Regiment of Foot

When Sharpe received his battlefield commission into the 74th Foot on 25 September 1803 he was twenty-six years old, virtually the same age as his new regiment. King George III had granted letters of service for the raising of the original regiment as recently as three months after Sharpe's birth. Formed to help bring the American Revolution to a speedy end, it was to be a big regiment of 1,082 soldiers, each company having 1 captain, 2 lieutenants, 1 ensign, 5 sergeants, 5 corporals, 2 drummers, 2 pipers and 100 privates. The recruits were to be at least 5'4" tall and aged between eighteen and thirty. At its first muster in April 1778 there were 987 men present of whom 192 were found to be over-age, 77 under-age, 149 too short and 17 in gaol. Although a Highland Regiment (its main recruiting area being Argyllshire), a high proportion were Lowlanders, mainly from Glasgow. Nine of the officers

FORMER OFFICERS RE-ENLISTING IN THE RANKS
William Surtees, author of *Twenty-Five Years in the Rifle Brigade* and one of the characters used by Bernard Cornwell in bringing to life Richard Sharpe, knew several soldiers who had previously held a commission, including a certain M'Laughlan who had been an officer in the light company of the 35th Foot (Surtees' former regiment) until gambling debts forced him to sell out. He rejoined as a volunteer and soldiered on, waiting for a non-purchase vacancy. In due course he was again commissioned. Yet again, for reasons unknown to Surtees, he lost his commission and in 1803 enlisted as a private in the 95th. Drunkenness and neglect of duty led to progressively more severe punishments. To escape it all, M'Laughlan tried to desert to the French by crossing the Channel in an open boat. Caught by a Royal Navy ship, he was sentenced by court martial to transportation for life as a felon. Had he been captured after actually joining the enemy he would surely have been executed.

Extracts from the Standing Orders of the 74th Highlanders, 1850

————⁓————

ALTHOUGH NOT WITHIN Sharpe's lifetime, he would undoubtedly have recognised most of these as coming from his old regiment – indeed from any British regiment of the nineteenth century:

Promotions by purchase

No officer's name will be included in the regimental returns for the purchase of promotion unless he is duly qualified in every respect, and has passed the examinations required by the orders of the army . . .

Drill

Every officer on joining the regiment for the first time, will go through the same course of drill and instruction as a recruit, and will not be dismissed until he is perfectly instructed in every part of the company, battalion, and light drill, and able himself to drill a squad and a company . . .

The Sergeant-Major

. . . his duties are generally the same as those of the adjutant, under whom he acts . . . He is to be treated with the greatest respect by all the non-commissioned officers and privates of the regiment, who must address him as 'Sir', and stand at attention when he speaks to them.

[This could have been written about any modern regimental sergeant major.]

Colours

The third Colour, which has been granted to the regiment for its pre-eminent services at the battle of Assaye, is to be carried on all occasions of parade and ceremony, and at all inspections, but not in the field.

Hair cuts

There will be a hair-cutter in every company; every man is to pay him one penny a month, and is to have his hair kept neatly and smoothly cut, as close as possible at the back [the queue had long gone], and of such length on the top of the head, that when combed straight down over the forehead it may be quite clear of the eyebrows. One short curl only will be allowed on each side.

Soldiers' wives

Although Captains cannot prevent non-commissioned officers and private soldiers from marrying if they please, they can, and must, point out to them the certain miserable consequences of the step, if they have not resources independent of the service.

were called Campbell (when Sharpe joined there were still six).

Service in Nova Scotia followed, with the regiment distinguishing itself in the defence of Penobscot. However, at the end of the war in 1783 the regiment was disbanded at Stirling after a life of barely six years. Four years later it was raised again by Major-General Sir Archibald Campbell, but with all the costs being borne by the East India Company. It was this battalion that took part in the capture of Seringapatam in 1799. Ensign Sharpe joined after the Battle of Assaye, when the 74th were left with 85 unwounded soldiers out of 480 and all 18 officers either dead (13) or wounded (5). This had led to one of those unheard-of occasions when a quartermaster (James Grant) drew his sword in anger (*see* Chapter 4). The regiment's supreme gallantry on this occasion won them the grant of a third Colour – the Assaye Colour. The word 'Assaye' was later incorporated into their cap badge, under an Indian elephant.

The 74th played a prominent role in the Peninsular War. They received no less than sixteen battle honours for their campaigns across Spain and Portugal including Bussaco, Badajoz, Salamanca and Vitoria. They were not, however, at Waterloo. They also missed the Indian Mutiny and Crimean War. A detachment was among the troops aboard the *Birkenhead* en route to South Africa in 1852 when the ship sank off the Cape of Good Hope with a huge loss of life. In 1881 the amalgamation of the 71st Foot and the 74th saw the old regiments forming the 1st and 2nd Battalions, respectively, of the Highland Light Infantry.

In the Great War the number of battalions rose to twenty-six. Highland Light Infantrymen fought in France, Belgium, the Dardanelles, Egypt and Mesopotamia. Famous battles such as Mons, Marne, Ypres, Neuve Chapelle and the Somme all featured on their Colours. The cost was exceedingly high: 598 officers and 9,428 other ranks were killed. The Second World War took them to the battlefields of France, the

THE LOSS OF THE BIRKENHEAD

In 1852 a steam troopship, the Birkenhead, was taking reinforcements to South Africa to participate in the Kaffir Wars when she struck a rock during darkness off Danger Point, near Simonstown. Instead of keeping her bows up against the rock, her captain put the engines in reverse, thus enlarging the hole. Water rushed in at an alarming rate and the ship began to founder. There were families on board and too few lifeboats to hold everyone. The troops, including the detachment of the 74th Foot, were paraded on deck and some detailed off to help the families and man the pumps. Those remaining stood silently in their ranks.

As the ship started to break up the captain gave the order 'Every man for himself.' The soldiers, however, waited for the order to come from their own officers. It was explained to them that if they swam to the overloaded boats and tried to get on board they would capsize them and the families would be lost. They were asked, not ordered, to remain where they were. Not a man moved. As the ship tilted and broke in two the soldiers were thrown into the sea. Only a handful of them survived the shark-infested waters by clinging to wreckage or swimming several miles to shore.

It is from this magnificent display of discipline and courage that the expression (not heard so often in these days of equality) 'women and children first' arose. Of the 638 people who sailed in the Birkenhead only 193 survived – including all the families. The King of Prussia considered the discipline of the troops so admirable that he ordered an account of the incident to be read out to every regiment in his army.

Western Desert (as part of the 8th Army), Italy, Normandy and Germany.

As part of the general reorganisation of the army in 1959 the Highland Light Infantry amalgamated with the Royal Scots Fusiliers to become the Royal Highland Fusiliers. By this time the 74th had a total of 73 battle honours and had won 12 Victoria Crosses (all but three in the Great War). Since 1959 the Royal Highland Fusiliers have served in Northern Ireland, the Gulf War, Bosnia and Kosovo. Their motto is *Nemo Nos Impune Lacesset*: No one molests us with impunity.

The 95th (Rifle) Regiment

By the time Sharpe reported for duty as a second lieutenant in the 1/95th at Woodbridge, Suffolk, in March 1806, the 95th Rifles had been in existence for six years. The commanding officer was Lieutenant-Colonel Thomas Sydney Beckwith, an officer who had led a detachment of the 95th on board Nelson's ship, the Elephant, at Copenhagen in 1801. There was also a second battalion under Lieutenant-Colonel Hamlet Wade stationed at Brabourne Lees, Kent.

Sharpe's first two years in the regiment were miserable. He lost his lover and his baby son; he was made quartermaster and missed out on being sent to either South America or Denmark. The only time he enjoyed was the three months spent learning to be a rifleman, mastering their drills and tactics, and becoming skilled in handling the Baker rifle. Sharpe found the discipline and new way of fighting very much to his liking; it suited his temperament and his independence – unlike the job of quartermaster. That appointment, coming on top of his traumatic double personal loss, tipped him over the edge of despair and depression. Only the good fortune of another special mission, this time in Copenhagen, restored his morale.

There were four landmarks in the development of the Rifle

Officer 74th foot c.1803

Regiments, which evolved into the famous Light Brigade and then the Light Division in the Peninsular War, eventually becoming today's Royal Green Jackets:

- The formation, in response to the defeat of General Braddock by the French and Indians in North America in the summer of 1755, of a new regiment called the 60th Royal Americans. Scarlet jackets, rigid linear formations, overburdened soldiers and the tactics of the open battlefields of Europe had all contributed to disaster. New ideas of how to fight in close, heavily forested country were developed by the Swiss commanding officer of the 1/60th, Lieutenant-Colonel Bouquet. He dressed his men in buckskin and homespun dyed dark green or brown, with black

95th RIFLEMAN ON CAMPAIGN

Usual issue black felt 'stovepipe' shako, with white metal buglehorn badge. Shako sometimes useful as an aiming rest when firing prone. When shako eventually fell to pieces, a soft, woollen forage cap, similar to a beret, was often worn.

Green cockade indicating marksman (normally black) with green woollen tuft above,

Green shako cord, riflemen being the only troops to have shako cord.

Hair long and heavy beard indicating this rifleman participating in long, hard campaign.

Rolled greatcoat on top of knapsack.

This rflm. has served with Sharpe for some time and been allowed to discard his stock. The 95th were still wearing them in 1813.

Black leather belts and accoutrements.

24-inch, brass handled sword bayonet more commonly used for chopping wood than against an enemy.

The uncomfortable 'Trotter' knapsack has been replaced with a soft calfskin one taken from a Frenchman.

Single white armband indicates a 'chosen man' who commanded a squad if the NCO was absent. The original L/Cpl.

Short, dark green (rudimentary camouflage) jacket with 3 rows of 9 white metal buttons but no lace. Black facings.

Powderhorn containing fine, loose powder for careful (but slower) loading for maximum accuracy.

General issue 'Italian' style, barrel-shaped, wooden waterbottle.

Cartridge pouch on single cross-belt with made up cartridges for more rapid loading.

Common cloth haversack containing rations such as salted beef/pork and hardtack biscuit-bread.

Waist pouch containing loose balls and patches for wrapping round balls prior to loading to ensure a tight fit in the barrel grooves.

Baker rifle. Flintlock, 30-inch long, grooved barrel. Effective range 200 yds. .615 calibre. Barrel 'browned' as distinct from polished. Weight 11 lb 2 ozs. Its greater accuracy was essential for skirmishing and picking off leaders, but rate of fire only 2 shots per min.

Brass covered 'butt box' containing rifle tools/cleaning kit.

Typical veteran's trousers – old, torn, patched and shrunk.

horn buttons made locally. Light equipment, simple drills and open formations were adopted. Mobility, marksmanship, alertness, concealment and initiative were stressed. The new methods proved extremely effective in subsequent engagements. By 1814 the 60th had eight battalions – more than any other regiment in the army (although they were all disbanded two years later).

- In 1797, shortly after Private Sharpe arrived in India, the 5/60th was armed with rifles and issued with green jackets; they substituted the buglehorn for the drum to direct movement, ceased to carry Colours, and abandoned the traditional ponderous and rigid style of marching. Thus they were transformed into true light infantry whose primary role was scouting and skirmishing. The first commanding officer, Lieutenant-Colonel de Rottenburg, prepared the *Regulations for the Exercise of Riflemen and Light Infantry*, which became the basis for training.

- In 1800, when Sergeant Sharpe was whiling away the long months in the Seringapatam armoury, Colonel Coote Manningham raised the Experimental Corps of Riflemen from the pick of fifteen regiments. They were armed with the Baker rifle and Manningham trained them in accordance with his famous *Military Lectures on the Duties of Riflemen*, based on de Rottenburg's regulations. The training and tactics followed principles familiar to any modern infantryman: camouflage, concealment, accurate shooting, effective use of ground as cover, speed of movement and the use of initiative by all ranks. An old Rifle Brigade song summed up the new techniques:

> Oh! Colonel Coote Manningham, he was the man,
> For he invented a capital plan,
> He raised a Corps of Riflemen
> To fight for England's glory!

REGIMENTAL PUNISHMENTS IN THE 95TH

Least severe was Confinement to Barracks, with or without 'coat turning' – sewing a 'C' on the offender's right sleeve, for which he was charged 2d. Next came confinement in the 'black hole' (guardroom cells) for a maximum of 8 days; this also involved coat turning and paying 3d. The most severe – punishment at the triangles, or flogging – could be awarded only by a court martial, with the sentence entered in the 'Black Book' of the regiment. It was usually carried out after evening parade. The cost of the cat-o'-nine-tails was charged to the offender's account.

For minor offences a company court martial would be assembled. Sergeants could not be tried by them, but a corporal could be tried, on receipt of a written order from the company commander to the sergeant-major, by a court composed of three sergeants and two corporals. A rifleman could be tried by a corporal, a 'chosen' man (a lance-corporal) and three riflemen. This court could pass sentences of extra duties, confinement to barracks, fines for the benefit of messes, and cobbing (spanking the backside with a tailor's sleeve board or similar object – done in private, not in front of the troops). Public punishments were for riflemen only; NCOs were reduced in rank, totally or partially.

> He dressed them all in jackets of green
> And placed them where they couldn't be seen
> And sent them in front, an invisible screen,
> To fight for England's glory!

Similarly, good man management and humanity tempered harsh discipline. In January 1801 new uniforms were issued, and in April Captain Sydney Beckwith took a company to Copenhagen to fight as marines with Nelson. It was here the Corps suffered its first death in action – Lieutenant James Grant. Copenhagen earned the Corps its first battle honour, and later the right to display a naval crown on its cap.

- During 1803, the year Sergeant Sharpe of the 33rd became Ensign Sharpe of the 74th, General Sir John Moore formed and trained the Light Brigade (later Light Division) at Shorncliffe Camp. The 95th was grouped with the 43rd and 52nd Foot, and under Moore, probably one of the finest ever trainers of British infantry, learned a different type of soldiering. Moore drew on his experience as a former major in the 60th, as well as on the work of de Rottenburg and Manningham. In January the 'Rifle Corps', as Manningham's Experimental Corps was generally called, was renamed the 95th (Rifle) Regiment (although unofficially 'Rifle Corps' continued to be used). In May the 2/95th was raised under Hamlet Wade. In 1805 the 95th saw action in Germany, 1806 in South America and the following year at Copenhagen. On this occasion, Beckwith was ashore commanding half of the 1/95th, unlike six years previously when he had commanded a company afloat.

Because the 95th was to become the regiment most associated with Sharpe, who continued to wear their uniform long after he had ceased to serve with them, it will be useful to look in more detail at how light infantry differed from the great bulk of British infantry at that time.

Regimental wives

MOST SERGEANTS and about 7 or 8 per cent of the soldiers were allowed to marry. Thus a 650-strong battalion might expect to have between 50–60 wives 'on strength' in England. Some of the women earned money by doing laundry for the troops and officers. They were permitted to live in barracks, perhaps in a 'married corner' of a barrack room – an arrangement one single soldier of the 33rd found 'revolting to decency'.

While many preserved their dignity, a number were 'turned out of barracks and struck off the list' having been found guilty of offences such as obscene language, drunkenness or fighting amongst themselves. More serious crimes such as theft were liable to be punished by flogging. In 1775 Winifred McCowen was court-martialled for stealing the town bull of Boston and sentenced to be 'tied to a cart's tail, and thereto to receive 100 lashes on her bare back in different portions in the most public parts of the town and Camp and to be imprisoned three months.' For 'the too frequent bestowing of her favours' on persons other than her husband, one wife was sentenced to an hour in a whirligig – a spinning chair that made the wretched victim violently ill or even unconscious. Officers caught misbehaving with soldiers' wives were cashiered.

Not all regimental wives were allowed to accompany the battalion overseas. There was a quota system, which permitted about six wives for every hundred men, inclusive of sergeants' wives, to sail. Wives with more than one child were automatically excluded from the ballot, which took the form of drawing lots or rolling dice on a drumhead. To be left behind was the cause of much wailing and anguish. Most wives shared with their husbands a fierce loyalty to the regiment and its officers. The regiment was, after all, the only home they both had. On campaign they tended the sick and wounded. During the dreadful retreat from Burgos in the Peninsular War one wife, Mrs Skiddy, carried her exhausted husband who had collapsed on the march 'on me back. Knapsack, firelock and all, strong as Samson, for the fear I was in. I carried him half a league [one and a half miles] after the regiment into the bivouac.'

The Light Brigade was trained to carry out tactical reconnaissance and to cover the advance and withdrawal of an army, a role that had previously been the sole prerogative of light cavalry. Constant alertness and readiness for action were instilled into all ranks. Marksmanship was constantly practised, with riflemen classified as first-, second- or third-class shots. A first-class shot was entitled to be called 'marksman' and to wear a green cockade. Shooting competitions were held, with the best company given the place of honour on the right on parade. Riflemen were trained to make every shot count, taking advantage of the rifle's greater range plus the ability of the firer to lie down to fire and reload, to pick off enemy officers or gun detachments. Although the barrel of the Baker was only thirty inches long compared with the musket's forty-six, the seven grooves made it accurate up to 300 yards. Good shooting was assisted by use of an extra-long sling to steady the aim. Use of rocks, bushes or even their shako (headgear) as a rest for the rifle was encouraged. Marshal Soult of France was later to write a despatch attributing heavy losses in Spain to the enemy being 'armed with a short rifle, selected for their marksmanship [so] whenever a superior officer goes to the front, he is usually hit.'

To make up for the shortness of the barrel all riflemen were equipped with a sword bayonet twenty-seven inches long instead of the usual triangular type. Swords were fixed only when absolutely necessary as they detracted from accuracy and could catch the sunlight, thus giving away a position (hence the modern custom of riflemen not having fixed swords on ceremonial parades). Officers' swords were lighter and slightly curved, with a buglehorn on the hilt instead of a Royal Cypher – although Sharpe was to continue to carry the straight, heavy-bladed cavalry sword throughout his time in the Peninsula.

Differences in drill were instituted to reflect and facilitate the new tactics. These derived from the practical aims of instilling alertness, eliminating unnecessary movements, minimising fatigue. The buglehorn, in Rifle parlance the 'horn', was of critical importance in the Light Brigade (and Division). Movement or changes in orders could not be controlled by shouted commands when the troops were in extended order on a battlefield. A horn was therefore carried by all buglers, while every officer and sergeant wore a whistle on his crossbelt. Exaggerated drill movements, long pauses between movements, stamping of feet, slapping of the rifle or crashing

MUSKET AND RIFLE – A COMPARISON

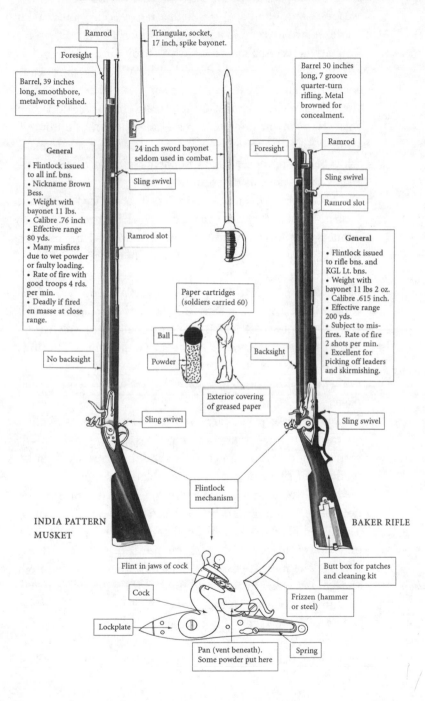

Ramrod

Foresight

Triangular, socket, 17 inch, spike bayonet.

Barrel, 39 inches long, smoothbore, metalwork polished.

Barrel 30 inches long, 7 groove quarter-turn rifling. Metal browned for concealment.

24 inch sword bayonet seldom used in combat.

Foresight

Ramrod

General

• Flintlock issued to all inf. bns.
• Nickname Brown Bess.
• Weight with bayonet 11 lbs.
• Calibre .76 inch
• Effective range 80 yds.
• Many misfires due to wet powder or faulty loading.
• Rate of fire with good troops 4 rds. per min.
• Deadly if fired en masse at close range.

Sling swivel

Sling swivel

Ramrod slot

Ramrod slot

General

• Flintlock issued to rifle bns. and KGL Lt. bns.
• Weight with bayonet 11 lbs 2 oz.
• Calibre .615 inch.
• Effective range 200 yds.
• Subject to misfires. Rate of fire 2 shots per min.
• Excellent for picking off leaders and skirmishing.

Paper cartridges (soldiers carried 60)

Ball

Powder

Backsight

No backsight

Exterior covering of greased paper

Sling swivel

Sling swivel

Flintlock mechanism

INDIA PATTERN MUSKET

BAKER RIFLE

Flint in jaws of cock

Butt box for patches and cleaning kit

Cock

Frizzen (hammer or steel)

Lockplate

Pan (vent beneath). Some powder put here

Spring

BRITISH FIRE
DISCIPLINE

Considerable
steadiness and fire
control was required
for a battalion to stand
in line and accept
casualties without
returning fire until it
was certain to produce
the maximum effect.
This fire discipline,
frequently coupled
with an immediate
bayonet charge,
secured the British
Army victory on many
battlefields. Paddy
Griffith, as detailed in
his book *Forward into
Battle*, has conducted
revealing research into
nineteen firefights in
which musketry range
is specifically
mentioned. In only
four instances (21 per
cent) was fire opened at
100 yards or more. In
nine (47 per cent) the
final volley was given at
20 yards or less. The
average range for
opening fire was 75.5
yards, while that for
closing fire was 30.4
yards. This gives an
overall average range of
British firefights,
taking a mean between
start and finish, of just
over 64 yards. Of
particular note is the
short range of the final
volley – fractionally
more than the length
of a cricket pitch, a
distance covered in a
few seconds if followed
by a rush with the
bayonet.

butts on the parade ground have no place in Rifle Regiments – weapons were (and are) too highly regarded. All movement was executed at as rapid a pace as possible. The need to move quickly in reconnaissance or when providing a screen was paramount. Riflemen had to be fit. Whereas the steady marching rate of the line infantry was 75 paces to the minute, the rifleman's was almost double that. On parade today an infantry regiment's quick march is 120 paces to the minute, while a Rifle Regiment's is 140 (or 180 double time). This is why you will never see a light infantry regiment march past – they always move at the double (run).

The wearing of buckskin in North America, the green jackets, black leather belts and, later, black buttons were fore-runners of modern camouflaged combat dress. Other modern items of dress trace their origins from around the time Sharpe joined the 1/95th. Cloth badges, buttons, boots, belts, scabbards, etc are all black. Until the Great War, officers of the Rifle Brigade wore black Sam Browne belts (instead of brown) with two shoulder straps so that from a distance they would appear to have the same equipment as their men. All buttons were of the same size so that if one was lost from a vital pocket it could be quickly replaced by one from a less essential place.

Colours were never carried. Their function of providing an easily seen rallying point for the regiment did not fit with the emphasis on concealment and the dispersed fighting methods of riflemen operating in isolated groups.

Sharpe would have approved of the respectful informality not only between officers but between officers and their men. This is another long tradition that has been retained. The only officer addressed as 'Sir' was the commanding officer, while in the mess Christian names were the rule for seniors and juniors alike. In the 60th and the Rifle Brigade, officers had no rank badges on their mess kit.

The 6th (or Light) Brigade fired the first shots of the Peninsular War at a Portuguese village called Obidos. It was near there that Lieutenant Bunbury of the 2/95th was killed

– a death that would allow Sharpe to obtain a long overdue promotion without purchase to lieutenant (but this anticipates events). The 95th expanded to three battalions and went on to gain sixteen battle honours. All three battalions were represented at Waterloo, where Sharpe was to come across his old company commander of six years earlier during the retreat to Corunna. In 1816 the 95th Rifles were taken out of the old numbered regiments of the line and formally re-titled 'Brigade'.

Two battalions fought in the Crimea, where they earned eight of the sixty-one Victoria Crosses awarded for that war, more than any other regiment. Another four were awarded for great gallantry in the Indian Mutiny. Two more were added during the South African War (Second Boer War) 1899–1902. During the Great War, twenty-two battalions fought in France, Flanders, Salonika, Gallipoli and the Middle East. Four years of ferocious fighting in atrocious conditions cost the regiment 11,575 dead. Ten VCs and 1,743 other decorations for bravery were won. The Rifle Brigade fought in France in 1940, North Africa and Italy, and landed in Normandy in June 1944 at the start of the liberation of Europe. They fought through France, Belgium and into Germany, ending the Second World War near Hamburg. Perhaps their most outstanding exploit of the war was in the North African desert at El Aqqaqir on an unknown ridge codenamed 'Snipe'. Here the 2nd Battalion, under Lieutenant-Colonel Victor Turner, fought off attacks by 100 German tanks, destroying 51 of them. At one stage, when one of the six-pounder guns they were using was down to a crew of two (an officer and sergeant), Turner acted as the loader. Turner was awarded the Victoria Cross. In total the regiment has won twenty-six VCs.

The endless reorganisation continued in 1966 with the formation of the Royal Green Jackets as part of the reductions and 'options for change' that have blighted the British Army over the last forty-five years. The 1st Battalion is derived (via several amalgamations) from the old 43rd and 52nd Foot that had trained with the 95th at Shorncliffe some 170 years earlier. The 2nd Battalion can trace its origins back to the 60th Royal Americans, while the 3rd Battalion originated with the Experimental Corps of Riflemen and the 95th – Sharpe's old comrades. At the time of writing, the Royal Green Jackets have been cut yet again to two battalions (the one to disappear: the 3rd Battalion that originated from Sharpe's old regiment).

The 33rd's failed Victoria Cross

PRIVATE PATRICK McGUIRE of the 33rd had the unique experience of being struck off the list of those recommended for the VC on the grounds of 'morality'. It was the result of an incident in the Crimean War. A Captain Calthorpe, an ADC at army headquarters, explained what happened in a letter dated 23 October 1854:

> You hear every day of heroic acts of bravery by soldiers: one I call to mind. A few days ago a private of the 33rd (Duke of Wellington's Regiment) was surprised and made prisoner by two Russians when an advanced Sentry. One of these worthies took possession of his musket and the other his pouch and marched him between them towards Sebastopol. The Englishman kept a wary watch and when he fancied his captors off their guard sprang on the one who had his musket, seized it and shot dead the other who carried the pouch as well as his own arms and accoutrements. Meanwhile the Russian from whom our fellow had taken his own musket . . . fired, missed and finally had his brains knocked out by the butt end of the Englishman's musket; after which the man coolly proceeded to take off the Russian accoutrements etc with which he returned laden to the post where he had been surprised, fired at by the Russian sentries, and cheered by our own pickets . . .

Queen Victoria, who had instituted the VC after the war, considered McGuire's actions 'of very doubtful morality' as it could lead to 'the inhuman practice of never taking prisoners'. In other words, if such an act was rewarded with a VC, Britain's future enemies might kill rather than capture soldiers who surrendered. However, it should be recorded that McGuire had by then already received the Distinguished Conduct Medal for gallantry in the field and a £5 gratuity – although one questions whether he had been a particularly alert sentry in the first place!

—◦∞◦—

3

Sharpe's Tiger

The story is set in India during the Fourth Mysore War against the Tippoo Sultan in 1799. Sharpe is a private in the 33rd Foot (led by Major John Shee), while Colonel Wellesley is acting deputy commander of the British forces under Lieutenant-General Harris. As the British forces advance on Seringapatam (now Sriringapatna), the Tippoo's capital, Sharpe is sentenced to be flogged. The punishment is stopped after 202 lashes to allow him to go on a special mission inside Seringapatam, with the promise of promotion if he is successful. He 'deserts' and joins a French unit fighting for the Tippoo. Betrayed (by *Sergeant Hakeswill*) and imprisoned, he nevertheless manages to escape in time to prevent heavy British casualties by prematurely exploding a mine set to annihilate them as they stormed through the breach. The success of the mission secures his promotion to sergeant.

A WEEK BEFORE CHRISTMAS, 1798, Colonel Arthur Wellesley obtained an important independent command – preparing the Army of Madras for an offensive against the Tippoo Sultan of Mysore. Two days before Christmas he was given the Arab horse, Diomed, that, four years later, was to be spiked under him at Assaye, an incident in which Sergeant Sharpe was to be intimately involved. Both these favours were the direct result of the bizarre, indeed tragic, events of 16 December. On that day Colonel Henry Ashton, the officer tasked with assembling the troops, fought two duels.

Ashton had been in command of the 12th Foot (East Suffolk) until his headquarters' duties compelled him to hand over to Major John Picton (elder brother of Sir Thomas Picton, who was to be one of Sharpe's divisional commanders in the Peninsula). A misunderstanding arose between Picton and Ashton concerning the actions of the other field officer with the 12th, Major Allen. An explosive mix of temper and slighted honour led to Picton challenging Colonel Ashton to a duel. Early on the morning of 16 December they faced each other with pistols. Picton fired first, but his weapon misfired. Ashton, who was an excellent shot, deliberately and disdainfully fired in the air. Honour was satisfied, so both protagonists shook hands. Within hours, however, it was Allen's turn to challenge Ashton. On both occasions he could have refused but foolishly did not. So, twice in one day, a colonel accepted to defend his honour against a subordinate – an event unique in the history of duelling. Again his opponent fired first, but this time with more effect. Ashton was hit in the side – a severe wound, probably through the liver. He staggered but remained standing. Although at that short range he could have easily evened the score, once more Ashton deliberately fired into the air. On hearing the news of his friend's injury, Wellesley rode all night from Fort St George, Madras, to be with him. He arrived on the eighteenth and, while Ashton lay dying, assumed command of the assembling troops in the Arcot, Arnee and Vellore area, which would otherwise have gone to the next senior officer – Picton. The two young colonels were visibly moved by the circumstances and, shortly before he died on the twenty-third, Ashton gave his charger, Diomed, to his friend. Major Allen was arrested and charged with murder; he died in March 1799, presumably of disease, while still in custody.

Three months earlier, a seasick Private Sharpe, along with about 400 soldiers of the 33rd, had been hurled ashore through the infamous surf on to the open beach below Fort St George. The 33rd had been ordered south from Calcutta (Bengal) to stiffen the Army of Madras. Wellesley and half the regiment had the misfortune to sail in the East Indiaman

WELLINGTON'S DUEL

Almost thirty years after Ashton's double duel, Wellesley (then Duke of Wellington and prime minister) challenged Lord Winchilsea to a duel. The challenge was taken up and the two met in Battersea Fields early on the morning of 21 March 1829. Wellington's doctor produced a pair of duelling pistols as the Duke did not own any. The doctor loaded both weapons. Wellington, anxious to proceed, said to his second, Lord Hardinge (who had lost an arm at the Battle of Ligny), 'Now then, Hardinge, look sharp and step out the ground. I have no time to waste, damn it!' An attempt to settle the affair verbally was unsuccessful so the noble lords squared off. After a few seconds Hardinge said, 'Gentlemen, are you ready? Fire!' Wellington aimed his pistol but, seeing Winchilsea hesitate, deliberately fired wide of him. Winchilsea smiled, raised his arm and fired into the air.

EIC SERVICE

Many men made their
entire careers with the
EIC and rose to high
rank. King's Regiments
(British regiments
with European troops)
were rated as greatly
superior to native
ones. A King's officer
was always senior to an
EIC officer. This was
exacerbated by the
EIC's reluctance to
promote its officers
(thereby saving
money). Often an EIC
battalion would be
commanded by a
captain with a
European adjutant,
assistant-surgeon and
six or eight subalterns.
   The EIC civil service
structure was also well
established. Educated
young men, boys of 13
even, came out from
England to join the
'Company' much as
others would join a
battalion as junior
subaltern. Instead of
ensign they held the
title 'writer' and were
entitled to put HEICS
(Honourable East
India Company
Service) after their
name. A writer copied
letters and checked
ships' cargoes. Not
many survived the
diseases and climate;
the odds of a young
EIC recruit seeing
home again were about
the same as those of a
subaltern leaving for
the trenches in World
War I.

Fitz William. A voyage that should have taken five days took twenty-five. The ship went aground in the muddy mouth of the Hooghly River. A thousand bags of saltpetre had to be thrown overboard while the troops sweated and heaved on the ropes for hours to drag her off. Thereafter, the ship leaked dangerously, necessitating the manning of pumps day and night. The drinking water was contaminated, so Sharpe, along with his commanding officer and virtually all on board, experienced the agonies of 'Bombay belly' (dysentery). Fifteen died from it. The ship's barrels had probably been filled from the Lall Diggee, a large open pond that provided much of Calcutta's water supply. A correspondent to the *Bengal Gazette* once wrote of this source, 'I saw a string of parria [sic] dogs without an ounce of hair on some of them, and in the last stage of mange, plunge in and refresh themselves very comfortably.'

An appalling voyage culminated in a frightening landing. With nothing to break their endless charge, monstrous green waves, crested with foam, raced for the shore from the darker blue waters of the Bay of Bengal. Only experienced local boatmen, operating special raft-type vessels held together with rope, could get men or cargo ashore at Madras. Soaked, exhausted and terrified, the soldiers could do nothing but trust the skill of the boatmen to catch a crest at precisely the right moment. To be overturned was to drown.

By the end of the eighteenth century the British were the dominant European power on the Indian subcontinent. They had gone there for trade and that was the reason they remained, making immense fortunes. Their rivals had been the Dutch, the Portuguese and, particularly, the French. When Sharpe arrived in February 1797, British control had long been exercised through the East India Company (EIC), which had grown into a government, complete with all the trappings of authority, including an extensive civil service. To protect its assets, the EIC was allowed to raise its own military forces (native troops officered by Europeans). All of

Ganges – holy river

HINDUS REGARD the Ganges as a sacred river and its water as holy water. Many cleansing ceremonies are carried out on its banks, including bathing to wash away sins. Ashes of the faithful, recently cremated, are often scattered onto the murky water. Millions make pilgrimages to the river every year. Of particular religious significance is the tongue of land at Allahabad where the Ganges and Jumna rivers join. Hundreds of thousands of devout Hindus repair to this spot to cleanse themselves. However, when Sharpe was in India some of the ceremonies were far more sinister.

Many old or sick Hindus wished to die on the banks of the river (or any river, as all rivers supposedly carry some-thing of the sacredness of the Ganges), and so when death seemed imminent they would be hurried down to the water's edge. If, however, they recovered or simply did not die as soon as expected, they were forbidden to return home. Indeed, their recovery might be seen as a sign that they were beyond blessing – perhaps the river had rejected them, an altogether bad sign. There was a village near Calcutta where many of those who had failed to die were taken. There the passing of the spirit was helped on its way by pouring gallons of Ganges water into the sick person's mouth. And if that failed, Ganges mud stuffed into the mouth and nostrils would be sure to do the trick.

which cost London nothing. The EIC's activities, administration, personnel (civil and military) were self-financing. One of its most senior officials went by the title 'Collector' – his task was to collect revenue, principally land tax.

Working under the Collector were a host of other officials. Foremost among these were the district officers, each responsible for administering an area that in some cases was the size of Wales. These all-powerful government representatives fulfilled a number of key functions, including that of magistrate. Such a man was William Sleeman, who took up the post of district officer some twenty years after Sharpe left India and struggled tirelessly to abolish the practice of widow-burning or suttee.

Hundreds, if not thousands, of Europeans (civilian as well as military) took Indian mistresses; some married them. Sharpe's lover Mary Bickerstaff, the widow of an army ser-

Indian wives of European soldiers

BRITISH ARTILLERYMAN Alexander Alexander gives an amusing glimpse of his domestic life in Ceylon in 1805, the year Sharpe left India for home:

I then began to look for a wife, or rather a nurse – love was out of the question. My affections were elsewhere all engrossed; but I must either take a wife or die.

My choice fell upon a Cingalese; she was of a clear bronze colour, smooth-skinned, healthy and very cleanly in her person and manner of cooking, which was her chief recommendation. Puncheh was of a good or bad temper just as she had any object to gain, forever crying out poverty, and always in want of either money or clothes. She imagined every person better off than herself; often pretended to be under the necessity to pawn her necklace and other ornaments, and boasted how much she was reduced since she came to live with me. Then she would pretend to be sick, and lie in bed for twenty-four hours together; and neither speak, nor take food or medicine, but lie and sulk. I was completely sick of her at times . . .

When these sullen fits came on, I in vain endeavoured to soothe or flatter her; I had no money to satisfy her extravagance, my victuals remained uncooked, and the hut in confusion. There was no alternative but to follow the example of the others. I applied the strap of my great coat, which never failed to effect a cure, and all went on well for a time. She bore me a son, a fine little boy, who died young. Often have I sat and looked with delight upon his infant gambols. As is the custom here, he smoked cigars as soon as he could walk about. It was strange to see the infant puffing the smoke into the air . . . and then running and placing his head upon his mother's bosom, to quench his thirst . . . What alone caused me to submit to her humours was that I now began to get stronger and better in my bowels, for my food was cleanly cooked and properly done.

geant, was the result of such a union. Later to become known as Anglo-Indians, those of mixed race often found themselves rejected by both the European and Indian communities, being neither one nor the other. Nevertheless, by the twentieth century they had grown into a clearly recognisable sector of the Indian population. Many were well educated and ambitious, and they were to be found throughout the civil service, the military and the police; at one time they were particularly prominent in the Indian railways, which they ran with considerable efficiency.

There were three British (EIC) Presidencies, or provinces, in India. In the north-east was the Bengal Presidency based on Calcutta with the centre of power in Fort William. Eight hundred miles to the south was the Madras Presidency. Another 600 miles to the north-west was the third, the Bombay Presidency, facing the Arabian Sea and based on the city of Bombay. At the head of each of the Madras and Bombay administrations was a governor who was subordinate to the governor-general in Fort William (Calcutta), although the huge distances made him more of a first among equals. Beyond and around these comparatively small enclaves were scores of native Indian rulers – the rajahs, the princes, and the sultans – who controlled a patchwork quilt of states, some as large as Spain, others as small as Surrey. They were absolute monarchs, motivated by pure self-interest – the retention of land, wealth and authority.

One such ruler was the Tippoo Sultan of Mysore. In 1799 he was forty-six, a cruel, bigoted Muslim who claimed descent from the Prophet but ruled over an overwhelmingly Hindu state. His father, Hyder Ali, had been half Afghan and comparatively light-skinned, but the Tippoo was short, flabby and much darker, with a pencil moustache and thick neck. Whatever his faults, he did not lack courage or ability as a soldier and administrator. Since the age of fourteen, when he took command of a cavalry unit, he had been a soldier. He had fought for his father against the British in the First Mysore War, 1766–9; the Second Mysore War, 1780–3; and,

SUTTEE

Widow burning might have been the fate of *Mary Bickerstaff* had she married the Hindu *Kunwar Singh*. It arose from the Hindu belief that a woman's husband is her god on earth. To be burnt on his funeral pyre was the only certain way to paradise for her. It was supposedly voluntary, but great pressure was put on the widow to submit. In Bengal she was tied to the corpse, however putrid, while men stood by with poles to push her back into the flames should she break free. In 1813 the EIC tried to check the practice by ordering that an Indian police officer be present to certify the woman was not drugged, pregnant or a minor, and that she went willingly. A few did. William Sleeman forbade *suttee* in his district in the 1820s but one widow insisted she was dead already and would feel no pain, refusing to eat or drink until Sleeman gave permission. After a week he did so. The fire was lit, the woman stepped in and lay down without a sound. *Suttee* was officially prohibited in 1829 in all three presidencies, but instances still occurred over a hundred years later.

after his father's death, he commanded the army in the Third Mysore War, 1789–92. By early 1799, with the help of the French, the Tippoo was ready to recoup some of his lost land and authority. Little Île de France (Mauritius) had declared its unswerving loyalty, although it could provide only about a hundred volunteers. Of infinitely greater significance was Bonaparte's victorious presence in Cairo. A French force landing at Mangalore (MAP 1) would receive the Tippoo's unstinting support – and the blessings of Allah. Such a landing was not impossible. Unease had been replaced by apprehension in Forts William and St George. This, at any rate, was the excuse the British needed to launch the Fourth Mysore War. Were the Tippoo to be deposed, British rule in southern India would be unchallenged.

From May 1798 British India was little short of a Wellesley family fiefdom. That was the month Richard Wellesley, the

The Tippoo's tigers

THE WORD *Tipu* is Kanarese for 'tiger'. The Tippoo Sultan was obsessed with tigers and they served as a sort of armorial bearing. His throne (which he swore not to use until he had defeated the British) was in tiger form; the support was a large wooden tiger carrying the throne on its back, its head covered in gold and its eyes and teeth formed of rock crystal. The throne's frame was octagonal, surrounded by a low rail on which were ten small tiger heads made of gold and beautifully inlaid with precious stones. The whole was covered in a thin sheet of gold and surmounted by a canopy fringed with thousands of pearls. Tiger stripes were incorporated in the uniforms of his troops; some mortars were in the form of crouching tigers, and the muzzles of cannons and hilts of swords were fashioned into tigers' heads. As we might keep watchdogs, the Tippoo kept tigers (one guarded Sharpe's dungeon at night). They were later shot by soldiers of the 33rd on Wellesley's orders. His two hunting cheetahs were not killed but sent as a gift, with six Indian keepers, to King George III. The Tippoo's tiger organ can be seen in London's Victoria and Albert Museum. It depicts a prostrate European soldier being savaged by a tiger, and when a handle is cranked it plays an organ inside the tiger, the sounds supposedly resembling the snarling of the beast and cries of the victim. Its voice, alas, is not what it was in Sharpe's day.

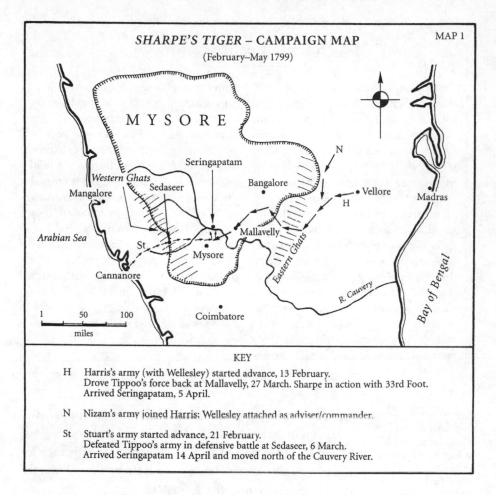

SHARPE'S TIGER – CAMPAIGN MAP   MAP 1
(February–May 1799)

MYSORE

Seringapatam

Western Ghats
Sedaseer
Mangalore   Bangalore

N

Vellore
H

Madras

Arabian Sea
St
Mysore
Mallavelly

Eastern Ghats

Cannanore

R. Cauvery

Bay of Bengal

1   50   100
miles

Coimbatore

KEY

H   Harris's army (with Wellesley) started advance, 13 February.
      Drove Tippoo's force back at Mallavelly, 27 March. Sharpe in action with 33rd Foot.
      Arrived Seringapatam, 5 April.

N   Nizam's army joined Harris; Wellesley attached as adviser/commander.

St   Stuart's army started advance, 21 February.
      Defeated Tippoo's army in defensive battle at Sedaseer, 6 March.
      Arrived Seringapatam 14 April and moved north of the Cauvery River.

Irish Lord Mornington, stepped ashore at Calcutta to a thunderous salute from the eighteen-pounder cannons on the walls of Fort William. The new governor-general had arrived. He brought with him as his private secretary his youngest brother, Henry. In April, during a brief stop on the voyage north, they had met Arthur in Madras.

Arriving on the same ship was Major-General David Baird, an officer who was to play an aggressive and significant role in the coming hostilities (and a key role in Sharpe's early career). Some fourteen years earlier he had been released after almost

THE BLACK HOLE OF CALCUTTA

Fort William was an immensely impressive fortification. It had been built to ensure that British Calcutta would never again be overrun, as it had been in 1756 when the Nabob of Bengal had attacked the city, causing total panic. Led by the governor,

The army on the march

To MOVE an army in India required about five camp followers for every man with a musket. When Harris and the Nizam advanced into Mysore, they did so in a vast parallelogram about seven miles long by three wide, with infantry forming the flanks and cavalry the front and rear. Within were siege guns, baggage, carts, *brinjarris* (grain merchants), servants, camp followers, their families, grass cutters (each horse required two men continuously cutting grass for fodder), all jumbled in an immense sea of animals. The beasts of burden included elephants, camels and horses, but the majority were bullocks – pack rather than draught animals – hired along with their owners to supply and carry the army. It is estimated that Harris's baggage and commissariat required 60,000 bullocks plus another 20,000 with his *brinjarris*. Add 36,000 with the Nizam, and the staggering total is almost 120,000. In effect, the army fed from a gigantic, ponderously moving bazaar that crossed the dry countryside under a choking cloud of red dust. As they moved, they consumed. Such a mass of men and animals stripped the surrounding country of anything edible as thoroughly as a plague of locusts. When General Stuart's force joined Harris in mid-April there were some 50,000 soldiers, 120,000 followers and 120,000 bullocks encamped around Seringapatam.

Roger Drake, most of the English had fled in boats into the middle of the Hooghly River, steadfastly refusing to return for the 146 left behind. The Nabob imprisoned these unfortunate men and their families in a small cell, said to be 18 feet long by 14 feet wide. Even if these measurements are understated, in the suffocating heat of an Indian summer night it is not surprising only 23 were alive next morning.

four years manacled in the Tippoo's cells at Seringapatam – the same cells that in a matter of months would house Sharpe, *McCandless, Lawford* and *Hakeswill*. Baird had little love for the natives; a characteristic that a year later would cost him the military governorship of Seringapatam.

The campaign plan involved squeezing the Tippoo between two very unequal arms of a pincer, the hoped-for outcome being that he would be crushed in his capital, Seringapatam (MAP 2). In overall command of the Madras Army was fifty-three-year-old Lieutenant-General George Harris, who had received a severe head wound when a bullet had furrowed his scalp at Bunker Hill during the American War of Independence (Sharpe would later notice that Harris was forever lifting the edge of his wig to scratch the old scar). His deputies were Major-General Baird and Colonel Wellesley. In February 1799 the Madras Army was about 20,000 strong, of which

Major-General Baird

BORN 1757, Baird served as a captain in India in the 73rd Foot (2nd Royal Highlanders). Severely wounded in the battle against Hyder Ali at Conjeveram in 1780. Taken prisoner and chained for 44 months in the Seringapatam dungeon that would house Sharpe, *Lawford, McCandless* and *Hakeswill*. When Baird's mother heard that captives were chained in pairs, she is reputed to have said, 'I pity the man who is chained to ma Davie!' He served in India again in 1791, then in the Cape of Good Hope before returning as Harris's senior deputy at Seringapatam in 1799. He was a large, powerful and courageous man, but had no love for the Indians and was jealous of the authority given to young Wellesley. He returned to the Cape of Good Hope (1805–6) and was at the attack on Copenhagen (1807).

Second-in-command to Moore at Corunna in 1809, shortly after Moore died he was hit by grapeshot in the left arm about an inch below the shoulder. He dismounted, stunned by the blow. On recovering his senses, he tried unsuccessfully to remount, then consented to be escorted (by his ADC and son, Captain William Baird) to the rear, where he was taken aboard the 110-gun ship Ville de Paris. Notwithstanding the intense pain from his shattered bone, Baird seemed calm. On his walk through Corunna he acknowledged the salutes of passing officers, none of whom realised he was wounded. Seeing his composure, the surgeon initially assumed that the wound must be slight, but on examining the arm he realised an amputation was essential. Baird did not want to lose his arm, but a second opinion from the surgeon of HMS Barfleur confirmed the limb could not be saved. The bone was splintered so near the shoulder that a normal amputation was impossible. Instead the arm had to be removed from the socket – an uncommon operation in those times. Carried out without anaesthetic, the prolonged agony is almost unimaginable and certainly indescribable. Baird sat, leaning his right arm on a table, without uttering one syllable of complaint except for the moment when the joint was finally separated, when a single cry of anguish escaped his lips.

The same shot had also inflicted another wound in his side from which he was to suffer for the rest of his life. Baird was promoted general 1814, but saw no more active service. He was to live for another 20 years, dying at the age of 72 in 1829.

PRESIDENCY ARMY
NICKNAMES

Each of the three
presidency armies
went by a nickname.
The Madras Army's
was 'the Mulls', from
mulmull, a type of
muslin in which the
EIC used to trade, or
from mulligatawny
soup, a popular
Indian dish. Bengal
Army soldiers were
'Qui-hyes' (rhyming
with 'pies'), from the
custom of shouting
Koi hai? ('Is anyone
there?') when
summoning a servant.
The Bombay Army's
nickname, the
'Ducks', came from
Bombay Duck, a dried
fish served over curry.

SERINGAPATAM
CASUALTIES

The British buried
some 9,000 of the
Tippoo's soldiers after
his defeat. The
number of wounded is
unknown. There were
287 cannons mounted
on the fort's walls plus
919 more in storage,
together with 99,000
muskets – many of
British manufacture.
The price the British
paid was
comparatively small:
just under 900
Europeans and 649
Indians killed,
wounded and missing.

only 4,300 were Europeans. The plan envisaged Harris marching from his assembly area at Vellore to Seringapatam, some 250 miles to the west. Before he reached Mysore he would be joined from the north by the Nizam of Hyderabad (recently seduced from French sympathies) with 20,000 native troops. Harris would depart on 13 February. Moving at under ten miles a day and resting every third day, he might expect to reach his destination around mid-April – if the Tippoo did not intervene beforehand.

The western arm of the pincer was somewhat flimsy, consisting of just over 6,000 troops of the Bombay Army under local (an important distinction when seniority issues were so sensitive) Lieutenant-General James Stuart. Stuart had made the unusual decision to split his force into two brigades on racial lines. Lieutenant-Colonel Dunlop had command of the European battalions, while Lieutenant-Colonel John Montresor led the EIC native units (1/2nd, 1/3rd and 1/4th Bengal Native Infantry). From the west coast at Cannanore, Stuart had only half the distance to march so he would start eight days later than Harris, and initially take up a defensive position in a pass in the Western Ghats.

The glaring weakness in the strategy was obvious: the Tippoo was occupying what strategists call an 'interior lines' position. He was sitting between two opponents who were a very long way away from each other and had virtually no means of communicating or co-ordinating their movements. He could strike one long before the other could intervene. And this is exactly what the Tippoo did. Selecting the weaker enemy, Stuart, he attacked the British position in the high pass near Sedaseer on 6 March. Because the pass was so long and narrow, Stuart had been able to deploy only three Bombay Infantry (EIC) battalions and six guns for its defence under the extremely capable command of Montresor. In a four-hour battle, against odds of five to one, Montresor's guns and native infantry smashed all assaults, even when the enemy managed to get into their rear. The skilful tactical handling of the situation by their commander, the steady,

Pay rates

DIFFERENCES IN PAY between Indian and British soldiers were enormous. Even so, sepoys lived comparatively well compared to the average villager or urban worker (as late as the twentieth century a grass cutter's pay was two rupees). In Sharpe's time, an Indian rupee was worth about two shillings (10 pence in today's money). Monthly pay rates, after stoppages:

	Indian	British
Private	6 rupees (60p)	30 shillings (Rs15 or £1.50)
Corporal	8 rupees (80p)	40 shillings (Rs20 or £2)
Sergeant	10 rupees (£1)	55 shillings (Rs28 or £2.80)
Officers	16–60 rupees (£1.60–£6)	120 shillings upwards (Rs60 or £6)

disciplined volleys of the infantry and the devastating use of the guns at close range were decisive in keeping the Tippoo's troops at bay. But by three o'clock that afternoon, both musket and artillery ammunition was running short. At this point Stuart himself led forward the 77th Foot (Hindoostan) – many years later the 2nd Battalion of the Middlesex Regiment – and the flank companies of the 75th Foot (Highland). These reinforcements came up the pass to take in rear those enemy that were attacking Montresor's rear. It clinched the engagement. The Tippoo turned away to find Harris, leaving almost 2,000 bodies on the battlefield.

The battle honour 'Sedaseer' was especially treasured by the three Bombay battalions that had fought so gallantly for so long. Two of them survived until Indian independence in 1947 as the 1st and 2nd Battalions of the 5th Maratha Light Infantry. The third became the Bombay Pioneers in 1929 and thus lost its identity. The Sedaseer legend was remembered outside the Indian Army for years afterwards. The present writer recalls an army camp in Aden in 1967 bearing the name 'Sedaseer Lines'.

On 27 March, near a town in Mysore called Mallavelly, Sharpe the soldier killed his first enemy in close combat. The

EUROPEAN NCOS IN SEPOY BATTALIONS

There was a small cadre of European NCOs in each EIC sepoy battalion. These consisted of the sergeant-major (who today would be the regimental sergeant-major); a quartermaster-sergeant, who usually retired rich if he did not die of drink; and one sergeant per company. Most had transferred from British battalions; the EIC offered not only an opportunity to remain in India, but also better pay and a number of perks including promotion. It was therefore not surprising that substantial numbers stayed on.

THUGS

Sleeman was made
responsible for
rooting out and
destroying the Thugs –
gangs of men who
murdered and stole
from travellers in the
name of religion. A
group would befriend
a party of travellers
then, on the signal of
their leader (often a
clap and a shout to
'Bring the tobacco!'),
each thug pounced on
his victim. They killed
by strangulation, using
a square
handkerchief, in one
corner of which was
knotted a silver coin
dedicated to the
Hindu goddess Kali.
Thugs believed they
were carrying out a
divine mission; one
claimed to have
murdered 719 people –
his only regret was he
did not reach 1,000.

Tippoo's army barred the British advance from a low ridge. Colonel Wellesley and the 33rd had been attached to the Nizam's army, the colonel to 'advise' the Nizam (Meer Allum), and the battalion to add backbone to the native troops. Wellesley's column bumped the enemy first and came under artillery fire. Harris ordered him to push on, which he did, with the 33rd leading a force of six EIC battalions. They formed line from column with each battalion echeloned back to the left rear of the one on its right. On the extreme right, out in front, was the 33rd under the temporary command of Major John Shee, an officer with a greater than average liking for the bottle. There were over 750 men advancing in a two-deep line, with the light company under *Captain Morris* on the left and Sharpe in the rear rank on the left of that. Wellesley had ridden forward on Diomed as a huge enemy column of two to three thousand infantry poured over the crest of the rise and rolled down towards the 33rd. Wellesley yelled the order: 'Thirty-third, halt! Half-right, face! Make ready!' The half-turn to the right meant that every man was standing at the best angle for firing from the shoulder to his front. The muskets were already loaded, so on the order 'Make ready' all the soldiers had to do was thumb the cock back and stand with their musket pointing forward from the waist. It is likely that bayonets were fixed as the battalion had been advancing to the attack, and from the fact that Wellesley was to wait until the enemy was too close for reloading before hand-to-hand fighting occurred. Then came the wait, followed by the great mass of warriors rushing down the gradual slope yelling war cries and thumping their drums. Still Wellesley waited. At a hundred yards there was no movement from the British line. At about seventy yards the order everybody had been anticipating rang out: 'Present!' Every musket came to the shoulder, those of the second rank projecting between the heads of the men in front. With the enemy a mere sixty yards away, the final order, 'Fire!' produced a sheet of flame, a thunderous roar and a blanket of white smoke that temporarily blotted out the enemy. Before

Pindarris

THESE BANDS of mounted bandits, up to several thousand strong, swept through the Deccan and Central India devouring all in their path until they met resolute opposition. It is thought they got their name from a fondness for a liquor called *pinda*. Although operating during Wellesley's (and Sharpe's) time in India, it was not until after he left that the Mahratta chiefs began to make use of their services for large-scale raids and light cavalry work. They were entirely mercenary, relying on plunder and pillage for their livelihood. Recruited from all over India, with a high proportion of discharged soldiers, criminals and vagabonds, they became such a scourge that a full-scale war, the Pindarri War of 1812–14, had to be mounted to bring them in check. Major-General Sir John Malcolm, who for a time was political adviser to Arthur Wellesley, had this to say on the subject:

> When they set out on an expedition they were neither encumbered by tents nor baggage; each horseman carried a few cakes for his own subsistence and some feeds of grain for his horses. The party usually consisting of two or three thousand good horse ... advanced at the rapid rate of forty or fifty miles a day, turning neither right nor left till they arrived at the country meant to be attacked. Then they divided and made a sweep of all the cattle and property they could find; committing at the same time the most horrid atrocities and destroying what they could not carry away ... If pursued they made marches of extraordinary length (sometimes upwards of sixty miles) ... If overtaken they dispersed and reassembled at an appointed rendezvous ...

In one raid alone, lasting eight days, Pindarris killed 182 villagers, wounded 505 and tortured 3,033. Their favourite method of persuasion was to tie a bag of hot ashes over their victim's mouth and nose and thump his back. The immediate result was the divulgence of the hiding place; the long term: ruination of the victim's lungs.

their vision cleared, the yell of 'Charge! Charge!' was taken up by the officers as they waved their companies forward with their swords. With bayonets levelled, the line surged forward into the shambles ahead of them.

In the mêlée, Sharpe confronted an Indian officer who, although he had a drawn sabre, fumbled to draw his pistol, then turned to run. Sharpe struck him in the side of the neck with his bayonet, parried a sabre slash, kicked him in the groin (in what was to become a favourite tactic), and slammed his musket butt into the officer's face before finally driving his bayonet into his throat. He then looted the dying man of a few coins. It had been easy, it had been quick – and Sharpe had enjoyed it.

Not all the enemy stood to cross swords with the bayonets. What fighting occurred was brief and bloody. In a matter of moments the Mysore infantry was streaming back over the crest the way it had come. The 33rd lost just two men; Baird's brigade, which had been victorious on the right, lost only twenty-nine. The army as a whole suffered only about seventy casualties, of whom forty-three were Europeans. The Tippoo had lost a thousand and had now been beaten twice in three weeks. Sedaseer and Mallavelly had provided a bitter taste of what to expect if the British and EIC battalions were engaged

Flogging

MAJOR SHEE exceeded his powers in two respects: trying Sharpe himself and awarding 2,000 lashes. He should have convened a drumhead regimental court martial of three officers. There was certainly time for this on a rest day – in the Peninsular War, General Crauford was known to hold them during a halt on the line of march. If Sharpe had been found guilty and sentenced, Shee, as his commanding officer, had the discretionary power to remit the whole, or part, of the punishment – something he was unlikely to do. Sentences varied from 25 to 1,200 lashes (the maximum permitted), which was calculated to kill or at the very least permanently disable. It was normally reserved for desertion to the enemy, robbery with violence or striking an officer. Only ten such awards were made during the Peninsular War, whereas over fifty men received 1,000 lashes. A surgeon was always present and could halt the punishment if he considered the man close to death. This was only a postponement (unless he had a humane commanding officer), as the culprit had to receive the remainder (in one or more instalments) when pronounced fit. In theory, if a soldier died under the lash the sentence was to be completed on his lifeless corpse. Drummers carried out the flogging and were supposed to carry a cat-o'-nine-tails in their pack. With heavy sentences several drummers would be involved, taking turns to give 25 lashes each.

Flogging – an example

THERE WERE a few men of iron who walked away from hundreds of lashes. One was Sergeant Thomas Mayberry of the 95th. He was sentenced to 700 for gambling with £200 of public funds, which had been entrusted to him to buy 'necessaries' for his men. A Corporal Morrisson and Private Divine were also implicated. When Mayberry was tied up, he was offered (as was then customary) the option of banishment. He refused, despite Morrisson and Divine, who were to get 300 and 100 respectively, entreating him to accept. Incredibly, Mayberry took his punishment without a murmur. Morrisson yelled and struggled so violently that the halberds collapsed and he had to be held by two men. Divine looked so frail that the Colonel took pity on him and he was let off with 25.

Mayberry, a man of immense strength and courage, almost won his stripes back in the breach at Badajoz. His company commander was so impressed by his actions (he had accounted for seven enemy) that he ordered him to the rear with the promise of his rank back. Mayberry, although covered in blood from several wounds, refused to retire. He was eventually killed by a sword-cut that split open his skull.

in the open. The sooner the Tippoo got behind the walls of Seringapatam, the safer he would feel.

The British were then about seven days' march from Seringapatam, two days of which would be needed to get the huge host across the Cauvery River. The route taken was far from direct, as Harris wanted to confuse the enemy. In all, some sixty miles of marching were necessary to get the army and its tens of thousands of camp followers and animals from Mallavelly to Seringapatam. On the day following the clash at Mallavelly, *Colonel Hector McCandless*, a senior EIC intelligence officer, was captured and taken to Seringapatam, while Sharpe was goaded into striking *Sergeant Hakeswill* and arrested.

On 30 March, exceeding his authority as a commanding officer, Major Shee sent Sharpe 'to the halberds' to receive 2,000 lashes. Hitting an NCO was so serious an offence that the case should have been heard by a general court martial, or at the very least a regimental court martial. Instead, Shee heard the case personally. Furthermore, the maximum number of lashes that could be awarded by any court was 1,200. Shee probably got away with these illegalities because the army was facing the enemy, and senior officers had their hands full with far more pressing matters. Also, he had the sentence carried out within two hours of passing it. Whatever the law, 1,200 would have killed Sharpe as surely as 2,000 had Wellesley's intervention on Harris's orders after 202 lashes not saved him. By the night of 31 March Sharpe and *Lieutenant Lawford*, having 'deserted' that morning, were in the cells in Seringapatam on their special mission to secure information from *McCandless*.

The Tippoo's stronghold had been cleverly sited to make the most of natural obstacles. The fortress sat securely on Seringapatam Island, protected on all sides by the north and south branches of the River Cauvery. Because the river was fordable almost anywhere, the Tippoo needed to hold out until the monsoon arrived – around 20 May. The rains would bring immediate flooding and six months' security. Thus if the British failed to take Seringapatam within eight weeks, they would be forced to withdraw. This was not long to conduct a full-scale siege.

A firm believer in the army adage that 'time spent on reconnaissance is seldom wasted', Wellesley rode forward on the afternoon of 4 April to examine the enemy's defences through his telescope. What he saw as he came up on the south side of Seringapatam Island was impressive (MAP 2). The encampment consisted of an outer fortification with an inner, much stronger, fortress at the north-western tip of the island. Wellesley estimated that the entire circumference must be at least two and a half miles. The southern wall of the inner fort was over 700 yards long with one main gate. The walls around the city were made of a mixture of large granite blocks with sections of bricks and mortar. The south face was bristling with guns – Wellesley counted almost a hundred. The only potential weakness he could identify lay in

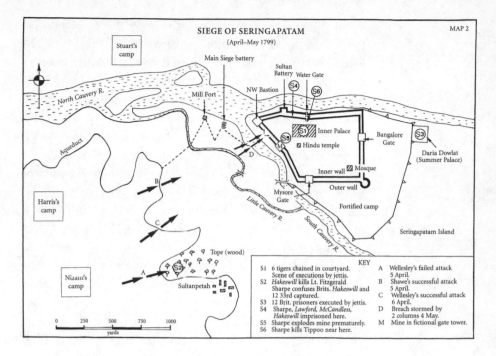

SIEGE OF SERINGAPATAM
(April–May 1799)

MAP 2

Stuart's camp

Main Siege battery

Sultan Battery   Water Gate

North Cauvery R.

Mill Fort

NW Bastion   S4   S6

Inner Palace   S1

Bangalore Gate   S3

Daria Dowlat (Summer Palace)

Aqueduct

S5   Hindu temple

M

Inner wall   Mosque

Outer wall

Harris's camp

B

Mysore Gate

Fortified camp

Little Cauvery R.

C

South Cauvery R.

Seringapatam Island

Tope (wood)

Nizam's camp

A

Sultanpetah

KEY

S1 6 tigers chained in courtyard. Scene of executions by jettis.
S2 Hakeswill kills Lt. Fitzgerald. Sharpe confuses Brits. Hakeswill and 12 33rd captured.
S3 12 Brit. prisoners executed by jettis.
S4 Sharpe, Lawford, McCandless, Hakeswill imprisoned here.
S5 Sharpe explodes mine prematurely.
S6 Sharpe kills Tippoo near here.

A Wellesley's failed attack 5 April.
B Shawe's successful attack 5 April.
C Wellesley's successful attack 6 April.
D Breach stormed by 2 columns 4 May.
M Mine in fictional gate tower.

0   250   500   750   1000
yards

the straightness of the walls; there were no bastions from which flanking fire could be brought down on attackers at the wall or a breach.

However it was not just the western side of the island that was defended. The Tippoo's 30,000 troops and several hundred guns were deployed not only on the fortress walls but also within the fortified camp outside the eastern and southern walls, behind the Little Cauvery and as far west as the aqueduct. Hidden from Wellesley's telescope as he carried out his reconnaissance was the inner wall, a particular strength of the fortress of which the British were unaware.

By the morning of 5 April, Harris and the Nizam had encamped their armies to the west of Seringapatam (MAP 2). Harris had to decide where to make a breach. This was always the key question for any besieger. His options were to attack from the north, east or west. The north seems not even to have been considered. Looking at the map, this appears a strange oversight. An attack from this direction would have avoided having to fight through the outer fortified camp (to the east of the fortress), and the enemy positions behind the aqueduct and the Little Cauvery in the west. In other words, a direct assault on the wall of the inner fort, allowing breaching batteries to be brought up close to the northern wall without direct enemy interference. Once that wall was stormed, the fortress was as good as taken. Perhaps the northern branch of the river, which was wider than the southern one, was thought too difficult. More likely Harris thought it would be too dangerous, difficult and time-consuming to move his entire force back over to the north of the river in full view of the enemy.

An attack from the east would have meant getting across on to the island, then breaching and storming the fortified camp; only then could the batteries open up on the inner fortress. Instead, Harris opted to attack from the west. This would involve fighting through and overcoming a series of defences and obstacles in depth, and looked possibly the most difficult of the three options. First the line of the aqueduct must be taken, then the Little Cauvery River, then the South Cauvery, before, finally, the outer wall of the inner fortress. From the attackers' start line there were some 1,200 yards of enemy positions and obstacles to overcome before a soldier could touch the walls.

The crucial requirement was to get the siege guns close enough – preferably within 400 yards – to the point in the walls selected for the breach. This would entail much preliminary fighting to clear the enemy from behind the aqueduct and the Little Cauvery, virtually to the banks of the South Cauvery. Until this was accomplished the main siege battery could not safely be established, ready to begin the real task of breaking in.

Harris ordered Wellesley to secure the area of Sultanpetah village, the wood to the north-west and the line of the aqueduct in that area, by a night attack on 5 April. Wellesley put the light and grenadier companies of the 33rd in the lead, followed by the rest of the battalion, with the 1/11th and

2/11th Madras Native Infantry in reserve. Some 750 yards to
the north, Lieutenant-Colonel Shawe with the 12th Foot (East
Suffolk), supported by the 1/1st and 2/3rd Madras Native
Infantry, was to carry out a similar operation. Wellesley personally led the flank companies of the 33rd.

The operation was to be Wellesley's only serious setback in his
lengthy career. After failure at Sultanpetah, he contemplated
night attack only as a last resort, for without meticulous
planning and prior reconnaissance it is often, if not always,
chaotic. Wellesley was confused as to the precise nature of
his task from the outset. When he received his orders, he
rode over to Harris and said, 'I do not know where you mean
... do me the favour to meet me in front of the lines ...'
There was no time for a proper reconnaissance; the night
was pitch-black and the wood (tope) was found to be east
of the aqueduct (itself fifteen yards wide and six feet deep on
top of an embankment) instead of to the west, as previously
thought.

   Silhouetted against the skyline as they clambered up the
slope of the aqueduct and plunged through the water, the
flank companies of the 33rd drew straggling fire. The width
and depth of the water came as a shock to the soldiers as
they half swam, half splashed across before slithering down
into the darkness of the trees. As they blundered around in
the thickets beyond the aqueduct, the Tippoo's defenders
launched a fierce attack. The first casualty on the British side
was control. Captain West and the grenadiers ended up nearly
a mile to the south; Major Shee with five battalion companies
went a mile to the north, where they eventually merged with
Shawe's force. The light company was pushed back in confused close-quarter fighting in the tangled bamboo and
brushwood of the tope. *Captain Morris*'s leadership was
ineffectual, while the only competent officer, Lieutenant Fitzgerald, had most of his arm torn away by a rocket and was
then mortally wounded by a bayonet thrust – murdered by
his own sergeant, *Hakeswill*. Sharpe, who had by then joined

a French unit fighting for the Tippoo, added to the shambles by yelling conflicting orders in English. Although casualties were light – only about twenty-five, including eight prisoners, one of whom was *Hakeswill* – the attack petered out. An embarrassed but wiser Wellesley reported his failure to Harris personally.

Shawe, in the north with the 12th, had little trouble taking his section of the aqueduct, but his two supporting battalions of native infantry had a dreadful night. Both were fired on by rockets and then became hopelessly confused in the darkness. The resultant indiscriminate and uncontrolled return fire caused panic and chaos. The companies could not distinguish who was who and the 2/3rd Madras, temporarily under Major Colin Campbell, 'paid no attention to orders', and succeeded in accidentally shooting and killing their commanding officer. The 1/1st Madras, under yet another Campbell, became equally entangled, confused and ineffective – although their commander managed to come through unscathed. All in all, an object lesson in the problems of fighting at night.

Finding himself virtually back at square one, Harris ordered another attack. The objective was, once again, to seize the entire length of the aqueduct. A fresh King's battalion, the Scotch Brigade, supported by two native units and four twelve-pounder brass field guns, was given the task. At least they could see where they were heading. Nevertheless, there was a hitch at the outset. The guns had opened their preliminary softening-up bombardment, the infantry assault column was poised on the start line – but where was Wellesley? The adjutant-general had despatched the necessary instructions to the units concerned, giving Wellesley, who continued to be duty brigade commander until noon, a chance to redeem himself. There was talk of Baird assuming command in his place until, at the last moment, Wellesley galloped up in a cloud of dust, having only just received his orders. The system of senior commanders taking over a particular operation did not seem to require them to plan it or give orders. It was sufficient for the commander to arrive at the eleventh hour, join the troops and give the signal for the advance to begin.

The exploding shells, the sight of the red jackets advancing, proved enough to send the enemy scampering back. The entire line of the aqueduct and the Sultanpetah tope that had caused so much grief a few hours earlier fell without the loss of a single soldier. The front line of the attackers was now the aqueduct. The advanced brigade headquarters was set up at the spot that Shawe had captured in the only successful part of the night attack (marked B on MAP 2). But they were still 1,500 yards from the walls.

It was to be another month before Seringapatam proper was stormed. During those weeks Stuart's force arrived (14 April). When he was a day's march away, Stuart fired two cannon shots – the prearranged signal for Harris to expect him within twenty-four hours. Harris replied by firing two shots in quick succession to show he understood. Once Stuart had set up camp north of the river, the British set about achieving their next objective: the heavily defended line of the Little Cauvery. Not until that was taken could the siege guns be pushed forward to positions from which they could do real damage to the walls.

A series of British attacks drove the Tippoo's troops back towards the western walls of the fortress. By 2 May, after taking a number of key points such as the Mill Fort, two of the three main siege batteries were within 380 and 340 yards of their target. A total of 29 cannons and 3 howitzers commenced their pounding. Except for two 24-pounders, these guns were all throwing 18-pound iron balls. The sustained bombardment began to tear down some 60 yards of curtain wall just south of the north-west bastion. Soon after the start, a huge explosion ripped the inside of the fortress as a magazine of rockets exploded.

Inside Seringapatam the Tippoo had presented Sharpe with a gold medallion for his efforts in the tope. However, on 25 April he and *Lawford* were betrayed. Thirteen British

Bullocks and brinjarris

—⟨∞⟩—

WITHOUT BULLOCKS no army could function in India. The roads were too poor for the large horse-drawn wagons used on campaign in Europe. Elephants (particularly suited to hauling heavy siege guns), camels and humans did some of the carrying, but bullocks did the bulk of the work. Many were draught animals pulling guns, carts and ammunition wagons, but the majority carried their loads in panniers. They were cheap and could, hopefully, live off the land – at least for short periods. Wellesley's correspondence reveals his preoccupation with supplies, and his command of the subject: 'the loads for pack bullocks must be 72 *pukka* ['genuine'] seers [about 144lb]'. Even the quality of the material used to make the sacks comes under scrutiny: 'The bags of rice must be proper bullock gunny bags, made of the best gunny.'

In the native regiments men were expected to carry a knapsack and musket, plus sixty rounds of ball ammunition. Other personal possessions such as sleeping mat, brass cooking pots and a cotton quilt for warmth at night were carried by hired bullocks at a cost to each soldier of around one and a half rupees a month. About ten bullocks would be needed per company for this purpose alone.

In addition to buying or hiring bullocks, the army made use of *brinjarris* – grain merchants who kept huge herds of pack bullocks to transport their goods. The *brinjarris* were a people in their own right; neither Hindu nor Muslim, they operated a system of semi-secret self-government, had their own laws, defended and policed themselves. Grain-trading was their hereditary occupation; they would buy cheap and transport grain hundreds of miles to where it was in short supply. It was difficult to beat them when it came to bargaining. Bullock drivers from birth, they knew their animals' capabilities and how to care for them. To ensure the *brinjarris* maintained a keen interest in protecting the grain and other goods they carried throughout the long march, the army did not purchase their stock at the outset but paid on delivery.

prisoners (eight captured on 5 April plus another five) from the 33rd were paraded for execution by the Tippoo's musclemen bodyguards, the *jettis*. One by one they died, either by a terrible twisting of the head through 180 degrees, or by having a nine-inch nail driven into their skull. Each man had to wait his turn, watching his comrades die, anticipating his own ghastly fate. *Hakeswill* was left till last. By this time he was beside himself in a frenzy of fear and convulsions.

Jetti

He saved his neck (literally) by screaming his betrayal of
Sharpe and *Lawford* just as the *jetti* began to turn his head.

The breach was pronounced practical on the evening of
3 May, the rubble from the broken wall having fallen forward
to provide a slope up which an infantryman with musket
could climb. But to get to that point still required the attacking force to cross the South Cauvery and the water-filled
ditch at the foot of the wall, although it was hoped most of
this water had drained away into the river after the pounding
the area had received. The plan involved two assault columns
attacking parallel to each other (MAP 2), both under the
direct personal command of the tall, bulky figure of Major-
General Baird. Wellesley commanded a reserve force in the
rear with over 4,000 men, his orders being to reinforce either
column as he saw fit. The intention was for each column to
clamber up the debris in the breach, turn left and right
to climb on to the walls before fighting their way round to
encircle the fortress. Each column was headed by a 'forlorn
hope' of volunteers. It consisted of a sergeant, carrying his
regiment's Colours, with twelve lightly equipped soldiers,

A sepoy enlists

SITA RAM, who joined the Bengal Army only a few years after Sharpe left India, served over forty-eight years before he was finally pensioned off at the age of sixty-five. His enlistment was arranged through the good offices of his uncle, a jemadar (lieutenant) in the regiment he wished to join. His account gives a fascinating insight into recruiting practices and how European officers were perceived by Indian villagers:

> We went to the Adjutant's house, which was four times the size of the headman's house in my village. He was on the verandah, with a long stick, measuring young men who were recruits. He was very young, not as tall as myself, and had no whiskers or moustache. His face was quite smooth and looked more like a woman's than a man's. This was the first *sahib* I had ever seen, and he did not fill me with much awe. I did not believe he could be much of a warrior with a face as smooth as that since among us it is considered a disgrace to be clean-shaven; in fact the smooth-faced soldier is usually the butt for many jokes. However he banged those young recruits' heads against the wall in a manner which showed he had no fear, and they looked as if they thought he was about to kill them.
>
> After he had finished the measuring, the Adjutant took notice of my uncle, and to my surprise spoke to him in my own language. He seemed glad to see him, asked after his welfare, and touched his sword [the uncle, as a mark of respect, would have offered the adjutant the hilt of his sword to touch – a custom maintained in the Indian Cavalry until the 1940s]. He then asked who I was, and on being informed that I had come to enlist and was my uncle's nephew, he told my uncle to take me to the Doctor *sahib*, to whom he wrote a letter. I was astonished at the speed of his writing . . .

followed by a subaltern (Lieutenant Lawrence on the left, Lieutenant Hill on the right) with another twenty-five men. The left column was commanded by Lieutenant-Colonel Dunlop from Stuart's force. Under him were six flank companies from Stuart's British regiments, the 12th and 33rd Foot, plus ten companies of Bengal sepoy flankers (in all, about 3,000 men). A matter of yards to the right the other column was under Lieutenant-Colonel Sherbrooke (Sharpe's old

A sepoy recruit's medical examination

SITA RAM'S account continues:

My uncle told me that the Doctor was married and had several children. He was at home and we were ordered into his presence. A chair was provided for my uncle, but no notice was taken of me so I squatted on the ground. My uncle made me stand up, and told me afterwards that it was bad manners to sit down in the presence of a *sahib*. After reading the note the Doctor ordered me to strip, but I was so ashamed I could not move, for there was a *memsahib* in the room. She was sitting at a table covered with a sheet, and feeding two children with eggs – those unclean things! I began to regret having followed my uncle, and remembered the priest's warning about being defiled. However I was ordered sharply to take off my clothes, and both the children began calling out – 'Papa says you are to take your clothes off! Don't you understand? Donkey, pig, owl!' – and the Doctor joined in, saying I was a fool and an ignorant villager. Then the children cried out – 'Oh, mamma, is he covered with hair?' I was so ashamed that I ran out on to the verandah, but my uncle came out and told me not to be afraid. No harm would be done to me. The Doctor then pushed me into an empty room and examined me, by thrusting his hand against my stomach, which nearly made me vomit. Then he opened my eyelids with such violence that tears came into my eyes, and he thumped my chest. After this he pronounced me fit and ceased tormenting me – to my great relief.

commanding officer at Boxtel). His force was composed of the flank companies of the Scotch Brigade and the Regiment de Meuron, the 73rd and 74th Foot and fourteen flank companies of Bombay and Madras sepoys (about 2,800 men). In total nearly 6,000 men, the majority of whom were Europeans, formed up in the trenches during the night of 3–4 May. They huddled, hidden, squashed together, sweating and swearing under a broiling sun until 1 p.m. the next day.

At that precise moment, Baird climbed stiffly out of his trench, drew his claymore and launched the assault. The two columns advanced, each on a platoon frontage, with Baird out in front, perspiration pouring down his brick-red face.

INDIAN RANKS

The Indian ranks and approximate British equivalents were:
sepoy – private
naik – corporal
havildar – sergeant
havildar-major – sergeant-major
jemadar – lieutenant
subadar – captain.
The ranks of lance-naik (lance-corporal) and subadar-major (major) did not exist in this period.

Just ahead of him were the two forlorn hopes. As the attackers approached the river, the British guns continued firing frantically at the summit of the breach and wall on either side. The columns surged forward under a galling fire into the 300-yard-wide river, whose passage had been marked out with white flags the previous night by Lieutenant Lalor of the 73rd. The water varied from ankle to waist deep. For the troops, splashing or wading across with muskets held high must have been a welcome relief from the intense heat. Within six minutes the forlorn hopes had climbed the breach and Sergeant Graham (of Dunlop's force) planted his Colours in the rubble at the top and announced himself 'Lieutenant Graham!' (a promotion he would expect to receive for being the first man into the breach). Regrettably, he was shot dead the next instant, one of only two casualties in the breach itself. But there was no stopping the rush: men from both columns scrambled up on to the outer walls on either side of the breach. There was some consternation at the depth of the ditch behind the outer wall, and that the inner wall was undamaged and manned by the enemy in large numbers. It was at this stage, before the attackers had got down into the space between the walls, that Sharpe, who had escaped from the dungeons, managed to prematurely explode the mine intended to destroy the assaulting force in this gap. In reality there was no mine.

The left column turned to force its way towards the northwest bastion. Under heavy musketry fire and unable to cross the ditch between walls, progress was slow. Then, to their front, they encountered a group of the enemy under a short, fat officer. They had no idea it was the Tippoo in person. From behind a traverse on the north wall, the podgy officer exposed himself to fire a succession of muskets, calmly firing shot after shot as his aides handed the loaded weapons to him. With one he killed Lieutenant Lalor. While this was going on, Captain Goodall of the King's 12th found a narrow bridge across the inner ditch and led his men over in single file. Once a lodgement had been secured on the inner wall the defenders were driven back with comparative ease. Despite the Tippoo's gallant efforts, resistance crumbled in the north. He was wounded and forced to retire.

Dunlop's men now pushed around the north wall towards the Sultan Battery, which surrounded the Tippoo's dungeons where Baird had been incarcerated for nearly four years and, until earlier that day, Sharpe, *Lawford, McCandless* and *Hakeswill*. The enemy attempted to make a stand both here and at the nearby Water Gate, which was actually a short tunnel through the walls, and there was confused hand-to-hand fighting with sword, bayonet and musket butt as attackers closed in from both ends.

Baird accompanied the right column under Sherbrooke. Resistance was spasmodic as his soldiers pushed steadily along the wall towards the Mysore Gate in a running fight of some 600 yards. The defence of this gate was overcome without much difficulty and the attackers pressed on eastwards along a 400-yard stretch of wall to the only bastion on the south-eastern corner. Another 400 yards northwards took them to the Bangalore Gate. With this secured, Sherbrooke had in a single hour captured some 1,400 yards of wall, including the Mysore and Bangalore gates. His troops then linked up with Dunlop's men, thus having taken the entire perimeter wall – a notable achievement.

The only place of significance remaining in enemy hands was the inner palace. Here would be the Tippoo's family, his concubines and his treasure – loot with a capital L. It was the custom of the times that if a garrison surrendered after a breach had been made and before it was stormed, then surrender would take place with honour and without pillage. This was not the case with Seringapatam. Military convention dictated that if a fortress resisted when a breach was stormed the attackers had free reign inside. An assault on a breach was always likely to be a bloody affair. Forlorn hopes would get blown away (that was why they were so called), while those coming behind could expect heavy losses and a bitter struggle to gain a foothold. If the assault succeeded – and

Prize money

WITH PAY LOW and expenses high, the thought of prize money was prominent in the minds of most soldiers. Booty was supposed to be pooled and distributed to all who participated in its capture according to a set scale based on rank. Naturally, this caused much discontentment as the general got a fortune, the private a pittance. Moreover, precise calculations as to who qualified and the proportions of each share could drag on for months – even ten years in some cases – by which time individuals had dispersed or died. If a soldier wanted to be sure of picking up a worthwhile sum, his best chance was to grab whatever plunder he could during the conquest, hence the rush for loot at Seringapatam (in which Sharpe did well to grab the Tippoo's jewels). Comparatively little made it into the official kitty after the 1799 sacking of the city, and distribution details are unknown. After the first surrender of Seringapatam, however, the shares were: colonel £297, lieutenant £52, British private £3 15s 9d, Indian subadar £7, jemadar £3 10s and sepoy £1 17s 6d.

By 1825 things had improved, particularly for the officers. After the second siege of Bhurtpore the commander-in-chief got £60,000, general £6,000, lieutenant £238, British private £4 (a miserly increase), subadar £28, jemadar £12 and sepoy £2 12s. The huge divide between British and Indian officers was blatantly unjustified, a subadar with forty years' service entitled to an eighth of a subaltern's share. No wonder prize money caused friction.

At Seringapatam the symbol of Mysorean power – the light green, silken standard with a red hand in its centre – was taken by Baird from the palace roof and sent to Fort William. The huge, gilded tiger's head from the Sultan's throne ended up in Windsor Castle, and the tiger organ in the Victoria and Albert Museum. The value of the treasure looted was estimated at £2 million, a fair proportion of which found its way into soldiers' hands as virtually every house in the city was raided. It was said that a single casket of jewels valued at £300,000 disappeared from the palace. The coins and jewels seized officially by the authorities were declared prize money. This meant that most senior officers became rich. Baird was presented with the Tippoo's jewel-encrusted sword, though Harris entered a six-year legal battle with a penny-pinching EIC to keep his allocation. The Privy Council finally decided in his favour.

most besiegers who reached this final stage did – the troops expected revenge and rewards for being forced to fight their way in.

With the capture of the walls it was the turn of the palace. Two officers – Major Allan, the deputy quartermaster-general, and a Major Beatson, the chief engineer – mutually decided to try to prevent the necessity of an attack on the palace by persuading the defenders to surrender. They conferred with Baird. He agreed they should try. Both managed to gain access (they were just in time to stop the 33rd from launching an attack) and talked the killadar (commandant), along with two of the Tippoo's sons, into surrendering. Of the Tippoo himself there was no sign.

A thorough search of the palace proved fruitless. The exact circumstances of his death will never be known. Fortescue's version has the Tippoo, who had been twice wounded, borne back to the Water Gate in the north wall. His followers tried to lift him into his palanquin to get him away, but they were too late. He was hit again and attacked by British soldiers hand-to-hand. He finally fell to a bullet through the temple, possibly fired by a soldier from the 12th Foot. He collapsed, and in the fury of the fighting by the inner wall Water Gate his body became covered with other corpses – possibly unrecognised. Later, when the fighting was over, one of his aides, who had probably feigned death under the palanquin, crawled out and indicated where he had died. Corpse after corpse was lifted and examined by torchlight until the flabby and bloody body of the Tippoo was revealed. He was wearing no jewels. The man who killed him never claimed the credit. But then neither did Sharpe.

When Wellesley, who had entered the fortress with a few aides, returned to his command outside, inside the drinking, looting, raping and murdering began. Baird showed little inclination to stop it. Perhaps at that time it was impossible to do so, perhaps it was too late to try. The soldiers had had to storm the breach – they knew their 'rights'. Perhaps Baird himself wanted revenge for his long years in those dreadful

OFFICERS' DEBTS

Sharpe's good fortune in picking up the Tippoo's jewels made him rich, but by the time he left India some six years later he was in debt. This was not unusual for a subaltern. After Sharpe left India, a committee examined the expenses facing junior officers. Equipment and uniform cost up to Rs1,800, which would have to be borrowed (unless a generous relative paid). As security, the officer would be compelled to insure his life; and because life was cheap in India, insurance costs were high. Even with the strictest economy, most subalterns would owe Rs6,000–7,000 by the time they were promoted captain. While as a captain he might prevent the debt rising, it was unlikely to be cleared until he became a major. Much depended on where he was stationed: outside Calcutta expenses increased, so debt was the norm. Most young officers accepted this as a fact of life, annoying but unavoidable. Credit was easy, life was likely to be short. If they lived to be a major it would be paid off. If not . . . well, they would not be around to worry.

HOOKAHS

The smoking of
hookahs (also referred
to as hubble-bubbles
or water-pipes) was a
part of British social
life in India until the
middle of the
nineteenth century.
Sharpe would almost
certainly have tried
one during his years in
the country. There
were even women who
smoked. Among the
many servants in a
typical Anglo-Indian
household would be a
hookahbadar whose
sole task was to look
after the *sahib*'s
hookahs and provide
the tobacco.

cells. Whatever the reasons, the night was given over to drunken shouts, shrieks, the sound of things being smashed and musket shots as the city was ransacked. Wellesley was later to describe Baird as

> a gallant, hard-headed, lionhearted officer, but he had no talent, no tact; had strong prejudices against the natives; and he was peculiarly disqualified from his manners, habits, etc and it was supposed his temper, for the management of them. He had been the Tippoo's prisoner for years. He had a strong feeling of the bad usage he had received during his captivity . . .

Perhaps because his thoughts troubled him Baird wrote a note to Harris asking to be relieved of command in the city due to exhaustion – although he later denied it. On the morning of 5 May Harris ordered Wellesley into Seringapatam to restore order. He was later to be confirmed military governor, much to the fury of the far senior Baird. Baird had a heated confrontation with Harris over the appointment. Not only did he write, vehemently protesting over what he saw as his being superseded by a junior, he remonstrated with Harris face to face, demanding that the matter be referred to the Duke of York. To his credit, the commander-in-chief did not allow himself to be browbeaten by this insubordination and told Baird to withdraw his letter or quit the army. Baird backed down.

Not that Wellesley was soft. He was to write in his *Despatches*: 'I came in to take command on the morning of the 5th, and by hanging, flogging, etc restored order among the troops. I hope I have gained the confidence of the people.' He had. When, eventually, Wellesley left India, the people of Seringapatam wrote thanking him for his governorship – a letter Baird would never have received.

4

Sharpe's Triumph

In July 1803, at the outset of the Deccan campaign of the Second Mahratta War, Sergeant Sharpe, in command of a small group of soldiers sent from Seringapatam to collect ammunition, is the sole survivor of a massacre at the small garrison of *Chasalgaon* carried out by a detachment from the Mahratta forces of Colonel Pohlmann under the command of EIC deserter, Lieutenant (then *Major*) Dodd. Sharpe subsequently accompanies *Colonel McCandless*, the senior EIC intelligence officer, in pursuit of *Major* Dodd. He is present at the taking of the town of Ahmednuggur on 11 August, and remains with *McCandless* despite being offered a commission in Pohlmann's army. Sharpe later takes over the duties of Wellesley's orderly when that soldier is killed at the start of the Battle of Assaye on 23 September. In that capacity he saves the general's life and is rewarded with a battlefield commission as an ensign in the 74th Foot. Inside Assaye, Sharpe's friend and supporter *Colonel McCandless* is murdered by *Sergeant Hakeswill.*

MUCH OF THE SERIOUS FIGHTING of the Second Mahratta War took place in 1803. The first such war, fought some twenty years earlier, had been inconclusive, while the third and final struggle took place 1817–18, mostly against locust-like hordes of Mahratta freebooters and outlaws. In 1803 the war to crush the Mahrattas involved two simultaneous campaigns. To the north, in Hindustan, General Lake was pitted against a Mahratta army commanded by the French

ANOTHER
BATTLEFIELD
COMMISSION

Wellesley did indeed promote a sergeant for great gallantry at Assaye, so Sharpe's commission is based on an actual incident. The soldier, Syud Hussein, was a havildar in the Native Cavalry. During a cavalry charge into the midst of the enemy he captured a standard and presented it to his commanding officer, who took Hussein with the standard to Wellesley. John Malcolm, who had served with Wellesley at Assaye and was to become Resident in Mysore, wrote to Wellington in 1818 recalling how, after being given the standard, 'you [Wellesley] patted him upon the back, and with that eloquent and correct knowledge in the native language for which you were celebrated, said, "*Acha havildar; jemadar.*" A jemadar he was made, and amid all his subsequent success in Persia and in India which have raised him to medals, pensions and a palanquin from Government his pride is the pat on the back he received at Assye [Assaye].' Hussein retired as a subadar.

adventurer, Pierre Perron. Lake stormed the city of Aligarh, scattered his enemies in a battle outside Delhi and then destroyed them completely at the Battle of Laswari on 1 November 1803. In the south, Wellesley marched across the Deccan plain to confront the combined armies of the Mahratta prince, Scindia, and his less powerful ally Berar. It was Wellesley's first campaign as a general with an independent command. In the four months from mid-August to mid-December Wellesley triumphed at Ahmednuggur, Assaye, Argaum and Gawilghur (the latter two feature in *Sharpe's Fortress*). These victories later prompted Napoleon's contemptuous comment that Wellington (Wellesley) was a mere 'Sepoy general'. Sharpe came of age as a soldier (and a ferocious killer) in this campaign.

The Mahrattas are a mixed people who, at the start of the nineteenth century, inhabited a huge swathe of central India stretching for 900 miles south of Delhi and from the Arabian Sea in the west to the Bay of Bengal in the east. They were, and remain, Hindus with their own language and customs. Physically small but tough, they are a people with a warrior tradition. Two hundred years ago they were fine horsemen who supplemented a primitive agricultural lifestyle with brigandage and plunder. Local chieftains were, of necessity, petty warlords who preyed on their neighbours. All villages were fortified, if only with mud walls – how similar it sounds to today's Afghanistan! Years of feuding and fighting in which villagers had been robbed of even their basic water vessels and brass cooking pots had caused much hunger and suffering. Nevertheless, at the time Wellesley left Seringapatam and established his base at Hurryhur in early 1803 the great Mahratta Confederation was still second only to the EIC as a political power.

The hereditary ruler of the Confederation, the Peshwa, was a young man of little talent called Bajee Rao II. His two most important feudal subordinates were Scindia and Holkar, whose territories overlapped. Confrontation was continuous and bloody. The Peshwa had formed an alliance with Scindia

The army in India

UNTIL 1858 the army in India consisted of the King's or Royal regiments (which always took precedence), the Company's Europeans, and the Company's native troops. There were in fact three EIC armies, one from each of the Presidencies – Bengal, Bombay and Madras. This arrangement came into being by accident and was maintained by sentiment, a liking for independence and the huge distances between them.

Troops arriving in India for the first time were unacclimatised and highly susceptible to a host of illnesses and risks unknown in England. If they survived the first year they developed some immunity and their stomachs reacted less violently to the mixture of germs, exotic foods and spices. An extreme example of how a battalion could suffer is provided by the 72nd Highlanders, who within three weeks of their arrival in Madras in March 1781 had shrunk from 500 to 50 men fit for duty. A regiment sent on a semi-permanent posting to India might remain there for many years, sometimes up to twenty. Officers and men would be killed, die of disease, or be sent home when time-expired, but the regiment stayed, made up by drafts sent out from home. The first King's Regiment to set foot in India was the 39th Foot (later the Dorsetshire Regiment). To commemorate this, and the Battle of Plassey in 1757, their cap badge was inscribed '*Primus in Indus*'.

Having survived the vagaries and hazards of climate, disease and the efforts of the enemy for a number of years, many time-expired soldiers did not wish to leave India. They had come to like the life; for some it was the only life they knew. Rather than return to England, they chose to join the Company's service, some as soldiers, a few as civilian employees. The Company's Europeans had originally been a dubious cocktail of Armenians, Portuguese, French and Eurasians (there were no Indian troops in these battalions), but by the end of the eighteenth century the great majority had transferred from Royal regiments. There were six European battalions in all, two to each of the three Presidency armies. The number of companies varied from eight to thirteen; sometimes they were paired to form a single regiment but more often they remained single, independent battalions. When they were finally transferred to the Crown the six battalions became His Majesty's 101st to 106th Regiments of Foot. Not until 1881 did they assume county titles: 1st Battalion Royal Munster Fusiliers (101st), 1st Battalion Royal Dublin Fusiliers (102nd), 2nd Battalion Royal Dublin Fusiliers (103rd), 2nd Battalion Royal Munster Fusiliers (104th), 2nd Battalion King's Own Yorkshire Light Infantry (105th), 2nd Battalion Durham Light Infantry (106th). All the Irish regiments were disbanded in 1922.

Finally, there were the Company's native battalions, recruited locally with a mixture of British and Indian officers, the soldiers being collectively referred to as sepoys. Their conditions of service are dealt with in subsequent boxes.

The British Army on the march in India – early 1800s

MAJOR THORN, in his *Memoir of the War in India*, wrote:

> The march of our army had the appearance of a moving town or citadel in the form of an oblong ... On one side moved the line of infantry, on the opposite that of the cavalry, parallel to and preserving its encamping distance as near as possible from the infantry, and keeping the heads of the columns abreast of one another. The front face was protected by the advanced-guard, consisting of all the picquets coming on duty, and the rear by all the picquets returning from duty, and then forming the rear-guard. The parks and columns of artillery moved on the inside of the square, always keeping [to] the high road, and next to the infantry, which moved at a short distance from it. The remainder of the space within the square was occupied by the baggage, cattle and followers of the camp ...
>
> The army encamped for the most part as it marched – the infantry and cavalry facing outwards ... [A] sudden transformation takes place on these occasions, when an Indian camp exhibits ... the appearance of a lively and populous city ... Throughout long and regular streets of shops, like booths at an English fair, may be seen in every direction ... Here *sheroffs*, or money-changers, are ready with their coins ... Every kind of luxury abounds; while some shops allure the hungry passenger with boiled or parched rice, others exhibit a profusion of rich viands [meats] with spices, curry materials and confectionery ... native agents are busily employed in vending wines, liquors and groceries. Here also are to be found goldsmiths and jewellers ... Besides these and various other traffickers, the camp exhibits the singular spectacle of female quacks, who practice cupping, sell drugs, and profess to cure disorders by charms. Nearly allied to these are the jugglers showing their dexterity by numerous arts of deception; and, to complete the motley assemblage, groups of dancing girls have their allotted station in the bazaar.

Though the above describes Lord Lake's army, which was fighting to the north of Wellesley, any differences would have been in scale rather than substance. Before Assaye, Wellesley left all his civilian clutter at Naulniah, with the 1/2nd Madras as baggage guard; this speeded up the last five miles considerably.

and two years earlier they had turned on Holkar, sacking his capital Indore – the credit for which should go to Colonel Sutherland, who commanded the troops while Scindia cavorted on cushions with his concubines. Within a year Holkar sought and obtained vengeance in a resounding victory at Poona. As with all Indian armies, many of the regimental and battalion commanders were British, most on leave of absence from the EIC. At Poona the Peshwa decamped with a sizeable chunk of his army before things became too dangerous. An unfortunate Captain Dawes who was left commanding the artillery and four regular battalions could not withstand Holkar's attacks – led by a Major Harding. A fine cavalry charge clinched the affair. Dawes and Harding died and the Peshwa lost his throne to Holkar's youngest son, Amrut Rao. It was time for the British (Wellesley) to intervene. Throughout these exciting times Sergeant Sharpe had continued to oil muskets and issue ammunition in the obscurity of the armoury at Seringapatam.

Wellesley's brother, as governor-general of India, made a deal with the ousted Peshwa to restore him to his throne provided he signed a treaty that made him a subsidiary of the British. He signed. Despite being the junior general, Wellesley was given the task of reinstating the Peshwa. In February 1803 he began the long haul north to Poona. Under his command, but marching entirely separately and many miles away in Hyderabad, was a subsidiary force under Colonel Stevenson. Wellesley's immediate superior, General Stuart, instructed him: 'Restore Bajee Rao, but don't involve us in a war!'

At Hurryhur Wellesley was already 150 miles from his main base at Seringapatam. Poona was well over 300 miles further north. In total, the equivalent of marching from central London to Wick on the north-east tip of Scotland. Little wonder Wellesley was as concerned with his supply line as he was with what the enemy might do. Without uninterrupted supplies he could not function. Over half of his daily corre-

COLONEL POHLMANN

Pohlmann did well for himself fighting for Scindia. He went from sergeant in a British Hanoverian regiment to colonel in command of Sutherland's compoo (contingent) – over 6,000 men with at least forty guns and 500 cavalry – the senior European officer in the Mahratta army at Assaye. He was fond of the trappings of his position, travelling by elephant surrounded by an ostentatiously uniformed bodyguard. With Scindia's departure, Pohlmann took command of the army – something Wellesley was unaware of. Assaye was his first defeat on the battlefield after several years of campaigning. Though his well-drilled battalions were more than a match for Indian opponents, they had never before confronted a British force and disintegrated during the retreat from Assaye. Pohlmann's immediate fate is uncertain, but he later reappeared as an officer in the EIC Army (unlike the fictional Pohlmann, who lost his life in *Sharpe's Trafalgar*).

Human sacrifices

IN SHARPE'S DAY, sinister rituals existed among certain tribes. The people of the Eastern Ghats, for example, offered *Khond* sacrifices to ensure good harvests. The sacrificial victims, called *Meriah*, were initially bought and kept, well treated and well fed, as servants. Then, when drought struck or crops were threatened by locusts, a *Meriah* would be selected, tied up, plied with copious amounts of alcohol and paraded around the village amid festivity, dancing and prayers. On the third day the ceremonial climax was reached and the victim, his senses at least partially deadened by drunkenness, met his horrific fate. Tribes carried out the sacrifice in different ways, but common to all was the tearing of flesh from the *Meriah*'s living body. These bleeding strips were then buried in the fields or slung from poles over the stream (presumably dried up) that would water the crops. Perhaps the victim who was drowned in pig's blood before dismemberment was the lucky one.

Elsewhere, mothers who had borne only one child in seven or more years would sacrifice their first-born to the Ganges, the sacred river of India, to appease the gods so that they would grant more children thereafter. This practice led to 7–9-year-old infants being taken, shrieking in terror, to be thrown to the crocodiles of the Ganges or the sharks at Sagar Point.

Such sacrifices drew the outright condemnation of the British authorities, but officials had to tread carefully where rituals were carried out in the name of religion. It was a risky business, even with an escort, venturing into remote villages to stamp out centuries-old customs. One official who succeeded was Captain John Campbell (no relation to Lieutenant Colin Campbell). Having summoned the chiefs to a formal gathering, he informed them that the 'Great Government' abhorred human sacrifice and asked if they could prove it cured drought. Were their crops worse, or their men stronger, than those in tribes that did not make such sacrifices? The chiefs retired to consider their verdict. Campbell had a long and worrying wait – if they refused to stop, force would have to be used. The elders' response, however, was positive. As they were now subjects of the 'Great Government' they would do as they were told: animals would be used instead of humans. They would explain this sudden relaxation of standards by telling the gods, 'Do not be angry with us; vent your wrath upon this gentleman, who is well able to bear it.' Not all tribes could be so easily persuaded.

spondence was devoted to bullocks and supplies. Wellesley bought bullocks (with EIC money), hired bullocks and used the *brinjarris*' bullocks. His staff officer Captain Barclay (whom Sharpe was to get to know at Assaye) wrote to the *brinjarry* agent that all *brinjarris* of Mysore (a state that produced a particularly strong breed of white bullock) and ceded districts were required immediately. Wellesley's correspondence also covered horse-keepers, gram kettles (in which fodder for horses was boiled), the rupee exchange rate, litters for wounded, bearers for carrying wounded, wheels for ammunition tumbrils, casks for arrack (a spirit distilled from grain or rice) plus a host of other items. He was determined to have a self-contained force that could march – and he succeeded admirably. After the march to Poona at the hottest time of year he was able to write: 'I never saw troops look better.'

Wellesley's cavalry arrived at Poona on 20 April. Holkar did not oppose them. As they rode in through the south gate Amrut Rao galloped out through the northern one. On 13 May, when the chicken's entrails looked encouraging and the stars were properly positioned, Bajee Rao sat himself on his throne once more – and immediately started to plot against the EIC with Scindia, the Rajah of Berar, and even Holkar.

The longer an army's line of communication to its base, the lower the number of troops available to fight a battle. This is due to the ever-increasing demands for convoy protection and security. Sharpe's regiment, the 33rd Foot, had been employed on such duties for almost four tedious, tiring years. *Sergeant Hakeswill* was particularly incensed that Sharpe had found himself such a cushy (and he considered lucrative) billet in the armoury at Seringapatam. In the summer of 1803 the 33rd was based at Arrakery, some sixty miles north of Seringapatam. The acting commanding officer, the alcoholic Irishman Major John Shee (who had awarded Sharpe 2,000 lashes), had died of a fit. His replacement was Lieutenant-Colonel Arthur Gore – a thoroughly competent soldier.

Although *Hakeswill* may have been jealous of Sharpe's job, it nearly cost him his life at the beginning of July. *Chasalgaon*

INDIAN COINAGE

Wellesley was always scrupulous when it came to the army paying its way. As far as possible, supplies were paid for with coinage acceptable to local farmers, villagers and merchants – no mean feat in India, where coins that would be accepted in one area were regarded as worthless in another. For example, there were two types of gold coins: 'mohurs' in the north and 'pagodas' (sometimes called 'fanams') in the south. A merchant in Mysore would be happy with either, but his counterpart in Poona would reject the 'pagodas'. Silver rupees were generally acceptable everywhere, but they varied in weight, size and appearance. To ensure the right money was available involved judicious money-changing and haggling, in which Wellesley took detailed interest. He would not tolerate cheating, and dealt severely with offenders. He was, however, forced to resort to counterfeit coins to overcome a similar currency problem in Spain some ten years later (*see Sharpe's Regiment*).

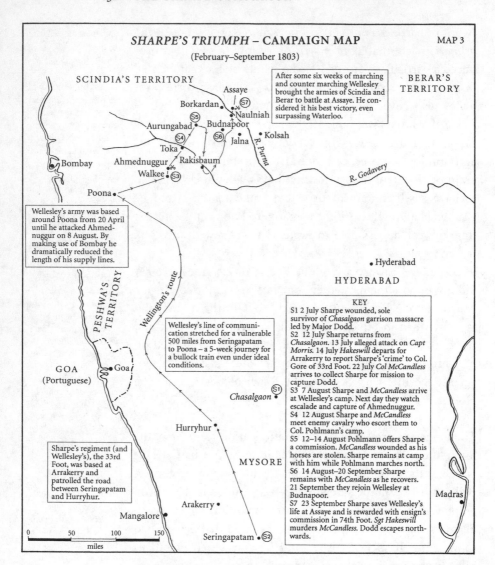

SHARPE'S TRIUMPH – CAMPAIGN MAP

(February–September 1803)

MAP 3

SCINDIA'S TERRITORY

BERAR'S TERRITORY

Assaye

Borkardan

Naulniah

After some six weeks of marching and counter marching Wellesley brought the armies of Scindia and Berar to battle at Assaye. He considered it his best victory, even surpassing Waterloo.

Aurungabad

Budnapoor

Toka

Jalna

Kolsah

R. Purna

Ahmednuggur

Rakisbaum

Walkee

Bombay

Poona

Wellesley's army was based around Poona from 20 April until he attacked Ahmednuggur on 8 August. By making use of Bombay he dramatically reduced the length of his supply lines.

R. Godavery

Hyderabad

HYDERABAD

PESHWA'S TERRITORY

Wellington's route

Wellesley's line of communication stretched for a vulnerable 500 miles from Seringapatam to Poona – a 5-week journey for a bullock train even under ideal conditions.

GOA (Portuguese)

Goa

Chasalgaon

Hurryhur

MYSORE

Sharpe's regiment (and Wellesley's), the 33rd Foot, was based at Arrakerry and patrolled the road between Seringapatam and Hurryhur.

Arakerry

Mangalore

Seringapatam

Madras

KEY

S1 2 July Sharpe wounded, sole survivor of *Chasalgaon* garrison massacre led by Major Dodd.
S2 12 July Sharpe returns from *Chasalgaon*. 13 July alleged attack on *Capt Morris*. 14 July *Hakeswill* departs for Arrakerry to report Sharpe's 'crime' to Col. Gore of 33rd Foot. 22 July *Col McCandless* arrives to collect Sharpe for mission to capture Dodd.
S3 7 August Sharpe and *McCandless* arrive at Wellesley's camp. Next day they watch escalade and capture of Ahmednuggur.
S4 12 August Sharpe and *McCandless* meet enemy cavalry who escort them to Col. Pohlmann's camp.
S5 12–14 August Pohlmann offers Sharpe a commission. *McCandless* wounded as his horses are stolen. Sharpe remains at camp with him while Pohlmann marches north.
S6 14 August–20 September Sharpe remains with *McCandless* as he recovers. 21 September they rejoin Wellesley at Budnapoor.
S7 23 September Sharpe saves Wellesley's life at Assaye and is rewarded with ensign's commission in 74th Foot. *Sgt Hakeswill* murders *McCandless*. Dodd escapes northwards.

0   50   100   150
miles

was one of several small forts used by detachments guarding the lines of communication. Sharpe had the misfortune to be there when *Major* Dodd and his men, disguised in British (EIC) uniforms, tricked their way in and slaughtered the garrison – all except Sharpe, who got away with a head wound.

Lieutenant William Dodd

———— ❧ ————

WHEN COLONEL WELLESLEY returned to Seringapatam in 1801 he discovered a number of officers had been guilty of 'ungentlemanly behaviour', embezzlement and theft from the arsenal stores. Such was his abhorrence of officers engaging in such practices that there was no hope of leniency for those at fault. When a court martial, having found Captain Shuttleworth (a surgeon) guilty of having an Indian tied up and flogged for refusing to give him straw for his horse without payment, let him off with a reprimand, Wellesley refused to approve the sentence: 'I never can agree in opinion with the court martial that this scandalous conduct is not unbecoming the character of a British officer and gentleman, and I can never approve a sentence that describes it in other terms than those of the strongest reprobation.' His objections, however, were overruled by his general (Braithwaite) so the 'slap on wrist' sentence stood.

Lieutenant Dodd's case was even more deplorable. Dodd, who features in *Sharpe's Triumph* and *Sharpe's Fortress,* was very much a real person. As an EIC officer stationed at Seedesegur he had an Indian goldsmith named Basur beaten to death, possibly because of financial dealings. One account has Dodd making the villagers swear that Basur had poisoned himself – although how death by beating can be made to look like poisoning is unclear. Also accused of torturing Indians, in order to extract money, by making them stand for long periods in the sun with heavy boxes on their heads, Dodd was tried by court martial in 1801 and sentenced to six months without pay and loss of seniority.

Wellesley was incensed by this leniency. This time he was able to get the court to reconsider by asking them to 'reflect on the disgrace . . . to the whole army'. The sentence was increased to a dishonourable discharge, although this required the approval of the Commander-in-Chief, India. Upon discharge, Wellesley intended to have Dodd tried for murder by a civilian court. Dodd, having got wind of what lay in store, deserted (in *Sharpe's Triumph* he took a number of sepoys with him, but there is no evidence of this in reality). He became a hunted man with a reward on his head. The wanted notice described him as straight and well-made, with sandy hair, small blue eyes, thin lips, able to speak reasonable Moorish (one wonders where he learned it), with a 'good deal of Irish accent in his speech'; he was last seen at midnight on 3 February 1802 on a boat in Bombay harbour 'carrying with him a stout Bay horse'.

When Sharpe, who had set out with Colonel *McCandless* to capture Dodd, caught up with him, he was a wealthy major in the Mahratta forces of Scindia. It seems he escaped justice.

THE SEPOYS' PAY
AND RATIONS

Sepoys were paid
seven rupees a month,
from which were
deducted various
stoppages amounting
to around one rupee.
As a general rule the
Bengal Army sepoy
would keep three and
send three home for
his family, but in the
Madras Army the
family usually
followed the soldier in
the field. Often sepoys
lived on two rupees a
month in order to
send home more.

Although rations
were provided, feeding
Indian soldiers was
seldom easy. The
staple food was grain,
which accounted for
90 per cent of the cost
of living for most
Indians. A man
needed two pounds a
day – but it had to be
the right sort of grain.
In northern India rice
was regarded as a
luxury for the rich.
Next in order of cost
came wheat and then
millet (similar to rye)
– the food of the poor.
Two rupees would
buy about 60lb of
wheat or 90lb of
millet. Peasant farmers
grew wheat for cash
and millet to eat. It is
a good food but makes
coarse, dark, bitter
flour. The sepoys, and
indeed the animals,
rejected it if they
could get wheat. In the
south, on the other

Wellesley, increasingly frustrated with the incompetence of the authorities at Bombay where he was trying to set up an alternative base, had begun casting covetous eyes on the city of Ahmednuggur only fifty miles to the north-east. It was, apparently, stuffed with exactly the sort of supplies he needed and as such made a highly desirable forward base for future operations to the north. He moved his force to the small town of Walkee, a mere seven miles from Ahmednuggur. And it was there, on 7 August, that Sharpe and *McCandless*, escorted by *Syud Sevajee* and his irregular horsemen, arrived in pouring rain after some three weeks on the road from Seringapatam. The campaign proper would start the following day – the downpour had led to a twenty-four-hour postponement.

Wellesley's informants on the enemy's strengths were reasonably precise. He was confronted by the walled city of Ahmednuggur and its fort some two miles away. The town was the more important target. The Indian word for it was *pettah*, a fortified town for the protection of the civilian dependants of the fort plus the numerous merchants inevitably associated with such a community. This one, surrounded by a high, strong wall, looked impressive, but unbeknown to Wellesley many of the sections lacked a walkway or fire-step inside because the ramparts were rounded on top in such a manner that there was no adequate foothold between them. The wall had twelve gates, forty bastions and a circumference of some 4,000 yards. Behind the walls other defence works had been constructed – all of which were concealed from Wellesley as he rode around the town, staring at it long and hard through his telescope.

Wellesley later wrote that the opposition consisted of '1,000 sepoys in white jackets, with five brass guns, smaller than our 6-pounders, commanded by three French officers, a little dark-coloured, who wear blue clothes. They have twelve one-pole tents.' He neglected to mention an additional 1,000 Arab mercenaries who were in the town. The sepoys were a detachment of regular troops, about 900 strong in two small battalions, from Colonel Pohlmann's far larger compoo (contingent) of eight battalions. The French officers mentioned by Wellesley were the English deserter, former Lieutenant, now *Major, William Dodd* commanding, with *Captain Pierre Joubert* as his second-in-command, assisted by *Lieutenant Sillière*. In the ensuing fight *McCandless* and Sharpe were given the task of capturing Dodd and bringing him to face British justice for murder and desertion – both capital offences.

The attack on the city of Ahmednuggur was all over in twenty minutes – well before breakfast. One of Wellesley's irregular cavalry commanders who, though paid by Wellesley, was officially one of the Peshwa's officers, later summed it up neatly: 'These English are a strange people, and their General a wonderful man. They came here in the morning, looked at the pettah [city] wall, walked over it, killed all the garrison, and returned for breakfast! What can withstand them?'

Wellesley, to the consternation of the defenders, opted for a quick escalade at three separate parts of the wall instead of blasting a breach in it. There is no doubt that his four twelve-pounder cannons would, at close range, have made short work of the somewhat flimsy walls. Wellesley, however, unaware that most of the wall did not have, could not have, defenders due to the lack of a walkway behind the ramparts, had assumed that with a garrison of around 2,000 and such a long circumference the defenders must, of necessity, spread themselves thinly – until they knew for certain where the main attack would take place. The positioning of a siege battery would tell them precisely that. A quick rush with ladders – an escalade – should achieve surprise. It did. Nevertheless, an escalade was always a risky option. On this occasion two things went wrong. First, the three assaults were not simultaneous. The left column attacked early, thus removing the element of surprise for the other two. Secondly, the ladders of the left column were placed against a part of the wall that had no fire-step or platform behind and was

hand, rice was the staple diet – though nine out of ten northern Indians would not eat it. It all made for a logistical nightmare as far as quartermasters were concerned.

WELLESLEY'S ASSAULT

(8 August 1803)

Dodd's *Cobras* manned the walls
further west and were not involved
in repelling the escalade.

The first escalade failed due to the
lack of a fire-step behind this section of the wall, which left troops
facing a 20ft drop.

A

B

Flank companies 78th

Picquets giving covering fire

HARNESS

KEY

A The left assault column under Lt-Col Harness
–600 men. Under heavy fire from flanking bastions the grenadier and light companies of the
78th Foot escaladed an undefended portion of
wall. The assault failed as the lack of a fire step
left the kilted Highlanders facing a sheer 20ft
drop.

B Harness ordered a second try directly on a
bastion. First man up, claymore in his teeth, was
Lt Colin Campbell (Grenadier Coy). Wounded
and knocked down twice, he secured a foothold
on the third attempt. His men followed, the bastion was taken, and Harness sent the picquets in.
As Campbell led his men to the gate to lift the
bar, the cannon outside fired blasting the gates
open and chopping a sepoy in half.

C The right assault column of 1,200 men under
Capt Vesey (EIC) was delayed by a rogue
artillery elephant. Two ladders were placed close
to a bastion and, despite one collapsing, *c.*300
men climbed over the wall before the second was
shot away.

D The centre assault column (1,650 men) under
Lt-Col Wallace attacked the gate, pushing the
muzzle of a cannon against the woodwork and
firing.

E Reserve units under Wellesley (3,600 men).

ON AHMEDNUGGUR

The defenders of the wall and
bastions were Arabs.

The wall was 20 feet high, made
of bricks and mud, without
protecting ditch or glacis. Bastions
were located at 100 yard intervals
along its 4,000 yard circumference.

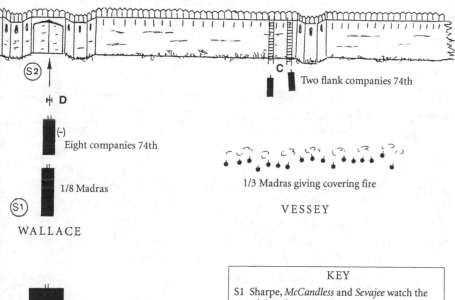

S2 ↑

╫ D

(-)

Eight companies 74th

1/8 Madras

S1

WALLACE

C

Two flank companies 74th

1/3 Madras giving covering fire

VESSEY

E

WELLESLEY

KEY

S1 Sharpe, *McCandless* and *Sevajee* watch the
assault but do not participate.
S2 Once the assault has succeeded, Sharpe,
McCandless and *Sevajee* enter city via gate in
pursuit of Dodd. Hoping to take him alive,
McCandless prevents Sharpe from shooting
Dodd, who escapes through the north gate.
Lt Silliere is killed defending *Simone Joubert*,
who Sharpe then rescues.

ELEPHANTS

As draught animals, elephants were in a class of their own due to their strength and intelligence. In addition to pulling siege guns, moving timber and drawing heavy pontoons, they were a symbol of authority for Indian princes and senior commanders, who rode them in preference to horses. The drawback was the expense of buying and maintaining them: each elephant's daily diet consisted of 40lb rice (enough for 20 men), 1lb ghee (clarified butter), 1lb date-palm juice and 40 coconut palm leaves (or equivalent). Owners of animals hired to the British often resorted to stealing fodder or under-feeding. As Wellesley wrote in his despatches (1802): 'I know the people who have charge of them [elephants] perfectly well, and I assure you that they are not to be trusted in the care of these valuable animals without European superintendence. I have worked more, probably than any other officer in the army, and I never saw them out of condition when they were under the eye of the agent; but whenever they have been detached

therefore undefended. Those attackers who reached the top of the ladders – and many did not – found the prospect of leaping twenty feet unappealing. The ladders were moved to a bastion.

By this time, with surprise long gone, it was left to the weight of covering fire from some 250 picquets, banging away at the top of the parapet, plus the courage of the soldiers climbing the ladders, to ensure success. A crucial factor in this attack was the leadership of Lieutenant Colin Campbell. He was wounded and knocked off a ladder twice but still climbed back up for a third attempt. At the top he flailed around with his heavy claymore, clearing a space while a steady stream of men clambered up to join him. Wellesley is said to have watched Campbell's daring escapade and asked for his name. He was fifty-three years too early for a Victoria Cross, but his bravery secured him immediate promotion to captain and a job on Wellesley's staff – where he would shortly become well acquainted with Sergeant Sharpe.

Campbell's success was instrumental in securing the city as he was able to fight his way round to open the gates from the inside. The timing was a little unfortunate because at that moment the cannon outside with the centre column fired through the woodwork. For one of the sepoys struggling to lift the bar, death was gruesome but instantaneous. On the right, Captain Vesey (whose men were fighting their way round the inside from the other direction) had been delayed by an artillery elephant, maddened by pain from a wound, that crashed through the ranks of the assault group from the 74th, scattering them. Vesey, having profited from watching Harness's initial failure at the undefended wall, placed his ladders in the re-entrant close to a bastion. Some 300 men scrambled over before one ladder broke and the other was shot away.

Sharpe, who was not required to participate, had watched the attack with professional interest, for this was the first time he had seen an escalade. When the gates opened he joined *McCandless* and their escort of horsemen as they rode

Lieutenant Colin Campbell

———◦≫◦———

SHARPE WAS NOT the only person to receive promotion for gallantry in this campaign, although his elevation from the ranks to officer status was by far the most unusual. For his inspiring leadership at Ahmednuggur, twenty-seven-year-old Lieutenant Colin Campbell of the 78th Foot (Ross-Shire Buffs) was promoted to captain.

In 1792 at the age of sixteen, Campbell had run away from his family in Perth, Scotland, to join a merchant ship sailing to the West Indies. On leaving the ship in Kingston, Jamaica, he was confronted in the fruit market by his brother, a Royal Navy lieutenant on a man-o'-war, and escorted home immediately. A year later, Campbell was a midshipman aboard an East Indiaman – but not for long. Within two years he had exchanged his blue jacket for a red one as a lieutenant in the Breadalbane Fencibles – a militia unit inconspicuous to the point of invisibility. This dead-end appointment lasted until 1779 when, in desperation, he accepted demotion to ensign in a West India Regiment. Perhaps seeking to avoid the ravages of yellow fever in the West Indies, he soon exchanged his commission (its value enhanced by a suitable sum) for a lieutenant's appointment in the 78th Foot – a far more prestigious regiment.

After winning promotion at Ahmednuggur, he was wounded at Assaye. Following the 1807 Copenhagen campaign he joined Wellesley in April 1809 as assistant adjutant-general in the Peninsula and received brevet lieutenant-colonel's rank a year later. He remained with Wellesley until 1814, much of the time as HQ commandant, and was present at nine battles or sieges. For his services in Spain he was awarded the Gold Cross with six clasps, and in 1814 he was knighted. The following year he reappeared at Wellington's Waterloo HQ as commandant. Promoted major-general in 1825, he served as governor of Nova Scotia (from 1833) and then of Ceylon (from 1839). In his last years in Ceylon Wellington wrote to him, 'We are both growing old. God knows if we shall ever meet again. Happen what may, I shall never forget our first meeting under the walls of Ahmednuggur.' Sir Colin died, aged seventy-one, about a week after arriving back in England, and was buried in St James's Church, Piccadilly. He should not be confused with his namesake Sir Colin Campbell, Lord Clyde.

into the city to hunt for Dodd. Their quarry, however, escaped with his men through the north gate. Sharpe could have shot him but was restrained by *McCandless*, who insisted on a live prisoner. Ahmednuggur was one of the very few actions where Sharpe did not kill anybody. He was caught up in some brawling while protecting *Simone Joubert* (with

they have fallen off in condition, and some have died, and frequent instances of frauds and thefts in feeding them have been discovered.'

whom he managed to share a bed that night), but nobody died. He was to make up for this the following month at Assaye.

After the fall of the city Wellesley turned on the nearby fort. It was an altogether more formidable stronghold with outer ditch, glacis and thicker, stronger, higher walls than those around the city. During the Second World War the British kept the Indian independence leaders locked up in this fort and today it is still an important Indian Army base. On 10 August Wellesley turned his twelve-pounders on the wall at a range of only 300 yards. With only four cannons it took until late afternoon the next day before the breach was thought practical (as the guns were by then running short of ammunition, the breach was not going to get much bigger in any case). The choice was therefore to storm the breach or wait two weeks for more shot. On the morning of the twelfth the attacking column formed up. The sight of the impending assault, combined with the knowledge of what had happened to the city, was enough to induce the killadar to surrender and march out with his property and 1,400 men. For Wellesley the entire affair had cost a mere 79 European and 62 sepoy casualties – all during the taking of the city. He now had an advance base full of supplies of all kinds necessary for further campaigning. Of even more importance was the fact that Ahmednuggur could be restocked from Bombay as required, thus shaving 400 miles off his lines of communication; it was likened to a prisoner being released from his ball and chain.

After Ahmednuggur, Wellesley pushed north. It took three days to cross the Godavery River and he arrived at Aurunga-bad on 29 August. There followed several weeks of marching and counter-marching as Wellesley and Colonel Stevenson tried to corner Scindia and Berar to bring them to battle. In the second half of September Wellesley received intelligence that the Mahrattas had encamped at Borkardan. On 21 September he rode to Stevenson's camp to confer and plan a joint advance on the enemy. That same day, Sharpe and *McCandless* (now recovered from his wound) rejoined the army. Sharpe was spotted by *Private Lowry* who reported his presence to *Sergeant Hakeswill,* then doing duty with the bullock train. *Hakeswill* rushed to *Colonel McCandless* waving Sharpe's arrest warrant – which the colonel invalidated by removing the 'e' from 'Sharpe'. The thwarted sergeant vowed murder.

Wellesley's plan involved his force and that of Stevenson marching by separate routes and then combining to attack Scindia at Borkardan. It is not usually considered good military sense to divide your forces when in close proximity to a numerically vastly superior enemy, but this is what Wellesley decided to do. The aim was to march separately but fight together, as one huge column on the march would be too slow. Speed was vital to ensure contact before Scindia could slip away.

At sunrise on 23 September Wellesley marched. By eleven o'clock he had covered the fourteen miles to the village of Naulniah, some ten miles south-east of Borkardan. Here a cavalry patrol brought word that the enemy was not in fact at Borkardan but to the east, spread out over several miles along the north bank of the Kaitna River. On learning that parts of the Mahratta army were only five miles away, Wellesley, accompanied by Captain Barclay and the newly promoted Campbell of Ahmednuggur fame, rode off immediately to reconnoitre (MAP 4). They were closely followed by Sharpe, *McCandless* and *Sevajee*. A discreet distance behind, Colonel Maxwell led forward the 19th Light Dragoons and the 4th Native Cavalry as the general's escort. Wellesley turned north-west towards Borkardan at the small village of Barahjala. Within three miles they climbed a gentle rise overlooking the Kaitna valley. A mile across the river an incredible sight confronted them. Wellesley gazed long and hard through his telescope.

Stretching for eight miles from Borkardan to Assaye was a huge tent city. Tens of thousands of men and animals

EUROPEAN
OFFICERS IN
NATIVE ARMIES

Indian princes,
recognising the
superiority of well-
trained, -armed and
-drilled infantry
battalions, soon began
recruiting European
officers as
mercenaries. For
many, the
inducements on offer
in terms of promotion
(there was no bar on
an EIC or British NCO
getting officer status),
pay, women and the
chances of loot were
hard to resist. No
wonder Sharpe was
sorely tempted by
Pohlmann's offer.
While the majority
were French, there
were a number of
English, German and
Irish – and at least one
American, a Colonel
J. P. Boyd – who
served the Peshwa.
Some had left under a
cloud, like Colonel
Sutherland (previous
commander of
Pohlmann's
compoo), who had
been cashiered from
the 73rd Foot as a
lieutenant. A sizeable
number of the British
were put in the
position of having to
fight their own
countrymen, and did
so in spite of generous
offers from the
governor-general to
abandon their
employers.

    Most were colourful

milled about on the north bank. Wellesley and his group, including Sharpe and *McCandless,* could see only a fraction of the host opposite as trees and folds in the ground obscured the view. It was enough, however, for Wellesley to draw several crucial conclusions. Firstly, that the enemy were much closer than expected. Secondly, that he was hugely out-numbered, particularly as Stevenson was still a day's march away. Thirdly, a quick attack would ensure a battle, and a battle was Wellesley's primary objective. He had no wish for the enemy to avoid a fight as they had in previous weeks. If he waited another day for Stevenson there was no guarantee of an action. And finally, if he attacked, he wanted to avoid a frontal advance across the river in the face of sustained and possibly overwhelming cannon fire. It was therefore vital to find an unguarded crossing place, hopefully on the enemy's flank.

As he watched, Wellesley became certain the enemy were breaking camp. Were they going to run or fight? After a few moments the telescope was snapped shut, the group remounted and, riding just below (south of) the crest, Wellesley led off in a brisk gallop due east. He wanted to check the enemy's left flank. They stopped about a mile from the village of Peepulgaon on the south bank of the Kaitna. Again the telescopes came out. This time Wellesley asked Sharpe to have a look at the bank opposite the village. What could he see? Sharpe saw buildings, another village. It was Waroor. Two villages opposite each other with a river flowing between meant there must be a ford – it was a simple, common-sense deduction. That was where he would cross the river. Wellesley held to his view despite the insistence of local farmers that the only fords were located at Kodully and Taunklee (they must have been either stupid or liars, prob-ably the latter). Before galloping back to Naulniah he briefed Maxwell to bring up his remaining two regiments and deploy them in a thin screen south of the river from Kodully to Taunklee.

Wellesley knew he was dramatically outnumbered – the

St Giles Rookery where Sharpe lived on his wits with Maggie Joyce for three years (1789–92).

Newgate Gaol, engraved by R Acon after a drawing by Thomas H Shepherd.

Storming of Seringapatam showing General Baird in the centre, directing the assault on the breach. Note how the attackers are clambering up the broken wall on the left. The man with

the Colours, top left, represents Sergeant Graham moments before he was killed. Bottom left and in the centre are excellent examples of the Tippoo's tiger-mouthed cannons and, bottom right, a soldier in a tiger-striped uniform.

Seringapatam:
The site of the breach seen from the south. The British assault came from the left. The actual breach has been repaired and the monument is to the battle.

The breach seen from across the South Cauvery – the repaired section of the wall is clearly visible below the monument centre left.

Seringapatam: a view of the entrance to the tunnel through the outer wall at the surviving Watergate. The Tippoo was killed near here by a shot through his temple.

British soldiers find the body of Tippoo Sultan – by which time Sharpe had stripped him of his jewels!

A view of the battlefield at Assaye looking west. It shows where the original Mahratta gun line was placed – eastern end anchored on the village, with the guns stretching away from the camera.

Gawilghur: the gateway to the inner fort where Lt. Col. Kenny and many more died in a fruitless attempt to take it.

Bernard Cornwell, posed with the gun that killed five men with one shot. Abandoned on the ramparts of the inner fort, it measures 22ft – the wooden carriage has long since rotted away.

Lieutenant Colonel the Honourable Arthur Wellesley,
later 1st Duke of Wellington, by John Hoppner.
Stratfield Saye.

Nelson is struck down on his quarterdeck at 1.15 p.m. He died about three hours later, down on the orlop deck.

Battle of Trafalgar – the surrender of the Redoutable.

exact figure was of no real significance. The largest enemy contingent was Pohlmann's compoo. Pohlmann (who was also in overall command of the entire army) led a compoo of eight infantry battalions, each comprising approximately 800 men commanded by a European or half-European officer. Within this force were four field guns and a howitzer, plus about 500 horsemen. In total something over 7,000 men – not far short of Wellesley's regular and reliable troops. Next in size was a compoo whose absent commander was an intelligent, middle-aged and apparently remarkably attractive lady by the name of Begum Somroo (the Indian version of her late husband's nickname 'Sombre'). She was the widow of Walter Rheinhart, a mercenary soldier previously in the service of Scindia. Before his death he had become a subordinate political vassal of Scindia and had delegated the command of his army to others. His widow had inherited his position. Her most notorious general was the huge Irishman George Thomas, a former sailor who could neither read nor write but, when sober, was a competent commander. Perhaps the demon drink had got the better of him by autumn 1803, because at Assaye Begum Somroo's compoo of five battalions, twenty-five cannons and about 500 cavalry was commanded by the Frenchman Colonel Saleur. Both these contingents were considered well trained, well drilled and expected to give a good account of themselves – particularly the artillery. Baptiste Filoze, the son of a Neapolitan father and an Indian mother, had nominal command of the third compoo. At Assaye this duty had been delegated to Major John Dupont, a Dutchman. Under him were four battalions, fifteen field guns together with 500 or more cavalry, pioneers and auxiliaries – another 4,000 men.

The regular backbone of the army facing Wellesley was therefore about 15,000 strong, of which 12,000 were infantry who also manned the forty-four field guns. If this component of the Mahrattas' vast army could be defeated the rest would run. Within this force it was the number of enemy guns that was especially worrying. Interestingly, most of the Mahratta

characters; two stand out. The first was a huge Irish sailor called George Thomas, who proved an effective commander despite the fact he could neither read nor write. He could have conquered a large part of India had he not been so fond of the bottle. The second was Benoît de Boigne, who started his career with the Mahratta chiefs in 1781 aged thirty-five. A highly competent professional soldier and, a rarity perhaps, an honest, public-spirited man, he administered huge tracts of territory with justice and competence. After only eleven years he retired to Europe with £100,000 (a multi-millionaire in today's money), married a girl of seventeen and bought himself a large estate in his native Savoy. He lived to enjoy his money, wife and property for another thirty years.

WELLESLEY'S APPROACH

(23 September 1803)

Camp of Scindia's 50,000–70,000
Mahratta infantry and cavalry

Borkardan

Singwarry
ford

KEY

A Approximate location of Wellesley's first
observation post (OP) at around noon.
B Wellesley's second OP from which he
deduced existence of ford between
Peepulgaon and Waroor.
C As his leading troops were crossing the
river around 3 p.m., Wellesley first observed
the heavy defences of Assaye village and
made his battle plan.
S1 On 22 September *Sgt Hakeswill* attempts
to arrest Sharpe but *McCandless* invalidates
the warrant.
S2 Sharpe and *McCandless* follow Wellesley
on his reconnaissance.
S3 Wellesley hands Sharpe his telescope to
study the ford.
S4 Wellesley's orderly (Pte Fletcher) is
killed by cannon fire and Sharpe takes over
his duties.
S5 Pohlmann conceals his treasure under
guard in Assaye. *Simone Joubert* shelters in
house nearby.

Col. Stevenson with 7,000 infantry,
1,000 cavalry and 30+ guns advancing
from Hussainabad some 5 miles
south.

TO ASSAYE

MAP 4

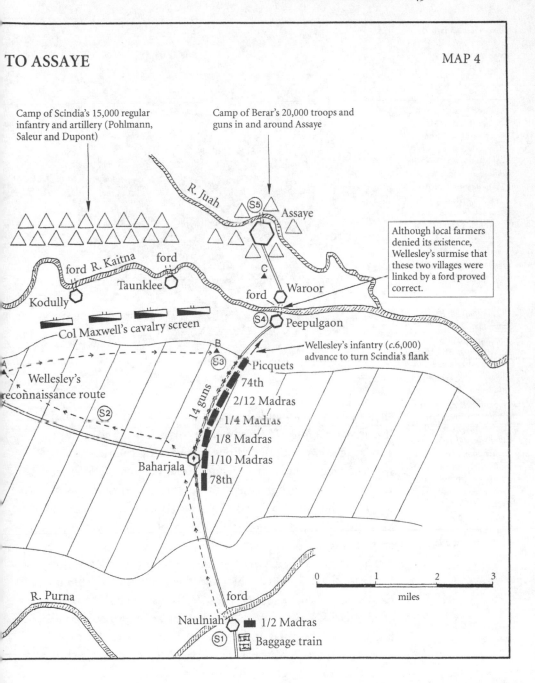

Camp of Scindia's 15,000 regular infantry and artillery (Pohlmann, Saleur and Dupont)

Camp of Berar's 20,000 troops and guns in and around Assaye

R. Juah

Assaye

Although local farmers denied its existence, Wellesley's surmise that these two villages were linked by a ford proved correct.

ford R. Kaitna ford

Taunklee

Kodully

Waroor

ford

Col Maxwell's cavalry screen

Peepulgaon

Wellesley's infantry (c.6,000) advance to turn Scindia's flank

Wellesley's reconnaissance route

Picquets

74th

2/12 Madras

1/4 Madras

1/8 Madras

1/10 Madras

78th

Baharjala

14 guns

R. Purna

ford

Naulniah

1/2 Madras

Baggage train

0   1   2   3

miles

ORGANISATION OF
SCINDIA'S
BATTALIONS

Major Dodd's force at
Assaye were regular
troops in battalions of
around 700 men and
forty officers. There
were only two white
or partly white officers
to a battalion (Dodd's
battalion had the two
Frenchmen, *Capt.
Joubert* and *Lt Silliere*)
and six Portuguese
gunners, one in charge
of each piece. Of
General Perron's forty
battalions (operating
against Lord Lake)
only 300 officers,
including those
supervising
ammunition
manufacture, were
Europeans. Attached
to each battalion were
four light 6-pounder
cannons and one 5.5
inch howitzer. A full
holding of
ammunition would
include 300 roundshot
and 100 grape
(canister) for each gun,
with 50 explosive
stone shells and 50
grape per howitzer.
Four to eight regular
battalions comprised a
compoo – a brigade
equivalent.

An escalade

artillery was commanded and manned by Portuguese and
Indian Christians. The remainder of Scindia and Berar's
army, excluding countless thousands of camp followers, consisted of over 70,000 men of whom about 15,000 were infantry
and the remainder horsemen. These were irregular troops of
doubtful morale, whose reaction to stiff opposition was more
likely to be flight than fight. Mixed up with them were
another fifty or so cannons.

The Battle of Assaye resulted in a resounding victory for
Wellesley. He had been right about the ford between Peepulgaon and Waroor, so he succeeded in avoiding a frontal
attack across a river. With an army of around 7,000 good
infantry, 2,000 regular and 6,500 irregular Mysore and Mahratta cavalry, plus fourteen guns, he defeated an enemy at
least six times bigger with almost a hundred guns. There
were moments, however, when victory was far from certain.

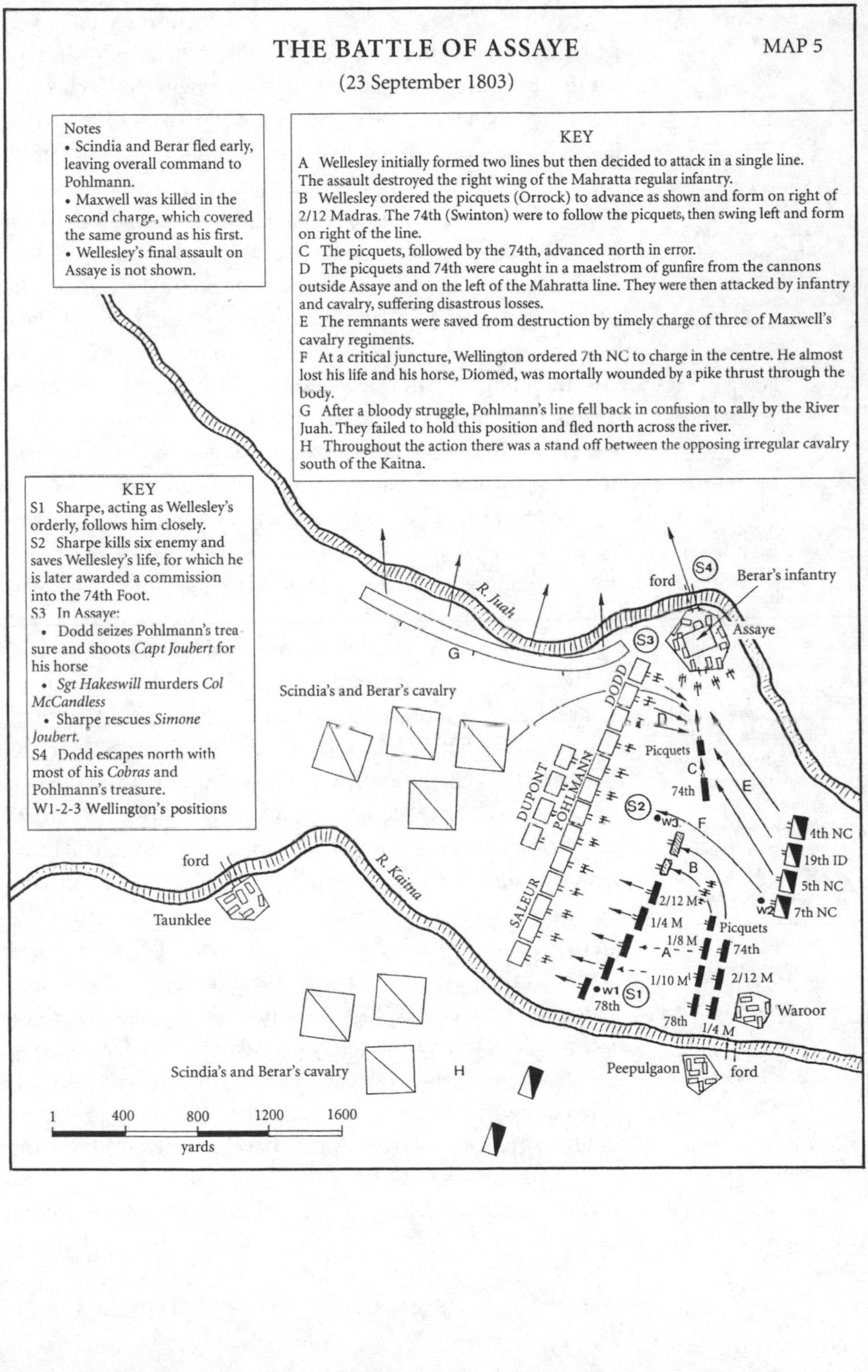
THE BATTLE OF ASSAYE
MAP 5
(23 September 1803)
Notes
• Scindia and Berar fled early, leaving overall command to Pohlmann.
• Maxwell was killed in the second charge, which covered the same ground as his first.
• Wellesley's final assault on Assaye is not shown.
KEY
A Wellesley initially formed two lines but then decided to attack in a single line. The assault destroyed the right wing of the Mahratta regular infantry.
B Wellesley ordered the picquets (Orrock) to advance as shown and form on right of 2/12 Madras. The 74th (Swinton) were to follow the picquets, then swing left and form on right of the line.
C The picquets, followed by the 74th, advanced north in error.
D The picquets and 74th were caught in a maelstrom of gunfire from the cannons outside Assaye and on the left of the Mahratta line. They were then attacked by infantry and cavalry, suffering disastrous losses.
E The remnants were saved from destruction by timely charge of three of Maxwell's cavalry regiments.
F At a critical juncture, Wellington ordered 7th NC to charge in the centre. He almost lost his life and his horse, Diomed, was mortally wounded by a pike thrust through the body.
G After a bloody struggle, Pohlmann's line fell back in confusion to rally by the River Juah. They failed to hold this position and fled north across the river.
H Throughout the action there was a stand off between the opposing irregular cavalry south of the Kaitna.
KEY
S1 Sharpe, acting as Wellesley's orderly, follows him closely.
S2 Sharpe kills six enemy and saves Wellesley's life, for which he is later awarded a commission into the 74th Foot.
S3 In Assaye:
• Dodd seizes Pohlmann's treasure and shoots Capt Joubert for his horse
• Sgt Hakeswill murders Col McCandless
• Sharpe rescues Simone Joubert.
S4 Dodd escapes north with most of his Cobras and Pohlmann's treasure.
W1-2-3 Wellington's positions
R. Juah
ford
S4
Berar's infantry
Assaye
S3
G
Scindia's and Berar's cavalry
DODD
D
Picquets
C
74th
DUPONT
POHLMANN
S2
W3
F
E
4th NC
19th ID
5th NC
7th NC
W2
B
ford
R. Kaitna
Taunklee
SALEUR
2/12 M
1/4 M
1/8 M
A
1/10 M
Picquets
74th
2/12 M
W1
S1
78th
78th
1/4 M
Waroor
Peepulgaon
ford
Scindia's and Berar's cavalry
H
1 400 800 1200 1600
yards

INDIAN ARMS AND
ARMOUR

Irregular Indian
troops carried a
bewildering array of
arms. In the early
nineteenth century
Colonel Mark Wilks,
in his *Historical
Sketches of South India*,
listed some of the
antiquated weapons
still in use: 'the
Parthian bow and
arrow, the iron club of
Sythia, sabres of every
age and nation, lances
of every length and
description,
matchlocks of every
form, and metallic
helmets of every
pattern.' Muskets were
often locally made
copies of European
models; a factory at
Agra produced
excellent replicas of
French muskets –
though the locks did
not last so well as on
the original.

The use of plate and
chainmail body
armour was not
unknown. It was so
heavy that armour-
clad troops trying to
swim a river risked
drowning. Some
horsemen wore
Chinese-style quilting,
which was debilitating
in the heat but seemed
capable of absorbing
the lighter blows and
cuts. While helmets
were common, the
majority of native
warriors wore a turban
made of many yards of
woollen cloth; when

The first of these occurred as he was fording the river, when he came under long-range artillery fire from cannons south of Assaye and realised that the enemy had changed front, deploying on a new line with both flanks secure. This left Wellesley committed to a frontal attack against hugely superior numbers, with the Mahratta regular battalions of Pohlmann formed behind a long line of cannons. To an impartial observer able to look down on both armies that afternoon, the British force would have seemed to be march-ing to almost certain disaster. Over-confident might have been an observer's least derogatory comment on what he saw unfolding; irresponsible and foolhardy would have surely sprung to mind too. Wellesley had wanted to avoid a frontal assault but was now committed to undertake one. He had hoped to surprise his enemy, but there was no surprise. The regular troops had been able to change front to the east with ease, well before the British had crossed the ford and formed up – something Wellesley had considered beyond their capa-bilities.

The Mahrattas' huge force not only had both flanks secured by rivers, but the left was doubly secured by the village of Assaye, which had been fortified and was covered by numer-ous cannons that would enfilade troops advancing across their front. Wellesley's plan envisaged a very thin line of infantry spread over almost a mile of front advancing for at least half a mile into the teeth of dozens of cannons backed up by a solid mass of infantry. Having failed to outflank his enemy, he found himself in a position where the only alternative to the complete extermination of his force was victory against odds of at least eight to one. Worse still, Scindia's vast host had had a restful day, unlike Wellesley's sweat-soaked, thirsty and weary troops, who had been lugging their heavy muskets and packs since dawn in a forced march of over twenty miles, most of it under the broiling, brassy midday sun. Our observer must have wondered about the sanity of such generalship.

The trouble started at the Peepulgaon ford. As Wellesley

himself splashed across (the water was only three feet deep and must have felt wonderful to thousands of sore feet) at the head of the column, he and his staff came under effective artillery fire at long range by heavy eighteen-pounder cannons. This was not good. The army had still to cross the river, let alone form up and attack, and yet already it began to suffer losses. Probably the first casualty was Wellesley's unlucky orderly, Private Fletcher of the 19th Dragoons, whose head was severed, though his body remained in the saddle for several seconds as his horse reared and plunged. Abandoning his musket in exchange for Fletcher's heavy cavalry sabre – a weapon with which he was entirely unfamiliar – Sharpe took over the orderly's duties, which involved keeping close to the general and leading his spare horse, loaded with extra water canteens. Behind him, the long snake of infantry began the crossing, an operation that would take considerable time.

Wellesley's lack of numbers meant that the further he advanced towards his enemy, the more exposed his right flank became. He had initially deployed in two lines, but quickly realised this would be unworkable and issued orders for the second line to move to the right of the leading line. The consequences could easily have cost him the battle long before his infantry reached the enemy guns.

The problem was that Lieutenant-Colonel Orrock, commanding the small, ad hoc battalion of picquets, misunderstood his orders (MAP 5). Instead of moving north and then swinging left into line to join the main attack, Orrock marched straight towards Assaye village, a bastion bristling with guns and muskets. The error was compounded when he was followed by 500 men of the 74th Foot (Sharpe's future regiment) under Major Samuel Swinton. Confusion worsened as Wellesley ordered the general advance to begin before the repositioning of the second line had been completed. The extending of the first line was to be done on the move and under artillery fire. Moreover, the attack had started without the support of Wellesley's fourteen guns,

wound round the head it provided an effective cushion against all but the severest sabre stroke. The British 19th Dragoons were supposedly trained to remove the turban with the point before striking the bare head, though the practicality of such a technique in a mêlée seems doubtful.

PICQUETS

Nowadays the word denotes small bodies of troops (infantry or cavalry), normally static, used to screen a defensive position, guarding against a surprise attack. A cavalry picquet would deploy a number of vedettes of two horsemen to cover a greater distance – each vedette remaining in sight of those on either side. However, the term had a somewhat different meaning in Sharpe's day, when picquets – like the infantrymen under Colonel Orrock's command – formed the advance guard on the line of march. Additional duties included protection of the force when halted or in camp. Because the work was arduous, they were changed every day.

Picquets were made up of one half-company (about fifty men under an officer) from each battalion in the force commanded by the duty field officer (major or above). With six infantry battalions engaged at Assaye, Orrock's force numbered around 300 (a weak battalion). Despite the potential disadvantages of entrusting defence of the force to troops from different

which were still struggling to get into position. A number of the bullocks dragging them were hit, rendering the guns immobile. At least one cannon was stuck in the stream. Wellesley's response – the only one available in the circumstances – was to speed up the frontal attack on the enemy's guns.

When Colonel Orrock, in error, continued to head towards Assaye instead of wheeling west, the 74th, whose orders were to form on the right of the picquets, followed. Whether Swinton knew that this was not the intended plan but carried on regardless, determined to support the picquets (among whom were a half-company of his battalion), will never be known. In any event, a large gap began to open up between the 74th and the 2/12th Madras. The picquets were the first to feel the effects of their commander's mistake, suffering grievously in consequence. When Orrock's men came within musket-shot of the village, the hail of fire from the enemy defenders – which included cannonballs ripping through the ranks – was soon enough to send them scrambling back in disorder on to the 74th. In the middle of an uncomfortable belt of thick cactus plants, surrounded by panicky picquets, under a deadly barrage of fire from most of the left wing of the enemy army, the 74th were brought to a halt. Suddenly, the firing slackened. The respite, however, was fleeting, just sufficient for a mob of Mahratta horsemen to appear and charge down on them with their long, curved chopping swords flashing in the sun. The 74th closed ranks around their Colours and stood their ground, encouraged by the skirl of bagpipes from a solitary piper. Casualties were horrendous. Only one officer was unwounded and all but about a hundred of the soldiers were down.

At this juncture reinforcements arrived from an unusual and unexpected source. Quartermaster James Grant had been bringing up some coolies carrying more ammunition, water and medical supplies, when he saw the predicament of his battalion. With a certain amount of fumbling with his unfamiliar sword hilt, Grant led forward an assortment of

Mahratta horseman

baggage guards, clerks and orderlies. If there was to be a last stand the quartermaster had every intention of being part of it. Three years later, when a disgruntled Sharpe was himself a quartermaster, he would have done well to recall that even they had sometimes to fight.

One cavalry charge was about to be countered by another. Colonel Patrick Maxwell commanded Wellesley's cavalry brigade of some 1,500 horsemen. It was composed of the 19th Light Dragoons together with three native regiments: the 4th, 5th and 7th Native Cavalry. Initially positioned on the right flank of the second line, Maxwell's task was to protect Wellesley's right flank. As he watched events unfold on the right – the picquets on the run and the 74th, reduced to a handful around their Colours, being charged by enemy horsemen – Maxwell knew it was decision time. With Wellesley nowhere in sight, he was the senior officer on the spot; he had to act. But there is evidence to suggest he hesitated, unsure whether to commit his brigade and risk exposing the army's right flank; there were, after all, many thousands of enemy troops still uncommitted. His British battalions, unused to fighting together and commanded by an officer who was unlikely to know them or his subordinate officers, the arrangement seemed to work, provided the troops were well trained and disciplined.

officers did not understand his apparent dithering. The brig-ade major (staff officer) Captain Grant cantered up to him, crying, 'Now, sir! Now is the time to save the 74th. Do, pray, order us to charge!' Maxwell obliged. He personally led forward the 19th Light Dragoons with the 4th Native Cavalry on his right and the 5th Native Cavalry on his left – about 1,100 horsemen. Wisely, he kept the 7th Native Cavalry back in reserve. Eleven hundred cavalrymen, in two lines, with sabres drawn and flashing in the sunlight must have made a splendid sight. It was almost twice the number involved in the famous Light Brigade charge at Balaclava some fifty years later. Above the din of battle the clear, stirring notes of Maxwell's trumpeter sounding the 'walk', 'trot', 'gallop' and then 'charge' could be heard as the brigade swept forward. The charge crashed into and through the enemy horsemen, saved the remnants of the 74th, and put to flight some infan-try units that had advanced on the 74th. But by then Maxwell had lost proper control. The wild excitement, the rush of adrenaline and the sheer joy of chasing a beaten foe carried most of the brigade away in a pursuit that took them over the Juah River. In later years this lack of control by the cavalry was repeated on numerous battlefields in the Peninsula and even at Waterloo. It was to cause Wellesley – or the Duke of Wellington, as he was by then – considerable anger, and it soured his relationship with his undoubtedly gallant cavalry.

Orrock's blunder led not only to Wellesley's right flank being exposed, but to his main attack taking place with five battalions instead of seven. These battalions, with the 78th Foot on the extreme left by the Kaitna River, advanced in echelon, the left leading. Wellesley positioned himself immediately behind the right of the 78th with Sharpe riding to his rear. The 78th must have been an intimidating sight as they slowly, steadily closed the distance on Pohlmann's right flank. A long, disciplined double line of scarlet tunics, feathered bonnets, swirling kilts, with muskets shouldered and bayonets fixed, Colours let fly in the centre, all backed by the scream and wail of pipes. The Indian gunners were

An officer's career in the Company's army

PROMOTION WENT by seniority and, despite the havoc wrought by the climate, was usually exceedingly slow. A subaltern might wait fifteen years to become captain. Many ambitious young men, frustrated with the prospect of a fifteen-year wait to be made up from subaltern to captain, abandoned their regiments for alternative employment within the King's Army, the civil service, or the 'political' branch (the diplomatic service). All three offered better pay, and they could keep their military rank, thus ensuring automatic, if slow, army promotion. It was in the political service that the most famous Indian administrators – such as Henry Lawrence and James Outram – made their names.

With the best men weeded out, many Indian regiments were left with the mediocre, the inferior and the idle. Most of the younger officers were good sportsmen, a few of them on cordial terms with the Indian aristocracy. England was many months away and leave to return, except on grounds of ill health, was seldom considered before a stay of ten years. In consequence they settled down to make the country their home, the native troops their children. Many became over-fond of the bottle; most took solace in the arms of an Indian mistress. In times of peace they lived comfortably in cantonments, with a great host of servants. In the field, the more senior often rode forth in palanquins, taking their servants with them. In the Afghan War of 1839 one brigadier found he needed sixty camels to carry all that he needed to keep himself comfortable. The combined effects of age, drink and climate ensured that any man of colonel's rank was virtually certain to be past his best – like Colonel Orrock at Assaye. No wonder that, in Sharpe's day, many important operations were conducted – and brilliantly so – by captains.

well trained; they rammed and fired, rammed and fired, blowing holes in the approaching line. But nothing they did could stop the 78th. When the battalion finally came to a halt, about sixty yards from the gunline, it was in accordance with an order. The line was about to deliver a volley – its first shots of the battle. 'Make ready! Present! Fire!' Then, instead of charging, the battalion calmly reloaded. It took about twenty seconds. 'Make ready! Present! Fire!' Just as the enemy gunners were struggling to recover, they were hit by another blast of fire. Then out of the smoke came the 78th at the double, bayonets levelled, bagpipes shrieking, Highlanders

From sepoy to subadar

ALTHOUGH PROUD to wear the red coat of a soldier, Sita Ram – being accustomed to cool, loose-fitting cotton garments – cursed its tightness, the restrictions of the crossbelts and the weight of his shako and musket. The pouch-belt and knapsack he deemed 'a load for a coolie [low caste servant or labourer]' (an Indian soldier's typical load was about half his own weight). His experiences on the drill square during basic training will strike a chord with many an old soldier:

The parade ground was covered by parties of six or eight men, performing the most extraordinary movements I had ever seen, and these to orders in a language of which I did not understand a single word. [English words of command were used in the Indian Army until the late 1960s.] I felt inclined to laugh, and stood astonished at the sight. However a violent wrench of my ear by the drill havildar soon brought me to my senses. I had to attend drill for many months, and one day I happened to forget how to do something and was so fiercely cuffed on the head by the drill havildar that I fell down senseless. I complained to my uncle [perhaps not a wise move] who was very angry with the drill havildar. Although he never dared to strike me again, from that day on he bullied me in every other way and used to abuse me at every opportunity. As I had gone to great pains to learn my duties, I resented this treatment very much and I had almost made up my mind to run away. The drill havildar told the Adjutant that I was obstinate and stupid, and would never make a soldier.

In his memoirs, published in 1873, Sita Ram reminisced about his British officers, many of whom were known by nicknames, such as "the Camel" – because he had a long neck' and "the Wrestler" – a real *sahib*, just as I imagined all *sahibs* to be . . . his chest as broad as Hanuman's, the monkey god.' He probably would not have approved of Ensign Sharpe! 'Most of our officers had Indian women living with them. They could speak our language much better than they do now and they mixed more with us.' (Having a local girlfriend has always been the quickest and most enjoyable way of learning a foreign language – many years later in the British Hong Kong Police it was called having 'a sleeping dictionary'.) Of the other ranks, Sita Ram comments: 'I was always very good friends with the English soldiers and they used to treat the sepoy with great kindness. And why not? Did we not do all their work? We performed all their duties in the heat. We stood sentry over their rum-casks. We gave them our food. Well, English soldiers are a different breed nowadays. They are neither as fine nor as tall as they used to be.'

He held interesting views, too, on the British soldier's fighting spirit:

I hardly know why they love fighting as much as they do, unless it is for grog. They would fight ten battles in succession for one bowl of grog. Their pay is very little so it cannot be for that. They also love looting but I have seen them give a cap full of rupees for one bottle of brandy. I have been told that the English doctors have discovered some kind of essence which is mixed with the soldiers' grog. Great care has to be taken not to mix too much otherwise the men would kill themselves in battle by their rashness . . . there must be some kind of elixir of life in ration rum; I have seen wounded men, all but dead, come to life after having some rum.

Sita Ram was promoted to subadar (the highest rank an Indian officer could attain) at the age of sixty-five, shortly before being pensioned off.

---

yelling. Twenty seconds was all they needed to cover the final sixty yards. The battalion swept through the cannons, making good use of bayonet and butt as they did so – but they did not stop. With a coolness and discipline that astounded those who saw it (including Sharpe), the 78th reformed beyond the guns and advanced on the enemy infantry. Another halt, another volley, followed yet again by a second. It was an amazing demonstration of how an infantry battalion should, and could, attack. Saleur's flank battalions had certainly seen enough – they fled.

The example set by the 78th was as much an inspiration to the four Madrassi battalions on its right as it was a deterrent to the enemy infantry ahead of them. These battalions stormed forward, still in echelon, so that the Mahratta line was hit a succession of blows. As the part of the line being hit crumbled, so their comrades to the left began to waver. Panic is infectious. Pohlmann's right and centre began to disintegrate as units turned and ran for the Juah River to the north. Here their officers succeeded in getting some of them sufficiently under control to form another, somewhat shaky, defensive front along the south bank of the river.

Although Wellesley's attack on Pohlmann's right was successful, mainly due to the inspiring example of the 78th Foot, and Maxwell had redeemed an impending disaster in the north, a most unusual situation had arisen in the centre. A number of British guns appear to have been taken by Mahratta cavalry that had avoided Maxwell and come south. Meanwhile some Indian gunners who had feigned death had courageously come to life to man their guns again. These cannons were now being fired into the backs of the infantry that had swept through them. Wellesley sent staff officers galloping off to bring back the 78th, keeping two battalions watching the great mass of Mahratta horsemen still uncommitted in the west and the other two on hand to face the infantry near the Juah River. He rode over to his last reserve – the 7th Native Cavalry. Wellesley personally led them forward, with Sharpe, the awkward infantryman on horseback, desperately trying to keep up.

It was during the frantic mêlée that followed around the cannons that Wellesley came as close to losing his life as he ever would in his long career. His horse Diomed had a pike thrust through his lungs, bringing Wellesley to the ground, where he had to use his drawn sword for a few brief moments until his assailants were driven off. During those frenzied minutes, Sergeant Sharpe earned his battlefield commission. Pushing Wellesley under a cannon, he went berserk with his sword, flailing, hacking and stabbing like a man possessed. Despite being slashed on the shoulder by a *tulwar* (Indian sword) he killed six opponents, including an officer. They died in a welter of blood with at least one severed head, a slit gullet, a split skull, a thrust through the throat and a disembowelment – an impressive achievement. Wellesley, shaken but unhurt, had his saddle and holsters shifted, then mounted his third horse of the day. Although Diomed was almost certainly dying, Wellesley, who was deeply attached to his horse, instructed that the pike be pulled from the animal's chest rather than have him shot immediately. It was a hopeless gesture.

Wellesley rode north with the bulk of the 7th Native Cavalry, followed by the ubiquitous 78th. He arrived in time to see Maxwell, who had returned from his ride around

The joys of promotion

JOHN SHIPP, who, uniquely, was twice commissioned and busted, was in India as a private soldier at the same time as Sergeant Sharpe in 1802. He wrote with great humour and insight into the lives of soldiers of his day, memorably describing a sergeant-major's wife as, 'his more consequential spouse, who is queen of the soldiers' wives, and mother of tipplers, and from whom an invitation-card to tea and cards is considered a ponderous obligation.' Of his remarkable rise from drummer boy to pay sergeant, Shipp wrote:

> I was transferred from the drummers' room and promoted to the rank of corporal. This was promotion indeed – three steps in one day! From drum-boy to private; from a battalion company to the Light Bobs [light company]; and from private to corporal! It was not long before I paraded myself in the tailor's shop, and tipped the master-snip a rupee to give me a good and neat cut, such as became a full corporal. By evening parade my blushing honours came thick upon me. The captain came upon parade, and read aloud the regimental orders of the day, laying great stress upon, 'to the rank of corporal, and to be obeyed accordingly.' . . . A corporal has to take command of small guards; is privileged to visit the sentinels whenever he pleases; his suggestions are frequently attended to by his superiors; and his orders must be promptly obeyed by those below him. There is certainly a pleasure in all this, and a man rises proportionally in his own esteem. In short, to confess the truth I now looked upon a drum-boy as little better than his drum.

Within six months Shipp was a sergeant and soon after that secured the much sought-after post of company pay sergeant (roughly equivalent to a modern company quartermaster-sergeant):

> The post of pay-sergeant is certainly one of importance . . . He feeds and clothes the men; lends them money at a moderate interest and on good security; sells them watches and seals on credit, at a price somewhat above what they cost, to be sure . . . it is not my intention to enter into a detail of the chicanery practised among the minor ranks of the army, let it suffice that I never served in a company in which every individual could not buy, sell, exchange, lend and borrow, on terms peculiar to themselves.

Not much has changed!

Army food – Ceylon 1803

AT THE TIME Sharpe was winning his commission at Assaye a garrison artilleryman, Alexander Alexander, was bemoaning army rations in Ceylon:

From the depression of mind I then lay under, but more especially from the miserable diet we got, I became extremely ill. I was never free from inveterate flux and other troubles; our food was not only bad in itself, but cooked by the black cooks belonging to the garrison, in the most dirty and careless manner and we, being strangers in the country, could not alter their slovenly fashions. When the meat was brought to the cooking place it was thrown down upon a dirty mat, and chopped up. Then [the] cooks sat down upon their hams, placing a knife between their toes, and cut it up into small pieces, and thus daubed all about, and without being even washed, it was boiled in curry. The rice being boiled at the same time in another earthen vessel called a chattie . . .

At night we got what was called supper, which consisted of a small cake of rice flour and water, and a liquid called coffee, although there was never a single grain of the berry in it. What we used for sugar was called jaggery, which was made up in cakes, very insipid and dirty; it bore no resemblance to the sugar used in Europe. At eight o'clock in the morning we got breakfast brought to us in the same manner; it consisted of the same cake, fish or bullocks liver, and jaggery water . . .

The beef, of which we had a pound a day, was given out along with the rice in the morning, for which sixpence a day was kept off our pay. But it was rather carrion than beef. The cattle, sometimes buffaloes, sometimes bullock, having been used in their husbandry were generally lean, old or diseased. The meat was soft, flabby, and full of membranous skin. It had a rank, heavy, loathsome odour, was offensive to both sight and smell, and hurt me more than the climate, and was, I am certain, the cause of much of the disease and death which thinned our numbers. The rice, too, was small, and of bad quality, full of dust and dirt, from which our rascally cooks were at no trouble to free it.

Assaye, preparing to charge again at the eastern part of Pohlmann's new line along the river. This time he only had about 600 sabres and they were formed up at a forty-five degree angle to the enemy rather than facing them directly. This meant that some change of direction on the move would be required if the attack was to hit the Mahratta infantry square on. Maxwell moved off, placing himself ahead of the line. Unfortunately, just as the brigade got into its stride, but before any adjustment of direction had been made, Maxwell was knocked from his saddle by a piece of grapeshot. At the moment of receiving this fatal wound he dropped his sword and at the same time involuntarily raised his right arm. To those nearby, seeing their commander fall was demoralising; some may even have thought his raised right arm was a signal to halt. Coupled with the angled alignment of the charge, it was enough to ensure the attack did not hit home. A few troopers on the right struck the left of Pohlmann's new line, but the great majority ended up riding parallel to it rather than into it. From this it was but a short step to riding away from it. Major John Blackiston, an officer who rode in this charge, later wrote: 'I suddenly found my horse swept round as it were by an eddy current. Away we galloped right shoulders forward along the enemy's line receiving their fire. We took to our heels manfully.'

Wellesley now brought up his infantry to attack the enemy's line along the river. The sight of another disciplined assault developing was enough to send the enemy splashing over the Juah in headlong retreat. The general turned his attention to the only remaining enemy position – Assaye. He organised some guns to open fire on the defenders from a range of 300 yards while the two British battalions formed up to attack. But Berar's irregular infantry in the village had seen more than enough. There was only minimal resistance as the British entered Assaye.

Scindia and Berar had long since disappeared, leaving Pohlmann in command. His entire army was now on the run, leaving behind a field littered with dead, wounded, and scores of brass cannons.

> The sun of the evening looked down from his throne,
> And beamed on the face of the dead and the dying,
> For the roar of the battle, like thunder, had flown,
> And red on Assaye the heaped carnage was lying.

THE BUTCHER'S BILL FOR ASSAYE

Mahratta losses are uncertain, but a body count is said to have totalled 1,200 dead, with an estimate of four times that number wounded and 102 cannons left on the field. The British losses were high in proportion to the number of troops engaged: 198 Europeans killed and 442 wounded, while the Indians suffered 258 dead and 695 wounded. These 1,593 casualties represented just under 27 per cent of those engaged – which exceeds Anglo-Allied losses at Waterloo by nearly 3 per cent. Had Orrock not made his blunder (resulting in the picquets being almost wiped out and 401 men lost from the 74th), the total losses would have been halved. Of the four EIC battalions that took part, the 2/12th Madras suffered the most with 212 casualties.

WELLESLEY'S
VIEWS ON ASSAYE

Many years later a friend in the diplomatic service asked Wellesley, by then Duke of Wellington, what had been the best thing he ever did in the way of fighting. The Duke replied 'Assaye'. Shortly after the battle he wrote: 'I cannot write in too strong terms of the conduct of the troops; they advanced in the best order and with greatest steadiness, under a most destructive fire, against a body of infantry far superior in number, who appeared determined to contend with them to the last ... The fire from their cannon was the hottest that has been known in this country ... [the troops] were exposed to a most terrible cannonade from Assaye ... I assure you that the fire was so heavy that I much doubted at one time whether I should be able to prevail upon our troops to advance ... All agree that the battle was the fiercest that has ever been seen in India. Our troops behaved admirably; the sepoys astonished me ... Scindia's French [officered] infantry was far better than the Tippoo's.'

Inside Assaye, while Dodd escaped northwards, Sharpe lost his friend and mentor *Colonel McCandless* at the murderous hands of *Sergeant Hakeswill*. At least Sharpe was on hand to save *Simone Joubert* from the proverbial 'fate worse than death'.

Wellesley was always proud of his triumph against the odds at Assaye. He even forgave Orrock his blunder. In fact he left him in command of the 1/8th Madras despite his low opinion of him. (Wellesley is recorded as saying: 'through habits of dissipation and idleness, he [Orrock] has become incapable of giving attention to an order to see what it means'.) Orrock had been in the EIC service for twenty-five years. He died, still in service, eight years later at Seringapatam.

The worst losses were suffered by the 74th – which was the reason Sharpe, when commissioned, was posted to them. The unwounded survivors consisted of about thirty to forty men grouped around the Colours. Well over four hundred bodies lay scattered on the ground south of Assaye. Wellesley, who had spent most of his time in the south, did not appreciate the true situation of this battalion. As he approached the commanding officer, Major Swinton – who, wounded in the leg and head, dazed and weak from loss of blood, was sitting seated on the ground with his back against the dead body of his horse – he called:

'Where's Major Swinton?'

'Here, sir!'

'They are on the run! Bring up your men, Swinton!'

'But they are all down, sir!'

Wellesley was never to forget this incident.

Stevenson arrived at Assaye twenty-four hours later. He had got lost en route and ended up marching via Borkardan. Thirty-six hours passed before the pursuit of Scindia and Berar began. The time was spent collecting and treating the wounded and burying the dead. Wellesley had over a thousand wounded men and insufficient surgeons or medical

The Vellore mutiny

THE MUTINIES in the Bengal Army during the 1850s were not the first such uprisings. In November 1805, shortly after Wellesley (and Sharpe) left India, General Sir John Craddock, Commander-in-Chief of the Madras Army, issued a thoughtless, humiliating and totally unnecessary order that alienated all Indian troops under his command, Muslim and Hindu alike. Instead of the turban, all were to wear a round hat with a leather cockade. In addition, they must adopt the leather stock round the neck, no jewellery could be worn (such as earrings), and no soldier was to have paint marks on his face. A 'hat-wearer' was a derogatory name for a Christian; leather of any kind was an abomination to Hindus, who regarded the cow as a sacred animal, while Muslims were suspicious it might be made from pigskin. Earrings were often linked with family rites from childhood and were meant to be worn until death. The paint marks on Hindus' foreheads were of religious significance, so to have them rubbed off on parade was deeply insulting.

A mutiny over this order might have been avoided had it not been for the agitation and subversive activities of the Tippoo Sultan of Mysore, whose father had been killed (by Sharpe) at Seringapatam. The Tippoo, with his innumerable sons and retainers, lived in a huge palace at Vellore, about a hundred miles west of Madras. They did all they could to encourage an uprising of the local garrisons. But it was not until July 1806 that the simmering pot finally boiled over.

In the fort at Vellore were four companies of the 69th Foot (South Lincolnshire) with the 1/1st, 2/1st and 2/23rd Madras Native Infantry. Some time after midnight on the sweltering night of 10 July the British sentries were shot down. The mutineers descended on the hospital, killing the patients, while simultaneously setting light to the barracks of the sleeping 69th, many of whom died in their beds. Officers were cut down as they stumbled from their houses; 14 British officers died, along with 115 other ranks, with many more wounded. The Tippoo's tiger standard was raised.

Sixteen miles away at Arcot were the 19th Light Dragoons who had done so well at Assaye. They arrived within two hours, along with two galloper guns and a squadron of Madras Native Cavalry. The mutineers had spent the remainder of the night looting and had made no effort to defend the walls; indeed, they left the outer gate open. Cannons were used to blast through the inner gates and the cavalry poured in, flailing away with their sabres.

The rebels paid a heavy price: some 350 died under the swords of the dragoons and native horsemen (who were equally enthusiastic in the hunt). The mutineers were tried and handed down harsh sentences: six were blown from cannons (tied to the muzzle and the gun fired), five were shot, eight hanged and five transported. The three regiments were disbanded. The unthinking order that started it was rescinded, the governor and commander-in-chief recalled.

supplies. All that could be done for most of them was to provide water, some dressings and protect them from marauders and the burning sun. The bodies lay in heaps, especially where the 74th had rallied round their Colours. Men were set to work digging pits near the Juah River north-west of Assaye for the British and allied dead. Most of the 631 British dead (198 European and 433 Indian) ended up in communal mass graves. (According to the author Jac Weller, the cemetery was marked as such on a one-inch Ordnance Survey map of the area dated 1912.) Five Indian officers and NCOs of the same family from the 1/8th Madras, a Muslim unit that assumed the title 'Wellesley's Own', were interred in a single grave; their comrades refused to mourn them as they had died doing their duty.

———— ✦ ————

5

Sharpe's Fortress

Covering the last few weeks of Wellesley's Deccan campaign in November and December 1803, the book opens with an unhappy Ensign Sharpe fighting with the 74th Foot at the Battle of Argaum on 29 November. His role in the action is insignificant and he feels inadequate and out of place as an officer. His brother officers have not accepted him. After the battle it is suggested he would be better off in the Experimental Corps of Riflemen (later the 95th Rifles) forming in England. In the meantime he is posted to the supply train as second-in-command to *Captain Torrance*. His discovery of theft and mismanagement in the stores and supply system soon leads to plots against his life involving *Torrance* and *Sergeant Hakeswill*.

Sharpe's adventures up to and including the storming of Gawilghur find him engaged in something of a killing spree. He despatches a *jetti*, *Torrance* and his Indian clerk, along with privates *Lowry* and *Kendrick* – all prior to the attack on Gawilghur. For the storming of the breach he forcibly takes command of the light company of his old regiment, the 33rd Foot. During the assault he kills at least one enemy soldier and *Colonel* Dodd with a claymore. The book ends with Sharpe forcing *Sergeant Hakeswill* into a deep snake pit.

WELLESLEY WAS UNABLE to organise an immediate pursuit of the defeated armies of Scindia and Berar after his victory at Assaye. This was largely due to the need to attend to the hundreds of casualties scattered around the battlefield.

General Lake's campaign in the north

WHILE WELLESLEY was fighting in the Deccan, General Gerald Lake was doing the same in Hindustan against a Mahratta force led (until his surrender in September 1803) by the Frenchman General Pierre Perron. Lake commanded about 11,000 troops of the 'Grand Army' composed mainly of EIC native soldiers with a small British contingent. After triumphs at Aligarh, Delhi and Laswari, there was a comparatively quiet year of minor operations against Mahratta brigands in 1804. Not until the following year, when both Wellesley and Sharpe were looking forward to leaving India, did the long run of British victories come to an end before the walls of Bhurtpore.

Although Lake's four assaults on this fortress failed, they serve to illustrate how well EIC battalions fought. Bhurtpore had a circumference of seven miles, the mud ramparts were 80–120 feet high and surrounded by a moat from which the colossal walls had been dug. Lake besieged the place with a mere 6,000 infantry (including the 31st Bengal Native Infantry), 2,000 cavalry, six iron 18-pounders and eight brass mortars. An escalade was impossible, so they relied on the meagre firepower of the siege train. The first assault was made on 9 January 1805 and beaten back; the roundshot that was supposed to make a breach was instead absorbed into the massive walls of dried mud. On 21 January there was a repeat performance. A third assault took place on 20 February, again ending in failure, with three British battalions refusing to go further. Philip Mason

describes the renewed attack on 21 February in his history of the Indian Army, *A Matter of Honour*:

Next day, Lake harangued the troops . . . he called for volunteers for a fourth assault. Such was the power of this fierce, obstinate old man, matchless in valour and energy, that when he had spoken every man volunteered . . . Men drove their bayonets into the walls and used the hilts to climb by [surely a unique method of making an escalade]. But a shower of logs and stones were rolled down on them, and so narrow was the way up that musketry fire could be concentrated on the leaders and as one man fell he brought down those below him. Nearly a thousand men were killed and wounded; the 31st Bengal Native Infantry lost 180 men killed and wounded out of about 400 in the short space of two hours . . .

The colours of the 31st had been near the summit, but they had been brought back . . . They were riddled with shot, tattered, unserviceable; a board of officers sat and orders were passed: they were to be replaced. The new colours arrived; they were to be consecrated next day but until that ceremony took place they were no more than coloured silk. They passed the night of their novitiate in the guardroom, sleeping side by side with the old, which tomorrow would be cremated. But in the morning nothing remained of the old colours; every fragment had disappeared and no British officer could learn what had become of them. It was a mystery, not pursued, soon forgotten.

Twenty-one years later Lord Combermere succeeded in taking Bhurtpore with a far larger force (again including the 31st). Even then siege batteries of 112 heavy cannons and 50 field guns could not blast a breach, so gigantic mines were used. As the 31st stormed into the fortress they carried aloft their new Colours and, tied to them, the ragged and torn remnants of the old ones. The men who had brought them home in defeat had given the cherished pieces of silk to their sons, who now carried them through the breach. Honour had been restored.

As his exhausted army bivouacked on the field, Wellesley himself lay down between one dead officer and another whose leg had been severed. For a long time he remained silent and motionless, his head bent low between his knees. Although in latter years he was to claim Assaye was his best victory, it cannot have looked that way at the time. Certainly he had triumphed over seemingly impossible odds, but success had come at a very high price. The tactics had been undistinguished, verging on amateurish. A third of his force (led by Stevenson) had been unavailable, he had failed to secure surprise, he had been compelled by events to launch a brutal frontal attack in the face of potentially overwhelming firepower and his orders had been misunderstood by a key subordinate. During the action his right flank (and therefore the battle) was only saved by the initiative of his cavalry commander (Maxwell). Finally, he was almost killed.

The general spent 24 September waiting for Stevenson. He needed his troops, but above all he needed his surgeons to help collect and treat the wounded. Not until the evening did his subordinate commander arrive. He had marched towards the sound of the guns (usually the right thing to do if in doubt), but had then been delayed during the night by navigational difficulties brought about by unreliable local guides. Although they had not fought a battle, Stevenson's men had been marching thirty-six hours. By the time they

EIC armies and caste

IN SHARPE'S DAY, the caste system pervaded every aspect of life for India's Hindu population. In simple terms, there were four main castes: the highest were the Brahmins (traditionally priests and scholars), then Rajputs (kings, princes, landowners and soldiers), Banias (traders, bankers, money-lenders) and Sudras (farmers, artisans, clerks and messengers). The vast majority had no proper caste; they were the 'untouchables' and their work (as sweepers, scavengers and cleaners) involved touching unclean things. Each caste, including the untouchables, had subdivisions; there were over 3,000 groups, which were in turn divided into sub-groups. Hindus could not marry outside their group or within their sub-group. Someone of high caste could not eat, drink or smoke with a person of lower caste, or even accept a drink of water from them. Anyone who broke the rules would be ostracised, and could only be cleansed through long penance and expensive ceremonies.

Remarkably, in the Madras and Bombay armies caste differences were set aside; soldiers ate together and barracked together without any regard to their social position. As one old subadar of the Madras Army put it, 'We put our religion in our knapsacks whenever our Colours were unfurled.' But the Bengal Army recruited only the higher castes and took great care not to infringe caste rules. One soldier of high caste asked for a discharge from the Bombay Army because a man of lower caste had been promoted, and then enlisted in the Bengal Army even though it meant suffering far more indignities. His reason: in the Bengal Army men took pride in their caste whereas in the Bombay Army their pride was in their battalion.

In the Bengal Army men of different castes were grouped together in the same companies within a battalion – a practice that continued even after the 1857 mutiny. The general pattern was to have mixed battalions with perhaps one or two companies of Muslims, one or two of Sikhs, one of Rajputs, Dogras, Pathans or Baluchis. The company became the soldier's family; it was there he hoped his son would find a future. There were exceptions, particularly in later years, when class (caste) battalions were formed composed entirely of, say, Sikhs, Mahrattas, Dogras or Garhwarlis.

An illustration of the importance of caste, even unto death, is provided by a Brahmin subadar of the Bengal Army. As he lay, desperately wounded and dying from loss of blood, the intense heat and a raging thirst, General Skinner (a British officer) knelt to give him a drink from his water bottle. Despite his pain, the wounded man turned away, groaning, 'My caste! My caste!' Skinner tried to persuade him with the reassurance that no one would see, no one would know, but still the subadar refused, whispering, 'God sees me.'

EIC battalion officers

DURING WELLESLEY'S TIME in India an EIC regiment normally consisted of two battalions under a British colonel or lieutenant-colonel. Each battalion had eight or ten companies, two of which were grenadier companies (light companies did not exist in Native units). Until 1796 it was common for sepoy battalions to be commanded by a captain, assisted by a European adjutant, assistant-surgeon and six or eight subalterns, as this cut the EIC's costs. A reorganisation was supposed to change all this, though Captain Vesey's role as commander of the 1/3rd Madras at Ahmednuggur shows that the old ways persisted as late as 1803.

According to the new regulations, a ten-company Native battalion would have twenty-two British officers – a lieutenant-colonel, a major, four captains, eleven lieutenants and five ensigns. Each company should therefore have been commanded by a captain or senior lieutenant, assisted by at least one other European junior officer. But all too often leave and sickness halved the number of officers, making it impossible to follow the new regulations.

A further twenty Indian officers – ten subadars and ten jemadars – made up the full establishment. This represented a distinct loss of prestige for the subadar who, under the old system, had commanded a company with four jemadars under him. There was now little difference in their duties, although the subadar continued to receive twice the pay and pension. The pension increased significantly after forty years' service, whatever the rank, so ancient havildars and jemadars clung on as long as they were physically able to march in the hope of being promoted into vacancies blocked by equally worn-out subadars waiting for their forty-year pension rise. The situation was detrimental to the morale and efficiency of officers who in effect became overpaid sergeants. Not until 1818 were the promotion prospects of a subadar improved slightly with the creation of the post 'subadar-major' – one for every battalion.

arrived they had lost as much sweat if not blood as Wellesley's men. All through the twenty-fifth Wellesley's army rested and attended the wounded. The next day Stevenson set out in pursuit, leaving Wellesley on the battlefield – it took a week for all the casualties to have their wounds dressed. Not until two weeks after the battle did Wellesley manage to deliver all his wounded into the safety of the fort at Ajanta, twenty miles north of Assaye. Meanwhile the unavoidable

MARCHING IN
INDIA (1)

There were three
major impediments to
maintaining a good
daily marching rate in
India: intense heat and
dust, the vast
distances to be
covered, and the
plodding pace of the
supply train of civilian
merchants, servants,
families and 'hangers-
on' that often hugely
outnumbered the
soldiers. The normal
routine was to march
at dawn (or earlier) to
avoid the blistering
heat of midday and
then make camp; six to
ten miles was
reckoned to be a good
day's progress.
Wellesley made a
considerable
improvement on this.
A few weeks after the
march to Poona at the
hottest time of year he
wrote, 'I never was in
such marching trim. I
marched the other
day twenty-three miles
in seven hours and a
half and all our
marches now are made
at the rate of three
miles an hour.' This
pace was kept up by
the whole force,
including the bullocks
and baggage. After
Assaye he wrote, 'We
marched sixty miles
with infantry in
twenty hours . . . It is
impossible for troops
to be in better order
than those under my
command.'

delay in any form of pursuit allowed the defeated Mahrattas sufficient respite to slip away; they had only been twelve miles from Assaye on the night following the battle.

Sharpe received Wellesley's grateful thanks for saving his life, promotion to ensign and, some time later, a telescope inscribed IN GRATITUDE. SEPTEMBER 23RD 1803. He joined his new regiment, what was left of the 74th, the following day. The battalion was in desperate need of replacements of all ranks. Almost 400 men from the 74th had fallen. The battalion's surgeon, Gallacher, and his assistant, Andrews, were swamped with casualties. By a truly remarkable effort on their part the lives of some 230 wounded were saved and, within a month (well in time for the next clash at Argaum), half of these were parading with their battalion.

Sharpe was posted to No. 6 Company under *Captain Urquhart*, where he found himself the only officer apart from the company commander. *Urquhart* was not particularly warm or welcoming, brusquely sending Sharpe away to get himself properly dressed! He had to transform himself from a sergeant of the 33rd Foot into something resembling an officer in the 74th Highlanders. In order to achieve this he managed to remove a tasselled, dark red officer's sash from a corpse without being spotted. Then he attended an auction of a dead officer's clothing and equipment. For a shilling he purchased the coat of *Lieutenant Blaine* and spent an hour fumbling with needle and thread, sewing up the hole in the front made by the musket ball that had killed *Blaine*, and trying, unsuccessfully, to remove the bloodstains. Another shilling bought him *Blaine*'s bonnet. He declined to purchase a claymore (he did not want to appear wealthy), instead keeping the curved cavalry sabre that he had used during the battle. He also kept his old trousers (fortunately the 74th were not wearing kilts) and his sergeant's boots. He certainly looked different, but it was really the red waist sash that now singled him out as an officer.

*   *   *

It was to take Wellesley two months to catch up with and confront Scindia again. Those weeks were spent marching and counter-marching some 300 miles. During this time Stevenson's force was again separated from Wellesley, but Stevenson was able to take the cities of Burhampoor and Asseergurh with little difficulty. The latter required a short siege, which was rewarded with the capture of a large quantity of military stores. The fall of these cities saw the surrender of ten of Scindia's European officers, who confirmed that Pohlmann's regular battalions had dispersed after Assaye. One of the officers to surrender was Major Dupont, the Frenchman who had commanded Filoze's compoo at the battle. There were, however, another ten still serving; eight with English names.

Colonel James Stevenson

AT THE TIME of the campaign against Scindia in 1803 Stevenson was a sick, elderly EIC cavalry officer, but his mind and willpower remained unimpaired. He never let Wellesley down and was one of his most trusted subordinates. Awaiting his arrival at Parterly before the Battle of Argaum, Wellesley saw a dust cloud and announced the arrival of Stevenson's force. 'How can you tell Colonel Stevenson's dust from any other dust?' he was asked. The answer was that Wellesley was expecting him at that precise time and trusted his reliability.

Stevenson was very much the old Company (EIC) officer with exceptionally long service in India. Although a cavalryman by training and experience (he had commanded the 1st EIC Cavalry Brigade in Wellesley's action at Malla-velly in 1799, and led the cavalry in operations against the freebooter Dhoondiah after he escaped from Seringapatam), he took over the administration of Mysore when Wellesley left Seringapatam in late 1800. In the hunt for Scindia and Berar, he commanded a mixed force of over 8,000 men, operating on his own with considerable success but at the same time co-operating within the framework of the campaign plan.

In December 1804 he finally gave in to his ailments and sailed for England. He died en route, probably without knowing that he had been promoted to major-general on 1 January 1805. Wellesley learned of his old friend's death when he called in at St Helena on his own voyage home. Stevenson's widow received an annual pension of £300.

MARCHING IN
INDIA (2)

'In India,' the Duke of
Wellington later told
Lord de Ros, 'we
always marched "by
the wheel." The men
who had charge of
these wheels attained
such extraordinary
correctness of judging
distance that they
could be depended on
almost as completely
without the wheel as
with it. The soldiers
were in messes of six
or eight; each mess
had its own native
cook and a bullock,
which carried the
men's knapsacks and
their cooking
materials, etc. The
native soldiers,
however, at that time
carried their
knapsacks on their
backs, but I believe
they now no longer do
so. An army in good
order in India would
march very nearly
three miles an hour.
Everything depended
on finding halting
stations at convenient
distances, 16 or 18
miles, where there was
water. Generally the
villages were by the
bank of what in winter
was a river, but in
summer was to all
outward appearance
perfectly dry, and a
mere bed of sand. The
water, however,
though unseen, was
always flowing at a
depth of from one to
three feet below this

Wellesley's strategy was to use Stevenson to seize places of importance while he concentrated on preventing his enemies from raiding in strength deep into friendly territory. It involved much hard marching, in which Ensign Sharpe was fully involved. During one eight-day period up to thirty miles a day was achieved, much of it under a broiling sun with siege guns. It is doubtful if this marching rate was ever surpassed by the British in India.

On 29 November Wellesley and Stevenson met at the village of Parterly (MAP 7). At about noon both officers climbed to the flat top of the fortified tower (still in existence) in the village. Wellesley stared north through his telescope. There through the heat haze, about seven miles away, was his enemy. They appeared to have formed line of battle. There was no obvious indication of withdrawal. He had to decide immediately whether to order his army forward again when they were already weary, having marched eighteen miles since dawn. Not only were the Mahrattas another seven miles away, but a major battle lay in prospect. The calculation was simple: either attack with an exhausted army or allow the enemy a chance to slip away. Wellesley had faced a similar situation once before, at Assaye. After all those weeks of trying to get to grips with his opponent there was, again, only one answer. Wellesley descended from the tower to issue his orders.

Two unusual features characterised the terrain south of Argaum where the clash was likely to occur. First, the approach, and the battlefield itself, was bisected almost exactly in two by a wide *nullah* (stream or gully). It wriggled its way roughly north–south and, this being the dry season, was filled with shallow pools. Wellesley, who had divided his army into four columns for the approach march, made use of the *nullah* as an inter-force boundary. To the west were Stevenson's two columns; closest to the *nullah* were the infantry (in order: picquets, 94th, 2/2nd, 2/9th, 1/11th, 2/11th and 1/6th Madras) with the cavalry, under Lieutenant-Colonel Sentleger of the 6th Native Cavalry, on the western flank. Immediately east of the *nullah* marched Wellesley's infantry

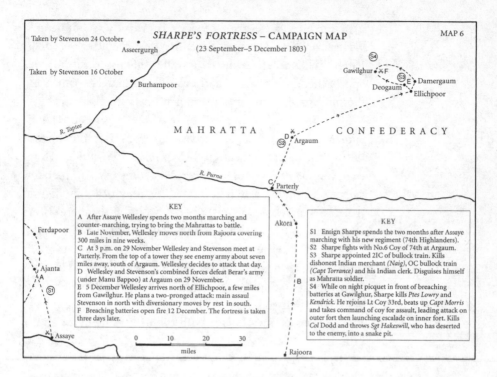

SHARPE'S FORTRESS – CAMPAIGN MAP

(23 September–5 December 1803)

MAP 6

Taken by Stevenson 24 October

Asseergurgh

Taken by Stevenson 16 October

Burhampoor

Gawilghur

Deogaum

Damergaum

Ellichpoor

R. Taptee

MAHRATTA   CONFEDERACY

Argaum

R. Purna

Parterly

KEY

A After Assaye Wellesley spends two months marching and counter-marching, trying to bring the Mahrattas to battle.
B Late November, Wellesley moves north from Rajoora covering 300 miles in nine weeks.
C At 3 p.m. on 29 November Wellesley and Stevenson meet at Parterly. From the top of a tower they see enemy army about seven miles away, south of Argaum. Wellesley decides to attack that day.
D Wellesley and Stevenson's combined forces defeat Berar's army (under Manu Bappoo) at Argaum on 29 November.
E 5 December Wellesley arrives north of Ellichpoor, a few miles from Gawilghur. He plans a two-pronged attack: main assaul Stevenson in north with diversionary moves by rest in south.
F Breaching batteries open fire 12 December. The fortress is taken three days later.

Ferdapoor

Akora

Ajanta

B

Assaye

0   10   20   30

miles

Rajoora

KEY

S1 Ensign Sharpe spends the two months after Assaye marching with his new regiment (74th Highlanders).
S2 Sharpe fights with No.6 Coy of 74th at Argaum.
S3 Sharpe appointed 2IC of bullock train. Kills dishonest Indian merchant (*Naig*), OC bullock train (*Capt Torrance*) and his Indian clerk. Disguises himself as Mahratta soldier.
S4 While on night picquet in front of breaching batteries at Gawilghur, Sharpe kills *Ptes Lowry* and *Kendrick*. He rejoins Lt Coy 33rd, beats up *Capt Morris* and takes command of coy for assault, leading attack on outer fort then launching escalade on inner fort. Kills *Col Dodd* and throws *Sgt Hakeswill*, who has deserted to the enemy, into a snake pit.

column (picquets, 2/12th, 1/10th Madras, 78th, 74th, 1/2nd, 1/ 3rd, and 1/4th Madras). His cavalry protected the eastern flank (MAP 7).

The second feature was that the flat plain was covered with growing millet and criss-crossed by narrow irrigation canals (in this respect the Argaum battlefield resembled Waterloo, which was covered for the most part in high-standing rye and wheat fields). The millet was exceptionally tall – up to nine feet. From the attackers' point of view, this posed potentially serious problems. The crop retained a furnace-like temperature, which made forcing a way through doubly ener-vating (one wonders how many men collapsed with heat exhaustion). Crossing these fields, the sweating infantryman could only tramp along blindly following the man in front, oblivious of what was happening a few yards away, and hav-ing not the remotest notion of where he was going – how familiar that situation is, even to modern infantrymen. Only

bed of sand. Scouts were sent forward to look for these dry rivers, and on the arrival of the army a great number of small wells were excavated the first thing. A few days afterwards the sand would blow into these holes, and after a short time no vestige of wells or excavations would remain.'

men on horseback had any idea of what was happening. Navigation thus became something of a nightmare. Fortunately the millet thinned as the enemy position was approached, so the army had basically to march north along the *nullah*, while mounted senior officers led the way.

Sharpe was with No. 6 Company of the 74th Foot (Highlanders) and thankful to be wearing trousers rather than a kilt as he progressed through the dense, scratchy millet. However, he was not a happy officer. His company commander, *Captain Urquhart*, barely tolerated his presence – he had no real duties anyway – and after two months his brother officers were still off-hand, unfriendly and obviously resentful towards the English ex-ranker who had been thrust into their midst. Life as a sergeant seemed far preferable. When his company paused for a while at the edge of the *nullah*, Sharpe wondered if his Gaelic-speaking comrades were discussing him. He felt as out of place with the men as he did with the officers.

Neither Scindia nor Berar was with the army awaiting Wellesley's advance. Command devolved on to Berar's younger brother, Manu Bappoo – a capable soldier who was grateful that these two militarily incompetent princes had failed to put in an appearance. He drew up his army immediately south of Argaum village, with fifteen regular infantry battalions in the centre, fronted by some forty cannons (MAP 7). The line was over three miles long; behind it was a somewhat disorganised mass of infantry as a reserve (which in the event was never engaged). On the right (western) wing was Scindia's cavalry, and on the left more irregular infantry, cavalry and artillery belonging to Berar's army. The whole stretched across the plain for well over five miles. Manu Bappoo's initial plan was for the centre to sit tight and pound the approaching enemy with cannon fire and then musketry, a combination expected to destroy any advance (it had almost worked at Assaye).

Wellesley's attack plan was simple almost to the point of

being foolhardy. His infantry columns were to wheel right about a mile from the enemy, march east for something over another mile, and then each unit would turn left so that the fifteen battalions would form a line in two ranks facing north. The guns would be interspersed between the battalions. On the flanks the cavalry would also form line. The result of this straightforward manoeuvre would be an extremely thin line of some 7,000 red-coated infantrymen strung out over three miles. Because the line was in two ranks there was a file for every 1.5 yards, or something over 2,300 men per mile. With much of the line hidden from enemy eyes by the millet, its fragile appearance would have encouraged Manu Bappoo to feel he had made the right decision to stand and fight.

Mahratta artillery

THE MAHRATTA ARMIES used an extraordinary mixture of cannons, ranging from the infantry regiments' light field pieces to virtually useless giants like the Great Gun of Agra – over 20 feet in length and theoretically capable of firing a 1,500-pound projectile. In his *Illustrated History of the British Empire in India*, E. H. Nolan writes that these cannons

> having the names of gods given to them, are painted in the most fantastic manner; and many of them, held in esteem for the services they are said to have already performed for the state, cannot now be dispensed with, although in every respect unfit for use. Were the guns even serviceable, the small supply of ammunition with which they are provided has always prevented the

Mahratta artillery from being formidable to their enemies.

The large guns had a long range but were too heavy to be moved. Any hit was due to luck rather than the gunners' skill. Major Blackiston, who was present at the Siege of Seringapatam, watched one of the huge cannons open fire:

> one of those enormous engines, called Malabar guns, was fired at our works. The man stationed on the flank of the battery, seeing the flash, gave the usual signal, 'Shot!' A moment or two afterwards, seeing a large body taking its curving course through the air he corrected himself by calling out 'Shell!' As the ponderous missile (for it was an enormous stone shot) approached, he could not tell what to make of it.

Mahratta artillery piece

Wellesley had no intention of making any flanking moves (the exhaustion of his troops, the shortage of time and the need to ensure a battle precluded this). With bayonets fixed, the seemingly endless line of infantry would walk steadily forward into the enemy gunfire and later musketry. Wellesley's own six-pounder guns would meanwhile advance with the infantry to halt about 500 yards from the enemy and fight a short artillery duel before the infantry assault went in – over a hundred years later infantry assault tactics had changed little. Wellesley relied on the sheer guts and staying power of his infantry to keep going. He had seen it succeed at Assaye and he counted on it again at Argaum.

As at Assaye, the British plan was almost scuppered at the outset when the leading elements came under long-range artillery fire before any line had been formed. This was remarkably good shooting from the Mahratta gunners. To open fire, even with heavy guns, at a range of over 2,000 yards, at such small, almost invisible columns would normally be considered a waste of ammunition. The distance, intervening trees, millet, slight undulations of ground would have made even the red-coated British infantry a poor target. That

SHARPE'S FORTRESS – THE BATTLE OF ARGAUM MAP 7
(29 November 1803)

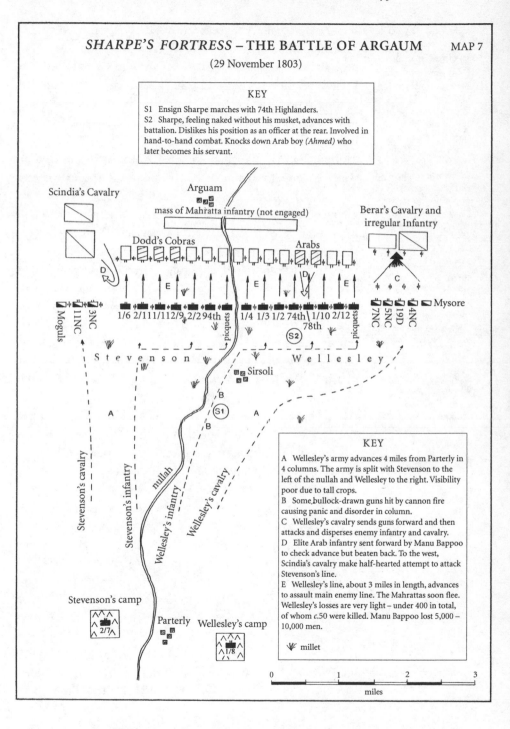

KEY

S1 Ensign Sharpe marches with 74th Highlanders.
S2 Sharpe, feeling naked without his musket, advances with battalion. Dislikes his position as an officer at the rear. Involved in hand-to-hand combat. Knocks down Arab boy (*Ahmed*) who later becomes his servant.

Scindia's Cavalry

Arguam

mass of Mahratta infantry (not engaged)

Berar's Cavalry and irregular Infantry

Dodd's Cobras

Arabs

D

E

E

D

E

C

Mysore

Moguls   1INC 3NC

1/6 2/111/112/9 2/2 94th   1/4 1/3 1/2 74th 1/10 2/12   7NC 5NC 19D 4NC
           picquets   78th   picquets

S2

S t e v e n s o n   W e l l e s l e y

Sirsoli

B

S1

A   A

Stevenson's cavalry

Stevenson's infantry

nullah

Wellesley's infantry

Wellesley's cavalry

KEY

A Wellesley's army advances 4 miles from Parterly in 4 columns. The army is split with Stevenson to the left of the nullah and Wellesley to the right. Visibility poor due to tall crops.
B Some bullock-drawn guns hit by cannon fire causing panic and disorder in column.
C Wellesley's cavalry sends guns forward and then attacks and disperses enemy infantry and cavalry.
D Elite Arab infantry sent forward by Manu Bappoo to check advance but beaten back. To the west, Scindia's cavalry make half-hearted attempt to attack Stevenson's line.
E Wellesley's line, about 3 miles in length, advances to assault main enemy line. The Mahrattas soon flee. Wellesley's losses are very light – under 400 in total, of whom *c.*50 were killed. Manu Bappoo lost 5,000 – 10,000 men.

𐑦 millet

Stevenson's camp

2/7

Parterly   Wellesley's camp

1/8

0   1   2   3

miles

REGULAR CAVALRY
IN INDIA

Until 1898 the 19th
Dragoons was the only
British cavalry
regiment in India.
Compared with
Indian horsemen they
were big men on big
horses whose charge
was to be feared – the
threat was frequently
sufficient to make the
opposition turn about.
They proved so
effective that the EIC
began to organise
regular Native cavalry
regiments, each with
three squadrons of two
troops. The standard
establishment was
nineteen Europeans
(two of whom were
senior NCOs) and 498
Natives. A troop would
have two or three
British officers, three
Indian officers, eight
Indian NCOs, one
trumpeter, one water-
carrier and seventy
troopers (privates).

the shots actually hit home must surely have been due to a combination of good gunnery and good luck, in equal proportions. A bullock-drawn six-pounder near the front of Wellesley's picquets was hit by an eighteen-pound cannonball at long range. The gun was destroyed but the bullocks survived. All ten of them turned and thundered back into the infantry behind. Another team followed, still pulling a cannon. For a while chaos reigned in the millet as soldiers scattered and the panic-stricken animals careered through the column. Some 250 sepoys in the leading battalion of picquets broke and rushed to the rear where they became intermingled with the battalions behind. Even Wellesley's personal intervention failed to stop the rot. He later wrote: 'the 1st of the 10th, and the 2nd of the 12th, and the native part of the picquets, broke and ran off, as soon as the cannonade had commenced although it was from a great distance, but not to be compared with that of Assaye.' Their own officers were able to rally them and they came forward again to participate in the attack. The next battalion in the column was the 78th Highlanders. Entirely unaffected by the panic ahead of them or the confusion and thrashing in the millet around them, the battalion marched steadily forward, pipes skirling, kilts swinging (unlike the 74th, they appear to have continued to wear kilts in India). A major setback was avoided. The only tangible result was delay.

Not until four-thirty in the afternoon was the line ready to move off. Wellesley had met with Stevenson (sick and ensconced in a *howdar* on the back of an elephant) at the village of Sirsoli. His orders had been for Stevenson and Wallace (in command of the infantry element of Wellesley's column) to advance steadily while he rode off to join the cavalry on the eastern flank. Apparently, Wellesley was concerned that with the death of Maxwell and the illness of his replacement, Lieutenant-Colonel Thomas Dallas, the cavalry lacked an experienced field officer. The senior officer on that flank was an EIC officer, Major Huddleston of the 7th Native Cavalry, who had only been promoted five months earlier.

The long line of red had about a mile to advance in the face of heavy enemy gun and then musket fire. To walk a mile at a brisk pace along a surfaced modern road takes about fifteen minutes, maybe a little more. To cover that distance across country, keep aligned with the hundreds of men to the left and right when most of them were invisible in the millet and, every hundred yards or so, negotiate a canal required a lot longer. No matter how well trained, no single company, let alone fifteen battalions, could keep their alignment in those circumstances. It was a drill sergeant's nightmare. The line edged forward, now bending, now breaking as mounted officers, looking left and right rather than at the enemy, strove to urge forward or check their men. Those British soldiers advancing at Argaum could not have expected to cross bayonets with their enemy for at least forty or fifty minutes. For all that time they were a target. Between each advancing battalion was a pair of light six-pounder cannons dragged by five pairs of white Mysore artillery bullocks. That they managed to keep up with the infantry over the drainage canals almost beggars belief.

While Stevenson's and Wallace's men struggled slowly forward, Wellesley was with the cavalry on the right. He advanced his horsemen in column until they were about 800 yards from the mass of Berar's irregular cavalry and infantry. There he deployed into line, halted and ordered the troopers to dismount. Next, the eight cavalry galloper guns were pushed forward another 200 yards or so. Their orders were to unlimber and open fire as soon as they were close enough to see clearly. As they carried out these instructions, Wellesley briefed his cavalry commanders. They were to wait until they saw the guns were having an effect, then charge – but not straight into one of the numerous canals! He then returned to the centre.

By this time the Mahratta artillery had been firing for well over an hour, mostly at a target that they could scarcely see through the smoke and tall grain. The gunners were exhausted, the guns were red hot, so the rate of firing had tailed

THE COST OF HORSES

When Wellesley offered to sell *Colonel McCandless* his spare horse for 400 guineas (*Sharpe's Triumph*) he was selling at a discount, although even at that price it represented almost a year's pay for the colonel. Quality European horses for use as officers' chargers fetched high prices because of their size and stamina. They represented a considerable investment and one that was worryingly at risk on operations. A trooper's horse, which had to be capable of carrying the trooper and his equipment, cost a fifth of the price of a charger at around £60. An ensign's gross salary was about £145 and a trooper's £36. In India, in addition to its rider, each horse usually required two servants to groom, water and feed it, and to collect forage.

off and its accuracy was much reduced. Although they could not know it, after the initial success the Mahratta cannons had done surprisingly little damage. There had been a lot of noise, a lot of smoke, but not a lot of casualties at the receiving end. When the British infantry got to within 500 yards of the enemy position, Wellesley ordered a halt. This was a pre-arranged signal that it was the turn of the gunners in the centre to go into action. The bullock teams wheeled round, the guns were unlimbered. When they opened fire at that range with cool guns and comparatively fresh gunners firing at three rounds a minute, the effect on the massed enemy was extremely unhealthy.

On the right the cavalry's cannons fired for around ten minutes into the crowded ranks ahead of them, firing an estimated 250 roundshot. Even if 50 per cent did no damage, the remainder would have ploughed through the stationary enemy horsemen, bowling over men and animals in disconcerting numbers. The 19th Light Dragoons, 4th, 5th and 7th Native Cavalry walked forward, picking their way with some care to avoid stumbling into the hidden ditches. As they came to within a hundred yards of the enemy horsemen, the nearest they dared get to charging was a brisk trot. Enough to give them some momentum which, combined with the support they had received from artillery fire and their disciplined formation, ensured a distinct advantage at the moment of impact. Sabres clashed with *tulwars* for a few brief moments, but before Wellesley's infantry in the centre had resumed their attack, the enemy cavalry in the east had melted away, dragging most of Berar's irregular infantry with them.

The high tide of battle was fast approaching. As the British again began to push through the thinning crops in the centre, Manu Bappoo signalled forward the two Arab battalions facing the two King's battalions of Highlanders (Sharpe's 74th and the 78th) in the centre of Wallace's line. Why only these units and not the whole line will never be known. He had by accident chosen to counter-attack two of the three best-trained and best-disciplined battalions in the entire force (the third being the 94th). The Arabs were his elite troops, eager for battle, fanatical in their fight for Allah (as many of their descendants were 200 years later fighting for the Taliban). Armed with sword, spear and buckler, well over a thousand warriors dashed forward, screaming their war cry *'Allah O Akbar!'*

Sharpe advanced with his company, feeling lost in his position as a supernumerary at the rear, and naked without a musket. When Manu Bappoo launched his Arabs in the attack on the 74th and 78th, Sharpe grabbed a musket and bayonet as his battalion halted but was ordered to his place in the rear of the company. Major Swinton yelled the orders, muskets were levelled and a volley crashed out. The Arabs kept coming, leaping over the crumpled bodies of their fallen comrades, still screaming, their huge drums thumping wildly. There was just time for the Highlanders to reload and commence platoon firing. At thirty paces every shot found a mark. Dozens of bodies fell. Swinton gesticulated frantically with his sword, dug in his spurs and darted forward. His shout went unheard, but his actions were unmistakable – the whole line levelled their bayonets and counter-charged. In the mêlée Sharpe wielded his clubbed musket with some effect, knocking unconscious an Arab boy (*Ahmed*) who later became his devoted follower. A few frenzied minutes of bayonet and butt against buckler and sword was enough to send the Arabs scrabbling back. Some soldiers fell, but not many. One of them was Lieutenant Langlands of the 74th, who was pinned to the ground by a spear through his thigh. He plucked it out and hurled it back.

Meanwhile on the flanks Stevenson's sepoy battalions had driven off a half-hearted attack by Scindia's horsemen, while Wellesley's regular cavalry on the right had scattered Berar's forces. When the British and sepoy infantry closed, the main Mahratta line collapsed to stream away northwards before heading east for sanctuary behind the mud walls of Gawilghur. At least 5,000 Mahrattas perished. Considering the circumstances of the action, Wellesley sustained miraculously

INDIAN SOLDIERS' DEVOTION TO GOOD EUROPEAN OFFICERS

Many European officers showed great kindness and affection for their sepoy soldiers, and often it was repaid in full. On one occasion a company with only one European officer had just finished a 23-mile march when the officer was badly mauled by a lion. Twelve sepoys volunteered to carry him to the nearest doctor, some 80 miles away. Leaving their uniforms, weapons and equipment with the company, they set off. The company, marching in stages, took over four days; the sepoys carrying their officer a mere nineteen hours. Taking it in turns to carry him, they kept up a continuous pace of over four miles an hour through the intense heat of the day. The officer's life was saved, but ten of the twelve sepoys were seriously ill. When they recovered, a special parade was held to thank them.

WELLINGTON'S
DESPATCHES

It was during his eight
years in India that
Wellesley began
writing detailed
despatches, covering
every conceivable topic,
military and civil, with
encyclopaedic
knowledge. He showed
deep concern for the
welfare of his troops,
for army finances,
appointments and
promotions,
intelligence-gathering,
equipment and
supplies – down to the
minutiae of feeding
bullocks. By 1832 his
correspondence
covered 15,000 pages.
Twelve volumes of
Wellington's Despatches
were published during
the Duke's lifetime by
Colonel Gurwood.
However, the Duke
had forbidden the
publication of
confidential letters and
had insisted on
Gurwood omitting the
names of individuals
whose competence is
questioned. The
resulting ' — appears to
be a kind of madman'
is frustrating for the
historian. The second
edition,
*Supplementary
Despatches*, published
1858–72 in fifteen
volumes by the second
Duke of Wellington, is
of much greater value as
it contains fewer
omissions, copious
notes and a well-
constructed index.

light losses. A total of 361 casualties were counted; of these
only 15 Europeans and 31 Indians died.

Sharpe emerged unscathed, but further depressed by
Colonel Wallace's suggestion that he might be more suited to
the new Experimental Corps of Riflemen forming in England.
Until that could be arranged Wallace told Major Swinton to
send him away from the battalion as second-in-command
of the baggage train. Its thoroughly competent commander,
Captain Mackay (killed at Assaye while disobeying instructions and charging with the cavalry), had been replaced by
an incompetent and corrupt *Captain Torrance* (assisted by
Sergeant Hakeswill) – a decidedly dangerous combination.

By 5 December Wellesley (with Stevenson) had marched forty
miles north-east to Ellichpoor, where he established a camp
and hospital. Thirteen miles to the north-west was the Mahrattas' final stronghold – the supposedly impregnable fortress
of Gawilghur (MAP 8). Wellesley rode forward to assess the
problem. He later commented that the great difficulty in
taking Gawilghur was not the attack itself so much as making
any approach at all. There were two options to be considered,
both involving the establishment of breaching batteries capable of knocking down a section of the walls.

The first was the southern approach following the 'road'
from Deogaum to Baury and then north-west to get into
positions to the south or west of the inner fort (although at
this stage it should be made clear that Wellesley had no
inkling that there were two forts to be taken). The difficulty
was that the ground was devoid of cover and the approaches
were narrow and steeply scarped, so much so that it was
doubtful whether guns could be sufficiently elevated to fire
with effect against the walls. Furthermore, the inner fort,
perched atop a precipitous hill, completely dominated the
area in which a besieging force and guns must assemble. Any
attempt to get guns into position south of the fortress would
entail a night approach, as artillery and troops along the
eastern, southern and western walls would have a clear shot

at anything that moved within two miles. Even supposing a breach could be made anywhere in the wall, how would the storming party climb the cliffs to get to it?

The alternative was to strike north from Damergaum, then generally westwards through the village of Mota to Lobada. Once there, the attackers would be on the same level as the outer fort, with only the walls to contend with – or so it was thought. The difficulty here was that the route was little more than a faint footpath along which a person or horse might climb rather than walk, but which was impassable to carts and bullock- or elephant-drawn guns. Nevertheless, Wellesley suspected that an assault from the north was the only way forward. Somehow he had to get the guns up there to Lobada. His thoughts were confirmed by the local killadar. Further reconnaissance revealed more details of the objective.

Gawilghur was both a fortress and a town with a substantial population (estimated to be at least 20,000). It sat on two hills, which in turn occupied the end of a narrow promontory that jutted southwards from a mass of high, rugged, jungle-covered hills. The rough track that ran north from Damergaum was nine miles long and climbed 2,000 feet through the hills. Many men – EIC engineers, pioneers and infantry working parties – would be needed to clear and improve the track in advance of the bullocks and elephants that hauled the cannons.

On 7 December Wellesley marched up to Deogaum to begin operations. Stevenson had drawn the short straw: his force had the task of getting the breaching battery guns through the hills to Lobada. But with Stevenson still far from fit, Wellesley had to resort to continuous hard riding in the scorching heat to supervise progress. On 9 December *Major Stokes*, Sharpe's old friend and boss from his armoury days at Seringapatam, was given the task of supervising the road and battery construction after the engineer in charge had been killed. By prodigious efforts of men and animals, by felling countless trees, digging out rocks and filling gullies with logs and soil, Stevenson reached Lobada in four days.

WELLESLEY'S USE OF FOOT MESSENGERS

Separated by hundreds of miles, Wellesley and Stevenson maintained communication by the use of messengers travelling on foot. These men, known as *dawks*, would keep running for enormous distances carrying a rattle in one hand to scare off wild beasts. They proved highly reliable – and would probably have made excellent modern marathon runners, covering five or six miles an hour.

SHARPE'S FORTRESS – THE APPROACH TO GAWILGHUR

(7–15 December 1803)

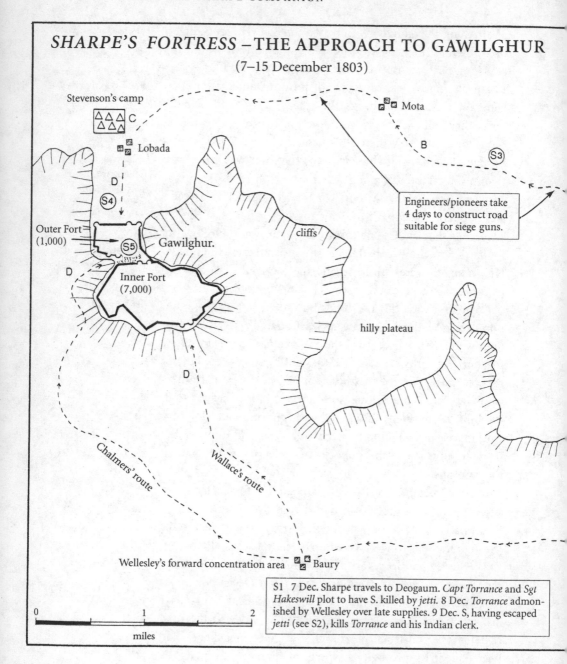

Stevenson's camp

C

Lobada

D

S4

Outer Fort
(1,000)

S5   Gawilghur.

Inner Fort
(7,000)

D

D

cliffs

hilly plateau

Mota

B

S3

Engineers/pioneers take
4 days to construct road
suitable for siege guns.

Chalmers' route

Wallace's route

Wellesley's forward concentration area   Baury

0   1   2

miles

S1   7 Dec. Sharpe travels to Deogaum. *Capt Torrance* and *Sgt
Hakeswill* plot to have S. killed by *jetti*. 8 Dec. *Torrance* admon-
ished by Wellesley over late supplies. 9 Dec. S, having escaped
jetti (see S2), kills *Torrance* and his Indian clerk.

MAP 8

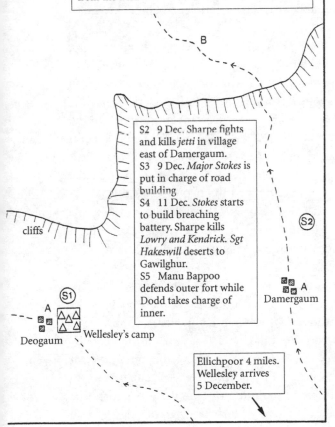

KEY

A 6 Dec. Damergaum and Deogaum secured.
7 Dec. Wellesley reaches Deogaum. 8–10 Dec. he
spends riding between Deogaum and the Lobada
area.
B Stevenson's besieging force took this route.
C Stevenson awaits siege guns at Lobada encampment. Siege battery construction begins 11 Dec.
D 15 Dec. Stevenson storms breach. Wallace makes
feint at southern gate while Chalmers approaches
from the west.

B

S2 9 Dec. Sharpe fights
and kills *jetti* in village
east of Damergaum.
S3 9 Dec. *Major Stokes* is
put in charge of road
building
S4 11 Dec. *Stokes* starts
to build breaching
battery. Sharpe kills
*Lowry and Kendrick. Sgt
Hakeswill* deserts to
Gawilghur.
S5 Manu Bappoo
defends outer fort while
Dodd takes charge of
inner.

cliffs

S2

S1

A

A
Damergaum

Deogaum Wellesley's camp

Ellichpoor 4 miles.
Wellesley arrives
5 December.

WELLESLEY'S HIGH
REGARD FOR THE
74TH

Wellesley was
immensely pleased
with the performance
of the 74th in India,
describing it as 'my
fighting regiment'. He
even went so far as to
reprieve one soldier
from a well-deserved
hanging – an act quite
out of character for a
firm disciplinarian –
explaining his leniency
thus: 'I think it very
desirable to avoid
punishing with death a
soldier belonging to
the 74th Regiment: and
therefore I propose to
offer the man to
commute his
punishment to
transportation for life
to Botany Bay. By this
means the
punishment of death
will be avoided, and
the 74th Regiment will
get rid of a bad soldier,
of which Colonel
Wallace is very
desirous.'

It was a magnificent achievement, to be followed on 11 December by a start on building emplacements for the breaching battery about 400 yards from the north wall of the outer fort. The garrison did nothing to interrupt or delay any of these activities. It was a serious error. Manu Bappoo probably appreciated that once the siege guns opened fire his walls would eventually crumble, but seemingly failed to realise that the only way to stop this was to prevent the guns getting to Lobada in the first place. A series of attacks and ambushes on the working parties in among the steep hills and forests might have achieved this. But, for whatever reason, the Mahratta commander remained indolent behind his mud-brick walls.

Sharpe, in the meantime, had been kidnapped after denouncing the theft of army supplies. Forced by his captors into combat with a *jetti*, he won the fight and went on to kill *Captain Torrance*, along with his Indian clerk. Following this, Sharpe spent the night of 11 December crawling around in the blackness in front of the siege battery emplacements looking to take revenge against *Sergeant Hakeswill* and his two underlings, *Lowry* and *Kendrick*, for their part in the abduction. He found and killed the two privates (by slitting their throats) but failed to find *Hakeswill*, who had deserted and sought refuge in Gawilghur, where he was given officer status and command of a company of Dodd's *Cobras*.

As MAP 9 makes clear, the capture of Gawilghur was a complicated affair. The inner and outer forts were separated by a deep ravine whose sides were, in many places, almost vertical. The southern part of the outer fort was not protected by a wall, the steepness of the ravine being thought sufficient defence. Across the ravine, however, a wall along the rim confronted attackers attempting to take the inner fort. The northern defences of the outer fort consisted of a double wall but no glacis. Having made a single wide breach in the outer wall, Stevenson's gunners would then have the task of making two more breaches in the inner wall. So steep was the slope

SHARPE'S FORTRESS – THE STORMING OF GAWILGHUR MAP 9
(15 December 1803)

Stevenson's camp

Lt-Col MacLean
reserve units

1/9M
1/6M
2/2M

Lobada

KEY

S1 12 Dec. breaching battery opens fire. Sharpe rejoins light company 33rd Foot for the assault.
S2 15 Dec. Sharpe enters breach with a few followers including *Sgt Lockhart* and *Pte Garrard*. They gain entry via right-hand inner breach.
S3 Sharpe (in reality Capt Campbell) spots a way to climb out of the ravine and, using a ladder, scale the wall. When *Capt Morris* rejects the idea, S. knocks him out and takes command 33rd lt coy. Armed with a claymore, he leads the escalade and attacks the gatehouse.
S4 Sharpe is wounded in chest and right cheek but kills *Col Dodd*. The four gates are unlocked, allowing attackers in.
S5 *Sgt Hakeswill* kills Beny Singh in his palace and steals his jewels but is confronted by Sharpe as he tries to flee. Sharpe forces him into snake pit and leaves him there.

enfilading batteries

2/1M
1/11M   Lt-Col Haliburton
2/7M

4 companies 94th Maj. Campbell
2/2, 1/6, 1/9 (3 flank companies)   Lt-Col Desse
Lt/94th, 94th, 95th (3 companies)
1/11M, 2/11M, 27M (flank companies)   Lt-Col Kenny
G/94th, 94th, 94th (3 companies)

breaching battery

A

S1

reservoir (tank)

Delhi Gate

double curtain wall

B   S2

water tanks

Outer Fort (garrison 1,000)

Southwest Gate

C   D Kenny   North Gate
Desse
deep ravine   S4

Chalmers   S3

Palace   S5

reservoir   snake pit
gardens

Inner Fort (garrison 7,000)

South Gate

KEY

A Stevenson's force (4,500) in three groups: Kenny's to storm breaches; Desse's to secure outer fort; Haliburton's to form tactical reserve.
B Breach taken. Delhi Gate outflanked. Outer fort taken.
C SW gate opened to allow fugitive garrison to escape. Most trapped and killed in ravine between Chalmers' force and their pursuers.
D Kenny and Desse line ravine. Kenny killed in vain assault on north gate. Capt Campbell (Sharpe) leads escalade on single ladder to outflank and open north gates. Inner fort falls.
E Wallace makes diversionary move towards south gate.

74th   diversionary battery

78th   E
Wallace

1/8M

Wellesley

0   1/4   1/2

mile

on which the walls were built that the bottom of the inner wall was (fortunately) visible to the besiegers. The final complication was that access to the breach was restricted by a large reservoir or water tank situated just north of the wall over which the breaching battery would fire. This effectively reduced the neck of land that could be used by the attackers to a mere 150 yards.

The normal garrison of Gawilghur consisted of 4,000 men under a Punjabi killadar called Beny Singh, but he had been joined by Manu Bappoo with a further 6–8,000 Mahrattas from Argaum (in *Sharpe's Fortress* the outer fort is commanded by Manu Bappoo, the inner by *Colonel* Dodd). Located around the walls were fifty pieces of artillery, some of truly monumental size. Jac Weller in his book *Wellington in India* describes seeing one in the 1960s, lying on the north side of the inner fort pointing northwards, too heavy to have been moved in 160 years. The wooden carriage had long since rotted away, but the wrought-iron barrel was twenty-two feet long, weighing an estimated eighty tons and in comparatively good condition. Surprisingly, the bore was only 12.5 inches across.

Although the plan was for Stevenson's force to breach and storm the walls in the north, Wellesley considered some diversionary effort was needed in the south despite the exposed and steep approach. On the night of 11 December an attempt was made to get the two remaining iron twelve-pounders forward. The ground was so precipitous that there was no possibility of dragging the guns on their carriages. The heavy nine-foot barrels, weighing over 4,000 pounds, had to be removed from the carriages and dragged, hauled and lifted by teams of sweating, cursing soldiers (even elephants could not negotiate some sections of the path) – and it all had to be done in the dark. For ten hours the struggle continued, with these burdensome monsters resisting every foot of progress while at the same time threatening to punish the slightest slip with crushed limbs. Just before dawn the task was adjudged impossible. The track was too steep, too uneven. The two offending barrels were dumped, covered with debris and abandoned. The following night, the twelfth, they tried again, but this time with two brass twelve-pounders and two 5.5-inch howitzers. These were eventually positioned within 500 yards of the South Gate.

The breaching battery opened fire on the outer wall of the outer fort on 12 December, the day Sharpe temporarily rejoined the light company of the 33rd to take part in the assault. The guns fired comparatively slowly, with a brief period between each shot to allow the barrels to cool slightly. If this was not done the intense heat of continuous firing, coupled with the blistering heat of the sun, could cause the cartridges to explode prematurely. With no earthen glacis to protect the base, every shot struck the wall directly and the old fortifications quickly began to crumble. Two enfilading batteries set back and to the east fired into the breaches at night to prevent repairs. At 10.30 a.m. on 15 December, after only three days of bombardment, the assault went in (MAP 9) – delayed by half an hour by killadar Beny Singh's fruitless attempt to negotiate over-generous surrender terms.

A total of around 4,000 men were grouped in columns behind the storming party – the kilted grenadiers of the 94th (Scotch Brigade) whose piper, lungs bursting with the effort, piped them forward. They were divided into three assault groups under lieutenant-colonels William Kenny (leading, to secure the breaches), Peter Desse (to capture the outer fort) and John Haliburton (follow up and reserve). Kenny had nine companies, just under 1,000 men. The grenadiers of the 94th were followed by two battalion companies of the same regiment supported by six flank companies from the 1/11th Madras, 2/11th Madras and 2/7th Madras. Desse led a further 1,000 made up of the remaining seven companies of the 94th under Major James Campbell and the flank companies of the 1/6th, 1/9th and 2/2nd Madras. Behind him was Haliburton with the battalion companies of the 1/11th, 2/11th and 2/7th Madras – around 2,000 men. Stevenson kept the battalion companies of three battalions (1/6th, 1/9th and 2/2nd

Madras) back near Lobada as a final reserve. The intention was to give the hard fighting to the 94th and the flank companies of the native EIC battalions.

Sharpe, who had joined the light company of his old regiment the 33rd Foot in the attacking column, was disgusted by the way its commander, *Captain Morris*, hung back. The reader should perhaps be reminded here that the 33rd Foot was not part of Wellesley's force at this time – all reference to it at Gawilghur is therefore fictitious. The light company that Sharpe would have joined was that of the 94th Highlanders, the leading company of Desse's column, formed up immediately behind Kenny's force.

The attackers swept forward without too much difficulty. A hail of canister from the breaching batteries flailed the breach from across the reservoir until the forlorn hope appeared below the breach. Resistance was fierce but brief. Kenny forced an entry with few losses. His men fanned out to secure the rest of the outer fort including the Delhi Gate – the main entrance at the north-eastern corner, which was soon opened. Sharpe and a handful of followers dashed ahead and into the breach. The defenders mostly fled to the south-west gate, which was opened to allow the fugitives out. Once outside, however, they were confronted by Chalmers and the left wing of the 78th Foot (Ross-Shire Buffs) who had climbed laboriously up from the plain below. Caught between their pursuers and this new, unexpected enemy, the fleeing soldiers were shot and bayoneted without mercy.

It was at this point that the attackers were confronted with the 'third wall' built virtually on top of the cliff-like northern rim of the ravine to protect the inner fort. Kenny and Desse led their men down into the ravine, spread them out and opened musket fire at the defenders who lined the walls above. The intention was to try to storm the North Gate. Kenny was to lead the way with the three companies of the 94th that had shortly before charged the breach. What was not understood was that entrance through the North Gate could only be achieved by smashing through four gates set behind one another and angled along a narrow passageway. Even with a cannon it would have been a dubious undertaking; without one it was suicidal. Kenny led the first attack personally and fell, mortally wounded, at the first gate. His followers were beaten back.

It is doubtful whether frontal attacks on the gates could ever have been successful. The passageway between them was angled in such a way that the inner gates were not visible from more than a few yards away. Even supposing cannons could be brought across (or up) the ravine in the first place when all approaches were swept by fire from the walls and gatehouse, their muzzles would have been almost touching the timber before they had a clear shot. Kenny would not have fully realised what he was up against when he attacked the first gate, but with hindsight the North Gate was almost certainly impregnable to direct assault. Fortunately, Sharpe (in reality a Captain Archibald Campbell of the light company, one of six commissioned Campbells in the 94th) had been carefully studying the climb up the cliffs to the base of the wall some 300 yards west of the North Gate through a telescope. He picked out a possible route and calculated that both hands would be needed for climbing, but at the top there was a sort of narrow ledge at the base of the wall, which was itself perhaps twelve feet high. If a ladder could be dragged up, an escalade seemed a possibility.

Captain Morris rejected the idea outright, so Sharpe knocked him unconscious, assumed command of his company and led a group of determined followers clutching a bamboo ladder down into the ravine. Slowly, they clawed their way up the other side, with frequent halts while the ladder was passed up. Amazingly, the escalade, led by Sharpe, clutching his sword, was not observed until too late. He scrambled up and over, jumped down and was quickly followed by others. The attackers turned east (left) to storm the North Gate from the inside.

The taking of the gatehouse involved a brutal battle at close quarters in which Sharpe was wounded three times (in

An escalade

THIS MEANT climbing walls with ladders. It was employed successfully by Wellesley at Ahmednuggur, Gawilghur and during the Peninsular War – the great sieges of Ciudad Rodrigo and Badajoz being famous examples. The principal advantage of the escalade was that it gave the attackers the possibility of surprise, because they could choose the section of wall at the last moment. There was no need for a lengthy bombardment that alerted defenders to the place where the main assault would come. Indeed, the escalade often succeeded where an assault on the breach failed. The garrison, having concentrated to repel the attackers at the breach, might be caught unawares by a sudden escalade at a remote part of the walls. Carrying out the escalade at night improved the chances of success.

But there were problems. An accurate estimate had to be made of the height of the wall (then two or three feet added, to allow for the ladder to lean at an angle). In 1812 at Badajoz the order was given that 30-foot ladders were required for the castle; twelve were taken but some were found to be 32 feet, others only 28. Six men were needed to carry each heavy, unwieldy ladder, and as they were conspicuous at the front of the assault they were likely to be among the first casualties. Trained defenders, once alerted, would aim their fire at the ladder-carrying parties. If a ladder was dropped, delays resulted while they picked it up, helped by soldiers who would have to stop firing and sling their muskets.

Climbing a ladder with someone dropping rocks on you, shooting at you, slashing with a sword, or trying to push the ladder over, was a thoroughly unpleasant experience. Both hands were needed to hang on, so a soldier had to sling his musket or let his sword hang from the wrist strap (some held their swords in their teeth). The knack lay in placing the ladder with the bottom as far from the base of the wall as possible and the top just below the battlements, then getting as many men on as would fit. This gave greater stability and the weight made it harder to push the ladder away from the wall. To reach the top, defenders would have to lean over, exposing themselves to fire from below – and their chances of being hit from short range were unhealthily high. A ladder that jutted up above the ramparts could be grasped by several defenders at once and pushed over with ease.

In a hand-to-hand fight at the top, the man on the wall had a distinct advantage over the man on the ladder. The latter had to rely on his comrades on the ground who would take aim at the top of the ladder and pick off any defender who popped into view. He was also vulnerable as he stuck his head above the wall, for a cunning defender might remain under cover until this opportunity arose to blow the enemy away. Once a man secured a foothold on the wall, however, he had simply to hold his ground until more men clambered up. If the escalade got this far, it was usually successful.

Peace (of sorts) with the Mahrattas

THE FALL OF Gawilghur convinced the
Mahratta leaders of the futility of further
resistance. By the close of 1803 Wellesley
had concluded treaties 'of perpetual
peace and friendship' with both Scindia
and the Raja, obtaining important con-
cessions to indemnify the EIC from the
costs of the war. Delhi, Agra, Broach and
Ahmednuggur, with territory yielding an
annual revenue of £3 million, passed into
British control.

The peace negotiations had their
amusing moments. Wellesley, in his
despatches, tells of an incident described
to him by Colonel John Malcolm:

Malcolm writes from Scindiah's
camp that at the first meeting Scindiah received him with great grav-

ity, which he had intended to pre-
serve throughout the visit. It rained
violently, and an officer of the
escort, Mr. Pepper, an Irishman, sat
under a flat part of the tent which
received a great part of the rain. At
length it burst through the tent
upon the head of Mr. Pepper, who
was concealed by the torrent that
fell, and was discovered after some
time by an 'Oh Jasus!' and a hideous
yell. Scindiah laughed violently, as
did all the others present; and the
gravity and dignity of the durbar
degenerated into a Malcolm riot –
after which they all departed on the
best of terms.

the hip, chest and right cheek – leaving a scar that was to
detract from his good looks for the rest of his life). His
opponents were Dodd and his *Cobras* (although there is no
evidence to show that Dodd fought at Gawilghur). Dodd
killed Sharpe's faithful Arab boy, *Ahmed*, before being shot
in the shoulder and then cut down by Sharpe (unlike Sharpe,
who preferred his straight cavalry sword, Campbell carried
a claymore). Shortly after this success, Sharpe encountered
Sergeant Hakeswill scurrying away with his loot. The confrontation resulted in *Hakeswill* being forced into a snake pit.

   The inner fort fell in the manner described above but with
credit for the escalade going to Captain Campbell rather than
Ensign Sharpe. While these attacks were being carried out
Wellesley had approached with the southern diversionary
column under Wallace. The two brass twelve-pounder

SHARPE MARCHES
WITH THE 74TH
In early 1804 Sharpe
participated with the
74th in operations
against the brigands or
'free-booters'. On
3 February Wellesley
was in camp with the
74th, two battalions of
native infantry and a
brigade of light
cavalry when he heard
that a large band of
brigands was on the
Deccan frontier. They
marched at once and
by noon the next day
had covered 40 miles.
On learning the
enemy was about 25

miles away, although his force had already marched 22 miles that morning, Wellesley set off the same evening. By noon the following day, after a dreadful night march over appalling roads, his troops had covered another 30 miles. The enemy was caught and defeated near a village called Munaskir. Wellesley's force had marched over 60 miles in less than thirty hours and then gone straight into action. He remarked, 'this was the greatest exertion I ever saw troops make in any country.' It was a feat neither Sharpe nor the 74th would ever equal.

THE 74TH LEAVES INDIA

Over 1,000 strong on its arrival in India sixteen years earlier, the 74th was a shadow of its former self with only 115 (most of them officers, NCOs and drummers) encamped on the beach to await transport home. Of the 60 wives and families who had accompanied the regiment to India in 1789, only two women and two children remained. Not all had died. Some women, having been widowed, had remarried into other regiments; others were sick or had remained to look after

cannons and the 5.5-inch howitzers that had been set up three days earlier, at the foot of the cliffs 500 yards from the wall, had opened fire. With maximum elevation of the cannons' barrels the shot could just hit the wall or the South Gate. However, damage inflicted was minimal. Indeed, some cannonballs are said to have bounced off and rolled back down the cliff towards the battery position. It did not matter, as the only purpose of this force was to represent a threat to keep some of the defenders away from the main action.

Once again Wellesley's casualties were extraordinarily light – 126. Mahratta losses, on the other hand, were severe. It is thought that at least half the 8,000 garrison perished, as no quarter was given; the rest would most likely have escaped by jumping, scrambling or tumbling down the cliffs. Manu Bappoo and the killadar Beny Singh died bravely, sword in hand, although not before the latter had poisoned his entire family (*Sharpe's Fortress* has the former shot by Dodd and the latter killed by *Hakeswill*).

Disappointingly, there was not much loot in Gawilghur, despite rumours to the contrary. Instead of jewels and gold and silver, several tons of copper coins valued at a mere 300,000 rupees were all that was found. Nevertheless, an abundance of military stores was seized, including 52 cannons, 150 half-pounder 'wall-pieces', matchlocks, even bows and arrows, along with 2,000 British Brown Bess muskets complete with belts, bayonets and cartridge boxes.

By January 1804 both Berar and Scindia had agreed peace terms. Treaties were signed. Wellesley in the south and General Lake to the north had both achieved dramatic successes. British prestige in India had never been higher.

In case the reader is reading this chapter before the novel, it may be of interest to include a quote from that part of Bernard Cornwell's historical note in which he describes the fort at Gawilghur as it is today:

> Gawilghur is still a mightily impressive fortress, sprawling over its vast headland high above the Deccan Plain. It is deserted

now, and was never again used as a stronghold after the storming on 15 December 1803. The fort was returned to the Mahrattas after they made peace with the British, and they never repaired the breaches, which are still there, and, though much overgrown, capable of being climbed. No such breaches remain in Europe, and it was instructive to discover just how steep they are, and how difficult to negotiate, even unencumbered by a musket or sword. The great iron gun which killed five of the attackers with a single shot still lies on its emplacement in the Inner Fort, though its carriage has long decayed and the barrel is disfigured with graffiti. Most of the buildings in the Inner Fort have vanished, or else are so overgrown as to be invisible. There is, alas, no snake pit there. The major gate houses are still intact, without their gates, and a visitor can only marvel at the suicidal bravery of the men who climbed from the ravine to enter the twisting deathtrap of the Inner Fort's northern gate.

A glance at Bernard's photographs in the picture section is recommended.

hospitalised husbands. As was usual, fit men had been given the option of transferring to other regiments (and claiming a bounty in the process) if they wished to stay in India. Thirteen officers embarked on the East Indiamen Lord Hawksbury and Baring, including Lt-Col Swinton and the QM, James Grant. Of the six who had fought at Assaye, one (Captain Moore) was disabled, three others were still suffering from their wounds. Sadly, three officers died on the voyage home, one of whom was Grant – perhaps Sharpe would have filled his post had he still been with the battalion.

They arrived in the Clyde in March 1806. The first monthly parade state issued at Dumbarton Castle showed an all-rank strength of 165 (including those still on passage home) out of an establishment of 1,035. One wonders how much leave those veteran NCOs received before marching all over the Highlands – recruiting. It would be four years before the regiment went on active service overseas again, to Portugal, under their old commander Wellesley (by then Lord Wellington).

Wellesley leaves India

BY EARLY 1805 Wellesley had had enough of India. Seven years there had taken its toll on his health – he suffered frequent spasms of lumbago, rheumatism and malaria. On 4 January 1805 he wrote: 'In regard to staying longer, the question is exactly whether the Court of Directors [of the EIC] or the King's Ministers have any claim upon me strong enough to induce me to anything so disagreeable to my feelings (leaving health out of the question) as to remain in this country.' Perhaps he recalled his friend William Hickey drawing his attention to a Dutchman's tombstone on which was inscribed the epitaph:

Mynheer Gludenstock lies
interred here,
Who intended to have gone home
last year.

Wellesley received numerous rewards and testimonials for his services to India. His Deccan officers presented him with a silver dinner service worth 2,000 guineas (now on display at his old London home, Apsley House). The British civilians of Calcutta gave him a £1,000 sword as a token of their gratitude. One of his most cherished testimonials was from the people of Seringapatam paying tribute to his time as military governor after the Tippoo's fall. Written in July 1804, when rumours of his departure reached the city's bazaars, it speaks volumes of his fairness, trustworthiness, efficiency and administrative ability in civil affairs:

We the native people of Seringapatam have reposed for five auspicious years under the shadow of your protection. May you long continue personally to dispense to us that full stream of security and happiness which we first received with wonder and continue to enjoy with gratitude; and, when greater affairs shall call you from us, may the God of all castes and all nations deign to hear with favour our humble and constant prayers for your health, your glory, and your happiness.

A more lighthearted but equally endearing memorial was the renaming of the jutting rock that towered above the village of Khandalla in the Western Ghats. Hitherto known locally as the 'Cobra's Head', it became the 'Duke's Nose'.

On 9 February 1805 Wellesley set out from Seringapatam following the same route he had marched six years earlier. He spent three weeks in Madras packing, preparing for the voyage and writing letters. The insignia of his Order of the Bath had arrived on an East Indiaman, the Lord Keith, where it remained for ten days until 'discovered by a passenger looking for his own baggage'. According to one story, Sir John Craddock, who had brought the insignia from England, pinned it on Wellesley's coat while he was sleeping.

6

Sharpe's Trafalgar*

After some six years in India Sharpe sails for England on the EIC merchantman *Calliope* to join the recently formed Experimental Corps of Riflemen, now expanded and renamed the 95th Rifles. Near the French island of Île de France (Mauritius) the captain of the *Calliope* gives the convoy the slip and deliberately surrenders his ship and valuable cargo to the French warship *Revenant*. Before reaching Île de France, however, the *Calliope* is recaptured by *HMS Pucelle*, commanded by Sharpe's friend *Captain Chase*. Sharpe transfers to *HMS Pucelle* along with *Lord William Hale* and his gorgeous young wife, *Lady Grace*, whom Sharpe has already bedded. *HMS Pucelle* sets off in pursuit of the *Revenant*, but before she can catch her both become embroiled in the Battle of Trafalgar. During the battle *HMS Pucelle* forms part of Nelson's column in his two-column attack on the Franco-Spanish fleet, and Sharpe is given command of some of the marines on board. *HMS Pucelle* breaks the enemy line between the Neptune and San Leandro, going on to assist Nelson's flagship, HMS Victory, in her bitter fight with the French Redoutable before clashing with the *Revenant*. In the course of the action Sharpe distinguishes himself leading a boarding party, wielding his cutlass with lethal effectiveness against at least five French seamen.

NAVAL COMMISSIONS

A commission in the navy could not be bought. All naval recruits in the early nineteenth century began their careers as ratings (ordinary crew members). Candidates for commissions had to pass an oral seamanship exam, and to have served six years at sea, two of which must have been served in the RN as a master's mate or midshipman. If a boy were well connected he would go to sea as an officer's servant and, under that officer's patronage, gain the sea time required. Less well-off boys would work their way up to petty officer (PO) rating and serve their time in the hope of qualifying for a commission. Men who had risen to the rank of mate in the merchant service could transfer into the navy as a PO. Merit was the main requirement for promotion.

* In this chapter British ships' names are prefaced with HMS as in HMS Victory; real French or Spanish ships have no preface e.g. the Redoutable; all fictional ships are in italics for example *HMS Pucelle* or *Revenant* (French).

BRITISH NAVAL
TOASTS

One wonders whether
Sharpe joined in the
traditional naval toasts
when he dined in the
captain's cabin on
HMS Pucelle.
Monday night: 'Our
  ships at sea.'
Tuesday night: 'Our
  men.'
Wednesday night:
  'Ourselves (as no
  one else is likely to
  concern themselves
  with our welfare).'
Thursday night: 'A
  bloody war or a
  sickly season.' Both
  helped promotion!
Friday night: 'A
  willing foe and sea
  room.'
Saturday night:
  'Sweethearts and
  wives – may they
  never meet.'
Sunday night: 'Absent
  friends.'

ON 21 OCTOBER 1805, Nelson, with twenty-seven line-of-battle ships, attacked the thirty-three ships of the combined French and Spanish fleets under the command of Vice-Admiral Villeneuve. The first British gun was fired at 12.20 p.m.; by 5 p.m. history's most famous sea battle was over, leaving the Franco-Spanish fleet virtually destroyed. By the conclusion of the subsequent engagement off Cape Finisterre on 4 November, thirteen French and eight Spanish ships had been lost – captured, sunk, blown up or wrecked in the storm that followed the Battle of Trafalgar. Although Britain did not lose a single ship, she paid a high price with the loss of her most famous commander, Lord Nelson. Whereas ships could always be replaced, an admiral of his genius seldom could. But the victory he secured off Cape Trafalgar marked the end of serious naval engagements in the Napoleonic Wars and left Britain in undisputed control of the world's waterways until the Second World War. This naval supremacy not only guaranteed her security from attack, it gave her worldwide trade, it gave her political, strategic, commercial and military power – it gave her the largest empire the world had ever known. All this was the legacy of Trafalgar.

Nevertheless, in terms of the situation in October 1805, the value of Nelson's stunning victory was not immediately apparent. A month previously, Napoleon had pulled the bulk of his troops out of Boulogne for the march against Austria. While Sharpe sailed round the Cape of Good Hope on *HMS Pucelle,* indulging himself to the full in his furtive affair with *Lady Grace Hale,* Napoleon had crossed the Rhine, then the Danube and, with masterly strategic skill, surrounded the Austrian Army at the Ulm. On the very day that Nelson crushed the French and Spanish fleet at Trafalgar, Napoleon had stood, singeing his coattails in front of a vast bonfire, as 27,000 Austrians filed past him in surrender. Within three weeks he had entered Vienna; two weeks later he crushed the combined armies of Austria and Russia at Austerlitz. It was a remarkable end to a 500-mile march by almost 200,000 men who had kept up an average of twelve to fifteen miles a day for five weeks – probably the fastest sustained march of comparable length by an army since the days of Ghenghis Khan.

The same troops who defeated Prussia, marched through the streets of Vienna and Berlin, and fought their way to Moscow had originally been destined for Britain. From mid-1803 the Napoleonic Wars had revolved around the Emperor's plans for the invasion of England. Boulogne was chosen as the main base for the invading army and a vast camp of 150,000 troops took shape along the coast on either side of the port, while specially constructed flat-bottomed boats for their transport were brought from all over France. The troops were given constant practice in embarkation and disembarkation. Napoleon calculated that once across the Channel he would reach London in four days, issue decrees abolishing the House of Lords, redistributing property and declaring England a republic. But to fulfil these dreams he needed to get this massive fleet of transports across the forty miles of sea unmolested. For this he needed control of the Channel, which in turn required the absence of the British fleet – and not for long; with careful planning and reasonable weather (always unpredictable) as little as eight hours might suffice. (Napoleon exaggerated somewhat when he exclaimed, 'Let us be masters of the Straits for six hours, and we shall be masters of the world.') Had the invasion forces secured a foothold in Kent there must be serious doubt whether the loss of London and then the country could have been prevented. The history of the world would have been very different if Napoleon had succeeded in crossing the Channel. There were, however, difficulties.

THE REAL ENEMY
During the Seven Years War (1756–63) the Royal Navy lost 1,512 men killed in battle, but 133,700 to disease and desertion. By the Napoleonic Wars, which lasted some 22 years, things had improved. During the ten major naval actions of the period, 1,875 men were killed in action, 72,000 died from diseases and another 13,000 from the weather or on-board accidents. Whilst in the West Indies (a notoriously unhealthy station), HMS Hannibal lost over 200 men to yellow fever – nearly four times the number killed on any British ship at Trafalgar. Six years prior to Trafalgar, of the 646 ships in the Royal Navy only 400 carried a surgeon, who was paid about £5 a month plus 2d per month per man embarked in his ship. Not surprisingly the larger ships were popular with medical men, while smaller ones, particularly those on overseas stations that really needed them, often went without.

'WATCHES'

At sea all warships kept two watches, starboard and larboard, with seamen, landsmen and petty officers on all parts of the ship divided between the two. One complete watch was on duty at all times, day or night, under the command of a watch-keeping officer (usually a lieutenant or the master on a large warship). Each watch lasted four hours, except for two 'dog watches' of two hours between four and eight in the evening. With an uneven number of watches in a day, times of duty varied. Each four-hour watch was divided into eight periods of half an hour, the sounding of the ship's bell indicating the passage of time. At the end of the first half-hour the bell was rung once, after the second twice and so on until at eight bells the watch changed. The half-hours were measured by a sand-filled glass that was turned by a petty officer known, on large warships, as the 'quartermaster of the glass'. The system did not allow seamen to get more than four hours' sleep at a time. No lights were allowed below decks at night for fear of fire. On

The acres of small transports could not all get out of the harbours in which they were assembled on a single tide. One half of the army would have to lie tossing (and crippled by seasickness) outside these ports for hours, waiting for the other half to get afloat. Then there was a forty-mile stretch of water to cross. If even a dozen British ships of the line were to get in amongst these helpless craft, the result would be slaughter. The obvious solution was for the French Navy to secure the Channel for those crucial eight hours. But this could not be achieved while the French fleet was scattered with warships stationed in widely separated ports such as Brest, Rochefort, L'Orient and Toulon, all of them prevented from sailing by British blockading squadrons.

When Spain entered the war at the end of 1804 Napoleon was able to add to his fleet the Spanish squadrons at Corunna, Ferrol, Cadiz and Cartagena – but these too were blockaded by the British. For two years Napoleon tried to find a strategy that would set his ships free so they could converge on the Channel. British policy was to maintain an endless, sleepless watch to keep those squadrons scattered and bottled up.

The latter half of 1803 had been a year of great excitement for Sharpe. He had fought under Wellesley in August at Ahmednuggur, in September at Assaye, in November at Argaum and, just before Christmas, at Gawilghur. For Nelson, 1803 marked the start of a seemingly endless period of disappointment, exasperation and boredom. It would be two and a half years before his ships would open fire on an enemy. He was destined to spend most of this time battling the fierce north-westerlies of the Gulf of Lyons while blockading Toulon. From May 1803 to August 1805 he left his ship only three times, and for less than an hour on each occasion. Admiral Cornwallis was positioned off Brest for three years without respite.

The hardships of the blockade were raw and unremitting. Week after week, month after month the men of the Royal Navy fought a battle against grinding weariness, foul food, bone-chilling winds and the threat of sickness or injury, superimposed on the numbing monotony of every day and night at sea. Collingwood, Nelson's second-in-command at Trafalgar, once spent twenty-two months at sea without even dropping anchor. On one occasion he wrote to his wife that he had 'not seen a leaf on a tree for fourteen months'. In seventeen years of sea-service (1793–1810) he was only in England for twelve months. But these conditions produced the toughest and most professional navy the world has ever seen. Britain won her naval battles not because she had more ships, or better ships, or heavier guns, but because she had

most ships the master-at-arms and his corporals had to inspect all the decks at midnight to ensure compliance with this standing order. In an emergency all hands (both watches) were required on deck.

The convoy system

WHEN ROYAL NAVY WARSHIPS escorted convoys of merchantmen across the Atlantic or to Murmansk during World War II they were employing a system that had been in operation for over two hundred years. As an island nation, Britain's survival depended on her merchant fleet (around 16,000 ships in 1790) trading all over the world. During the Napoleonic Wars escort duties were usually performed by 4th or 5th or unrated ships (frigates, brigs or sloops) and a surprisingly small number were involved. In 1808 only 15 frigates were permanently assigned to escorting convoys; where possible, larger rated ships that needed to change station were used instead.

As Sharpe discovered in Bombay, merchant ships had to assemble by a specified date of sailing. If they missed a convoy there could be a long wait for the next. Convoys were organised in accordance with the Admiralty's signal book. Merchant captains would apply to the escort commander's ship for a copy of instructions setting out how the convoy would be run and including vital signals such as, 'Alter course to larboard one point', 'Ships astern to make more sail' or 'Convoy to move closer together'. At night or in fog, signalling would employ lights, flares or guns. A large convoy of over one hundred ships would often be formed in a rectangle of equal columns with the men-o'-war escorts ahead and to windward, and possibly several sloops between columns. The convoy's speed was dictated by the slowest ship – frustrating merchants for whom time was money.

The system was usually successful, though there were disasters (one of the worst being the loss of 48 ships out of 200 off the Naze of Norway in 1810). It is estimated that only 0.6 per cent of ships travelling in convoy were lost, as against 6.8 per cent of stragglers.

GROG

As part of his daily ration, a seaman was entitled to either a pint of wine or half-pint of rum. In 1740 the commander in the Caribbean, Admiral Vernon – known as 'Old Grogram' because he wore a coat made of grogram, a coarse material stiffened with gum – decreed that the men's rum be mixed with water. The amount of water added varied at the discretion of the captain and depended on the climate and the availability of fresh water. The mixing took place in the presence of a master's mate, who also supervised its issue to the men twice a day. Because of the fire risk – a cask of rum once caught fire on HMS Glasgow as it was being issued in the hold – it was drawn from a cask on the open deck.

vastly superior seamen. As one officer of the time said, 'I have seen Spanish line-of-battle ships twenty-four hours unmooring; as many minutes are sufficient for a well-manned British ship to perform the same operation.' These seamen and their iron blockades thwarted Napoleon's plans, changing the fate of the world in much the same way that British airmen did in 1940, when once again the Channel was Britain's moat against invasion. (Now we have the tunnel and, at the time of writing, hordes of illegal immigrants.)

Napoleon's strategy depended on his ships evading the blockading squadrons, thus forcing them to scatter to various parts of the world in search of his missing fleet. His ships would then converge at a pre-arranged rendezvous and set sail for the Channel to protect the invasion flotillas. After several abortive attempts to put this plan into operation during 1804 and early 1805, Villeneuve used a gale to elude Nelson off Toulon and sail for the West Indies. Nelson, being for once badly served by his frigates whose duty it was to tread on the heels of the French and report their direction, sailed first towards Egypt. When he realised his error he then had to claw his way back through the Straits of Gibraltar in the teeth of strong westerly gales: 'I cannot get a fair wind or even a side wind. Dead foul! Dead foul!' It was to take him twenty-six days to cross the Atlantic, travelling the 4,000 miles at an average speed of around five or six knots. On 4 June 1805, after exchanging salutes with the guns of Fort Charles, he dropped anchor in Carlisle Bay, Barbados. A little later the cannons crashed out again with a twenty-one-gun salute for the King's birthday. Grog was served. But where were the French?

Yet more false information led Nelson south towards Trinidad instead of north to Martinique. Having departed Barbados on 5 June, he approached Trinidad on the eighth with the marine drummers beating to quarters ready for action. It was a huge disappointment for every man on every ship to find the bay at Port of Spain empty. Nelson was beside himself with frustration. He took his fleet north to

Antigua only to find that Villeneuve had vanished yet again, heading eastwards – back to Europe.

Villeneuve arrived at the French island of Martinique on 14 May 1805, the voyage having taken thirty-five days. Of the other squadrons that were supposed to join him only two ships arrived; the rest had been unable to escape the British blockades. While waiting he achieved nothing, apart from taking HMS Diamond Rock – a tiny islet at the entrance to Fort Royal (Martinique). General Reille, who was to fight at Waterloo almost exactly ten years later, commented: 'We have been masters of the sea for three weeks with a landing force of 7–8,000 men and have not been able to attack a single island.' On hearing that Nelson was on his heels Villeneuve sailed, in considerable haste, intending, in accordance with his orders, to pick up the other squadrons and appear in the Channel in overwhelming strength to escort *l'Armée d'Angleterre* across to England. The Admiralty sent Sir Robert Calder with fifteen ships of the line to intercept Villeneuve. Following an indecisive action off Cape Finisterre on 22 July (for which Calder was later to be court-martialled), Villeneuve was deflected to Vigo Bay and then Ferrol.

The flag signalling Calder's court martial was hoisted on HMS Prince of Wales two days before Christmas 1805. The relevant part of the charge sheet read out to the accused and the five admirals and seven captains of the court stated that

THE SLUSH FUND

Yet another modern expression with naval origins. Today a slush fund finances corrupt dealings or bribes. In Nelson's day, one of the perks of the ship's cook was to sell 'slush' – the fat that rose to the surface when he boiled meat in the ship's copper. The cook would skim it off and sell it to the purser for making into candles or to use as a water-resistant coating on masts, spars or rigging.

British Naval Captain 1805

Vice-Admiral Calder had 'not done his utmost to renew the said engagement, and to take or destroy every ship of the enemy, which it was his duty to engage accordingly'. In what today would probably be an infringement of human rights, the court sat throughout the Christmas holiday. On 26 December Calder was adjudged guilty as charged, though the court ruled that as his conduct had not been 'actuated by cowardice or disaffection, but has arisen solely from an error of judgement' a severe reprimand would suffice. It marked the end of his active career, although many naval officers thought he had been harshly treated.

Villeneuve, meanwhile, had set sail from Ferrol on 13 August with twenty-nine ships. He should have been heading for Brest and then into the Channel where Napoleon was watching eagerly for the white topsails of his fleet to appear. However, faced with a choice between confronting Cornwallis (who was guarding Brest) or Collingwood's tiny squadron at Cadiz, Villeneuve's nerve failed him. Declining to face Cornwallis, he swung south instead for Cadiz. Napoleon gave way to a tempestuous tirade when his fleet failed to appear off Boulogne. His secretary has described how he paced up and down with agitated steps. With a voice that shook, and in half-strangled exclamations, he cried, 'What a navy! What sacrifices for nothing! What an admiral! All hope is gone! That Villeneuve, instead of entering the Channel, has taken refuge in Ferrol [he had not yet heard of his admiral's flight even further south to Cadiz]. It is all over. He will be blockaded there.' Almost immediately he abandoned his invasion plans and began dictating the orders to send his army into Austria. The Trafalgar campaign was over though the battle had yet to be fought.

Sharpe was still on the high seas in pursuit of the French ship of the line, *Revenant* (*see* MAP 10), when Wellesley arrived home from India after a somewhat less adventurous voyage than Sharpe's. Soon after his return, on 12 September, Wellesley had his one and only meeting with Nelson, who

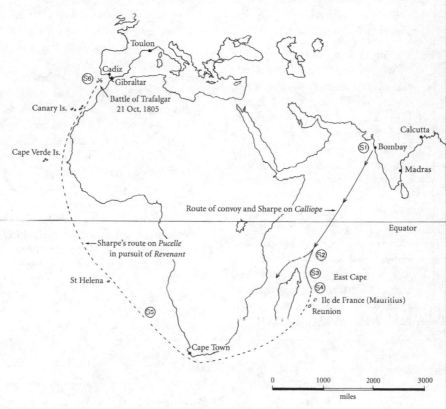

MAP 10

SHARPE'S TRAFALGAR–CAMPAIGN MAP

(End June–20 October 1805)

Toulon

Cadiz
(S6) Gibraltar
Battle of Trafalgar
21 Oct. 1805

Canary Is.

Calcutta

(S1) Bombay

Cape Verde Is.

Madras

Route of convoy and Sharpe on *Calliope* →

Equator

←Sharpe's route on *Pucelle*
in pursuit of *Revenant*

(S2)

(S3) East Cape

St Helena

(S4)

Ile de France (Mauritius)
Reunion

(S5)

Cape Town

| 0 | 1000 | 2000 | 3000 |

miles

KEY

S1 28 June Sharpe sails from Bombay on merchantman *Calliope* after six years in India. Bound for England to join 95th Rifles.
S2 15 July *Calliope* abandons convoy during night.
S3 20 July *Calliope* surrenders to French warship *Revenant*.
S4 20–25 July *Calliope* heads for Mauritius with Sharpe on board. *Revenant* sails for Cadiz. 25 July HMS *Pucelle* recaptures *Calliope*, which is ordered to England via Cape Town. Sharpe transfers to *Pucelle* and sails in pursuit of *Revenant*.
S5 7 Sept. *Revenant* sighted. Sharpe kills *Braithwaite* by breaking his neck. *Pucelle* unable to catch *Revenant*.
S6 20 Oct. *Pucelle* joins Nelson's fleet while *Revenant* joins Franco-Spanish fleet. Next day the two ships clash during Battle of Trafalgar.

Wellesley (Wellington) meets Nelson

THESE TWO great leaders met briefly around 12 September 1805. Initially Nelson did not impress Wellesley, as is apparent from his account:

I went to the Colonial Office in Downing Street, and there I was shown into the little waiting room on the right side, where I found, also waiting to see the Secretary of State, a gentleman, whom, from his likeness to his pictures and the loss of an arm, I immediately recognised as Lord Nelson. He could not know who I was, but he entered at once into conversation with me, if I can call it conversation, for it was almost all on his side and all about himself, and in reality in a style so vain and so silly as to surprise and almost disgust me. I suppose something that I happened to say may have made him guess that I was *somebody* and he went out of the room for a moment, I have no doubt to ask the office-keeper who I was, for when he came back he was altogether a different man, both in manner and matter. All that I thought a charlatan style had vanished, and he talked of the state of this country ... in fact he talked like an officer and a statesman. The Secretary of State kept us long waiting, and certainly, for at least half or three-quarters of an hour, and I don't know that I ever had a conversation that interested me more. Now, if the Secretary of State had been punctual and admitted Lord Nelson in the first quarter of an hour, I should have had the same impression of a light and trivial character that other people have had.

had been enjoying a four-week break with his beloved Emma and their young daughter Horatia. The meeting came about by accident, as both commanders had been summoned to appointments with cabinet ministers in the Colonial Office. They spent a few minutes in conversation in the waiting room before being called in to see their respective ministers. Two days later, Nelson walked down the beach at Southsea to his waiting barge, cheered by a large crowd of well-wishers. That afternoon HMS Victory sailed. Nelson was never to see his beloved country or Emma again. By 28 September he had taken over command from Vice-Admiral Collingwood. After peering through his telescope at the mass of masts in the harbour he wrote in his diary: 'Nearly calm ... Saw the

Royal Navy officers

JUNIOR OFFICERS were lieutenants (the equivalent of an army captain) of varying degrees of seniority. They could either serve on a rated ship or command a small, unrated vessel. On a large 1st- or 2nd-rated warship there was a complement of six lieutenants numbered from 1st to 6th in seniority (although at Trafalgar HMS Victory had nine). The first lieutenant was second-in-command to the captain (e.g. *Lieutenant Haskell* on *HMS Pucelle*); after a major victory such as Trafalgar he could expect immediate promotion to commander – in which case he would take charge of a large sloop with a lieutenant as his number two – or, exceptionally, post captain. Lieutenants were the only officers to receive the same pay (£8 8s per month in 1807) no matter the rate of the ship on which they served.

The lowest senior officer rank was post captain, in command of a ship of the 6th rate (small frigate) or above. At Trafalgar, Captain Blackwood commanded the 5th-rate 36-gun frigate HMS Euryalus, *Captain Chase* the 3rd-rate 74-gun *HMS Pucelle* and Captain Hardy HMS Victory (1st rate). For his first three years a post captain was equal to an army lieutenant-colonel, after that to a colonel – and he got to wear two gold epaulettes instead of one. Seniority, dating from commission as a captain, determined subsequent promotion, but pay depended on his ship's rating: in 1807 monthly pay for a 1st rate was £32 4s, a 3rd rate £23 2s, and 5th rate £16 16s. Thus Hardy, though three years junior to Blackwood, received almost twice the pay for commanding Victory.

Senior captains were in line for promotion to 'flag rank' (so called because admirals were allowed to fly their own flag). In 1805 there were three flag ranks – rear-admiral, vice-admiral and admiral – each divided into three squadrons to form nine grades of admiral. The squadrons were blue (the most junior), white and red (senior). Grades could be jumped, but in theory a rear-admiral of the blue had to serve as rear-admiral white and then red before promotion to vice-admiral blue, and so on – an extremely cumbersome system. Nelson was a vice-admiral of the white at Trafalgar; Collingwood, his second-in-command, vice-admiral of the blue.

enemy's fleet in Cadiz, amounting to 35 or 36 sail of the line.' He had finally caught up with Villeneuve. He was just over three weeks away from death and a naval victory that has outshone all others, before or since.

Villeneuve had received orders on 27 September to sail for Naples to support a landing of 4,000 troops there, but it was not until 19 October brought the combination of a fair wind

Warship rates

RATING WAS a method of classifying a ship's size based on the number of gun ports (though if carronades were carried on higher decks the actual number of guns could exceed gun ports). Of the six rates, the first four were ships of the line (battleships) with two or three gun decks, with frigates rated 5th and 6th. Smaller vessels such as brigs, sloops or cutters were unrated. Generally, the larger the ship the higher the rate, the more senior its captain, the more guns, crew and marines it carried. *Captain Chase*'s ship *HMS Pucelle* was a 74-gun, two-decker, 3rd-rate ship of the line. Her complement would have been a captain, 6 lieutenants, captain RM, 3 lieutenants RM, master, surgeon, carpenter, boatswain, gunner, purser, 3 master's mates, 16 midshipmen and 640 crew. Official complements at Trafalgar were:

Rate	Guns	Seamen
1st	100+	837 (Victory had 820 and 102 guns + 2 carronades)
2nd	90–98	738 (e.g. 98-gun Neptune)
3rd	64–80	491–738 (e.g. 74-gun *Pucelle*)
4th	50–60	343 (e.g. 64-gun Africa)
5th	32–46	215–294 (e.g. 36-gun frigate Euryalus)
6th	14–30	185–195 (small frigates, none at Trafalgar)
unrated	4–12	18–121 (e.g. cutter Entreprenante 8 carronades, the schooner Pickle 10 carronades)

and news that the admiral sent to replace him was on his way that he ordered his fleet to put to sea. Only seven ships of the line had cleared the harbour by the time the wind dropped. Getting the remaining ships to sea was a tediously slow business with little wind, confused orders and sailors who had spent many idle weeks in port. Nelson's main fleet of twenty-seven ships of the line was some fifty miles away over the horizon, waiting, watching and praying that their enemy would come out. A line of frigates from Cadiz to the fleet ensured Nelson received timely information on every move Villeneuve made. It was HMS Sirius, the closest frigate

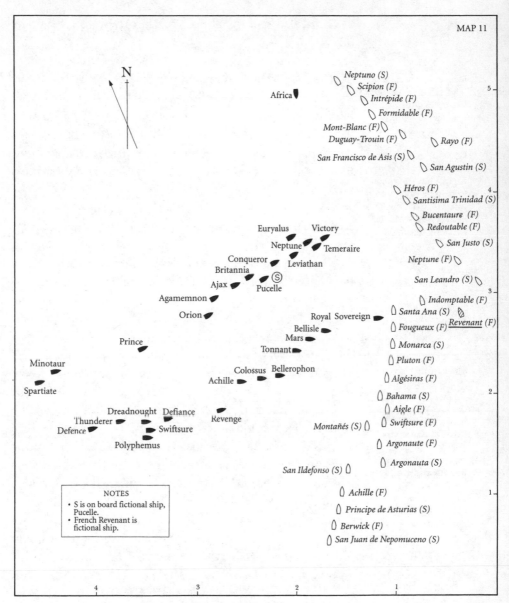

MAP 11

N

Neptuno (S)
Scipion (F)
Intrépide (F)
Africa
Formidable (F)
5

Mont-Blanc (F)
Duguay-Trouin (F)
Rayo (F)
San Francisco de Asis (S)
San Agustin (S)

Héros (F)
Santisima Trinidad (S)
4

Bucentaure (F)
Redoutable (F)

Euryalus   Victory
Neptune   Temeraire
San Justo (S)
Conqueror   Leviathan
Britannia
Neptune (F)
Ajax   (S)
Pucelle
San Leandro (S)
Agamemnon
3
Indomptable (F)
Orion
Royal Sovereign
Santa Ana (S)
Fougueux (F) Revenant (F)
Bellisle
Mars
Monarca (S)
Prince
Tonnant
Pluton (F)
Algésiras (F)
Minotaur
Colossus Bellerophon
Bahama (S)
2
Achille
Aigle (F)
Spartiate
Dreadnought Defiance
Montañés (S)
Swiftsure (F)
Thunderer   Revenge
Defence   Swiftsure
Argonaute (F)
Polyphemus
Argonauta (S)

San Ildefonso (S)

Achille (F)
1
Principe de Asturias (S)

Berwick (F)
San Juan de Nepomuceno (S)

NOTES
• S is on board fictional ship,
Pucelle.
• French Revenant is
fictional ship.

4   3   2   1

TRAFALGAR – THE APPROACH TO BATTLE

(Around noon, 21 October 1805)

THE CAT-O'-NINE-
TAILS

The 'cat' has given us three everyday sayings. 'A cat has nine lives' refers to the nine lengths of cord that made up the lash. To 'let the cat out of the bag' refers to the lash being taken from the red bag in which it was kept. While 'no room to swing a cat' derives from floggings taking place on deck as there was insufficient head room below. Regulations imposed a maximum of 12 lashes, but this was regularly exceeded (though punishment was still less severe than in the army where sentences of 500 lashes were common). The cords were about 18 inches long and worked into a handle of rope. Because it was impossible to lock up personal possessions, theft from a shipmate was considered such a heinous crime that a special 'thieves' cat' with three knots on each lash was used to punish offenders.

to Cadiz, that sent signal no. 370: 'Enemy ships are coming out of port.'

On 20 October Villeneuve succeeded in getting his entire fleet out of port and sailing, on a very light breeze, south-east towards the Straits of Gibraltar. During the day, as the British fleet moved slowly to intercept the enemy, *HMS Pucelle* with Sharpe on board joined the fleet and was instructed to merge with Nelson's windward column. Accordingly, *Captain Chase* took station between HMS Conqueror and HMS Britannia (MAP 11).

Nelson's intention was to attack the enemy line in two columns (or, more accurately, groups). He would lead the weather (windward) column of thirteen ships while Collingwood commanded the lee (leeward) column about a mile to the south. The plan was to cut off the enemy rear and destroy any ships caught between the columns before those in the van could turn and join the battle. Nelson had the advantage of the weather gauge – i.e., the enemy was downwind of him – a position generally favoured by the more aggressive British admirals because it gave the holder the initiative over when, where and whether to attack, and once firing started the smoke quickly cleared, blown towards the enemy. French commanders, on the other hand, viewed the weather gauge as a risky proposition because if a stiff breeze came up the ships might heel over with their lower gun ports submerged and unusable. Furthermore, at close range, the heel tended to tip the deck in the enemy's direction, exposing those on the upper decks to musket shots. And should retreat prove necessary, it was no simple matter for a vessel to turn and retire against the wind, whereas the lee gauge offered undamaged ships the chance of a quick escape. These considerations notwithstanding, Nelson was glad of the weather gauge at Trafalgar.

The two sides' strategy in the battle that followed was a reversal of tactics on land, where it was invariably the French who attacked in column against a thin line of British troops. Usually such attacks ended in victory for the line, whose

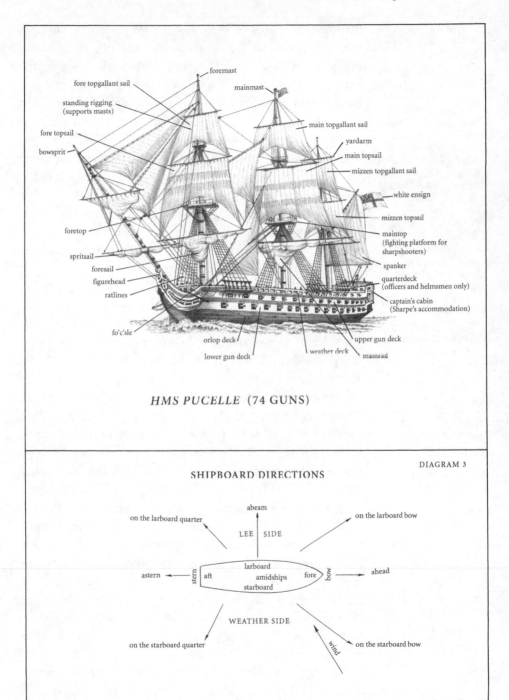

fore topgallant sail

foremast

standing rigging
(supports masts)

mainmast

fore topsail

main topgallant sail

bowsprit

yardarm

main topsail

mizzen topgallant sail

white ensign

mizzen topsail

foretop

maintop
(fighting platform for
sharpshooters)

spritsail

spanker

foresail

quarterdeck
(officers and helmsmen only)

figurehead

ratlines

captain's cabin
(Sharpe's accommodation)

fo'c'sle

upper gun deck

orlop deck

lower gun deck

weather deck

mainsail

HMS PUCELLE (74 GUNS)

SHIPBOARD DIRECTIONS

DIAGRAM 3

abeam

on the larboard quarter

on the larboard bow

LEE   SIDE

astern

stern   aft

larboard
amidships
starboard

fore   bow

ahead

WEATHER SIDE

on the starboard quarter

wind

on the starboard bow

SHIPS OF THE SAME
NAME ON OPPOSING
SIDES
Custom dictated that a
warship lost to the
enemy was replaced
with a new vessel of the
same name, while any
ship that was seized
would join the
captor's fleet under its
existing name. Thus at
Trafalgar the British
fleet included the
former French ships
HMS Téméraire and
Belleisle, while both
British and French
fleets boasted a
Neptune, an Achille
and a Swiftsure (the
Spanish, too, had a
Neptuno). It certainly
complicated sorting
out the details of who
did what to whom
afterwards.

firepower was greater than that of the column. Thus, in theory, Nelson was taking a considerable risk in following this strategy and, in naval terms, deliberately allowing the enemy to 'cross his T'. The leading ship of the column, as it came within effective range of the line, might be exposed to concentrated fire from the broadsides of as many as five enemy ships. If the wind was slight, as it was at Trafalgar, then the leading ship of the column could be under sustained fire, and unable to reply effectively, for some twenty minutes. French gunners were taught to fire high to hit the masts, yards and rigging (often using chainshot). With reasonable shooting, three or four ships could expect to cripple an attacker before she reached the line. In practice, however, things were not quite so straightforward.

A glance at DIAGRAM 4 will be helpful here. Ships B1 and B2 have crossed the T of ship A as it approaches them. The danger for A's captain is that, while he cannot bring any guns to bear on his enemy, several (in this case two) of theirs can pound him at will as he sails towards them. However, as the diagram shows, though B1 and B2 can hit him while he is in fire zone 1 (and even then they are aiming at a small, almost head-on target at long range), once he reaches fire zone 2 their guns cannot swivel sufficiently in the gun ports to fire upon him. The only way they can continue to target him is if they turn into the wind (luff up), but that would entail heaving-to (stopping), thus disrupting the line of battle. Such a move would almost certainly be unpopular with their admiral. The supposed dangers of allowing the enemy to cross the T were therefore more theoretical than real – something Nelson was fully aware of when he attacked the combined fleet at Trafalgar.

There were other reasons Nelson adopted this tactic instead of following the traditional approach of forming a line parallel to the enemy and slugging it out ship to ship as the lines sailed in the same direction. Firstly, he needed to sail straight at the enemy in order to catch them. He desperately wanted a battle; Villeneuve did not. There was no likelihood of

DIAGRAM 4

FIRE ZONES AND RAKING IN THEORY

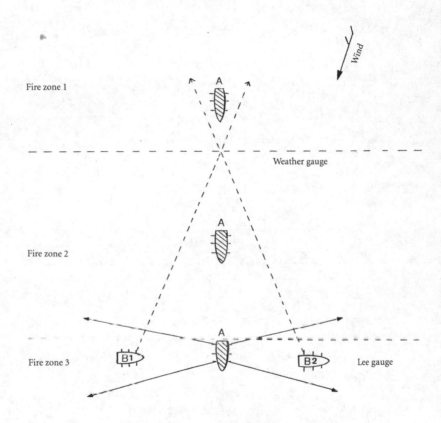

Fire zone 1

Fire zone 2

Fire zone 3

Weather gauge

Lee gauge

Wind

KEY

Ship A has the weather gauge and is sailing to break the line of ships B1 and B2, both with the lee gauge. While ship A is in fire zone 1 it can be hit by shots from both B1 and B2, although neither can fire their whole broadside.
In fire zone 2, however, ship A cannot be hit by either B1 or B2 because their gunports restrict the angle of fire. So unless B1 and B2 luff up (turns into the wind to change direction and thus bring some guns to bear), ship A will have a fire-free passage through fire zone 2.
As ship A enters fire zone 3 the line is broken. The three ships are now only about a pistol shot apart. Ship A is in a position to fire both broadsides, raking B1 and B2, which now present a vulnerable target. The effect would be devastating, most likely leaving both vessels crippled for the rest of the battle.

AIMING A GUN

The gun captain's view of the target at various ranges.

1,200 metres

top of barrel

At 1,200 metres
Strong likelihood of shot missing the hull and doing only minor damage
to masts, sails or rigging.

600 metres

top of barrel

At 600 metres
A good chance of hitting the target. The main point of aim is the hull.

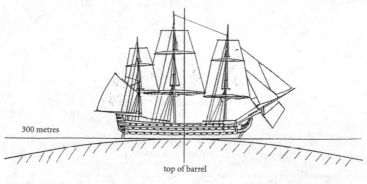

300 metres

top of barrel

At 300 metres
To hit the hull at this range the aim is just below the waterline.

the French Admiral waiting for Nelson to catch up and then obligingly forming a parallel line for battle. Secondly, Nelson was convinced (and rightly so) that such tactics would take the enemy by surprise. Given the comparatively low standard of seamanship and gunnery of French and Spanish crews, and the fire-zone problems discussed above, he was confident his columns would cut the enemy line before their fire could cause enough damage to make his ships unmanageable. Having broken through, every captain in the British fleet shared the same goal: to get into a position to rake an enemy ship.

To be raked was deadly, both for the ship and her crew. The attacking vessel would sail across her quarry's bow or stern with only a few yards of water between them. Then, as she passed slowly across the line of the enemy, she was able to fire her entire broadside of 30–35 guns along the length of the enemy ship. A full rake was from stern to bow or vice versa. Rather than a simultaneous broadside, the guns would fire shot after shot in succession as they came to bear. If an attacker broke through a line between two enemy ships it was possible to rake both, one with the larboard (port) broadside, the other with the starboard. Ships at the receiving end of such fire seldom recovered much of their fighting ability. Another glance at DIAGRAM 4 will explain this. Once ship A has broken the enemy line and entered fire zone 3, the distance between A3 and B1 and B2 might be as little as a pistol shot (30 yards or less). Ship A can now fire both broadsides, thus raking B1 and B2. When firing at this close range the guns would invariably be loaded with reduced charges and be double or even treble-shotted – with grape rammed in too for good measure. Ship B1 is best placed to survive an attack because the sturdier fore part of the vessel would bear the brunt; shot might glance off the curved surfaces or lodge in the solid bulkheads without perforating them, and there was no glass to shatter. Ship B2, on the other hand, is in the worst possible position with the lightly constructed glass windows to the captain's cabin and ward-

FIRING ON THE ROLL

A warship at sea was always in motion, whether pitching up and down in heavy seas or rolling from side to side in light winds. Allowance had to be made for this motion when choosing the moment to fire. The British, who preferred to aim for the hull in the hope of destroying enemy guns and creating a deadly splinter-storm to kill or maim the gun crews, would fire on the downward roll because, even if they fired a fraction late, the shot might still find its target as it ricocheted off the water. The French and Spanish were trained to fire on the upward roll, targeting the masts and rigging to destroy manoeuvrability and clear the upper deck for boarding. These firing tactics were consistent with the British preference for the weather gauge (which placed them upwind of the enemy, their guns low as the ship heeled) and the French for the lee (with guns pointing high).

Known as 'smashers' in the navy, carronades were named after their developer and manufacturer, the Carron Iron Company of Falkirk. Invented in the 1770s, they continued in use until after the American Civil War. Offering the same range of calibres as long guns, they were half the weight and length, and required fewer crew to man them. This enabled ships to carry heavier broadsides with weapons mounted on higher decks. HMS Victory's two 68-pdrs, mounted on the fo'c'sle, could unleash a hurricane of grapeshot across enemy decks prior to boarding. They were popular with merchant ships, where the standard armament of four 4-pdr long guns was often replaced with four 12-pdr carronades. Smaller versions could be fitted to ships' boats – useful in amphibious operations or cutting-out expeditions. They were sometimes used ashore in fortresses or martello towers. The main disadvantages were shortness of effective range (about half that of long guns) and reduced accuracy due to the shorter barrel.

room at the aft (rear) exposed to enemy fire. Flying splinters and shards of glass would add a lethal shrapnel to the cannon-balls sweeping the length of the deck. When *HMS Pucelle* was raked from the stern by the *Revenant,* the first lieutenant, *Haskell,* was cut in half, a quartermaster at the wheel was killed, the wheel itself was smashed, the mizzen mast collapsed, gun crews were decimated and a quarterdeck carronade was knocked off its carriage. As *Captain Chase* said to the frightened young *Midshipman Collier,* 'And a word of advice, Mister Collier. When you command a ship of your own, take great care never to be raked.'

The dawn of 21 October 1805 broke bright but misty. The sea was calm with the lightest of winds coming from the west and a lazy Atlantic swell rolling at long intervals towards the Straits. At last, the two fleets were visible to each other – at a distance. The speed of Nelson's fleet has been likened to the shuffling walk of an old man. It was desperately frustrating. Six hours would pass and it would be noon before either side could fire the first shot.

Then, at around eight o'clock, Villeneuve's combined fleet, having reached the halfway point between Cadiz and the Straits, 'wore together', i.e. turned 180 degrees so that all the ships were heading back towards Cadiz, sailing in reverse order. Rather than engage in an action on a lee shore – the rocky coast of Cape Trafalgar was only seven or eight miles to the east – their commander-in-chief had decided to scramble towards shelter, hoping that, if the British did attack, refuge would be near at hand.

If his intention was to avoid a battle, Villeneuve had made a grave error in wearing. Had he continued towards the Straits or Cartagena it is possible that Nelson would not have been able to catch him, or at best would only have caught up with the laggards. Instead, Nelson's fleet took advantage of the greater degree of manoeuvrability afforded by the weather gauge and slowly closed the distance while the combined fleet, hampered by lack of wind (with wind speeds of about a mile and a half per hour) and sloppy seamanship, took the best part of two hours to complete the turn. The variable quality of Villeneuve's crews was exposed as ships struggled to find their positions in the new line. Instead of sailing in close order (half a cable, or a hundred yards, between ships), the fleet disintegrated into a ragged, crescent-shaped formation, with the line sagging in the middle as ships lost too much leeway. In the four hours that passed between the decision to wear and the firing of the first shot, Nelson had covered some six miles towards the concave centre of Villeneuve's line while the combined fleet had made little progress in either direction. Captain Churruca of the 74-gun Spanish ship San Juan Nepomuceno observed to his first lieutenant: 'Our fleet is doomed. The French admiral does not understand his business. He has compromised us all.'

Lieutenant Paul Nicholas, RM, of the 74-gun HMS Belleisle, wrote:

> As the day dawned the horizon appeared covered with ships. The whole force of the enemy was discovered standing to the southward, distant about nine miles, between us and the coast near Trafalgar. I was awakened by the cheers of the crew and by their rushing up the hatchways to get a glimpse of the hostile fleet. The delight manifestly exceeded anything I ever witnessed . . .

Sharpe watched with fascination as *HMS Pucelle* prepared for battle. Parties of men tore down the canvas partitions to berths and cabins, carrying them below the waterline so that even *Chase*'s cabin and Sharpe's meagre bed space, together with the wardroom, were open to the gun decks, which then stretched unbroken from the stern windows to the bows. Topmen were aloft, hanging the yards with chains to reduce the chance of their being shot away. The boatswain supervised the setting up of extra support for the masts. Stays and backstays were snaked across and back again with rope to give added strength. All running rigging that could be spared was brought down to the deck. Splinter nets were spread from

NELSON'S PRAYER BEFORE BATTLE

'May the Great God whom I worship, grant to my Country, and for the benefit of Europe in general, a great and glorious Victory; and may no misconduct in anyone tarnish it; and may humanity after Victory be the predominant feature in the British Fleet. For myself, individually, I commit my life to Him who made me, and may His blessing light upon my endeavours for serving my Country faithfully. To Him I resign myself and the just cause which is entrusted to me to defend.'

Midshipmen

A MIDSHIPMAN (French equivalent 'Aspirant', Spanish 'Guardia Marina') was, in modern parlance, a cadet who expected to learn an officer's duties during two years' on-the-job training at sea. As a gentleman and potential officer, a 'Middy' was entitled to be addressed as 'Sir' by his juniors and 'Mr' by his seniors. They could be identified in full dress uniform by white cloth patches with a brass button on each on either side of the upright collar. To this day the white patch is still worn by officer cadets of all three services. The present writer recalls getting into serious trouble at RMA Sandhurst when the buttons were not gleaming and the cloth smoothly and immaculately whitened.

The age of midshipmen varied. Twelve-year-old *Harry Collier* of *HMS Pucelle* was exceptionally young. About 70 per cent of midshipmen were between sixteen and twenty-five. The youngest on HMS Victory at Trafalgar was sixteen-year-old James Poad; the oldest, Daniel Harrington, was twenty-nine. The oldest known midshipman (he died a lieutenant in 1802) was the famous Billy Culmer. Born in 1733, he served as a midshipman with Lord Howe in 1757 and was still at sea in that rating thirty-three years later, aged fifty-seven. Tough, hard drinking, hard swearing, Culmer must have terrified the younger lads in his mess! To be promoted lieutenant, midshipmen had to pass a stiff verbal examination. Somehow, after all those years, and many failures, Culmer was persuaded to take the exam again. Old enough to be the father of the captains seated in front of him, he quickly lost patience with the questioning. When asked what he would do in a theoretical situation he considered impossible, Culmer told the board it was humbug, and if that really was the position he would let the ship 'go ashore [founder] and be damned, and wish you were all aboard her'. He passed!

Midshipmen were accommodated below the waterline in the cockpit on the orlop deck. Although cramped, dark and smelly, at least space was not shared with the guns – though the mess table served as the surgeon's operating table in action. It was there that they ate, drank, studied and slung their hammocks. In 1793 Midshipman Richard Parker was court-martialled and busted for refusing a direct order to take up his hammock. It made him a 'lower deck lawyer' with a grievance; four years later he was hanged for leading the Nore mutineers. For minor disciplinary infringements a midshipman could be banished to the topgallant crosstrees of the main mast for several hours. Exposed and over 100 feet up, in bad weather the unfortunate middy would have to lash himself to the mast to stay put (though at least one admiral has claimed he did most of his reading at the masthead when he was a boy). In battle they acted as the captain's ADCs (messengers), keeping the log, assisting the signal lieutenant or commanding up to eight guns on the forecastle or gun decks. The British fleet at Trafalgar carried 460 midshipmen, of whom 13 were killed and 41 wounded – about a 12 per cent casualty rate.

the rigging above head level to catch wreckage falling from aloft. Sand was scattered on the decks to prevent the crew slipping in blood, hammocks were bundled up tightly and placed in netting around the gunwales.

Tearing himself away from all the disciplined activity on the weather deck and aloft, Sharpe clambered down the stairs to the upper gun deck. What he saw was impressive. On either side was a battery of fourteen 18-pounder guns; each group of four guns was assigned to a quarter gunner (junior petty officer) in command of two crews consisting of a gun captain and ten gunners, each crew being responsible for a pair of opposite guns. Guns were normally kept loaded at sea. The shot racks round the hatch combings were filled with clean, greased shot. Shot garlands, rope rings to retain shot on deck, were placed near the guns and filled, but the pieces themselves would not be cast loose (untied from their tackle) until the enemy was much closer. The deck as a whole was under the command of a senior lieutenant assisted by a junior lieutenant and several midshipmen.

Sharpe, fearful of getting in the way, clambered back up to the quarterdeck without visiting the lower gun deck. He had seen a lot but by no means all of the frantic activity stirred by the marine drummers beating to quarters. He had not seen the elaborate and vital precautions taken to prevent a spark or flame setting off an explosion that would have blown *HMS Pucelle* apart in a split-second sheet of flame. He did not see the gunner (a warrant officer) and his crew open the fore- and after-magazines, first emptying their pockets of all metal objects and donning felt slippers. Behind screens of wet felt (called 'fearnoughts') and marine-guarded copper doors, the yeomen of the powder rooms (petty officers) carried out their duties illuminated by the scant glow of lanterns housed in adjacent light rooms, separated by windows of double glass from the felt-lined and carpeted magazines.

In the fore-magazine were rows of copper-hooped barrels and oblong wooden cartridge cases. There was a handling

HAMMOCKS

Hammocks (derived from the Carib word *hamorca* for a bed suspended between two poles) were first officially issued in the RN in 1597. Seamen hung them from hooks in the deck beams. When not in use they were rolled and lashed into a tight bundle which had to be small enough to pass through a hoop under the critical eye of a bosun's mate (hence the phrase 'put through the hoop'). They were then stowed in netting around the perimeter of the upper deck to offer some protection from musket balls or flying splinters. Properly lashed, a hammock also made a serviceable life belt. When a seaman died at sea his body was sewn up in his hammock, with roundshot placed at his head and foot. The sailmaker finished the job by passing the final stitch through the man's nose to ensure he was really dead. If this procedure failed to rouse the corpse it could confidently be assumed there was no chance of recovery, so the body was pushed overboard.

GUN POSITIONS AND CARRONADE

Gun stowed, showing how
muzzle lashing was used.

Gun run in for loading

Gun run out for firing

1815 Carronade run out.
Note elevating screw.

space for packing loose powder into cartridges (thick paper bags) when those already made up were expended. Beyond a small opening in the bulkhead, through a funnel of fearnought, cartridges stored in wooden-handled and lidded containers could be passed to the hoist, which took them up to the orlop deck. There they would be received by the first man of a human chain and passed from hand to hand along passageways and up through hatches until finally being handed to the powdermen of the gun crews. Each gun crew had a powderman or boy to keep his pair of (opposite) guns supplied with cartridges. Sharpe had assumed it was the boys who had done this duty, dashing up and down the hatchways and along the decks, feeding their gun. Standing on a gun deck, he quickly realised the impractical nature of such a system. Firstly, there were never enough boys on a ship to allocate one per gun. Secondly, to have people running along decks in action would be a recipe for chaos. Sharpe was informed that most of the boys would be employed with wet swabs, dousing any loose powder that fell on the deck. This was the origin of the name 'powder-monkey'.

On the orlop deck the carpenter and his mates were getting out wooden plugs of various sizes to be hammered into any holes that were made in the hull. The surgeon, *Pickering*, and his assistants (called loblolly men) together with the purser, *Cowper*, had repaired below to the cockpit (on the orlop deck) to set out the medicines, bandages and instruments necessary to tackle the flood of anticipated casualties. They lit a hanging stove for hot water, cleared the table, hung several lanterns over it and set an empty salt-beef cask alongside for discarded limbs. Donning white aprons, they stood by for their first customers.

John Cash, a seaman on the 80-gun HMS Tonnant (fourth in Collingwood's lee column), wrote to his mother describing an incident during the slow crawl towards the enemy: 'Our good captain [Charles Tyler] called all hands and said "My lads this will be a glorious day for us, and the ground-work of a speedy return to our homes for all."' Not particularly

MORE NAUTICAL SAYINGS

In Portsmouth, where shore leave was often forbidden for fear that pressed men (landlubbers who had been press-ganged into service) would desert, local prostitutes were allowed aboard warships to 'improve morale'. Each morning the bosun's mates would shout for the occupants of the hammocks to 'Show a leg!' If the leg that appeared was smooth and shapely the lady was allowed to sleep in; if hairy, the petty officer would roust the occupant, sometimes by cutting the rope at the head end.

Hammocks were not ideally suited to the activities of these ladies, who much preferred to ply their trade in the space between the guns. Some even gave birth on the gun deck. As it was seldom certain who the father was, the baby would be entered in the Deck Log as a 'son of a gun'.

Floggings occasionally took place on the gun deck, with the victim tied to a barrel, hence 'they had me over a barrel'. Seamen referred to this situation as being married to the gunner's daughter – from which there was no respite.

The guns

GUNS, as distinct from carronades, were classified according to the weight of the roundshot (cannonball) they fired. At Trafalgar HMS Victory had thirty 32-pounders (lower-deck guns because of their weight); twenty-eight 24-pounders (middle deck); thirty long 12-pounders (upper deck); twelve short 12-pounders (quarterdeck); two medium 12-pounders (fo'c'sle) plus two 68-pounder carronades – a total of 102 guns and two carronades. Small ships carried 18-, 9- and 6-pounders. On the gun decks, guns were divided into larboard and starboard batteries. The weight of one of Victory's single-shotted broadsides (all guns in either battery firing together), was 1,148lb; her first broadside at Trafalgar was treble-shotted (as the range was so close) and weighed 3,240lb or 1.5 tons (it is estimated that in total she fired 28.32 tons during the battle). The maximum effective ranges, in yards, were: 32-pdr 2,640, 24-pdr 1,980, 12-pdr 1,320, 68-pdr carronade 1,280. Historically, a nation's territorial limit extended three miles from the coast because that was twice the effective range of a 24-pounder naval gun.

The crew consisted of six or seven men and a powder man (sometimes a boy).

This was enough to load and fire, but insufficient to run out the gun after each firing. Sometimes marines could provide extra muscle; if not, the crew from the opposite battery were used (a ship would usually fire one broadside at a time). To avoid confusion, if a starboard battery crew went to assist on a larboard gun they would always work on its starboard side. When targets presented themselves on both sides of the ship, only alternate guns would be manned and fired. Such decisions rested with the senior gun-deck lieutenant, while the changeover and firing came under the control and supervision of the other gun-deck officer, master's mates and midshipmen.

Other things being equal, the ship that fired the fastest won the engagement. Getting in the first rake gave an advantage that could be maintained if crews continued to load and fire more often than the enemy. Here British crews were supreme. The twelve-man British crew of a 24-pounder could fire once every 90 seconds, whereas a French or Spanish crew took twice as long. This advantage was compounded threefold by the British practice of targeting the enemy's hull to kill and maim gunners.

inspiring, but he went on to order something much more practical and appreciated: 'He [Tyler] then ordered bread and cheese and butter and beer for every man at the guns. I was one of them, and, believe me, we ate and drank, and were as cheerful as ever we had been over a pot of beer.'

Firing sequence for guns

GUNS WERE MOUNTED on wheeled wooden carriages, balanced on two trunnions – short metal projections on either side of the barrel. The sequence of orders given/actions taken (assuming the gun had been stowed and pre-loaded) was:

'Silence!'

'Cast loose your gun!' – remove muzzle lashings.

'Level your gun!' – push quoin (wedge) under breech to lower muzzle.

'Take out your tompion!' – remove muzzle cap/plug.

'Prime!' – gun captain to insert priming wire (spike) into touch hole at top rear of barrel. On piercing cartridge, he cries 'Home' and rammer is withdrawn. He then pours fine gunpowder down hole.

'Run out your gun!' – crew haul gun forward so muzzle protrudes from gun port.

'Point your gun!' – gun captain takes aim, peering along barrel, making adjustments for elevation or alignment.

'Fire!' – when locked on target, gun captain yanks lanyard attached to flintlock, sparking ignites powder which fires main charge. Ball is ejected at velocity of c.500 yards per second. Gun recoils, sending carriage back about two yards before breeching ropes check its progress.

'Worm and sponge!' – barrel is cleared of burning embers using wet sponge on end of rammer.

'Load with cartridge!' – charge of gunpowder in paper or cloth bag is rammed into barrel.

'Load with shot and wad your shot!' – ball then wad (to prevent ball rolling out) are placed in barrel.

'Ram home shot and wad!'

'Prime!' – the whole sequence is repeated.

If a rope severed and a gun broke loose, serious damage could be done by 3.5 tons of iron rolling around the deck. The term 'loose cannon', nowadays used to describe someone who presents an uncontrollable hazard, dates back to the threat posed by an untethered gun rolling about the deck.

Captains on many of the combined fleet's ships were also offering words of encouragement to their men. At eleven o'clock, Churruca, the deeply religious captain of the Spanish San Juan Nepomuceno, assembled his crew on deck. First, he had the chaplain absolve all and administer the Sacrament. Then he spoke: 'Children, in God's name I promise eternal blessedness to all those who today do their duty. Those who fail in it will be instantly shot down; and if any escape my eyes, or those of the gallant officers whom I have the honour to command, be sure that for the rest of their lives the stings

SIGNALLING

The officer or midshipman responsible for flag signals had a difficult job. Midshipman Hercules Robinson on the frigate HMS Euryalus at Trafalgar watched his fellow midshipman and signalman sorting and hoisting hundreds of flags that morning and thought 'they would die of it'. The large, coloured flags were hoisted to the upper yardarms or mastheads. There were ten numeral flags, one assigned to each number from 0 through 9. These were also used for the 26 letters of the alphabet, with two-flag hoists for double figures. Each ship had a codebook in which common words and phrases were allotted numbers from 26 upwards. Mistakes could have serious repercussions – particularly in the case of signals to and from the admiral's flagship, or frigates serving as scouts. On one occasion HMS Euryalus signalled: 'Nineteen under sail all the rest top yards hoisted except rear steady admiral and one line of battle ship.' The message required 56 flag hoists, so it's perhaps excusable that 'rear steady admiral' was substituted in place of 'Spanish rear admiral'.

of conscience shall render them wretched and miserable.' Somewhat different from Tyler's beer and cheese! Churruca was a man of exceptional gallantry and devotion to duty who had insisted on breaking off his honeymoon to join his ship – at a time when the Spanish government owed him nine years' back pay! He was destined to die a dreadful death that day. At around 2 p.m., with his ship surrounded by three enemy vessels, he was hit and his leg almost torn off at the hip. Lying on the deck in a welter of his own blood, he is said to have cried out, 'It is nothing. Go on firing!' Refusing to be carried below, he ordered his flag to be nailed to the mast. It was to be his last order. Shortly after his death the Nepomuceno struck his Colours – hauling down his ensign as a sign of surrender.

Many plans of the battle depict two neat columns of British ships, one behind the other, bearing down at right angles on a symmetrical line representing the combined fleet. The reality was quite different. Both Collingwood and Nelson's ships came into the action in bunches – more straggling groups than lines. Distances between ships varied from a few yards to half a mile. Lieutenant Benjamin Clements of HMS Tonnant stated, 'We went down in no order but every man to take his bird.' Captain Edward Codrington of the 74-gun HMS Orion said, 'We all scrambled into battle as soon as we could.' He was so impressed by the sight of the two fleets nearing each other that he called all his officers up from the gun decks to see it. (Codrington went on to become an admiral and lived to be eighty-one – long enough to see his eldest son, a midshipman, drowned at sea, but not quite long enough to see another son become a full general and a third an admiral of the fleet.) A Spanish witness agreed that the British ships' approach looked anything but orderly, exclaiming that they were 'coming down like mad Englishmen in confusion and disorder.'

To assist with recognition, Nelson had ordered that every ship have the white St George's ensign at the top mast, with a union flag from the main topmast stay and another from

Lieutenant John Pasco

PASCO WAS the signal officer on HMS Victory at Trafalgar, and his name will forever be associated with the drafting of Nelson's famous signal. As the fleets closed, Nelson turned to Pasco and said, 'I wish to say to the Fleet "England confides that every man will do his duty."' Because of the need for speed, Pasco suggested that the word 'expects' – for which there was a single flag – be substituted for 'confides', which would have had to be spelt out. Nelson agreed.

Pasco, being three years senior to the first lieutenant, Quilliam, would normally have stepped into that position on joining the ship. Nelson, however, left the arrangement unchanged. At 11 a.m. on the day of battle, Pasco followed Nelson to his cabin, intent on making a report and tactfully querying his official status. On entering the cabin, he found Nelson on his knees in prayer. When Nelson rose, Pasco made his report but felt the time inappropriate to raise this personal matter. It is highly unlikely Nelson would have sanctioned the change at that stage in any case.

Pasco was badly wounded in the right side and arm at Trafalgar, for which he received a pension of £250 a year, but was only promoted commander, whereas Quilliam was made a post captain. Things worked out for Pasco in the end, though: he eventually made rear-admiral and lived until 1853 while Quilliam, who died in 1839, never rose above captain.

---

the fore topgallant stay. As the fleets gradually came together Nelson ordered his signal lieutenant, Pasco, to hoist the flags for the message that was to live for ever in the nation's history books: 'England expects that every man will do his duty.' For those interested in trivia, the inscription of this signal on Nelson's column in Trafalgar Square, London, has omitted the word 'that'. Only one other signal was subsequently run up the Victory's halyards: 'Engage the enemy more closely.'

Collingwood's lee column, something under a mile south of Nelson's weather column, would hit the enemy line first. At its head was Collingwood's flagship HMS Royal Sovereign which, as she sailed into gunshot range, was well ahead of the following ship, HMS Belleisle. In fact the lee column was not a column at all but rather a gaggle of ships each making their best speed with little thought for position or order in the formation. Collingwood had soon abandoned any attempt to

'THERE'S A FLAP ON'

This English expression, to describe a state of panic or frenzied activity, has its origins in the custom of signalling between warships with flags. The current use dates from World War I when the British fleet at Scapa Flow under Admiral Jellicoe was ordered to intercept the German High Seas Fleet and the signal was given, by flags, to scores of ships all at once. That particular 'flap' culminated in the Battle of Jutland.

NOISE

The continuous indescribable, thunderous din of a gun deck in action is seldom mentioned in accounts of naval battles. Today anyone firing a pistol on a range must wear ear-defenders; the best the gun crews could do at Trafalgar was to tie a bandana round the head – which, of course, was useless. Once firing started, speech was impossible. Orders were given by sign or bellowing in a person's ear. It was common for gun crew members to be deaf for days afterwards. A Frenchman on the 74-gun Fougueux has described how the noise affected him: 'The captain ordered me to climb outboard and see if the wreckage of the mainsail was not in danger of being set on fire from the main deck guns. I obeyed; but as I clambered from the gangway into the chains one of the enemy fired her whole starboard broadside. The din and concussion were fearful; so tremendous that I almost fell headlong into the sea. Blood gushed from my nose and ears.'

maintain an orthodox column and signalled his ships to sail on 'a line of bearing', i.e. to sail line abreast and head directly for the nearest enemy at their best speed. Even so it was two hours after HMS Royal Sovereign broke the enemy line that the slowest ships such as HMS Defence joined the battle. Understandably these latecomers suffered little in comparison to those at the forefront of the attack. HMS Prince, for example, had no casualties at all.

Both the Royal Sovereign and HMS Victory took hits as they closed with the enemy. Nevertheless the combination of inaccurate gunnery aiming too high and the dead fire zone ensured that both ships broke the line as intended. The Royal Sovereign cut in astern of Vice-Admiral Alava's flagship the Santa Ana. Her broadside raked the Spanish ship with deadly effect, disabling 14 guns and killing around a hundred of her crew. HMS Victory hit the enemy some thirty minutes later, her captain, Hardy, steering to pass within touching distance of the stern of Villeneuve's flagship, the Bucentaure. On her fo'c'sle Boatswain William Willmet waited beside the lar-board 68-pounder carronade, one of HMS Victory's two 'smashers'. It had been loaded with roundshot plus a keg of 500 musket balls. As the carronade came into line with the enemy's stern windows, Willmet yanked his firing lanyard. There followed a continuous thundering roar as gun after gun of the larboard broadside flung their hot metal the length of the unfortunate Bucentaure.

Shortly after this, HMS Victory and the French ship Redoutable crashed together and their yards locked. It was a favourite tactic of the combined fleet to grapple an enemy ship, then shower the decks with grenades and musket fire from sharpshooters positioned in the tops; as a result, the majority of British casualties were officers and men who had been exposed to fire on the poop, quarterdeck and fo'c'sle. Pursuing this tactic, the Redoutable shut most of her larboard gunports to prevent boarding while French marines in the rigging threw grenades and fired their muskets at the Victory's decks. Nelson had forbidden British seamen and

Types of shot

Solid shot: the influence of this spherical 'cannonball' projectile was so pervasive that even today ammunition is counted in 'rounds'. Cast in solid iron using clay moulds designed to produce balls slightly less in diameter than the bore of the gun, roundshot replaced the old stone shot of the sixteenth century. At close range a 32lb ball could penetrate 2.5 feet of wood, creating a hail of splinters that could kill or maim. Few shots were aimed below the waterline as the resulting holes could be plugged, making it rare for a ship to be sunk by gunfire. The allocation of roundshot per gun was steadily increased because of the large number of guns carried and the need to keep firing for several hours to force an enemy into submission. By the late 1780s the 'foreign allowance' for a British ship of the line was 80 per gun. The 74-gun HMS Pucelle was carrying about 7,400 roundshot weighing some 80 tons.

Dismantling shot: several specialist types of shot, primarily for use against rigging (although capable of cutting through people as easily as ropes). Popular with the French because of their favoured tactic of aiming for masts and rigging (they carried c.10 dismantling shots per gun compared to 3 on a British ship). The various forms included:

— Bar shot: solid iron balls or hemispheres joined by an iron bar, thus resembling a dumbbell.

— Expanding or elongated bar shot: balls joined by two pieces of iron so that one could slide into the other for loading. When fired, the shot expanded in flight to double its length, increasing the potential to cut stays or rigging.

— Chain shot: balls joined by a length of chain.

—Star shot: four or five bars that folded around a ring, forming a whirling star when fired.

Anti-personnel shot: a number of small iron balls, each one or two inches in diameter, trussed up in a canvas bag approximately the diameter of the gun bore. It resembled a bunch of grapes, hence the term 'grapeshot'. On firing, the bag would burst to produce a deadly cone of shot. Replaced in the late eighteenth century by tiered shot, which consisted of three layers, each of three shot, separated by perforated iron plates and kept together by a central spindle, all encased in a canvas bag. Grape was particularly effective at close range against men on an open deck or exposed in a ship's boat. French ships usually carried c.10 per gun, the British 3–10.

marines from fighting from the tops on Victory, so it is sadly ironic that at 1.20 p.m., as he walked the quarterdeck with Hardy, a French sniper's musket ball struck Nelson on the top of his left shoulder and smashed into his spine. He knew

Though it was an incredible achievement to live through the most famous sea and land battles in history, Sharpe was not the only person to fight at both Trafalgar and Waterloo. Two officers are known by name. The first was *Capitan de Frigata* Don Miguel Ricardo de Alava who was an ADC to Admiral Gravina on the Principe de Asturias. His father, Vice-Admiral de Alava, flew his own admiral's flag on the Santa Ana. When Spain was no longer an ally of France, de Alava joined the Spanish Army as a colonel and served on Wellington's staff during the Peninsular War. He was later the Spanish representative at the Duke's Waterloo HQ.

The other was Major Antoine Drouot, an artillery officer who had been in charge of upgrading the gunnery of Villeneuve's fleet. During the battle he was on board the Indomptable, which put up a gallant fight against HMS Belleisle. Drouot later accompanied Napoleon during his short exile on Elba,

immediately that the wound would be fatal. He was carried down to the orlop deck where the surgeon, William Beatty, was called to attend him.

The admiral's wounding was soon avenged by an eighteen-year-old midshipman called John Pollard and a fifty-four-year-old quartermaster and yeoman of signals, John King. Both were on Victory's poop when Nelson fell. Pollard's attention was drawn to three musket-armed men on the mizzen top of the Redoutable whence the fatal shot had come. He picked up a musket from a dead marine and fired back, helped by King, who supplied him with ammunition. King was hit either through the mouth or forehead and died instantly. Half a century later there was some controversy as to whether another midshipman, Francis Collingwood (no relation to the admiral of that name), should share some of the credit for shooting down the French marksmen. The position is best explained by Pollard himself, who wrote to *The Times* on 13 May 1863.

> It is true my old shipmate Collingwood, who has now been dead some years, did come in the poop for a short time. I had discovered the men crouching in the tops of the Redoutable, and pointed them out to him, when he took up a musket and fired once; he then left the poop, I conclude to return to his station on the quarterdeck. I remained firing till there was not a man to be seen in the top; the last one I saw coming down the mizzen rigging, and he fell from my fire also. King, the quartermaster, was killed while in the act of handing me a parcel of ballcartridge, long after Collingwood had left the poop. I remained there till some time after the action was concluded . . .

Pollard never rose above lieutenant during his service, much of his later years being spent in charge of a coastguard station. He received his Greenwich pension in 1853, retired with the rank of commander in 1864, and died four years later aged eighty-one.

By the time *HMS Pucelle* (in reality HMS Téméraire) came up and laid herself along the starboard side of the Redoutable to assist Victory, Nelson was dying. Caught and crushed between the guns of two ships, the Redoutable was doomed. Her captain, Lucas, later wrote:

> At this minute the mainmast fell on board the Redoutable. All the stern was absolutely stove-in; the rudder-stock, the tiller, the two tiller-sweeps, the stern-post, the wing transoms, the transom knees were shot to pieces. All the guns were shattered or dismounted. The two sides of the ship were utterly cut to pieces. Four of our six pumps were shattered, as well as our ladders so that communication between the lower and upper decks was extremely difficult. All our decks were covered with dead, buried beneath debris and splinters . . . [but some of the wounded] still cried 'Vive l'Empereur! We're not yet taken.'

By 2 p.m. Lucas's ship was in danger of foundering so he ordered the Colours to be struck. Some 522 of the crew were and at Waterloo was acting commander of the Imperial Guard.

It is claimed that two British midshipmen were officers in Wellington's army at Waterloo and that one of Nelson's seamen fought there as a colour-sergeant. A handful of French veterans were almost certainly present at both battles as the 2nd and 93rd Ligne fought as marines at Trafalgar and as line regiments at Waterloo.

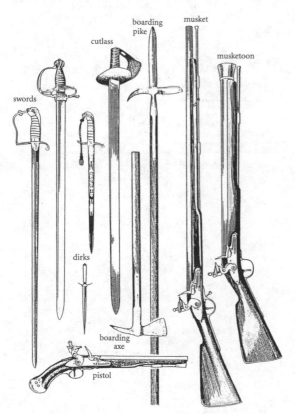

Small Arms

HMS PUCELLE AT THE BATTLE OF TRAFALFGAR

DIAGRAM 5

(From 1–2.30 p.m. on 21 October 1805)

PHASE 1

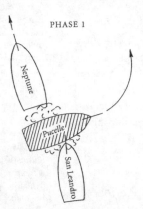

- *Capt Chase* takes the *Pucelle* into the tiny gap between the <u>Neptune</u> and <u>San Leandro</u>.
- *Pucelle* rakes stern of <u>Neptune</u> with double-shotted cannon and grape. Massive damage and serious casualties inflicted. <u>Neptune's</u> mizzen mast falls.
- <u>San Leandro</u> rams the *Pucelle* but backs off and sails away when threatened with boarding.
- *Pucelle* turns north to where HMS <u>Victory</u> is heavily engaged and hidden in dense smoke.

PHASE 2

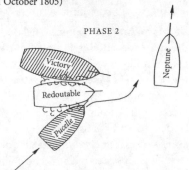

- <u>Victory</u> and <u>Redoutable</u> lock together, with the French ship relying on musketry to clear the <u>Victory's</u> decks prior to boarding while the latter continues to fire broadsides into the <u>Redoutable's</u> hull. Nelson is mortally wounded by a musket ball.
- *Chase* brings the *Pucelle* (in reality the <u>Téméraire</u>) alongside the <u>Redoutable</u> and opens fire. Some shots penetrate the enemy vessel and strike the <u>Victory</u>, and vice versa.
- *Sharpe* climbs into the maintop and uses the 7-barrelled gun to good effect.
- After passing <u>Redoutable</u>, the *Pucelle* tries to sail after <u>Neptune</u> with the object of securing her as a prize.

PHASE 3

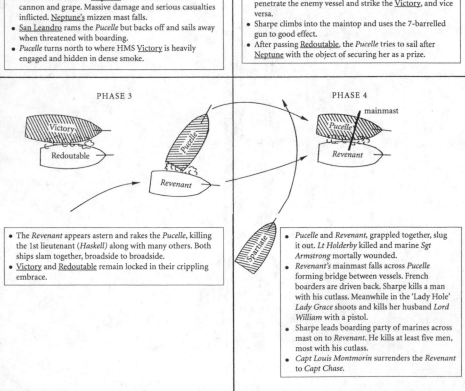

- The *Revenant* appears astern and rakes the *Pucelle*, killing the 1st lieutenant (*Haskell*) along with many others. Both ships slam together, broadside to broadside.
- <u>Victory</u> and <u>Redoutable</u> remain locked in their crippling embrace.

PHASE 4

- *Pucelle* and *Revenant*, grappled together, slug it out. *Lt Holderby* killed and marine *Sgt Armstrong* mortally wounded.
- *Revenant's* mainmast falls across *Pucelle* forming bridge between vessels. French boarders are driven back. Sharpe kills a man with his cutlass. Meanwhile in the 'Lady Hole' *Lady Grace* shoots and kills her husband *Lord William* with a pistol.
- Sharpe leads boarding party of marines across mast on to *Revenant*. He kills at least five men, most with his cutlass.
- *Capt Louis Montmorin* surrenders the *Revenant* to *Capt Chase*.

Royal Marines

THE CORPS OF MARINES, which originated in 1664 as the Duke of Albany's Maritime Regiment, was given the title Royal in 1802. By 1814 the corps numbered 31,000. In the early days they bore muskets and manned the sides of the weather deck (and sometimes the tops) during close action, provided extra muscle in the gun crews and formed boarding parties, or fought ashore with landing parties – tasks that had previously fallen to infantry regiments serving at sea. Although they were not seamen, and never worked aloft in the rigging, they were required to assist in pulling, hauling, cleaning, working the pumps or manning the capstan when raising the anchors. There was always a marine sentry on the captain's cabin, the spirit store and the magazines. Some learnt seamanship and transferred into the navy, which marginally improved their pay and status (a marine with under seven years got 19s 3d per month, an ordinary seaman £1 5s 6d). The all-rank establishment of marines was: 1st rate 145, 2nd rate 130, 3rd rate 80–110, 4th rate 50, 5th rate 35–45, 6th rate 25, sloop 15 (under a sergeant).

Their muskets were either 'bright sea service' (shiny barrel normally reserved for parades ashore) or 'black sea service' (rust-resistant metal barrel), with a triangular bayonet. Officers had swords while the sergeants carried pikes. The uniform was scarlet, with blue facings (collar, cuffs, lapels) denoting a 'Royal' corps. Even the most junior RM officer had a gold epaulette on his right shoulder, something only permitted to junior post captains in the navy – a cause of some grumbling in the wardroom.

The corps was organised administratively into four 'divisions' based at Chatham, Portsmouth, Plymouth and Woolwich. Each had up to 48 companies of marines and an artillery company. In practice, virtually all personnel were scattered in detachments throughout the fleet. In 1808 the 1st Marine Battalion was formed; it garrisoned Lisbon and took part in the landings along the north coast of Spain, including Santander. A 2nd Battalion was formed in 1812 and both saw service in North America in 1813, as did a third created that year.

dead or wounded – the highest number of casualties of any ship in either fleet.

Meanwhile on HMS Victory twenty-year-old Second Lieutenant Lewis Rotely, RM, was deeply affected by what he saw and heard:

> We were engaging on both sides; every gun was going off. A
> man should witness a battle in a three-decker from the middle

WARRANT
OFFICERS (WO)
AND PETTY
OFFICERS (PO)

Because there were so
many specialists on a
large warship, the rank
structure below
commissioned level
was complex. The most
senior WO on any ship
was the master, who
was virtually
equivalent to a
lieutenant. He had his
own instruments and
charts, and his most
crucial responsibility
was navigation. The
other WOs were
boatswain (rigging,
sails, tackle, anchors,
ropes); gunner (guns,
powder, ammo);
surgeon; carpenter
(maintenance of hull,
masts, yards, spars);
purser (victualling);
master-at-arms (chief
of the ship's police)
and cook. Below these
were a host of senior
and junior POs
including the
chaplain, midshipmen
and various 'mates'
(e.g. master's mate,
gunner's mate, etc),
armourer, sailmaker,
quartermaster
(whereas in the army
the QM was
responsible for
supplies and rations, a
naval QM was an
experienced seaman
who manned the wheel
of a ship), captain of the
tops, coxswain (*John
Hopper*, the coxswain
of *Chase*'s gig on *HMS
Pucelle,* was a PO), etc.

deck, for it beggars all description: it bewilders the senses of sight and hearing. There was the fire from above, the fire from below, besides the fire from the deck I was upon, the guns recoiling with violence, reports louder than thunder, the decks heaving and the sides straining. I fancied myself in the infernal regions, where every man appeared a devil. Lips might move, but orders and hearing were out of the question; every thing was done by signs.

Later Rotely fought up on the poop deck:

The poop became a slaughter house, and soon the two senior lieutenants of marines and half the original forty [of those deployed on the poop] were placed hors de combat. Captain Adair's party [Royal Marines] was reduced to less than ten men, himself wounded in the forehead by splinters, yet still using his musket with effect. One of his last orders to me was, 'Rotely, fire away as fast as you can!' when a ball struck him on the back of the neck and he was a corpse in a moment.

The battle continued in the dying wind, the dense smoke reducing visibility to zero. Ships drifted slowly about each other while officers on the quarterdeck desperately sought to identify ships as they loomed slowly out of the banks of smoke. Some ships were grappled together while their crews fought it out, as Sharpe did on *HMS Pucelle*, with cutlass, tomahawk, pistol or pike. The battle devolved into a murderous mêlée with ships of both sides having to face the fire of several of the enemy simultaneously. It was just what Nelson wanted – 'a pell-mell' battle where training, discipline, seamanship and speed of firing counted more than courage. Many ships were attacked from both sides. The ranges were so close that charges had to be reduced to prevent shot going through one ship to hit a friendly vessel on the other side. HMS Belleisle was at one time attacked by four ships simultaneously: her masts were shot away, her mizzen crashing down on her after-guns. By 3.25 p.m. she was a hulk with her Colours nailed to the mizzen stump. The French Intrépide later claimed to be the only ship in naval history to have borne the fire of five ships in succession – HMS Africa, Leviathan, Ajax, Agamemnon and Orion.

Two hours after the battle had started, the combined fleet's van under Admiral Dumanoir finally wore or tacked back to the fight, but only two ships, the Intrépide and Neptuno, came to Villeneuve's assistance. The others fired a few token shots or turned for Cadiz. Dumanoir was court-martialled for his tardiness and timidity. One by one the French and Spanish vessels struck their Colours or sailed away. Captain Hardy reported to Nelson that the battle was won. The dying admiral murmured, 'Now I'm satisfied. Thank God I've done my duty.' He died at 4.30 p.m.

Of the combined fleet, seventeen vessels were captured by

Jeanette of the Achille

AT AROUND 5 P.M. the French ship Achille exploded. She had been burning for some time and the fire had finally reached her magazine. The unfortunate ship disappeared in a sheet of flame followed by a mushroom cloud of black smoke that hung in the still air like a volcanic eruption. British ships nearby launched boats to pick up survivors. Among them was a black pig, swimming strongly, and a naked woman clinging to a spar. The frigate HMS Euryalus grabbed the pig and had pork for supper, while the schooner HMS Pickle rescued the young woman. She was treated with great gallantry. Lieutenant Lapenotiere's crew, now outnumbered four to one by prisoners, gave her trousers and a jacket and treated her burns. Along with many others, she was transferred to HMS Revenge where Captain Moorsom ordered up two purser's shirts to be made into a petticoat, and shoes and stockings were found to fit her.

Her name was Jeanette. She had stowed away, in disguise, to be with her husband, but in the dreadful confusion of the fire could not find him and was left with the wounded down on the orlop deck. There she stayed until the fire was so intense that it burned through the deck above and cannons came crashing through. She then climbed out of a gun-room port and sat on the rudder chains. This proved to be a painful perch as molten lead from the rudder trunk dripped down on to her neck and shoulders, forcing her to strip off her clothes and leap into the water. She swam to a spar, but the men already clinging to it kicked and bit her until she was forced to let go. Luckily, she was able to grab another, unoccupied, piece of wreckage and it was from there she was picked up. Her story had a happy ending in that her husband was found a few days later among the prisoners.

The Santisima Trinidad

THIS HUGE SHIP, flying the flag of the Spanish Rear-Admiral Cisneros was, in 1805, the largest man-o'-war in the world with her 220-ft gun deck, 58-ft beam and a depth, from keel to upper deck, of 48 ft. Originally built of Cuban cedar in 1770 as a three-decker with 116 guns, a fourth gun deck was subsequently added so that by 1805 she carried 136 guns and a complement of 1,048 officers and men. Her name was derived from the figurehead, a large white-painted group representing the 'Most Sacred Trinity'.

During the battle she came under fire at various times from HMS Téméraire, Leviathan, Neptune, Conqueror and Africa. By the end of the afternoon she was a total wreck, her sides smashed in, her masts gone, most of her guns destroyed and 313 of her officers and crew killed or wounded. Even so, she would have made a magnificent prize, but the storm that followed the battle finished her. Before she went down, however, HMS Ajax's first lieutenant reported: 'Everything alive was taken out down to the ship's cat.' His boat, the last to leave the stricken ship, returned to take in a cat that ran out on the muzzle of one of the lower-deck guns, mewing piteously for assistance. A British officer described the Santisima Trinidad's end: 'Night came on – the swell ran high – three lower-deck ports were open, and in a few minutes the tremendous ruins of the largest ship in the world were buried in the deep. The waves passed over her, she gave a lurch, and went down.'

the British, although some of these prizes were lost or destroyed – Achille blew up, San Agustin and Intrépide burned, Redoutable sank, Santisima Trinidad and Argonauta were scuttled; and in the violent storm that occurred soon after the battle Monarca, Fougueux, Aigle and Berwick were all wrecked. On 23 October a sortie from Cadiz by four French ships succeeded in recapturing the Santa Ana and Algésiras, but three ships were wrecked in the process. No British ships were lost, though a number – including the dismasted HMS Victory, which had to be towed to Gibraltar – sustained severe damage. In round figures, the British lost 450 men killed and 1,250 wounded, while the French and Spanish suffered 4,400 killed and 2,550 wounded. Many more were captured or drowned during the storms following the battle.

Burial at sea

LIEUTENANT-COLONEL OATTS, in Volume 2 of *Proud Heritage*, his history of the Highland Light Infantry, gives a moving account of the burial of an officer of the 74th on the voyage home:

On 27 January 1806 the Lord Hawksbury lay with her main yards aback and her colours at half mast. The entry-port in the leeward bulkhead was open, and opposite to it about thirty of the 74th were drawn up on deck, resting on their arms reversed. The length of their muskets enabled them while in this position to place their cheeks on the top of their hands and gaze upon the corpse which half a dozen of their comrades were carrying with much difficulty across the heaving deck. It was placed at the entry-port, draped in the union flag, then consisting only of the crosses of Saints Andrew and George. On its breast was a Highland broadsword, whose blade had last seen the light at the battle of Assaye.

[There was no chaplain] so the captain of the ship was ready with his prayer book:

'Forasmuch as it has pleased Almighty God to take unto himself the soul of our dear brother here departed ... We now commit his body to the Deep ...'

Flag and broadsword were removed, the plank lifted and the body of Quartermaster James Grant slid out through the entry port. The captain replaced his hat, closed his prayer-book and glanced aloft.

'Mains'l haul!'

The yards came round, jib and forestaysail filled, and the ship sank down into the trough.

'Head braces! Off all haul!'

The Lord Hawksbury heeled over and held on her course. The entry-port closed with a bang. The colours fluttered to the masthead, remained there for a moment, and were then hauled down. Astern a few gulls swept over the wake, under which the mortal remains of the gallant Quartermaster sank to their last resting place, two hundred fathoms down.

During action such niceties were abandoned and corpses were tossed unceremoniously over the side. Such was the fate of Nelson's secretary, John Scott, who was virtually cut in half by a roundshot while on the quarterdeck with Nelson. When Nelson himself fell mortally wounded, much of the blood on his coat was Scott's.

7

Sharpe's Prey

In the summer of 1807 the British fleet sailed for Copenhagen for the second time (the first was in 1801 when Lord Nelson secured a brilliant victory) to prevent the neutral Danish fleet falling into French hands. Sharpe, having deserted his post and come to London to try (unsuccessfully) to sell his commission, seeks out his boyhood tormentor *Jem Hocking*, still 'master' of the Wapping foundling home, kills him and takes his money. As he plans his escape, a chance encounter with his old mentor, Lieutenant-General Sir David Baird, leads to a special mission. Sharpe is to act as 'minder' to a Guards officer, *Captain John Lavisser*, who is being sent to Denmark with a large chest of the government's golden guineas with the object of applying persuasion, bribery or threats to convince the neutral Danes to hand their fleet into British custody for the duration of hostilities with the French.

While Copenhagen comes under indiscriminate bombardment by British besiegers, Sharpe pursues the treacherous *Lavisser,* and the stolen gold, around the city. In addition to being present with the 95th at Wellesley's successful engagement with the Danes at Køge, Sharpe prevents the Danes setting fire to their own fleet, kills nine men (including *Lavisser*), beds another woman and recovers most of the gold. All at the cost of a minor scalp wound.

ON 14 JUNE 1807 the Emperor Napoleon's victory over Tsar Alexander of Russia at Friedland effectively brought to an end the 4th Coalition (Britain, Prussia and Russia) allied against him. A week later, an armistice was declared between France and Russia, and on 25 June a historic meeting was staged on a raft in the middle of the river at Tilsit at which Napoleon set out to flatter, dazzle and overawe the Tsar Alexander and humiliate the King of Prussia, Frederick William. He succeeded admirably on both counts. General Savary of France wrote of the initial meeting:

> The Emperor Napoleon . . . ordered a large raft to be floated in the midst of the river, on which was built a well-enclosed and elegantly decorated apartment, having two doors on opposite sides, each of which opened into an antechamber . . . The roof was surmounted by two weathercocks: one displaying the eagle of Russia, the other the eagle of France. The two outer doors were also surmounted by the eagles of the two countries.
>
> The raft was precisely in the middle of the river, with the two doors of the salon facing the opposite two banks.
>
> The two sovereigns appeared on the banks of the river, and embarked at the same moment. But the Emperor Napoleon, having a good boat, manned by Marines of the Guard, arrived first on the raft, entered the room and went to the opposite door, which he opened, and then stationed himself on the edge of the raft to receive the Emperor Alexander, who had not yet arrived, not having such good oarsmen as the Emperor Napoleon.

The Tsar allegedly opened the conversation by saying, 'I hate the English as much as you do yourself.' To which Napoleon responded, 'If that is the case, then peace is already made.'

Within a fortnight France, Russia and Prussia had signed a peace treaty. Russia lost little in the way of territory, whereas

GENERAL LORD
WILLIAM
CATHCART

Something of a
nonentity as a general,
Cathcart was born in
1755 and spent part of
his childhood in
St Petersburg where his
father, the ninth
Baron Cathcart, was
British ambassador. At
twenty-one William
succeeded to the
barony and joined the
army. He served in
America during the
War of Independence,
and for a time
commanded an
irregular corps called
the 'British Legion'.
From 1793–5 he
soldiered in the Low
Countries with the 29th
Foot (Worcestershire).
He rose steadily in
rank, becoming
commander-in-chief
in Ireland (1803–5),
then commander of
the British expedition
to Hanover. After the
successful
Copenhagen
campaign he was
created a viscount.
Promoted full general
in 1812, he was posted
to Russia as
ambassador and
military commissioner
to the allies' HQ. As
such he had a close
view of Napoleon's
fateful march on
Moscow. He became
an earl in 1814 and
lived to the grand old
age of eighty-eight,
surviving long enough
to see his son, George,

Prussia was ruthlessly carved up. Despite the flirtatious endeavours of Frederick William's wife, Napoleon stripped away Prussia's possessions west of the Elbe (to create a kingdom called Westphalia for his brother Jerome) and in Poland. However it was not this that sent the British fleet (and Sharpe) scurrying to Copenhagen at the end of July. A combination of an efficient British intelligence network and what would today be described as 'leaks' ensured that the secret clauses of the treaty did not remain secret for long. One such article proposed that France and Russia would persuade other European nations to close their ports to British ships, threatening trade. But what really galvanised the British government was Napoleon's plan to incorporate the large Danish fleet (some 20 ships of the line, 17 frigates and 60 other vessels including 12 brigs and 24 sloops) into his own depleted marine. This would more than compensate the French for their losses at Trafalgar less than two years earlier.

For the Danish fleet to pass into French hands would have been catastrophic for Britain. She acted accordingly, despite being at peace with Denmark. Whether by diplomatic means or by force, the Danish navy would be secured – or neutralised. George Canning, the British Foreign Secretary, masterminded the diplomatic effort. At one o'clock in the morning of 18 July a messenger roused diplomat Francis Jackson from his bed in Northamptonshire. His instructions were to travel to London at once, then onward to Yarmouth, sailing within twelve hours for Kiel, where the Crown Prince of Denmark was then residing, to persuade him to hand over the Danish fleet into British safekeeping until a general peace treaty, when the ships would be restored to Denmark. It was a demand that had little prospect of success (there is no evidence that Jackson was empowered to bribe the Crown Prince as was Sharpe's antagonist, *Lavisser*). To back up this forlorn diplomatic mission with the threat of force, a large naval and military 'stick' was assembled and despatched to the Baltic.

Army operations, should they become necessary, were to be commanded by Lieutenant-General Sir William Cathcart.

Admiral James Gambier

AN UNPOPULAR and incompetent admiral, Gambier was nicknamed 'Dismal Jimmy' by his men. Born October 1756 in the Bahamas, where his father was lieutenant-governor, he joined the navy at the age of eleven. Family interest procured him rapid promotion: post captain at the exceptionally young age of twenty-two (though Nelson was even younger, securing the same rank at twenty). He was present at the capture of Charlestown in 1780 and received a gold medal for his services at the Battle of the Glorious First of June in 1794. The following year he was made rear-admiral and a Lord of the Admiralty.

Ostentatiously religious – no other admiral was ever known to heave to on a Sunday for divine service – his religious and humanitarian scruples persuaded him to side with Cathcart and delay opening the bombardment of Copenhagen for as long as possible, until finally goaded into action by the diplomat, Mr Jackson. Nevertheless he received the thanks of parliament, along with a peerage and a huge slice of the prize money. The following year, at the age of fifty-two, he left the Admiralty to take command of the Channel Fleet, but a missed opportunity to destroy the French fleet in the Basque Roads (he hung back instead of supporting the Commander-in-Chief Lord Cochrane) led to his court martial. After a partisan court acquitted him of neglect of duty, he returned to command a disappointed Channel Fleet. In 1814 he was involved in negotiating the peace treaty with America. In 1830 he became, due mostly to seniority, Admiral of the Fleet – the very pinnacle of a naval career. He died in 1833 aged seventy-six.

Cathcart was already in the Baltic, having landed at Rugen Island (on the present German coast north of Berlin) on 16 July to join the 7,000 troops of the King's German Legion (KGL) – part of the British Army that had arrived about a week earlier. Prior to the signing of the Treaty at Tilsit (finalised on 9 July) their task had been to co-operate with the Swedish and Prussian troops at Stralsund against the French. Now they were earmarked for Copenhagen. The naval side of the operation was under Admiral James Gambier, an officer better known for his evangelical religious views – heaving the fleet to for prayers, and distributing tracts around the lower deck – than naval competence.

become a lieutenant-general. George, a Waterloo veteran, died twelve years after his father, leading the 4th Division at the Battle of Inkerman in the Crimean War.

*   *   *

THE DIRTY HALF HUNDRED

Captain Willsen's regiment, the 50th Foot (later the Queen's Own Royal West Kent Regiment), secured this nickname not, as might be imagined, by some glorious battlefield action that reduced their number to fifty men, but for a much more mundane reason. Their uniform facings were black and, when wet, the dye tended to run. Soldiers using their cuffs to wipe sweat from their brow would leave a streak of dye on their forehead. As they were the 50th regiment, they became known as the 'Dirty Half Hundred'.

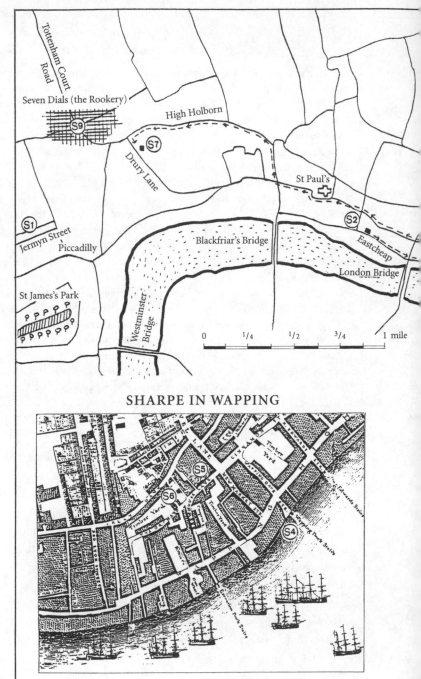

SHARPE IN WAPPING

MAP 12

SHARPE IN LONDON 1807

(26–27 July 1807)

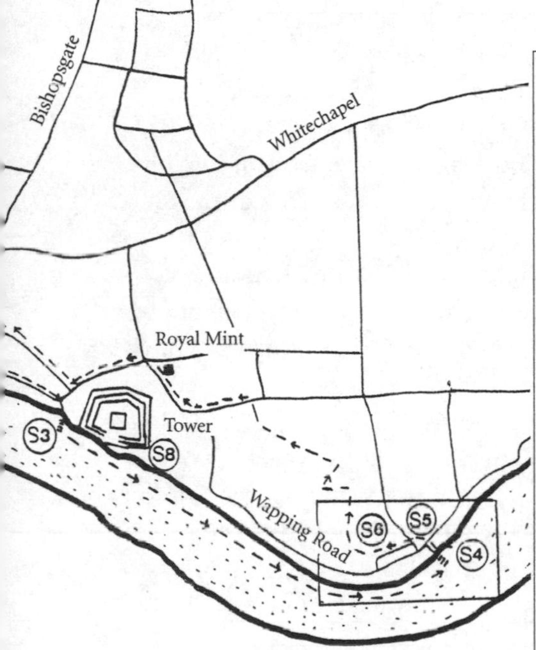

Bishopsgate

Whitechapel

Royal Mint

Tower

S3

S8

Wapping Road

S6

S5

S4

KEY

S1 At Horace Jackson's Hall of Arms in Jermyn St. *Capt Henry Willsen* has fencing match with *Lord Marsden* before meeting *Capt the Hon John Lavisser*, 1st Foot Guards. Later *Lavisser* has *Willsen* murdered near Piccadilly.

S2 26 July Sharpe, disillusioned with army life, tries to sell his commission at Army Agents' office in Eastcheap.

S3 En route to Wapping, Sharpe takes boat from Tower Hill stairs.

S4, S5 and S6 see insert

S7 Sharpe meets Lt-Gen Sir David Baird in *French Horn* (nicknamed *French Prick*) tavern off Drury Lane. Baird recruits S. for special mission to Copenhagen as a 'minder' to *Lavisser*.

S8 27 July Sharpe meets Baird and *Lavisser* (who has charge of large quantity of gold) at the Tower prior to departing for Harwich.

S9 Seven Dials or the Rookery was where Sharpe was brought up by *Maggie Joyce*, having run away from the foundling home in Wapping.

S4 landed at Wapping Dock stairs and made his way via Wapping High St–New Market St (Wapping Lane in novel) to Brewhouse Lane.

S5 S. revisits Foundling Home where he spent childhood under evil 'master' *Jem Hocking*. Deceives *Hocking* into believing he is recruiting drummer boys.

S6 Later that evening, S. meets *Hocking* in *Malone's* tavern, Vinegar St. After killing *Hocking* he flees westwards, pursued by thugs.

KGL CAVALRY

For the Copenhagen campaign of 1807 all Cathcart's cavalry were from the KGL, under the command of Maj-Gen von Linsingen. His brigade consisted of four squadrons each of the 1st, 2nd and 3rd Light Dragoons, all clad in hussar-type uniforms and referred to as 'hussars' despite their official status in the Army List as light dragoons. The authority for the change was published in the *London Gazette*, 28 Dec. 1813: 'His Royal Highness the Prince Regent has been pleased, in the name and on behalf of His Majesty to direct that from the 25th instant . . . and that the three Regiments of Light Dragoons shall be termed the 1st, 2nd, and 3rd Regiments of Hussars of the King's German Legion.'

Wellesley praised the regiments' performance at and after the action at Køge. In an act that showed that his gift of a telescope to Sharpe for his gallantry at Assaye was not unique, he presented Lt Jansen of the 3rd Light Dragoons, who was wounded at Køge, with a case of pistols, and a suitably flattering letter, in token of his distinguished conduct.

The bulk of the British battle fleet, consisting of 20 ships of the line, 40 frigates and other vessels, sailed from Yarmouth on 26 July, the day after Sharpe's murderous escapade in Wapping. Sharpe, along with *Lavisser* (who, unbeknown to Sharpe, had already killed an unwanted minder, *Captain Willsen)* and the gold, followed a day later from Harwich aboard a fast frigate. The remaining 380 transports, under escort by more warships, departed from a number of Essex and Kentish ports such as Harwich and Deal on 29 July, aiming to rendezvous with the fleet in ten days at the Helsingør Roads.

For the 18,000 soldiers embarking – 560 KGL cavalry, 1,500 KGL infantry, 14,000 British infantry in fifteen battalions plus 1,700 British and German gunners – the journey promised to be a grim one. Packed into the lower decks, most would experience the sordid horrors of seasickness for the first time within hours of sailing. Lieutenant-Colonel Alexander Napier, commanding the 1/92nd (later to become the Gordon Highlanders), knew what a sea journey could be like and was determined to lessen its effects on his men. Just prior to embarkation he published the following Regimental Order:

> Lieut-Colonel Napier desires that officers commanding different transports on which the 92nd are embarked will pay particular attention to the cleanliness of the ships; they will keep both men, women and children [each battalion was allowed a small quota of wives and children to accompany it overseas] on deck during the day when weather permits; bedding to be brought on deck in fine weather, and men to dine on deck. Ships to be fumigated three times a week.

Fresh water was in short supply and extremely strictly controlled. A sentry guarded the barrels and no water could be drawn without the authority of the officer of the watch. Soldiers had to drink at the cask, or if they wanted to cook anything they had to show the food on a plate to the officer of the watch first. No basins for washing water were allowed.

The contingent from Sharpe's regiment consisted of ten companies: five from the 1/95th under Lieutenant-Colonel

Five 'Napoleonic' Napiers

LIEUTENANT-COLONEL ALEXANDER NAPIER OF BLACKSTONE, commander of the 1/92nd, was one of three army officers named Napier who took part in the Copenhagen campaign of 1807. He was killed at the Battle of Corunna in January 1809 while commanding the picquets of General Hope's division.

Captain Charles Napier was an officer in the 50th Foot. He was captured at Corunna but later rose to be a lieutenant-general. His main claim to fame was his conquest of Scinde Province in India in 1843, when he supposedly sent the single-word despatch 'Peccavi' – completely foxing HQ staff until someone remembered his schoolboy Latin and correctly translated it as 'I have sinned'. He died in 1853 aged seventy-one.

Charles's youngest brother, Captain William Napier, served with the 1/43rd in Denmark and accompanied von Linsingen in his flank march prior to the action at Køge, which left him with a very poor opinion of the KGL officers and men (see box p.248). He served throughout the Peninsular War, and was present at virtually all the major battles and sieges including Salamanca and Badajoz. He was wounded twice, once seriously when a musket ball narrowly missed his spine. In 1819 he went on half-pay as a lieutenant-colonel to begin writing his classic History of the Peninsular War (published 1828–40). Promoted major general and appointed Lieutenant-Governor of Guernsey in 1842, he resigned after three years and in 1849 moved to Scinde House, Clapham Park, where his old back wound forced him to spend months at a time in bed. He died in 1860 aged seventy-five, four months after promotion to full general.

The middle brother, George Napier, missed out on the 1807 campaign but fought in the Peninsular War. He became Governor of the Cape of Good Hope and, like his brothers, rose to be a full general, dying in 1855 aged seventy-one.

The fifth 'Napoleonic' Napier, also named Charles, was a naval officer. He became a midshipman in 1800, ultimately reaching vice-admiral some fifty years later. The highlights of his career included being struck off the Navy List for switching to the Portuguese navy to take command of their fleet in 1833 then, after reinstatement, receiving command of the Channel Fleet in 1846. Finally he was given the Baltic Fleet during the Crimean War, but caused an outcry when he refused to attack Cronstadt. That was his last command. He died in 1853 aged sixty-seven.

Thomas Sydney Beckwith (who had served under Nelson at Copenhagen six years before), and five from the 2/95th under Lieutenant-Colonel Hamlet Wade. Wade's quartermaster-sergeant was one William Surtees, a disgruntled NCO whom

THE BOATSWAIN'S
(BOSUN'S) CALL

Sharpe heard the shrill sound of the bosun's call (wrongly called a whistle by landlubbers) when boarding HMS Cleopatra for his voyage to Denmark. Bosuns and their mates used a variety of notes to communicate in three ways: the 'call' was a distinctive sound giving a command that would be understood by the crew without the order having to be shouted (e.g. 'call all hands' or 'call the larboard watch'); the second was a 'pipe' or signal for the crew to stand by for a verbal order; the third was a salute. Probably the most familiar 'pipe' was 'pipe down', an expression still in everyday use. 'Pipe still' meant every man was to stand at attention, probably to salute a passing ship. A skilled bosun could produce about eight notes. The range of sounds possible, and the frequency of their use, led to bosun's mates being nicknamed 'Spithead Nightingales'.

Wade had refused to appoint as acting quartermaster (a decision unconnected to Sharpe's absence). On the twenty-sixth, as the main body of the British fleet set sail, the two half-battalions left Deal to join the transport flotilla off Harwich. Three days later it was the transports' turn to sail for the rendezvous off Helsingør (Elsinore) and Kronborg Castle – places well known to anyone familiar with Shakespeare's *Hamlet*.

Gambier's ships passed round the northern tip of Denmark on 1 August. There he detached a squadron of four ships of the line, three frigates and ten brigs under Commodore Keats tasked with sailing into the Great Belt to prevent reinforcements reaching Zealand, and thus Copenhagen, from the mainland. By the third, Gambier was exchanging salutes with the guns in Kronborg Castle before dropping anchor to await his transports. By the eighth they had arrived, but the vast armada of vessels had to sit quietly swinging on their cables awaiting the outcome of Mr Jackson's diplomatic discussions and the arrival of the army commander, Cathcart, from Stralsund. On 12 August the general joined his command well in advance of the main KGL contingent. Two days later Jackson scrambled awkwardly up the side of the 98-gun flagship, HMS Prince of Wales, to announce the failure of his mission. The military option would be required. Early on the fifteenth half the seamen and many of the troops strained for hours on scores of capstan bars dragging up the anchors to allow the huge flotilla to move south.

Owing to some unusually capricious currents, contrary winds, poor seamanship, or perhaps a combination of all these factors, Sharpe did not arrive off Copenhagen until late on 12 August. The following night, on the beach near Herfølge, Sharpe narrowly escaped with his life after *Lavisser's* servant, *Barker*, tried to kill him. While Sharpe was making his way first to Køge and then, hidden in the hay on the back of a farm cart, to Copenhagen, the fleet was looking for a suitable landing site on the shore between Helsingør and the capital city. Agreeing the precise location for an amphibious landing is fraught with the difficulties of compromise between the conflicting requirements of navy and army – a modern example being the selection of San Carlos Water in the Falklands. However, on the sixteenth Gambier and Cathcart were lucky, they found a good spot acceptable to both off a village called Vedbæk (MAP 13). As the soldiers were being rowed ashore, Sharpe was struggling, sweating and squirming to escape through the chimney of *Skovgaard*'s house in Vester Fælled in the northern suburbs of Copenhagen. At about the time his 95th Rifles came ashore some ten miles to the north, Sharpe was killing three Frenchmen before heading back into the city.

Disembarkation began at 5 a.m. with Wellesley's reserve brigade, under the close protection of the guns of numerous small brigs and bomb vessels loaded with grapeshot, ready to clear the beach should any enemy appear. Surtees, the quartermaster-sergeant of the 2/95th, was impressed. He later wrote: 'The most perfect arrangements had been made by

A bomb vessel

KRONBORG CASTLE AND HELSINGØR ROADS 1807

To Sharpe, Kronborg Castle looked more like a palace. It was here that Shakespeare had Hamlet pronounce 'Something is rotten in the state of Denmark.'
On the right is a Danish brig, while in the foreground to the left a two-decker ship of the line sails to her anchorage.
Helsingør Roads (harbour) lies behind the headland left of the castle, where masts of ships at anchor can be seen.

The British fleet arrived here 3 Aug. 1807. The troop transports joined them 7–8 Aug., and Gen. Cathcart arrived 12 Aug.

After the Danes refused to hand over their fleet, on 15 Aug. the British sailed some 12 miles south and began to disembark troops the next day.

On 15 Aug. Sharpe, *Lavisser* and *Barker* landed on the beach near Køge, 50 miles south of Kronborg Castle.

Bomb vessels

SHARPE SAW his first bomb vessels in Harwich harbour at the start of his voyage to Denmark. HMS Vesuvius, aboard which Sharpe met *Captain Chase* prior to leading him into the inner harbour at Copenhagen, was an actual bomb vessel. Unlike other ships, 'bombs', as they were known, had a consistent naming policy: vessels were named after volcanoes, or in a way that suggested fire or hell (for example Sulphur and Explosion). In 1807 the RN had about twenty such vessels (up from only two in 1793). Until 1813, when six Vesuvius-class bombs were purpose-built for attacks on the American coast, the majority were converted merchant ships of 300–400 tons. Square-rigged, constructed to bombard enemy towns or forts guarding a harbour with high-trajectory fire, bomb vessels were specialised fighting ships with a complement of just under 70 men (commanded by a lieutenant, as they were not rated ships). By the 1790s they were ship-rigged (i.e. they had three masts), where before they had been ketch-rigged (with only two). The third mast improved balance but obstructed the guns, so on Sharpe's Vesuvius two large mortars were mounted on either side of the mast on rotating turntables.

Each shot weighed over 200lb and, since recoil is proportional to the weight of the projectile, the downward thrust, or deck blow, was considerable. To alleviate this, the deck was reinforced with beams, while the space below was packed tightly with old rope to act as a shock absorber. The mortars were designed, not to knock down walls or penetrate thick timber, but to destroy buildings – usually by firing incendiary bombs – or to kill people with the explosions. They certainly made their contribution to the devastation of Copenhagen in 1807.

THE KING'S GERMAN LEGION (KGL)

When Hanover was overrun in 1803, King George III (as Elector of Hanover) authorised the formation of a King's German Regiment from the town's citizens. It quickly expanded into the KGL, eventually comprising eight line

Sir Home Popham [second-in-command to Gambier], who superintended the landing of the troops; and nothing could exceed the beauty and regularity in which the different divisions of boats approached the shore . . .' It was not, however, the green-jacketed riflemen of the 95th who had the honour of being the first infantrymen to set foot on Danish sand but soldiers wearing red coats and kilts. They belonged to the light company of the 1/92nd and had landed behind a battery of light artillery and some KGL cavalry. Like all troops landing that morning they had been warned in General Orders that Britain was not at war with Denmark so the 'rules of engagement', to use a modern expression, permitted opening fire only if resistance was encountered. There was no opposition, the only casualty being the unfortunate Private James Duncan of the 1/92nd who was shot and killed by an 'accidental discharge'. He was described as 'a fine young soldier, and his untimely death caused great grief to his comrades'. One wonders what happened to the culprit!

Of Cathcart's army only 40 per cent came ashore during the sixteenth: Wellesley's reserve force of four battalions (five companies each of 1st and 2nd 95th, 1/43rd, 2/52nd and 1/92nd), the two brigades of Lieutenant-General Ludlow's 1st Division (Guards Brigade – 1st Coldstream and 1/3rd Guards – and the 1st Brigade with the 1/28th and 1/79th), plus Major-General Grosvenor's 2nd Brigade (1/28th and 1/79th), part of Baird's 2nd Division. Thus ten battalions out of the twenty-five that would eventually come ashore had landed that day. Because the landing had gone so smoothly, with no resistance from the Danes, Cathcart was able to get three columns on the road south by mid-afternoon. The next day the 3rd Brigade (1/32nd, 1/50th and 1/82nd), part of Baird's division under Major-General Spencer, landed at Skovshoved to join the move to encircle the city. The following day Major-General von Linsingen disembarked the bulk of the KGL Cavalry Brigade near Charlottenbund, immediately deploying inland to the east to protect Cathcart's flank and rear. With Brigadier-General Macfarlane's 4th Brigade (1/7th and 1/8th) late arriving from England, it was not until 21 August that Baird, the man responsible for Sharpe's mission, had his complete division ashore. By then Copenhagen was encircled and there had been some indecisive fighting.

and two light battalions, five regiments of cavalry (three hussars, two dragoons) plus six artillery batteries and a handful of engineer officers. The KGL became an integral part of the British Army, fighting with great distinction in the Peninsula and at Waterloo – where Wellington had more troops that spoke German (KGL, Nassauers, Brunswickers and Hanoverians) than English. Their dragoons gained lasting fame for breaking two French infantry squares at Garcia Hernandez in 1812 – an exceptionally rare achievement. However, if Captain Napier is to be believed (see box p. 248) their behaviour off the battlefield in Denmark left a lot to be desired – although it must be said that soldiers of all nations have behaved abominably on numerous occasions throughout history.

The Danes, having rejected outright Jackson's humiliating suggestion that they hand over their fleet to the British, quickly realised that they would have to fight if they wanted to keep it. Fighting meant the defence of Copenhagen, where the fleet was snugly tucked away in the inner harbour (MAP 13). The defences of the city had been constructed with

KGL looters

COLONEL NAPIER'S namesake, Captain William Napier, was detached with three companies of the 1/43rd to accompany Major-General von Linsingen on his march to Køge and during the pursuit that followed. When describing the appalling behaviour of his KGL comrades he did not mince his words:

> The general asked an old grey-haired peasant which way his countrymen had fled. The old man proudly answered he would not tell; and [von Linsingen] immediately made his orderly shoot him dead. His brigade-major had in my hearing two days before ordered Major McLeod to shoot all peasants he met with; but he pronounced it *pheasants,* and McLeod laughingly promised he would certainly obey that order. I saw General [von Linsingen] in his uniform groping in a common sewer for money, and I ordered a soldier of my own, named Peter Hayes, whom the general had called to aid him, to quit such an infamous work and behave like a soldier. The general afterwards performed a very indecent and cruel act, and finished by rearing in person a ladder against the church to enable his men to rob the place.

On another occasion Captain Napier was ordered to escort some 400 prisoners, including a number of women. He commented:

> I reached the army without the loss of a prisoner, if I except some women, who had been taken, I fear, for a shameful purpose, but delivered to me as prisoners of war! I thought it scandalous to carry them through the country and to shut them up at night with the men, and therefore left them in the first village I halted at.
>
> During this march and previous to it, my company never took so much as a cherry from a bough . . . although General [von Linsingen] called upon them to join his Germans in the disgraceful scenes that were enacted . . . at the time I did, at the risk of my commission, tell General [von Linsingen] my opinion of his conduct when he was encouraging my men to plunder; and because the 43rd Regiment was falsely and injuriously reported by him to have committed the outrages which his own Germans perpetrated under his eyes and with his approbation; nay, more, with his personal assistance.

Napier later summed up his experiences when writing to his mother: 'I can assure you that, from the General of the Germans down to the smallest drumboy in the legion, the earth never groaned with such a set of infamous murdering villains.' Strong words but, seemingly, justified.

such a situation in mind and appeared formidable. Copenhagen is built partly on the large island of Zealand and partly
on the much smaller one of Amager. The narrow passage
between the two formed the harbour and arsenal. The
defences towards the sea were very strong. There were block-
ships, sunk and converted into batteries, to enfilade the passage by which Nelson had approached in 1801. There were
regular works on Amager, fitted with the heaviest ordnance to
protect the harbour, and there was the Sixtus or Three-Crown
Battery on a shoal due north of the city, powerfully armed
with eighty guns and howitzers. On the northern side the
citadel was in perfect repair, with double ditch fortifications
plus thirty guns and eleven mortars well supplied with
ammunition. Extended ramparts, a deep ditch, outworks, a
glacis and covered way protected the western side of the city.
There was sufficient ordnance to enfilade the approach roads
and deliver a crossfire in every direction. In total there were
some 430 guns and mortars defending Copenhagen –
an impressive array. Some 500 to 600 yards beyond the
inland walls and ditches stretched three wide inundations
that acted as an enormous outer moat. Three tunnels and
gates led out westwards carrying roads round the northern
and southern ends and two across causeways through the
centre (MAP 13). The Danes' problems, however, lay not in
their fixed defences but in the command, quantity and quality
of the garrison.

   Responsibility for Copenhagen's defence rested on the aged
shoulders of seventy-two-year-old General Ernst Peymann
(the newly promoted *Major Lavisser*, who was part Danish
and a clandestine Danish agent, was attached to Peymann as
an ADC). He was a militia soldier who had never before
commanded regular troops. His commander-in-chief, the
Crown Prince, having ordered him to hold the city and certainly not to surrender the fleet (under the command of
Captain Steen Bille), had departed to rejoin the main Danish
Army in Holstein. Peymann was thus left holding the short
straw. His garrison comprised a mere 4,300 regular troops,

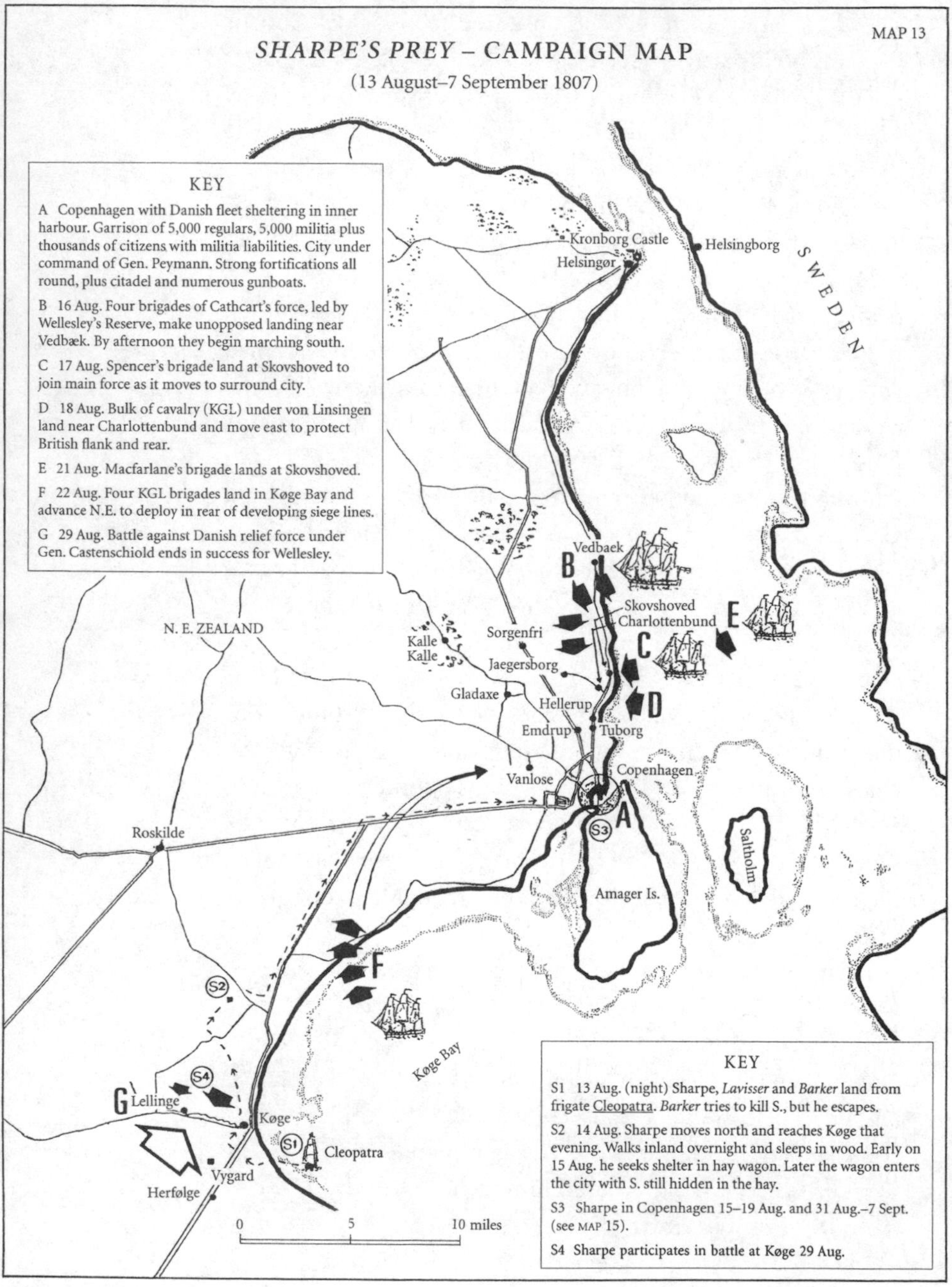

SHARPE'S PREY – CAMPAIGN MAP

(13 August–7 September 1807)

MAP 13

KEY

A Copenhagen with Danish fleet sheltering in inner harbour. Garrison of 5,000 regulars, 5,000 militia plus thousands of citizens with militia liabilities. City under command of Gen. Peymann. Strong fortifications all round, plus citadel and numerous gunboats.

B 16 Aug. Four brigades of Cathcart's force, led by Wellesley's Reserve, make unopposed landing near Vedbæk. By afternoon they begin marching south.

C 17 Aug. Spencer's brigade land at Skovshoved to join main force as it moves to surround city.

D 18 Aug. Bulk of cavalry (KGL) under von Linsingen land near Charlottenbund and move east to protect British flank and rear.

E 21 Aug. Macfarlane's brigade lands at Skovshoved.

F 22 Aug. Four KGL brigades land in Køge Bay and advance N.E. to deploy in rear of developing siege lines.

G 29 Aug. Battle against Danish relief force under Gen. Castenschiold ends in success for Wellesley.

SWEDEN

Kronborg Castle

Helsingborg

Helsingør

N. E. ZEALAND

Vedbaek

B

Skovshoved
Charlottenbund

E

Sorgenfri

Kalle
Kalle

C

Jaegersborg

D

Gladaxe

Hellerup

Emdrup

Tuborg

Vanlose

Copenhagen

A

Roskilde

S3

Amager Is.

Saltholm

F

S2

Køge Bay

G Lellinge

S4

Køge

S1 Cleopatra

Vygard

Herfølge

0   5   10 miles

KEY

S1 13 Aug. (night) Sharpe, *Lavisser* and *Barker* land from frigate <u>Cleopatra</u>. *Barker* tries to kill S., but he escapes.

S2 14 Aug. Sharpe moves north and reaches Køge that evening. Walks inland overnight and sleeps in wood. Early on 15 Aug. he seeks shelter in hay wagon. Later the wagon enters the city with S. still hidden in the hay.

S3 Sharpe in Copenhagen 15–19 Aug. and 31 Aug.–7 Sept. (see MAP 15).

S4 Sharpe participates in battle at Køge 29 Aug.

some 2,400 badly equipped militiamen, three Volunteer Corps totalling 1,200 men, a citizen militia (the body into which *Aksel Bang* was hastily commissioned) of 5,000, and 7 engineers – in all almost 13,000 men, the majority of whom were semi-trained or untrained civilians in uniform.

By 18 August the British had surrounded Copenhagen, although they were not yet ready to besiege it. To the east was Baird's 2nd Division with his left flank on the coast road, in the centre Wellesley's reserve, and in the west Ludlow's 1st Division comprised of guardsmen, Highlanders and lads from rural Gloucestershire. Cathcart's force was not complete until the arrival, on 22 August, of the KGL force from Stralsund under Major-General von Drechsel. They came ashore in Køge Bay and marched up to form the second line in the rear of Cathcart's army.

It was on the eighteenth that Sharpe left the city with *Jens*, the Danish militiaman. *Jens* was taking part in a brave but foolish sortie; Sharpe was attempting to rejoin the British Army by mingling with the attackers. The sortie involved over 2,000 Danes on the left of the British lines, near the shore, supported by the fire of gunboats from position F on MAP 15. It is uncertain which route the attackers took from the city, but it appears that Sharpe and *Jens* exited through the northernmost of the two tunnels under the city ramparts, crossed the central causeway over the inundation and then headed north for something over a mile. *Major Lavisser* led this particular column of militiamen, and during the action *Jens* saved Sharpe when *Barker* fired a pistol at him. In reality the Danish sortie came up against four companies of the 2/95th Rifles, four of the 1/23rd (Welch) Fusiliers, two of the 1/4th (King's Own Lancaster) supported by two light field guns – in all about 1,000 men. Surtees, who was present, dismissed the Danish efforts in one sentence: 'the moment the armies came into contact, they [the Danes] instantly gave way, leaving a considerable number of killed and wounded behind them, and retreated into the town.' *Jens* was killed, but Sharpe succeeded in rejoining the British Army and was

HMS CLEOPATRA

The 32-gun frigate that took Sharpe and his party to Denmark was a real ship, built twenty-eight years earlier in Bristol. In April 1805, two years before Sharpe boarded her, she was briefly captured by the French after her captain, Sir Robert Lawrie, gave chase to a large frigate north-west of the Bahamas. When the Cleopatra caught up with the other ship, it broke out the French colours and fired two broadsides at her from less than a hundred yards. The 46-gun Ville de Milan, with its 18-pounders on the main deck, then engaged in a lengthy exchange of fire which damaged both ships' rigging. After a shot destroyed the Cleopatra's wheel, rendering her rudder immovable, the French ship rammed her bowsprit over the Cleopatra's quarterdeck and the French crew attempted to board. Although initially driven back by musket fire, a second attempt was successful and Lawrie was forced to surrender. The Cleopatra had put up a gallant fight against a ship that heavily outgunned her and had a crew of 400 compared to her 200. She lost 22 killed and 36 wounded, including 2 lieutenants and the master. Fortunately, a few days later she was recaptured by HMS Leander. In 1808 she was the victor in another battle against a French frigate (the 48-gun Topaze) off Guadeloupe in the West Indies, where she saw out her service before sailing home to be paid off for the last time in 1814.

taken to Baird's headquarters near the village of Emdrup. From there he was directed to rejoin the 1/95th.

There was a second attempt at a sortie, in which Sharpe did not participate, on 24 August when, in the words of historian J. W. Fortescue, 'the garrison made a feeble show of a general sortie by all the outlets from the city, only to be driven back at every point.' Cathcart's General Orders for 23 August had stipulated a British advance, a further tightening of the encirclement, but this was called off as many units became involved in driving the Danes back the way they had come. The standard of military competence of the average Danish militia unit is well illustrated by the experience of the 1/92nd on that afternoon. The Highlanders' leading company, sent to chase the Danes from an outlying village, entered the village quietly and with caution. They found no troops, only a sentry who had fallen asleep at his post. He was terrified 'out of his wits when he woke to find himself in the hands of a Highland sergeant!' The unit to which he belonged had not bothered – or had forgotten – to relieve him before scurrying back to Copenhagen, although the posting of sentries does establish at least a modicum of military talent.

The British lines had by this time reached the suburbs of the city on the western side of the inundations. The five days between the two Danish sorties (18–24 August) had been spent dragging forward artillery and beginning to construct siege battery positions from which to pound the city. Guns could now be positioned within 700 yards of the walls (MAP 15). The counter-battery fire from the Danes was heavy and continuous, but their gunners were hampered by not being able to see targets hidden by trees and buildings in the western suburbs. Nevertheless, it was not until 2 September that the British guns opened up for the first time.

On 26 August, Cathcart received warning that a relieving force was approaching from the south of Zealand and Wellesley was put in command of a mixed force to intercept and destroy it. He divided his command of some 7,500 men into two and gave the German, Major-General von Linsingen, command of 3,500 (made up of six squadrons of KGL light cavalry, three companies of the 1/43rd under Captain William Napier, five companies of 2/95th under Lieutenant-Colonel Wade, the 6th Line Battalion KGL and four cannons). Colonel Hohnstedt commanded the infantry, Colonel Alten the cavalry. Wellesley retained the remaining 4,000 (two squadrons of KGL cavalry, five companies 1/95th, seven companies 1/43rd, the 1/52nd, the 1/92nd and twelve guns) under his personal control. Sharpe, meanwhile, had joined the half-battalion of the 1/95th under Colonel Beckwith and been posted to No. 2 Company under *Captain Warren Dunnett*. His reception was frosty. *Dunnett* could see no good reason why he should be lumbered with the quartermaster and therefore declined to give him any command or authority.

Wellesley's plan was to send von Linsingen west and then south with the object of carrying out a sweep to get behind the Danes and cut off their retreat, while he marched directly along the road towards Roskilde. Both forces set out on the twenty-sixth. For von Linsingen it was to prove a particularly exhausting and fruitless march. The enemy was reported to have retired south and thus escaped the encircling move. Wellesley withdrew to between Roskilde and Copenhagen to protect the siege lines from any incursions from the south or west.

Although both Cathcart and Wellesley insisted that all troops refrain from any sort of plundering or misbehaviour on the line of march, there were a number of serious lapses during this time. According to the Regimental Orders of the 1/92nd for 27 August, near Roskilde:

> Lieut-Colonel Napier has observed with extreme concern the bad conduct of the great part of the regiment in regard to plundering the houses on the road. The regiment used to be a pattern to others on all marches, but they have now shown a very different one. A great deal has been done through mere mischief and wantonness, and he is sorry to be obliged to say

Quartermasters

WHEN SHARPE transferred into the 95th Rifles as a second lieutenant he was initially given a combatant officer's post but, because of his long other-rank service, was soon appointed quartermaster (QM). This was one of the posts within an infantry battalion often given to an officer who had risen from the ranks (another was adjutant). In peacetime they could also expect postings as recruiting officer or barrack master. According to *The Regimental Companion,* published in 1811: 'The quartermaster is not to do any duty other than quarter-master while the regiment is on actual service. His duty is, to take care of the ammunition and stores of the regiment; to attend to all deliveries of coals, forage, etc and to prevent frauds from being committed against the public service.' It was an administrative job of crucial importance but a non-combatant post. As such, it was looked down on by others, which irked Sharpe considerably.

Sharpe had won his commission on the battlefield as a sergeant, so it seemed logical that his fighting experience would secure him a combatant role. But the army saw things differently. As an ex-ranker and senior NCO, Sharpe knew soldiers intimately, he understood company and battalion administration, knew every piece of equipment and weapon, and understood the cheating and trickery that went on in the ranks. The system of having ex-rankers as quartermasters has persisted to the present day and, until recently, had become entrenched in that special quartermaster commissions were given to senior warrant officers who had worked their way up the NCO promotion ladder. No officer with a combatant commission could be a quartermaster. Likewise a quartermaster would never command troops in a combat role, except in dire emergency when no other officer was available. In the modern army where such long-service former NCOs are commissioned they get a 'late entry commission' and are usually employed as QMs, motor transport officers, or as the unit welfare officer.

Captain Dunnett was far from exceptional in his dislike of ranker officers. This was based on the prejudice that only a gentleman could be an officer. But Sharpe, as quartermaster, was accepted for what he was – a courageous NCO who had been rewarded with a commission and given a job that fitted his background and experience. The position of promoted sergeants was invariably difficult and required a man of exceptional character to make good. Even the soldiers preferred a 'proper' officer.

the officers have not done their duty in preventing it . . . it is strictly forbidden to any man to go into any house on the march . . . any offender will be punished [with a flogging] immediately when the regiment halts.

On the twenty-eighth, acting on reports that the Danish relieving force was near Køge, Wellesley issued orders for another move against them. Again von Linsingen was to take his force inland using a road that ran about three miles from, but roughly parallel to, the coast, while Wellesley headed down the road that hugged the shore. When the enemy was met he would attack and hold them in front while von Linsingen moved round their left to envelop their flank and rear. The following day, about two miles north of Køge the KGL Hussars ahead of Wellesley's column were brought to a halt by the sight of the Danes drawn up a mile ahead of them on rising ground. Wellesley, as usual, rode forward to peer through his telescope. He could make out what appeared to be a line of three, perhaps four, infantry battalions with cavalry on either flank. Behind them stood a dark mass of what was obviously a large infantry reserve. If any more troops were on the reverse slope they were invisible, as was the town of Køge. There were some cannons by the coast road and along the enemy front (MAP 14).

The Danish force was made up of around 12,000 troops, including at least three regular battalions, cavalry, and artillery. These were heavily outnumbered by militia and hastily recruited levies (Surtees claimed up to 5,000 were armed with only pikes), all under the command of another elderly, inexperienced officer, Lieutenant-General Castenschiold. Wellesley ordered his force forward to deploy. The 1/95th companies and the light company of the 1/92nd were pushed ahead as skirmishers. The main attacking force had the 1/92nd on the left with their flank covered by the sea, the seven companies of the 1/43rd in the centre, the 1/52nd on the right. All three battalions formed in lines two deep. Guarding the right were two squadrons of KGL cavalry under Colonel von Reden. Wellesley looked long and hard to the

MRS SEMPLE AND OTHERS IN TROUBLE

Even on active service, British battalions were permitted to take a few wives overseas. This privilege was granted to only 10 families, although many more 'wives' went unofficially. One of the official wives on the Copenhagen campaign was a Mrs Semple, whose husband was in the 1/92nd Highlanders. According to Lt-Col. Napier, the excessive drunkenness in the battalion was due 'to the practice of the women bringing brandy and wine from Roskeld' – with Mrs Semple particularly at fault. 'Mrs Semple of the 1st Company having been found in the act, her provisions are to be stopped.' This was mild compared to the punishment meted out to a fellow offender: 'it was the intention of Lieut.-Colonel Napier that she should be drummed through the quarters of the regiment, but out of respect to the character of her husband, the lieut.-colonel will be satisfied with her disappearance for ever – and he gives her 48 hours to do so.' Alas, it is not known what she had done, or if she did indeed disappear.

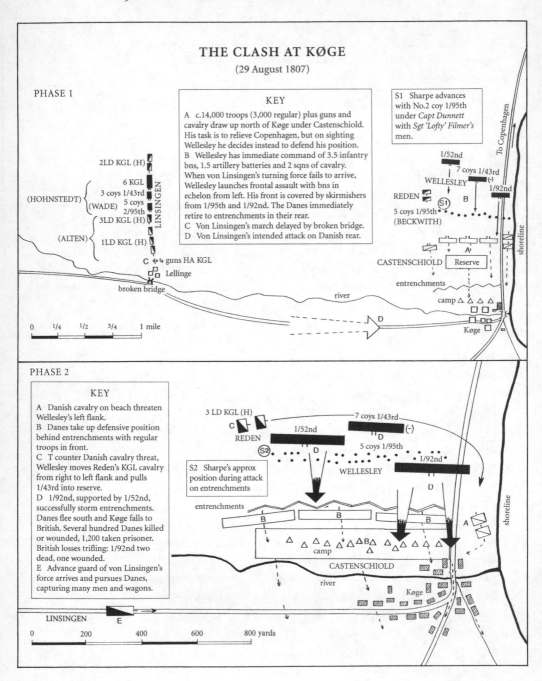

THE CLASH AT KØGE

(29 August 1807)

PHASE 1

KEY

A c.14,000 troops (3,000 regular) plus guns and cavalry draw up north of Køge under Castenschiold. His task is to relieve Copenhagen, but on sighting Wellesley he decides instead to defend his position.
B Wellesley has immediate command of 3.5 infantry bns, 1.5 artillery batteries and 2 sqns of cavalry. When von Linsingen's turning force fails to arrive, Wellesley launches frontal assault with bns in echelon from left. His front is covered by skirmishers from 1/95th and 1/92nd. The Danes immediately retire to entrenchments in their rear.
C Von Linsingen's march delayed by broken bridge.
D Von Linsingen's intended attack on Danish rear.

S1 Sharpe advances with No.2 coy 1/95th under *Capt Dunnett* with *Sgt 'Lofty' Filmer's* men.

2LD KGL (H)

6 KGL
(HOHNSTEDT)   3 coys 1/43rd
(WADE)   5 coys
2/95th
3LD KGL (H)
(ALTEN)   1LD KGL (H)

LINSINGEN

C ⊣ 4 guns HA KGL
☐☐ Lellinge
⊢ broken bridge

0   1/4   1/2   3/4   1 mile

To Copenhagen

1/52nd
7 coys 1/43rd
WELLESLEY   (-)
REDEN   1/92nd
S1   B
5 coys 1/95th
(BECKWITH)

shoreline

A
CASTENSCHIOLD   Reserve

entrenchments

river

camp △ △ △
☐ ☐
D   ☐☐
Køge ☐

PHASE 2

KEY

A Danish cavalry on beach threaten Wellesley's left flank.
B Danes take up defensive position behind entrenchments with regular troops in front.
C T counter Danish cavalry threat, Wellesley moves Reden's KGL cavalry from right to left flank and pulls 1/43rd into reserve.
D 1/92nd, supported by 1/52nd, successfully storm entrenchments. Danes flee south and Køge falls to British. Several hundred Danes killed or wounded, 1,200 taken prisoner. British losses trifling: 1/92nd two dead, one wounded.
E Advance guard of von Linsingen's force arrives and pursues Danes, capturing many men and wagons.

S2 Sharpe's approx position during attack on entrenchments

3 LD KGL (H)
C
REDEN
S2

7 coys 1/43rd
1/52nd   (-)
D
5 coys 1/95th
D   WELLESLEY
1/92nd
D

entrenchments
B   B   B   A   shoreline

△
△ △ △ △△B△ △ △ △ △
camp   △
CASTENSCHIOLD

river
Køge

LINSINGEN   E

0   200   400   600   800 yards

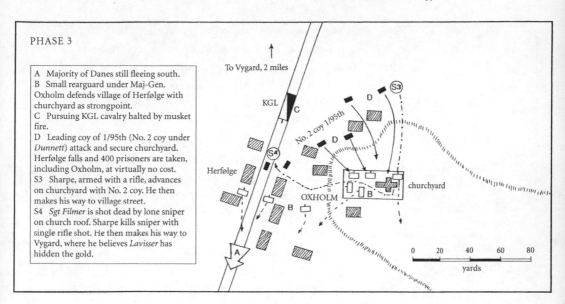

PHASE 3

A Majority of Danes still fleeing south.
B Small rearguard under Maj-Gen.
Oxholm defends village of Herfølge with
churchyard as strongpoint.
C Pursuing KGL cavalry halted by musket
fire.
D Leading coy of 1/95th (No. 2 coy under
Dunnett) attack and secure churchyard.
Herfølge falls and 400 prisoners are taken,
including Oxholm, at virtually no cost.
S3 Sharpe, armed with a rifle, advances
on churchyard with No. 2 coy. He then
makes his way to village street.
S4 *Sgt Filmer* is shot dead by lone sniper
on church roof. Sharpe kills sniper with
single rifle shot. He then makes his way to
Vygard, where he believes *Lavisser* has
hidden the gold.

To Vygard, 2 miles

KGL

No. 2 coy 1/95th

Herfølge

OXHOLM

churchyard

0   20   40   60   80

yards

west. There was no sign of von Linsingen. He decided to
wait. At this point, recognising Sharpe, he stopped for a quick
word with him – much to the annoyance of *Dunnett*.

Sharpe, armed with a rifle borrowed from one of the sick,
joined the 95th skirmishers and attached himself to *Sergeant
'Lofty' Filmer*, an NCO of noticeably short stature. When,
after about an hour, Wellesley's patience with von Linsingen's
non-appearance ran out, Sharpe and his fellow skirmishers
moved up the slope towards the Danish position. All three
British battalions in line attacked, supported initially by artillery fire along the line of the road. There was nothing subtle
about a straightforward frontal assault by infantry. Up to this
time Wellesley's battle plans (Mallavelly, Argaum and Assaye)
had all resulted in marching straight at the enemy position.
(The US Marine Corps' unofficial and frivolous tactical doc-
trine of Korea and Vietnam – 'hey-diddle-diddle, straight up
the middle' – springs to mind.) That said, Wellesley had a
shrewd idea of the worth of his enemy and of his own infantry's steadiness. His battalions advanced in echelon, the left-
hand one (1/92nd) leading. In the centre was the 1/43rd and

some distance back on the right the 1/52nd. The British guns firing along the road and the sight of the three red-coated lines of steady infantry advancing behind the galling fire of the 1/95th's rifles, which easily outranged the muskets of the Danish skirmishers, proved too much for even the Danish regulars to stomach. Long before any bayonets crossed, the Danes retreated rapidly to entrenchments that had been dug north of the town in front of their encampment.

Wellesley rode up the slope to assess the new situation. Worried about the threat of a cavalry attack from the beach area to the left flank of the 1/92nd if the advance was continued immediately, he ordered Colonel von Reden to bring his two squadrons from the right flank to the extreme left. Once they were in position, and the 1/43rd had been pulled back into reserve in a second line, the 1/92nd stormed forward and took the entrenchment, driving the Danes back through the town. The retreat quickly turned into a rout. At about this time, as Køge was taken, von Linsingen's force finally appeared from the right to hasten the flight of the Danes. Thus far it had cost the 1/92nd two killed and one wounded. The whole affair barely rated the term 'battle'. It was remarkable, however, as the only engagement in which Sharpe participated but did nothing of note.

Surtees, our informative quartermaster-sergeant of the 2/95th, who was in practice doing the quartermaster's job, was responsible for the wagons of his half-battalion as it marched with von Linsingen. Interestingly, he throws no light on the reason for the latter's late arrival – no mention of a broken bridge or difficult crossing of the river – though he does describe some awkward circumstances and navigation problems which will be familiar to modern quartermasters:

> I had charge of the baggage, which was carried on light German wagons . . . I found it impracticable to continue in the same direction the troops had gone, for they presently left all traces of a road, and struck right across the country – and as I knew I should be expected to have the baggage with them that night if possible, I determined to run all hazards, and

Quartermaster-Sergeant William Surtees

SURTEES, author of the journal *Twenty-Five Years in the Rifle Brigade,* was a fascinating character. Like Sharpe, he worked his way up through the ranks to become a quartermaster (in June 1809), eventually resigning through ill-health as a captain quartermaster in 1826. He died four years later in Corbridge, Northumberland, the village of his birth, at the age of forty-nine. His had been a rough life; after enlisting at seventeen in the local militia he had joined the 56th Foot (West Essex) and then the light battalion – where he was for a time commanded by a Lt-Col. Sharpe of the 9th Foot – and he saw many years' continuous active service throughout the Peninsular War (though he missed Waterloo).

An ambitious and competent soldier, he rose rapidly to corporal, sergeant and then company pay sergeant. When the 2/95th was formed Sergeant Surtees was openly aggrieved that he did not get the vacant appointment of sergeant-major. He took to the bottle, but a warning from his company commander brought him to his senses. In October 1805 he was with the 1/95th when they embarked for Germany. In his journal he recalls events on board the troopship during a violent storm: 'In the midst of the confusion attendant on such circumstances, the master (with what intention I know not, whether to drown dull care, or fortify him against his exposure to the watery element) went below, and swallowed the best part of a bottle of brandy ... My commanding officer now became quite alarmed ... and after consultation among our officers, an attempt was made to deprive him of the command, and entrust it to the mate ... who determined on running the vessel high and dry, as he termed it, on the sandy beach, near the Jade River. At this proposal, however, the master stormed and blasphemed like a madman ... he went so far, and became so outrageous, that our commanding officer talked of hanging him up at the yard-arm ... The poor mate sat down on the companion[way] and cried like a child, partly owing to the abuse the captain gave him, and partly, I imagine, from the hopelessness of our situation. The captain told the major he had been several times wrecked ... and exposed for a considerable length of time in the water; and that he was not afraid to encounter it again. This, however, was but poor consolation to landsmen, who had not been accustomed to such duckings.' The master's answer was to hoist the mainsail, which 'every moment threatened to carry away the mast'. They eventually made a 'providential' escape from the bay and landed at Cuxhaven on 18 November 1805 after being saved from ploughing into some rocks by the shouted warnings of a cabin boy. (Sharpe, only just back from Trafalgar, missed this exciting voyage with the 1/95th.)

proceeded along the great high-road in hopes of afterwards being enabled to find them ... I own it was a hazardous undertaking, for a very small party of the enemy would easily have captured both me and my baggage; but I knew my commanding-officer [Wade] to be such a person as to pay little attention to excuses of any kind when he wished a thing to be done, and withal he loved his comforts, and would not have been easily pacified had he been deprived of them.

Surtees was lucky; he met no enemy and by good fortune was able to deliver his precious wagons to his commanding officer that evening. Despite his daring and initiative in bringing up the rations and officers' baggage on this occasion, Surtees had to wait nearly another two years before he was commissioned as quartermaster – a good example of how promotion to quartermaster normally came after years in the ranks, many of them spent as a senior NCO. Surtees had enlisted at seventeen and when made quartermaster had eleven years' service. Sharpe, by comparison, was still just fifteen on enlistment and had risen to sergeant when, after ten years' service, he was commissioned – initially as a combatant officer.

Von Linsingen had indeed been delayed by unforeseen terrain difficulties, although this does not explain his not informing Wellesley of the situation. First, he had tried to cross the river at a place rendered impassable by a large morass, and then found the bridge at Lellinge had collapsed. Major Munter, who commanded the pioneers of 6th KGL, repaired it sufficiently in half an hour to allow troops to cross in single file. Von Linsingen's approach to the town was opposed very briefly by enemy skirmishers who had been positioned in the high branches of trees in a wood through which his force had to pass. Such deployment serves to underline the inexperience of the Danish commanders. Anything but mobile, finding it difficult to reload without falling, these unfortunate snipers could at best get away one shot – the smoke from which would reveal their position to the enemy. Captain William Napier, later Sir W. F. P. Napier the great

Peninsula historian, was in command of the detachment of the 1/43rd that accompanied von Linsingen and would not allow his men to fire on them, 'pitying their helpless and cruel situation'.

The pursuit of the Danes, led by the KGL cavalry, was swift and vigorous. Surprisingly, while the Danish regulars for the most part kept running, some militia or levies showed more spirit. As Beamish's *History of the King's German Legion* records:

> Although the Danish regular troops fled with precipitation, throwing away their arms and appointments, the new levies showed much spirit. Some of these raw recruits fired upon the cavalry from the windows of the houses in Køge, and suffered themselves to be bayoneted by the [following] infantry; others took shelter behind the sheaves of corn in the fields, and from thence fired on their pursuers. The greater part of these were either cut down or made prisoners, but not without loss to the legion hussars.

The German cavalry lost one officer killed and one officer and sixteen men wounded in this skirmish. Wellesley and his troops were much surprised to discover that the Danish levies wore wooden clogs instead of shoes or boots – hardly conducive to mobility or silent movement. Surtees rightly deemed this footwear 'a very inconvenient kind I should imagine for a rapid retreat'. As a result, Køge came to be referred to as the 'Battle of the Clogs'.

The Danes' final attempt to stop the rot occurred in the small village of Herfølge, about four miles south-west of Køge and close to where Sharpe had come ashore sixteen days earlier. Major-General Oxholm had arrived at Herfølge with fresh troops from the south to take up positions in the village and the churchyard, which was on a small hill and thus dominated the buildings and approaches. The advancing KGL horsemen were halted by musket fire and forced to await the arrival of the first infantry – the 1/95th. These light infantrymen quickly opened fire and skirmished forward. *Dunnett*'s company attacked the churchyard with great verve and speed. It was in Herfølge that *Sergeant Filmer* was shot and Sharpe, with deadly effect, used his rifle for the first time that day on the NCO's killer. The defenders soon surrendered and Oxholm, along with four hundred men, was taken prisoner. Two days after this engagement Sharpe was to seek out *Lavisser*'s house at nearby Vygård, hunting for the gold, only to be arrested (briefly) by *Dunnett* for plundering – a capital offence.

The casualty score for the day was decidedly unbalanced. Although no figures for Danish dead or wounded are available for this encounter, some 56 officers were captured, as were over 1,100 soldiers, at least ten cannons, countless discarded weapons and a large number of stores or ammunition wagons. Fortescue, without differentiating between this action and the army's skirmishing since the landing, puts British losses from 16–31 August at 172: 2 officers and 27 men killed, 6 officers and 116 men wounded, 21 men missing. Surtees nonetheless found the whole business disappointing, complaining of having not fired more than eight or ten shots since he came ashore – although for the battalion quartermaster-sergeant this sounds a more than satisfactory amount.

By 31 August the British batteries had been built (MAP 15) in the western suburbs, within range of the city centre. There were fifteen siege battery positions (that is, excluding field artillery), including three for the newly developed Congreve rockets. Some forty-one mortars, thirty-five 24-pounders and four howitzers stood ready to fire. Although the 24-pounders had been removed from warships and brought ashore, the fleet still retained enormous firepower including bomb vessels and rocket-firing ships. The gunners now had nothing to do but await the order to open fire.

That same day the Danes launched what was supposed to be a general sortie, gallantly led by General Peymann in person. It was a rather feeble affair that was easily repelled by the picket line of Baird's 2nd Division. Nevertheless, both

Baird and Peymann were wounded, the latter more seriously
– although he retained command, issuing orders from his
bed for the remainder of the siege.

The British had been ashore for two weeks but had yet to
begin a full-scale assault on the city. Cathcart, Gambier and
Jackson did not have to refer back to England when making
a decision to bombard Copenhagen; they had the authority
– indeed, uncompromising instructions – to open an attack
if the Danes refused to hand over their fleet. So why the
hesitation? The reason was the military commanders' awareness that a bombardment of the city would cause countless
civilian casualties; what today's military term 'collateral damage' was unavoidable. Mr Jackson, apparently, was made of
sterner stuff. As the British Government's representative on
the spot he could, and did, insist that the service commanders
carry out their duty. In other circumstances, had there been
ample time, a proper siege could have been undertaken with
the attackers concentrating their fire on the outer walls,
making a breach and storming it. This method would have
avoided shelling civilians or causing damage in the town, but
the process might have taken months. Instead the British
now contemplated firing on Copenhagen to cause maximum
damage to buildings and death to its citizens in order to
force a quick surrender – this at a time when Denmark was
not even at war with Britain.

On 31 August one last attempt was made to persuade the
wounded Peymann to spare the city the horrors of bombardment by delivering the fleet into British hands. If this were
done the British force would evacuate Denmark, restore all
captured property and carry off the fleet with the solemn
undertaking to return it on the signature of a general peace.
The answer was another indignant refusal. Still Cathcart,
whose guns awaited his order, hesitated. Much to the annoyance of Jackson, the general waited another two days in the
hope that the Danes would see sense. They did not. At
7.30 p.m. on 2 September the batteries opened fire.

*   *   *

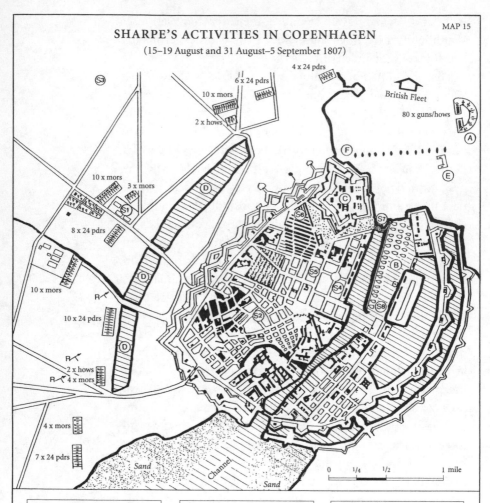

SHARPE'S ACTIVITIES IN COPENHAGEN

(15–19 August and 31 August–5 September 1807)

MAP 15

4 x 24 pdrs

6 x 24 pdrs

10 x mors

2 x hows

British Fleet

80 x guns/hows

F

E

A

10 x mors

3 x mors

D

C

S7

S6

10 x mors

S1

8 x 24 pdrs

D

S3

B

R

10 x 24 pdrs

S5

D

S4

S8

R

2 x hows

S2

R   4 x mors

4 x mors

7 x 24 pdrs

Sand

Channel

Sand

0   1/4   1/2   1 mile

A Sixtus or Three Crown Battery, built on piles at mouth of harbour with timber bulwarks backed by earth berms but with no overhead cover. Barracks, magazine and furnace for hot shot, 68 x 24-pdr guns, 4 light field guns and 8 howitzers.
B Inner Harbour with Danish fleet sheltering inside.
C Citadel with 30 guns and 11 mortars.
D Inundations.
E Little Crown Battery–without guns.
F Position of Danish gunboats when forced back during siege.
R Positions of British rocket batteries

KEY

S1 Suburb of Vester Fælled, location of *Ole Skovgaard's* house where Sharpe was imprisoned but escaped via chimney. Here *Skovgaard* was tortured and Sharpe killed 3 Frenchmen (16 Aug.)
S2 Ulfedt's Plads, site of *Skovgaard's* townhouse and warehouse. Sharpe imprisoned *Aksel Bang* here after he tried to arrest him (2 Sept.) and slept here with *Astrid* (3 Sept.).
S3 Danes engage in skirmish with British as Sharpe rejoins British Army (18 Aug.).
S4 Amalienborg Palace, winter palace of Royal Family, where Danish commanders held planning meetings.

S5 *Lavisser's* house in Bredgade where he hid the stolen gold. Sharpe driven off by musket fire on night of 2 Sept. S. returns with *Hopper* and *Clouter*, attacks the house and kills a Frenchman. After the siege he collects the gold (5 Sept.).
S6 Nyboder, poor area of city where *Astrid's* orphanage/hospital was located. Ruined in bombardment. Here S. kills *Bang, Barker* and *Lavisser* on 4 Sept.
S7 Sharpe, *Capt Chase* and seamen land here night of 31 Aug. en route to Danish fleet to prevent it being set alight.
S8 Sharpe, *Chase* and others board *Christian VII*, 96-gun Danish flagship.

During the lull before the storm Sharpe, having left the 95th, was involved in a number of escapades. On the night of 31 August he guided a party of British naval ratings including *Hopper* and *Clouter,* led by *Captain Chase* of HMS *Pucelle* (on which he had fought at Trafalgar), to the Danish fleet in Copenhagen's inner harbour. They succeeded in getting aboard the unmanned ships and neutralising the incendiary devices which had been intended to destroy the fleet. The Crown Prince did send orders, one of which was captured, to destroy the fleet rather than allow it to fall into British hands, but there is no evidence that it was ever attempted. Perhaps Peymann felt he could hold out long enough to make it unnecessary, or that the British taking the fleet intact, with the possibility of getting it back at some later date, was preferable to its complete destruction. It is possible too that the order never got through to the high command, cut off as Peymann was within a city under bombardment.

Over the following four days Sharpe embarked on a number of missions, some official, some personal, in the city. These included saving his latest lady-friend, *Astrid,* ensuring the safety of her father, *Skovgaard,* killing *Lavisser* and finding the gold. He succeeded in all these tasks while the city around him went up in flames. The wooden buildings of Copenhagen made a gigantic bonfire. For twelve hours the shells, bombs and rockets rained down on the defenceless citizens, then the deluge stopped. The Danish defenders continued to fire from the walls at targets they could not properly see, but for the inhabitants there was a respite. In case the reader might think this pause was to allow the Danes to change their minds about surrendering their ships, this was not the case; the batteries were merely restocking their ammunition. On the night of 3 September the brutal bombardment started up again, although it was noticeably less severe as the supply of shells and bombs was limited. There followed another day of horror in the city with hundreds of dead and injured. The conflagration roared unchecked, hospitals were over-whelmed, but, perhaps due to the slight slackening of inten-

Naval mortars

THESE WERE short-barrelled (2–4 times as long as the bore diameter), high-angle muzzle-loaders borrowed from the army, where they were mostly used in siege warfare to fire explosive shells or 'carcass shot' (incendiaries) at buildings, shore batteries or over the walls of fortifications. They were also used to support landings and cutting-out expeditions or attacks on ships blockaded in a port. There were two main types, 13 inch and 10 inch, and a bomb vessel would usually have one of each on traversing turntables. By 1807 they were manned by the Royal Marine Artillery, formed for this purpose because mortars required a greater degree of specialist skill to operate than guns. Elaborate precautions were needed to keep the shells safe on board, while keeping them on target required a high degree of accuracy in assessing the range and considerable experience in handling the timed fuse, which had to be trimmed to the right length to ensure the burning time matched the flight time. Too short, and the shell would burst over or before reaching the target, too long and it would land fizzing on the ground or on deck, giving the enemy time to extinguish it or push it into the sea. The first Victoria Cross ever awarded went to Mr Charles Lucas, a mate on HMS Hecla. While bombarding a Baltic fort in 1854 during the Crimean War, a shell landed on the Hecla's deck and Lucas ran forward to throw it over the side before it exploded.

Although mortars were not designed for ship-against-ship action, in 1808 the bomb vessel HMS Thunderer used them in her heroic defence of a convoy that had come under attack from twenty-five Danish gunboats. She fought for five hours, firing her carronades, together with shells and 1lb balls from her mortars, until the Danes were driven off, taking with them only twelve out of the seventy vessels under the Thunderer's protection.

---

sity of the bombardment during the night, Peymann still refused to give in. More ammunition was brought up to the batteries for the third night of the bombardment. The renewed ferocity proved too much. On 5 September Peymann pleaded for a ceasefire. It was granted immediately.

That same day, Sharpe sailed home on leave on the *Pucelle*. He had completed his mission well, had recovered some of the gold for the British Government (and a lot more besides, which he donated to the rebuilding of *Astrid*'s orphanage). For political reasons his continued presence in Copenhagen was considered unwise, so General Baird authorised his early departure – the 95th would spend another seven weeks in Denmark before they too came home.

Those three weeks in 1807 were a disaster for Denmark. She lost her fleet and her capital city was devastated, many parts not being rebuilt for a generation. Over 300 houses were completely burned out, a thousand more were badly damaged, along with the cathedral, churches and the university. Britain seized all the various naval and military stores, together with the cannons in the arsenal. The British also took possession of eighteen ships of the line, ten frigates, five corvettes, six brigs and about twenty-five other vessels. A number of partially built ships were destroyed. This added up to a huge financial loss for the Danes – an estimated 30 million thalers. Despite a violent storm on the voyage home which deprived the victors of a number of prizes, the booty was immense. Both Cathcart and Gambier were said to have shared £300,000 while almost £1,000,000 was due to the troops.

The human cost was high, too. During the siege and bombardment the Danish Army suffered 135 dead and 300 wounded, the navy 53 dead and 50 wounded. Civilian losses in Copenhagen amounted to 1,600 dead and over 1,000 injured, while a further 1,200 soldiers and seamen had gone missing (deserted).

Finally there were Denmark's territorial losses. This incredibly short campaign pushed her into an alliance with France, which cost her Norway (to Sweden) while Britain secured Heligoland, a tiny island in the North Sea, that she kept for eighty-three years (it became a useful depot for smuggling British goods into the Continent) before handing it over to Germany – it is only thirty-odd miles from the German coast.

Sharpe came home on leave, still in the 95th, still a quartermaster, still poor and still disgruntled.

DANISH PRISONERS

Nearly a thousand Danish prisoners were taken during the campaign. They were shipped back to England and transferred to the notorious prison ships – rotten and leaky hulks of former warships crammed full of prisoners, mostly French, from the wars in Europe. It was a grim experience, even for men hardened by years of marching and fighting. Lieutenant John Kincaid, then an officer in the North York Militia (he later joined the 95th Rifles), was responsible for guarding c.800 Danish prisoners on HMS Irresistible. He wrote with obvious feeling for their undeserved fate: 'found guilty of defending their property against their invaders [the British] ... I can answer for it that they were made as miserable as any body of men detected in such a heinous crime had a right to be, for of all diabolical constructions in the shape of prisons, the hulks claim by right a pre-eminence.'

Let's join the ladies!

THE BRITISH TROOPS remained in Denmark for a few weeks after the capitulation of Copenhagen. Inevitably, the victors' thoughts turned to booze and women. Rifleman Harris, in his book *A Dorset Rifleman*, published in 1848, gives a splendid account of where these thoughts led:

> Occasionally, we had some pleasant adventures among the blue-eyed Danish lasses, for the Rifles were always terrible fellows in that way [I doubt things have changed much]. A party of us occupied a gentleman's house. The family . . . consisted of the owner of the mansion, his wife, five very handsome daughters, and their servants. On the first night we were treated with the utmost civility, although it cannot have been pleasant to have a company of foreign soldiers in the house. It was doubtless thought best to do everything possible to conciliate such guests, so on this night everything was set before us as if we were their equals, and a large party of green-jackets unceremoniously sat down to tea with the family.
>
> One young lady presided over the urn serving out the tea whilst the others sat on each side of their father and mother . . . Five beautiful girls in a drawing room were rather awkward companions for a set of rough and ready, bold and unscrupulous Riflemen . . . bye and bye, some of them expressed themselves dissatisfied with tea and toast, and demanded something stronger. Liquors were accordingly served to them. This was followed by more familiarity. The ice once broken, respect for the host and hostess was quickly lost as I feared would prove the case. Several of the men started pulling the young ladies about, kissing them, and proceeding to other acts of rudeness [delicately put]. I saw that unless I interfered matters would quickly get worse, so I jumped up and endeavoured to restore order. I upbraided the men for behaving like blackguards after the kindness we had been shown. My remonstrance had some effect, and when I added that I would immediately report to an officer the first man I saw ill-use the ladies, I succeeded in extricating them from their persecutors. The father and mother were extremely grateful to me . . .

TIMELINE – SHARPE'S EARLY LIFE (1777–1808)

ABBREVIATIONS

GLOSSARY

BIBLIOGRAPHY

TIMELINE – SHARPE'S EARLY LIFE (1777–1808)

Year	Month	Sharpe	Other Events
1777	26 Jun	Born London near Howick Place, Westminster	In American War of Independence British defeated at Princeton and Saratoga
1780	Jun	Aged 3 sent to foundling home in Brewhouse Lane	Mother killed in Gordon Riots
1789	Jul	Aged 12 sold to chimney sweep. Runs away to St Giles Rookery. Taken in by *Maggie Joyce*, owner of gin-house-cum-brothel. Lives on wits, mostly by thieving.	Paris mob storm Bastille: French Revolution begins
1792	Sept	Aged 15 kills drunken gang leader attacking *Maggie Joyce*. Flees to Yorkshire. Finds work in tavern.	French capture Brussels
1793	Mar	Kills Yorkshire tavern owner in fight. Runs away again	Louis XVI executed. Reign of Terror begins. Maj. Wesley (later Wellesley, later D. of Wellington) takes command 33rd
	16 Apr	Enlisted by *Sgt Hakeswill* into 33rd Foot while still just 15. Recruit training	

1794	Jun	To Holland with 33rd as pte.	D. of Y's expedition to
	15 Sept	First action at Boxtel	Holland
1795	Jan	Suffers frostbite in worst winter in living memory.	Napoleon C-in-C Italy. Brit. withdraws from
	15 Apr	Returns to England to Warley, Essex.	Europe after disastrous campaign
	16 Nov	Sails from Portsmouth for W.I. but hurricane forces return. With 33rd to Lymington.	33rd suffers 200 dead, 192 sick. Only 6 in action.
	17 Dec	Promoted corporal aged 18	
1796	6 Jan	Reduced to private for drunkenness and neglect of duty as guard commander over Christmas/New Year festivities.	Napoleon enters Milan Col Wesley joins 33rd at Cape Town
	Apr	Sails for India with 33rd	
1797	17 Feb	Arrives Calcutta.	Jervis and Nelson
	Aug	Sails with 33rd; expedition to Manila. Recalled on reaching Penang.	defeat Spanish at Cape St Vincent
1798	28 Sept	Arrived Madras from Calcutta for campaign against Tippoo Sultan	
1799	13 Feb	Marches as pte against Mahrattas.	4th Mysore War begins Col Wellesley 3IC to
	27 Mar	Kills Indian officer at Mallavelly.	Gen. Harris. 33rd under Maj. Shee.
	30 Mar	Flogged for hitting *Sgt Hakeswill*. Sent on special op. inside Seringapatam.	Napoleon conquers Egypt.
	2 Apr	Wounded in side by lance en route to Seringapatam.	

	6 Apr–4 May	Special ops in city, kills 6 including Tippoo. Prevents detonation of mine.	
	5 May	Promoted sergeant for actions in Seringapatam aged almost 22.	
	Jun	Appointed armoury sergeant at Seringapatam.	
1800		Armoury sergeant at Seringapatam	33rd patrolling and guarding supply routes north. Napoleon defeats Austrians at Marengo.
1801		Armoury sergeant at Seringapatam	Hyde Parker and Nelson defeat Danes off Copenhagen.
1802		Armoury sergeant at Seringapatam	Peace of Amiens between Britain and France.
1803	2 Jul	Wounded in head while on detached duty at *Chasalgaon*	2nd Mahratta War begins
	16 Jul	On special ops to find Dodd.	
	11 Aug	Present at capture of Ahmednuggur.	Renewal of war between Britain and France.
	23 Sept	Wellesley's orderly at Battle of Assaye. Kills 6 and saves Wellesley's life.	
	25 Sept	Commissioned ensign in 74th Foot aged 26.	
	29 Nov	Coy officer No. 6 Coy 74th at Battle of Argaum. Kills one man.	
	5 Dec	Sent as 2IC bullock train.	

	9 Dec	Kidnapped, kills one *jetti*, escapes; kills OC bullock train and clerk.	
	11 Dec	Kills 2 men of 33rd for plotting to kill him.	
	15 Dec	Takes part in assault on Gawilghur, wounded in hip, rib and cheek. Kills 2 men (including Dodd).	
1804	Feb	As ensign in 74th takes part in campaign against Pindarris. Marches 60 km in 30 hrs.	Napoleon proclaimed emperor.
	Apr–Dec	Stationed at Poona. Garrison duties, often sick with fevers, runs up debts, depressed.	
1805	Jan–May	At Poona	Wellesley leaves India in Mar.
	28 Jun	Aged 28 leaves India on *Calliope* (merchantman)	
	20 Jul	Captured by French when *Calliope* surrenders to *Revenant*. Kills French officer.	
	25 Jul	Transferred to 74-gun *Pucelle* after it recaptures *Calliope*.	
	7 Sept	Kills civilian enemy on *Pucelle*.	1/95 under Lt-Col
	21 Oct	On board *Pucelle* at Battle of Trafalgar. Kills 6 enemy plus others with Nock gun during battle.	Beckwith embarks for Germany 30 Oct. Napoleon victorious at Austerlitz.
	16 Nov	Arrives England.	
1806	Jan–Feb	Lives with *Lady Grace* while on leave	1/95th returns 19 Feb move to Woodbridge, Suffolk.

	Mar	Reluctantly reports for duty 1/95th posted to No.3 Coy as 2nd Lt.	2/95th raised in May. Napoleon enters Berlin.
	Jun	*Lady Grace* dies in childbirth along with baby son. Sharpe devastated.	1/95th move to join 2/95th at Brabourne Lees, Kent.
	Aug	Made QM 1/95th.	3 coys 2/95th to S.
	Oct	Remains as QM in England	America followed by 5 coys 1/95th.
1807	Jan–Jun	QM 1/95th at Brabourne Lees. Acute depression, in debt, wants to quit army.	
	Jul	Told he must remain as rear party QM to await arrival of coys from S. America	Remaining coys 1/95th and 2/95th warned for expedition to Denmark.
	26 Jul	To London. Fails to sell commission. Visits foundling home at Wapping. Kills his old master (*Hocking*).	95th coys embarked at Deal. 1/95th under Beckwith, 2/95th under Wade.
	27 Jul	Meets Gen. Baird: given special op in Denmark. Departs Harwich.	Napoleon victorious at Friedland 14 Jun.
	13 Aug	Lands Køge Bay south of Copenhagen.	
	16 Aug	Kills 3 Frenchmen.	
	18 Aug	Rejoins Brit Army outside Copenhagen.	
	29 Aug	Sent to 1/95th. Present at Battle of Køge with 1/95th.	
	3 Sept	Kills Dane at Herfølge. Kills Frenchman in Copenhagen.	British besiege and bombard Copenhagen.

	4 Sept	Kills 3 in Copenhagen. Slightly wounded in head.	City surrenders 7 Sept.
	21 Oct	Sails for Yarmouth with 1/95th.	
1808	Apr	Still QM 1/95th.	3 Coys 1/95th sent with Sir John Moore's
	May	Transfers to 2/95th as QM. Based at Hythe under Lt-Col Wade.	expedition to Sweden.

Abbreviations used in Text and Glossary

The Sharpe Books (in historical chronological order)

ST	*Sharpe's Tiger*	SC	*Sharpe's Company*
STr	*Sharpe's Triumph*	SS	*Sharpe's Sword*
SF	*Sharpe's Fortress*	SEn	*Sharpe's Enemy*
STraf	*Sharpe's Trafalgar*	SH	*Sharpe's Honour*
SP	*Sharpe's Prey*	SRegt	*Sharpe's Regiment*
SR	*Sharpe's Rifles*	SSge	*Sharpe's Siege*
SHav	*Sharpe's Havoc*	SRev	*Sharpe's Revenge*
SE	*Sharpe's Eagle*	SW	*Sharpe's Waterloo*
SG	*Sharpe's Gold*	SD	*Sharpe's Devil*
SB	*Sharpe's Battle*		

ADC	aide-de-camp	cav.	cavalry
adjt	adjutant	col	colonel
adm.	admiral	comd(s)	commander(s)
AG	adjutant-general	coy	company
ammo.	ammunition		
AQMG	assistant quartermaster-general	fmn	formation
arty	artillery	EIC	East India Company
asst.comm.	assistant-commissary		
AWI	American War of Independence	gen.	general
		gren.	grenadier
bn	battalion	fmn	formation
bde	brigade	Fr.	French
capt.	captain	HQ	headquarters

inf.	infantry	Pen. War	Peninsular War
		pdr	pounder
KGL	King's German Legion	pte	private
lt	lieutenant	Regt	regiment
lt-col	lieutenant-colonel	rflm.	rifleman
lt coy	light company	RM	Royal Marines
		RN	Royal Navy
maj.	major	RSM	regimental
maj-gen.	major-general		sergeant-major
NCO	non-commissioned	sgt	sergeant
	officer	sgt-maj.	sergeant-major
		sqn	squadron
QM	quartermaster	sub.	subaltern
QMG	quartermaster-general		
QMS	quartermaster-sergeant	2IC	second in command

Glossary

adjutant Regtl/bn staff officer responsible for drill, discipline and personnel matters. Usually captain, often with other-rank service.

Ahmed 13-year-old Arab boy who fought against Sharpe at the Battle of Argaum in 1803. Sharpe knocked him down and later rescued him from probable execution. He became Sharpe's devoted servant and follower, but was killed by *Colonel* Dodd in the fight for the gatehouse at Gawilghur. In *SF.*

Allen, Maj. Officer in 12th Foot in India 1798 who shot and mortally wounded his former CO, Col. Ashton, in a duel. This led to Wellesley receiving Ashton's horse, Diomed, and the task of preparing the Army of Madras for 4th Mysore War against Tippoo Sultan. Allen died a few months later while still in custody.

Amalienborg Palace (MAP 15) Winter palace of the Danish royal family in central Copenhagen. Consisted of 4 palaces (King's, Crown Prince's, Hereditary Prince's and Duke's palaces) grouped round a courtyard. Here Danish commanders held their planning meetings during the siege in *SP.*

Argaum One of Wellesley's victories in India fought on 29 Nov. 1803. Sharpe ensign in 74th Foot.

Armstrong, Sgt RM NCO on board *HMS Pucelle* at Trafalgar, where he was mortally wounded fighting alongside Sharpe. In *STraf.*

Army Agents Civilian businessmen acting as middlemen between adjutant-general/paymaster-general and regiments in matters of pay, clothing issue, and sale/purchase of commissions. Individuals wishing to buy a commission would deposit the necessary sum of money and letter of recommendation from their colonel with the relevant regimental agent, who would forward details to the AG's office. If there was no vacancy in the officer's own regiment, the agent would find an opening in another regiment in his 'portfolio' – for a fee. A commission could be sold through an agent only if it had been paid for in the first place; Sharpe's had been awarded for valour on the battlefield, so his visit to *Messrs Bolling and Brown* was unsuccessful (in reality Messrs Greenwood and Cox acted for the 95th Rifles).

Ashton, Col Henry Formerly of 12th Foot. Friend of Wellesley, killed in a duel. His horse, Diomed, was bequeathed to Wellesley and subsequently killed at Assaye.

Assaye Village in India, site of Wellesley's victory over greatly superior forces on 23 Sept. 1803. Sharpe, a sgt on special duties, was commissioned ensign into 74th Foot for saving Wellesley's life at this battle.

Assaye Colour Third Colour of the 74th Foot, carried on parade but not in the field, awarded in recognition of the regiment's outstanding gallantry and heavy losses at the Battle of Assaye 1803.

Baird, Lt-Gen. Sir David b.1757. Captured and imprisoned for 44 months in Seringapatam by the Tippoo Sultan in 1780. Deputy to Lt-Gen. Harris at Siege of Seringapatam in 1799, and led the storming of the breach. Was instrumental in sending *Lt Lawford* (and therefore Sharpe) on the special mission into Seringapatam in 1799. As a divisional commander Copenhagen 1807 was again Sharpe's mentor in another special mission. Badly wounded at Corunna in 1809. Thereafter, due to various enmities, received no further field command. Gen. 1814. C-in-C Ireland 1820–22. Died 1829 aged 72.

Baker, Ezekiel Inventor of the rifle that bore his name and with which Sharpe and all Brit. rifle battalions were eventually armed during Napoleonic Wars. Had a 30-inch, 7-groove, quarter-turn barrel. Accurate up to 300 yards, but could only be loaded about twice a minute. Excellent for skirmishers and picking off enemy officers or gun crews.

Bang, Mr Aksel Danish assistant to *Ole Skovgaard* in Copenhagen in 1807 who wanted to marry his daughter, *Astrid*. This (obviously) led to problems with Sharpe. *Bang* later betrayed *Skovgaard* and tried to have Sharpe arrested. Sharpe imprisoned him and later shot and killed him. In *SP*.

Barclay, Capt. William EIC officer from Shetland Islands who was on Wellesley's staff in the Second Mahratta War as deputy adjutant-general. Also ran HQ intelligence department.

Barker No other name given. Thug who accompanied *Capt. Lavisser* to Denmark as bodyguard in 1807. Failed to kill Sharpe on two occasions. Sharpe ultimately killed him by shooting him with a pistol. In *SP*.

battalion (bn) Tactical infantry unit varying from 500 to 1,000 men (sometimes less). British bns usually divided into 10 coys and commanded by lt-col. EIC bns followed British system but had European officers down to coy comds plus a nucleus of senior European NCOs mainly for drill and musketry training.

Beckwith, Lt-Col Thomas Sydney b. 1772. Came from army family (his father, Maj-Gen. John, led 20th Foot at Minden 1759; his nephew, Maj. Charles, was AQMG at Waterloo, where he lost a leg). Founder member of 95th Rifles – took command 1802. Having fought at Copenhagen in 1801 with Nelson, returned 1807 with Wellington and led 5 coys 1/95th. Sharpe's CO from March 1806; appointed him QM and later arranged his transfer to 2/95th. Fought under Moore in Corunna campaign then commanded 1/95th in the Light Brigade in the Peninsula until 1811. Returned home sick. AQMG in Canada, took part in American War 1812. Maj-Gen. 1814. C-in-C Bombay 1829. Lt-Gen. 1830. Died in India 1821 aged 59.

Belling, Mr Army Agent in Eastcheap, London. It was to him (and his partner *Mr Brown*) that Sharpe tried unsuccessfully to sell his commission in July 1807 in *SP*.

Beny Singh Subordinate of Berar who was killadar (commandant) of Gawilghur when it was attacked by

Wellesley in December 1803. Before the capture of the fortress he poisoned all his family before dying bravely fighting to defend the inner fort. In *SF* he is a fat, cowardly individual who killed *Sevajee*'s father and is himself killed by *Sergeant Hakeswill* on Dodd's orders.

Bhonsha, Rajah of Berar Mahratta prince allied with Scindia. His forces were present at Assaye, but he did not command them personally.

Blackiston, Maj. John Wellesley's engineer officer during the Second Mahratta War. Present at Ahmednuggur and Assaye.

Borkardan (MAPS 3 and 4) Fortified city 9 miles west of Assaye on River Kaitna where Mahratta army were thought to be assembled mid-September 1803. Wellesley planned to attack them here until he learned of encampment near Assaye. Site of Scindia's durbar (council of war) in *STr*.

Boxtel Small Dutch town; scene of Sharpe's first action when 33rd Foot under Lt-Col. Sherbrooke (not Wesley, who was bde commander) participated in the skilful withdrawal of main Brit. force on 15 Sept. 1794.

Brabourne Lees Small town in Kent where 95th was stationed. Sharpe moved here with 1/95th in August 1806 and after being appointed QM remained till July 1807 while coys from both bns departed for S. America.

Braithwaite, Mr Malachi Secretary to *Lord William Hale* on homeward voyage from India, summer 1805. He was in love with *Lady Grace Hale* and, consumed with jealousy at her affair with Sharpe, tried to blackmail the lovers by threatening to tell *Lord William*. Sharpe broke his neck, but he had left a letter to *Lord William*, to be opened on his death, informing him of the affair. The subsequent confrontation between *Lord William* and *Lady Grace* resulted in her shooting him dead during the Battle of Trafalgar. In *STraf*.

Bredgade (MAP 15) Wealthy area of Copenhagen, location of *Capt. Lavisser*'s grandfather's house, where he hid the stolen gold. Driven off by musket fire 2–3 Sept., Sharpe later returned with *Hopper* and *Clouter* to attack the house; he finally collected the gold after the siege. In *SP*.

Brewhouse Lane (MAP 12) Location of the foundling home for destitute orphans in Wapping, London, where Sharpe spent his early boyhood (1780–89). The lane still exists, some 200 metres from Wapping tube station.

brigade Tactical military fmn of c.3,000 men containing 2 or 3 bns. Until 1809 was highest (largest) formation in Brit. Army. Commanded by maj-gen. in Brit. Army, a *général de brigade* in Fr.

brigade major (BM) Staff officer attached to inf. bde.

brinjarris Grain merchants contracted to supply Brit. Army on campaign in India.

Brown Bess Nickname of Brit. smoothbore musket. 'To hug Brown Bess' meant to enlist.

Brown, Mr Army Agent working in Eastcheap, London. It was to him (and his partner *Mr Belling*) that Sharpe tried unsuccessfully to sell his commission in July 1807. In *SP*.

Bunbury, Lt Coy officer in 2/95th; first Brit. soldier killed in Pen. War, near Obidos, in Aug. 1808. Sharpe promoted lt into his vacancy.

Bursay, Lt Brutal ex-ranker French officer sent from the *Revenant* to command the *Calliope* as a prize after she was captured in July 1805. Killed by Sharpe with a sword thrust through the throat when he tried to rape *Lady Grace Hale*. In *STraf.*

Butters, Colonel Wellesley's chief engineer officer in the 1803 campaign against the Mahrattas. In *SF.*

Calliope EIC merchant ship under *Capt. Peculiar Cromwell* that sailed from Bombay late June 1805, carrying Sharpe home to England. Captured by the French warship *Revenant* near Mauritius on 20 July; recaptured by *HMS Pucelle* five days later. It eventually sailed for England via Cape Town, but Sharpe had transferred to *HMS Pucelle.*

canister Artillery projectile of lead balls in tin container. Resembled giant shotgun cartridge and had similar effects at short range. Also known as case-shot.

Canning, George b. 1770. British Secretary of State for Foreign Affairs in 1807. Leaked information on the clauses of the Treaty of Tilsit led him to take prompt and resolute action to seize the Danish fleet. In 1822 he was appointed governor-general of India, and in 1827 became prime minister, only to die, aged 57, after just 100 days in office, having caught a cold at the funeral of the Duke of York.

Castenschiold, Lt-Gen. Commanded Danish force that intended to march to the relief of Copenhagen in Aug. 1807. He was attacked and defeated by Wellesley near Køge on 29 Aug.

carronade Large-calibre, short-range cannon used on ships for firing canister.

Cathcart, General Lord William b. 1757. C-in-C of Brit. forces Denmark 1807 and was thus Sharpe's overall commander. Died 1843.

Chalmers, Lt-Col J. M. Regarded as one of Wellesley's best EIC bn commanders. He commanded the 1/2nd Madras, which was left out of the Battle of Assaye as baggage guard. At Gawilghur in December 1803 he led the left wing of the 78th Foot in a diversionary attack on the western side of the fortress – killing many of the enemy as they fled from the outer fort.

Chasalgaon (MAP 3) Small fort on the frontier with Hyderabad, garrisoned by EIC troops tasked with patrolling and protecting Wellesley's supply lines north from Seringapatam. Sharpe was sole survivor of massacre by *Major* Dodd's troops on 1 July 1803. In *STr.*

Chase, Capt. Joel RN 35-year-old commander of 74-gun ship of the line *HMS Pucelle*. Befriended Sharpe in Bombay after the latter rescued him from difficult confrontation with Indian merchants. Later returned the favour by recapturing the *Calliope,* on which Sharpe was sailing, after it had been surrendered to the French near Mauritius. *Pucelle* joined Nelson's fleet at Battle of Trafalgar with Sharpe on board. Chase survived to encounter Sharpe again at Copenhagen in 1807, where he led a naval party that prevented Danish fleet being deliberately destroyed by fire. In *STraf, SP.*

Chase, Florence Wife of *Capt. Joel Chase,* commander of *HMS Pucelle*. She lived in Devon. In *STraf.*

Cleopatra, HMS 32-gun frigate built in Bristol in 1779. In 1807 commanded by Capt. R. Simpson RN. Carried Sharpe to Denmark with *Capt. Lavisser* in

August 1807. Paid off for first time July 1814.

Clouter Large black seaman and former slave from the island of St Helena. In charge of the first gun to fire on the French from *HMS Pucelle* at Trafalgar. Saved Sharpe's life by killing a Frenchman with a pike during hectic mêlée on the *Pucelle* during the battle. With Sharpe for some of his time in Copenhagen in 1807. In *STraf, SP*.

cobbing Corporal punishment involving beating buttocks with flat piece of wood; meted out for minor offences in 95th Rifles.

Cobras The nickname given by *Maj*. Dodd to his elite inf. bns. In *STr*.

Collier, Midshipman Harry 12-year-old serving as midshipman on *HMS Pucelle*. Sharpe befriended him. He was given the task of recording the signals at the Battle of Trafalgar to keep his mind off the carnage. Survived the action unscathed. Commanded boat taking naval party to defuse incendiary devices on Danish fleet in Copenhagen 1807. In *STraf, SP*.

Colours Bn flags that represented the honour of a unit. Brit. bns had a King's and a Regtl Colour carried in battle by ensigns and protected by sgts (later colour-sgts). To lose a Colour meant disgrace. Fr. equivalent: Eagle.

commissariat Agency of Treasury responsible for supply of food, clothing, weapons and equipment in the field. Commissary officers were attached to all formations and dispersed along the army's lines of communication organising convoys, requisitioning, purchasing and moving supplies – a nightmare task, and commissary officers were personally liable for any financial losses.

company (coy) Basic inf. sub-unit of 60–120 men; usually commanded by capt.

compoo Indian term for large contingent of troops. Most were about the size of a British bde but size varied considerably. Colonel Pohlmann's compoo at the Battle of Assaye had 13 battalions.

Congreve rockets Invented by Sir William Congreve; mounted on long sticks like modern fireworks. First used in action 1805 firing from boats in salvoes. Erratic in flight; more inaccurate than guns. Limited lethality, although noise and sparks frightened horses. Used during Siege of Copenhagen 1807. Rocket troop of RHA formed 1813, used briefly in Pen. War and at Waterloo.

Connors, Pte Company clerk in the light company 33rd Foot at Gawilghur, December 1803. In *SF*.

Copenhagen Capital city of Denmark, scene of Brit. naval victory in 1801 and siege in 1807 when much of the city was destroyed by fire and Brit. forces captured entire Danish fleet. Sharpe was on special mission in the city during siege (in *SP*). Wellington's favourite horse during Pen. War and Waterloo was named Copenhagen after the 1807 bombardment.

Cowper, Mr Purser on *HMS Pucelle* at Trafalgar, Oct. 1805. In *STraf*.

Cromwell, Capt. Peculiar Corrupt ex-RN officer who transferred to EIC merchant service to make more money. As captain of the *Calliope* he surrendered his ship to the French *Revenant* in return for large share of prize. Survived Trafalgar (on board *Revenant*), but later faced trial for his treachery. In *STraf*.

Crosby, Maj. Drunken, disagreeable

EIC officer in command at *Chasalgaon* in summer of 1803. He was shot by *Maj.* Dodd when the fort was overrun. In *STr*.

cushoon Circumcised Muslim soldier in Tippoo Sultan's army.

cutting-out expedition An attack on a ship at anchor, usually by night, by several ships' boats full of seamen or soldiers. The attackers board the ship and capture it, then sail it away as a prize.

Dalton, Maj. Arthur Officer 96th Foot, sailing home from India on *Calliope* in 1805 to begin his retirement. Sought Sharpe's advice on fighting in India for history book he was writing on the subject. In *STraf*.

Daria Dowlat Tippoo Sultan's summer palace in Seringapatam where Brit. prisoners (except for *Sgt Hakeswill*) were executed by his *jettis* in 1799.

Davi Lal 13-year-old Indian boy befriended by Sharpe; served as messenger/interpreter during the latter part of Sharpe's time at Seringapatam armoury. Nicknamed 'hedgehog' due to his spiky hair. Murdered by Dodd's men at *Chasalgaon* on 1 July 1803. In *STr*.

Dilip Middle-aged Indian clerk who worked for *Captain Torrance* and collaborated with him in theft of army supplies and 'cooking the books'. *Torrance* blamed him when asked to explain irregularities and delays to Wellesley. *Dilip* was hanged by *Sgt Hakeswill* so that he could not incriminate both himself and *Torrance*. In *SF*.

Diomed Grey Arab charger given to Wellesley by Col. Ashton as he lay dying from a duelling wound in 1799.

Diomed died from pike wound after B. of Assaye, 1803, despite Wellesley having the pike removed to improve chance of recovery.

Dodd, Lt William British officer who deserted after being convicted of having an Indian merchant beaten to death. Joined Mahrattas' army (promoted to maj. by Col. Pohlmann) and, despite reward on his head, was never captured. Led the massacre at *Chasalgaon* in July 1803. *Col McCandless* and Sharpe sent on special mission to arrest him. He fought at Argaum and Gawilghur, where he wounded Sharpe in the hip with his sword but was then killed by him. In *STr, SF*.

Dornberg, Baroness Mathilde von Wife of *Baron von Dornberg* (Pohlmann). Accompanied her husband on board *Calliope* for voyage from Bombay to Europe in summer 1805. Present on the *Revenant* at the Battle of Trafalgar. In *STraf*.

'Dukes, the' Modern nickname of the Duke of Wellington's Regiment, the old 33rd Foot. One of only ten regiments to avoid amalgamation and the subsequent loss of their old title.

Dunbar, Lt RN Officer on HMS Cleopatra during Danish campaign 1807. In *SP*.

Dunlop, Lt-Col Commanded left assault column storming breach at Seringapatam on 4 May 1799.

Dunnett, Capt. Warren Officer in 1/95th who commanded No. 2 Coy at Copenhagen in 1807. Sharpe, whom he detested, was attached to his coy for the battle at Køge 29 Aug. 1807.

Dupont, Maj. John James Dutch mercenary officer who commanded several bns of Scindia's regular infantry at Battle of Assaye in Sept. 1803.

Dyce, Capt. Andrew The likely actual coy commander of No. 6 Coy 74th (Sharpe's coy) in 1803.

East India Company (EIC) Incorporated by royal charter in 1600 to exploit trade with India and Far East, made immense profits. Under Charles II obtained rights to acquire territory, coin money, raise troops, make alliances, make war or peace, and exercise civil or criminal jurisdiction. Handed over functions to Brit. govt in 1858.

Elliot, Maj. Engineer officer tasked with building the road through the jungle for the siege guns at the siege of Gawilghur in December 1803. He was killed and the task was taken over by Sharpe's friend, *Major Stokes*.

enfilade Term used to describe fire coming from flank.

escalade Attack on walls of fort using ladders.

facings Collars, cuffs and lapels of uniform jacket. Regts had varying colours: 33rd scarlet, 74th white, 95th black.

Fairley, Mr Ebenezer Rich merchant travelling home to England from Bombay in 1805 on board the same ship *(Calliope)* as Sharpe. In *STraf*.

fencibles Militia-type units of bn strength only for service in home defence.

Filmer, Sgt 'Lofty' Senior NCO of small stature in *Capt. Dunnett's* No. 2 Coy 1/95th at Køge 29 Aug. 1807, shot dead by sniper on church roof at Herfølge (Sharpe, attached to No. 2 Coy at the time, then shot the sniper). In *SP*.

first lieutenant Second-in-command of a warship. Today the RN call this officer 'No. 1', the Americans 'XO' (Executive Officer). Usually the senior lt aboard.

Flaherty, Pte Soldier 33rd Foot, one of six men sent by *Sgt Hakeswill* to arrest Sharpe shortly before Battle of Assaye. In *STr*.

Fletcher, Pte Daniel Soldier in 19th Dragoons who was Wellesley's orderly. Sharpe took over his duties after he was killed by a cannonball crossing the River Kaitna at the start of Battle of Assaye, and was thus in a position to save Wellesley's life later in the action. In *STr*.

forlorn hope Small group of soldiers, usually volunteers under a junior officer (sometimes a sergeant), who led the storming party into breach in besieged fortress to draw enemy fire. Officers and sergeants who survived usually rewarded with promotion.

French Horn (Frog Prick) Tavern Tavern near Drury Lane, London frequented by army officers. Sharpe fled there after killing *Jem Hocking* in July 1807 and met Lt-Gen. Sir David Baird who sent him on special mission to Copenhagen.

galloper guns Six-pdr guns drawn by horses, as distinct from bullocks, in India to accompany cav.

Gambier, Adm. Sir James b. 1756. Zealously religious, unpopular officer who was C-in-C of the British Fleet at Copenhagen in 1807. Not renowned for his competence, although seniority took him, eventually, to highest rank in RN: Adm. of the Fleet. Died 1833 aged 76.

Garrard, Pte Tom Comrade of Sharpe in light coy 33rd Foot in India. Took part in attack on Gawilghur December

1803. Promoted sgt, then commissioned into Port. Army in Pen. War. In *SF*.

Gawilghur, Siege of Indian town and fortress. Brit. under Wellesley stormed and captured it 15 Dec. 1803. Ensign Sharpe (in 74th) took over lt coy 33rd for escalade. In *SF*.

Goodall, Capt. Commanded lt coy of 12th Foot at storming of Seringapatam, 1799.

Gopal, Subadar Indian officer and *Maj*. Dodd's second-in-command when his troops massacred the entire garrison, except for Sharpe, at *Chasalgaon* on 1 July 1803.

Gordon Riots Large-scale anti-Catholic riots in London 1780 during which considerable damage was done to property and c.850 lives were lost, many when troops opened fire. Sharpe's mother was among the dead.

Gordon, Capt. Nephew of Lt-Gen. Baird and his ADC during 1807 campaign in Denmark. In *SP*.

Gore, Lt-Col Arthur Took command of 33rd Foot on the death of Maj. Shee in March 1802. *Sgt Hakeswill* and *Capt. Morris* tricked Gore into signing an arrest warrant for Sharpe in June 1803.

Goslitt Yard Small, filthy alleyway in which *Maggie Joyce* ran a gin-shop-cum-brothel. Sharpe was given sanctuary there when, aged twelve, he ran away from a chimney sweep. He lived there for three years before again going on the run after killing a man who attacked *Maggie*.

Green, Sgt Senior NCO in lt coy 33rd Foot. Took part, with Sharpe, in the attack on Gawilghur in December 1803. In *SF*.

grenadier company (gren. coy) Elite coy composed of strongest men. Posted on right flank of bn line on parade or in battle. Title originated from C18 when they carried grenades.

Hakeswill, Sgt Obadiah b. 1769. Evil senior NCO of 33rd Foot – became Sharpe's main enemy in India and thereafter. Sentenced to be hanged, aged 12, by Sussex Assizes; cut down by his uncle and survived, albeit with heavy scarring, deformed neck and facial twitch. Henceforth regarded himself as impossible to kill. He venerated mothers in general, and his own, '*Biddy' Hakeswill*, in particular. Joined 33rd Foot as drummer boy in 1781; took great pleasure in flogging duties. In 1793 he enlisted Sharpe (whom he called 'Sharpie'). Thereafter he was forever plotting against Sharpe, causing him to be flogged in India in 1799. *Hakeswill* murdered Lt Fitzgerald at Seringapatam in 1799 and *Col. Hector McCandless* at Assaye in 1803. He deserted to the Mahrattas inside Gawilghur in Dec. 1803 and commanded enemy coy, but escaped punishment by claiming to have been captured. Invalided out in 1806 but re-enlisted into newly forming *S. Essex* in 1808. In *ST, STr, SF*.

Hale, Lady Grace Formerly *Grace de Laverre Gould*, 3rd daughter of *Earl of Selby*. Beautiful young wife of *Lord William Hale*. She and Sharpe became lovers during the voyage home from India, first on the *Calliope* and then on *HMS Pucelle* in the summer of 1805. She shot and killed her husband during the Battle of Trafalgar as he was threatening to kill her, having discovered the affair. She became pregnant by Sharpe and they lived together in England

until her death in childbirth. In *STraf,*
SP.

Hale, Lord William Pompous and pol-
itically ambitious member of the EIC
Board of Control who was sailing
home from Bombay on the *Calliope* in
1805. Married to *Lady Grace*. On dis-
covering her affair with Sharpe, threatened to kill his wife with a pistol while
hiding below decks during the Battle of
Trafalgar. *Lady Grace* managed to kill
him instead. In *STraf.*

Harness, Lt-Col William Commanded
the 2nd Brigade during Wellesley's
Indian campaign against Scindia, summer 1802. Present at Ahmednuggur
(commanded first column to attempt
escalade), and Assaye. He was unable
to command at Argaum on 29 Nov.
1802; Wellesley wrote: 'Colonel Harness
was taken ill a day or two before the
battle. He was so unwell as to be deliri-
ous; I was obliged to order him into
his palanquin.' He died on 1 January
1804.

Harper, Pte Patrick Augustine DoB
unknown; probably 1780 in Tangaveane
(which ceased to exist due to the
potato famine of 1840) in Donegal, Ireland. Fourth of eleven children. Left
home after argument involving extra
work because of his size (in 1809 he
was 6'4" and weighed 14 stone). Got
drunk and woke up to find he was in
the army. Initially cav. regt, but transferred to 95th Rifles in 1803; almost certainly his regt used a request for drafts
to offload a troublemaker. He was a
drunk, a brawler and hated the
'system' after crushing of Fr. invasion
of Ireland and the ensuing Irish
rebellion of 1798. Fiercely proud of
background and heritage, but aware of

stigma of being Irish in Brit. Army;
focal point for dissenters. Took part in
disastrous expedition to S. America in
1805, fighting at Montevideo and
Buenos Aires. Posted to 1/95th in May
1805. Fought at Copenhagen in 1807 in
No. 2 Coy under *Capt. Dunnett*. Later
became a sgt and good friend of
Sharpe. In *SP.*

Harris, Lt-Gen. George b. 1746. Commanded Madras Army in 4th Mysore
War against Tippoo Sultan; also combined force that took Seringapatam in
1799. On his orders Sharpe's flogging
was stopped and he was sent on special
mission. In *ST.*

Harris, Rflm. Benjamin Soldier in
1/95th during campaign in Denmark in
summer of 1807. Later fought in Portugal and Spain, including retreat to Corunna 1809. Took part in the Walcheren
expedition later that year. Invalided out
in 1810 and later wrote the now famous
account of his experiences, *The Recollections of Benjamin Harris* published in
1848.

Haskell, Lt First Lt (2IC) of *HMS
Pucelle*. Wounded in the arm and then
cut in half by a cannonball fired from
the *Revenant* at Battle of Trafalgar. In
STraf.

havildar Sergeant in an Indian inf. bn.

Herfølge (MAP 15) Village 5 miles SW
of Køge, Zealand, Denmark. Site of
Danish rearguard action under Maj-
Gen. Oxholm to halt pursuing British
after victory at Køge 29 Aug. 1807. The
Danes defended the churchyard but
were quickly defeated by the 1/95th. *Sgt
Filmer* was shot and killed by a sniper,
who in turn was killed by Sharpe with
a rifle shot. Some 400 Danes were captured here.

Hicks, Ensign Timothy Officer 33rd Foot lt coy in India. At Siege of Seringapatam, 1799. In *ST*.

Hill, Lt Officer of 74th Foot; led storming party of right column in breach at Seringapatam, 4 May 1799.

Hocking, Jem Sadistic and corrupt 'master' of the foundling home in Brewhouse Lane, Wapping, where Sharpe was incarcerated as a boy. He suffered endless cruelties under *Hocking,* and returned in 1807 to seek revenge. Not recognising Sharpe, *Hocking* tried to sell him young boys (as drummers) and girls for less respectable duties. Sharpe robbed him and slit his throat. In *SP*.

Holderby, Lt Killed in action by roundshot on *HMS Pucelle* at Trafalgar. In *STraf*.

Holkar, Jeswunt Rao Most powerful of several rival Mahratta princes who, when not fighting the British, were fighting each other. Defeated combined armies of Peshwa and Scindia at Poona in October 1802. Remained neutral during Wellesley's campaign against Scindia in summer 1803. Died of overindulgence in brandy 1811.

holystone Block of sandstone used to scour decks. So called because large blocks were similar shape and size to bible, smaller blocks resembled prayer books – and they had to be used while on your knees.

Hopper, Coxswain John Petty officer (naval NCO) in charge of the captain's gig on *HMS Pucelle*. Involved in the confrontation with cheating Indian merchant's followers in Bombay June 1805. Made friends with Sharpe. Commanded starboard carronade on quarterdeck at Trafalgar. Assisted

Sharpe in Copenhagen 1807. In *STraf, SP*.

Horrocks, Lt 4th Lieutenant *HMS Pucelle* 1805. Commanded the small prize crew of *Calliope* for voyage home after recapture – and so missed B. of Trafalgar. In *STraf*.

Horse Guards Buildings in Whitehall, London, used by the commander-in-chief of British Army. Modern equivalent: MoD.

howitzer Short-barrelled cannon for high-angle fire.

Hughes, Capt. Sharpe's first coy commander 33rd Foot who asked for him in lt coy (Sharpe had been destined for gren. coy). Died of flux in Calcutta 1798. Replaced by *Capt. Morris*. In *ST*.

Huntingdon, Earl of Raised the 33rd Foot, the regiment Sharpe enlisted in, in 1702.

Hurryhur (MAP 3) Indian town in Mysore c.150 miles north of Seringapatam. Base of the 33rd in summer 1803, from which they patrolled Wellesley's lines of communication. In *STr*.

Jackson, Horace Owner of Hall of Arms of his name in Jermyn St, London in 1807. Former pugilist. In *SP*.

Jackson, Mr Francis British career diplomat whose mission (Aug. 1807) was to persuade the Danes to hand over their fleet into British safe custody. He failed and so the British bombarded Copenhagen and took the fleet by force. He, rather than the military commanders, had the authority of the government to decide whether the Danes should be attacked.

Jama Tall Indian with a limp, brother of corrupt Indian merchant *Naig*. After

Naig was hung, *Jama* sought revenge on Sharpe by having *Sgt Hakeswill* kidnap him and hand him over to be killed by a *jetti*. In *SF*.

Jem Old sailor on *Calliope* in charge of No. 5 gun, the weapon Sharpe was assigned to crew in emergencies. In *STraf.*

jemadar Indian officer equivalent to lieutenant.

Jens Danish militiaman (full name unknown) who befriended Sharpe during the first Danish sortie from Copenhagen on 18 Aug. 1807. He saved Sharpe's life by pushing him aside just as *Barker* fired a pistol at him. After the fighting, Sharpe gave *Jens* a pistol and told him to take it to *Skovgaard* in the city. *Jens* was killed en route. In *SP*.

jettis Professional Indian strongmen employed by Tippoo Sultan to execute prisoners by twisting their head through 180 degrees or driving 9-inch nail into skull.

Joubert, Capt. Pierre Small, weak, timid Frenchman serving as an officer with Mahratta forces of Scindia in 1803. Was acting commander of one of Col. Pohlmann's bns until replaced by *Maj.* Dodd after *Chasalgaon* massacre. Continuously bullied by Dodd. Married to *Simone Joubert*. Dodd eventually shot him in Assaye to steal his horse and escape after the defeat of Pohlmann's army on 23 Sept. 1803. In *STr.*

Joubert, Madame Simone Attractive wife of *Capt. Joubert*. She married him to exchange the monotony of life in Mauritius for the excitement of India. Sharpe met her in Ahmednuggur, where she had been left behind after Dodd's retreat, and gave her some of the Tippoo's diamonds. He slept with her on the night of 8/9 August 1803. He and *McCandless* escorted her back to her husband as an excuse to scout Scindia's army. In *STr.*

Joyce, Maggie Owner of lodging-house-cum-brothel-cum-gin-shop in St Giles Rookery. Took Sharpe in when he ran away from foundling home. Taught him to live on his wits; first woman to bed him.

Kendrick, Pte Soldier in 33rd Foot. One of *Sgt Hakeswill*'s cronies, involved in plot to kill Sharpe. He was himself killed by Sharpe with a sword on 11 Dec. 1803 in front of the breaching battery at Gawilghur. In *STr, SF*.

Kenny, Lt-Col EIC officer who commanded 1/11th Madras in 1803 campaign against Mahrattas. He led assault on breaches at Gawilghur on 15 Dec. 1803 and was mortally wounded during attack on gate of inner fort.

Keppel, Ensign George 16-year-old officer who carried the Regtl Colour of 3/24th at Waterloo.

Køge (MAP 13) Small coastal town 25 miles SW of Copenhagen. Scene of Wellesley's successful engagement with the Danish Army 29 Aug. 1807. Sharpe participated in the action with the 1/95th although (unusually) he was not involved in any fighting.

Kronborg Castle (MAP 13) Famous Danish castle adjacent to Helsingør on NE tip of Zealand, Denmark. Famous as setting for Shakespeare's *Hamlet*. Both Brit. fleet and HMS Cleopatra (with Sharpe on board) exchanged salutes with the castle as they arrived opposite. The fleet lay at anchor close by from 3–15 Aug. before moving south to land troops on 16 Aug. 1807.

Kunwar Singh Hindu commander of Appah Rao's bodyguard in Seringapatam, 1799. Fell in love with *Mary Bickerstaff*, mixed-race widow of Brit. sgt and Sharpe's lover. In *ST*.

Lalor, Lt 73rd Foot; used flags to mark route for assault on breach across South Cauvery R. at Siege of Seringapatam in 1799. Shot and killed by Tippoo Sultan.

Lavisser, Capt. the Hon. John Treacherous officer of 1st Foot Guards tasked with taking huge sum of gold to Denmark in 1807 to persuade and/or bribe the Danes to hand their fleet to British. Part Danish, he went over to the Danes on arrival but was also secretly working for the French. He hid the gold and repeatedly tried to have Sharpe, who had replaced *Willsen* as his 'minder', murdered. Eventually killed by Sharpe, who forced him off the balcony of a burning house into the flames. In *SP*.

Lawford, Lt the Hon. William Coy officer 33rd Foot in India when Sharpe was a pte; nephew of *Col. McCandless*, EIC intelligence officer. *Lawford* and Sharpe pretended to be deserters to undertake special mission inside Seringapatam. Taught Sharpe to read and write in Tippoo Sultan's dungeon. Later *Lt-Col. Sir William*. In *ST*.

Lawrence, Lt Officer of 77th Foot; led storming party of left attacking column on breach at Seringapatam, 4 May 1799.

lee or leeward Side opposite to that from which the wind is blowing.

Leonard, Capt. EIC officer, 2IC of garrison at *Chasalgaon*, India, summer 1803. *Maj.* Dodd killed him with a sword when the garrison was massacred on 1 July. Sharpe, although wounded, was the only survivor. In *STr*.

light company (lt coy) Brit. Army elite bn coy composed of agile men and good marksmen for use as skirmishers; on left flank of line on parade. Towards end of Pen. War issued with muskets with rudimentary backsights.

Linsingen, Maj-Gen. Charles Christian von Officer in command KGL cavalry bde during Zealand campaign, summer 1807. He commanded the mixed flanking force from Wellesley's army at the action near Køge on 29 Aug. Failed to arrive in time to participate in the main attack. Severely criticised by Capt. Napier for his personal participation in looting and for ordering the murder of at least one Danish civilian. Fought in the Peninsular War. Rose to full general and inspector-general of cavalry in the Hanoverian army. Died Hanover 1830.

Llewellyn, Capt. Llewellyn RM officer in command of the marines on *HMS Pucelle*. Became Sharpe's immediate superior when he was attached to the marines during Battle of Trafalgar in October 1805. In *STraf*.

Lockhart, Sergeant Eli Senior NCO 19th Dragoons. Befriended Sharpe late 1803 and assisted in hanging of corrupt Indian merchant *Naig*. Took part in assault on Gawilghur on 15 Dec. 1803 and saved Sharpe's life by shooting Dodd in the shoulder as he was about to kill Sharpe (who then put an end to Dodd). Later married the widow *Mrs Clare Wall*. In *SF*.

Lowry, Pte Soldier 33rd Foot. One of *Sgt Hakeswill's* cronies in plot to get Sharpe killed. He was himself killed by

Sharpe with a sword during the night of 11 Dec. 1803 in front of the breaching battery at Gawilghur. In *STr, SF*.

luff up The order to put the helm towards the lee side of the ship – thus moving the bows windward, into the wind. 'Keep your luff' meant to keep the ship as close to the wind as possible.

McCallum, Cpl Junior NCO in Sharpe's coy 74th Foot at Battle of Argaum 29 Nov. 1803. In *SF*.

McCandless, Col Hector 60-year-old Calvinist Scot, formerly of the Scotch Brigade. Senior EIC intelligence officer at Harris's HQ in 1799 campaign against Tippoo Sultan. Captured and imprisoned in Seringapatam. *Lt Lawford* (his nephew) and Sharpe sent to contact him inside the city. Present at the taking of Ahmednuggur. Sharpe accompanied him again at the Battle of Assaye in 1803 when *McCandless* was shot and killed by *Sgt Hakeswill*. In *ST, STr*.

Mackay, Capt. Hugh Officer 4th Native Cavalry; in charge of entire military bullock train for campaign against Scindia in summer 1803 – an important post that he fulfilled brilliantly. *Sgt Hakeswill* with his 6 men who were on their way to arrest Sharpe were attached to his bullock train at Ahmednuggur on 14 August. Before Battle of Argaum 29 Nov. 1803 Mackay asked Wellesley's permission to rejoin his squadron for the battle – he was refused. He went anyway, and was killed charging at the head of his men.

Mallavelly (MAP 1) Scene of first clash between Brit. under Lt-Gen. Harris and Tippoo Sultan's forces on 27 Mar. 1799;

33rd Foot with Pte Sharpe in lt coy led advance. Sharpe killed his first enemy (Indian officer) in close combat and looted body.

Malone's Tavern (Vinegar Alehouse) Tavern in Vinegar Street, Wapping, owned by *Jem Hocking* where he did most of his shady business. Sharpe killed him by slitting his throat. It got its name from the deceased owner, '*Beaky' Malone*, but was sometimes called the *Vinegar Alehouse* because of its location. In *SP*.

Malone, 'Lumpy' Son of '*Beaky'* *Malone* (deceased), ringmaster of the dogfights held in backyard storeroom of the *Malone Tavern* in 1807. In *SP*.

Mangalore (MAP 1) Main Mysore port on W. coast of India controlled by Tippoo Sultan in 1798. Fr. troops coming to India would probably have landed here.

Manningham, Col Coote Formed the Experimental Corps of Riflemen in 1800 from the pick of 15 regiments.

Manu Bappoo Younger brother of Berar; 35-year-old Mahratta leader of Berar's forces at Argaum. Died fighting during the storming of Gawilghur on 15 Dec. 1803.

Maxwell, Lt-Col Patrick CO of King's 19th Dragoons in India in 1803. He commanded Wellesley's regular cavalry at Assaye. Led two charges during the battle, the first highly successful, the second less so. He lost his life during the second charge.

Meer Allum Nizam (ruler) of Indian state of Hyderabad who led army allied to Brit. against Tippoo Sultan in 1799. Wellesley was his adviser (de facto commander) during Siege of Seringapatam.

Montmorin, Capt. Louis Commanded

the French 74-gun *Revenant* that operated out of Mauritius in 1805 hunting
merchant ships to seize as prizes.
Montmorin captured the *Calliope* in col-
laboration with her captain, *Peculiar
Cromwell*. Sailed for Cadiz, but joined
combined French and Spanish fleet in
time to fight at Trafalgar. There he
fought against *HMS Pucelle* but was
forced to surrender to her after heavy
losses. In *STraf.*

Moore, Lt-Gen. Sir John b. Glasgow
1761. Ensign in 51st Foot at 15. Served
in Hamilton's Regt during AWI, briefly
in 60th Rifles, then transferred back to
51st. In 1792 was involved in the operations in Corsica; wounded at taking of
Calvi. Went as brig-gen. to W. Indies
where he distinguished himself at the
capture of St Lucia. As maj-gen.
defeated Irish during 1798 rebellion at
B. of Vinegar Hill. Commanded bde in
1899 expedition to Holland; again
wounded. Commanded reserve bde in
Egypt, wounded at B. of Alexandria.
Renowned for training of light troops
at Shorncliffe in 1803, particularly the
43rd, 52nd and 95th, which later
became the famous Light Bde. In 1808
sent to Sweden to help in war against
Russia, France and Denmark, but
forced to return after refusing to agree
king's plans. Ordered to Portugal
where his retreat to Corunna and death
after a victorious battle have become a
highlight of Brit. military history.

Morris, Capt. Charles Lt coy comd.
33rd in India. Plotted with *Sgt Hakeswill* to have Sharpe arrested for striking NCO; Sharpe sentenced to 2,000
lashes. Sharpe knocked *Morris* out and
took over his coy just before escalade
at Gawilghur in Dec. 1803. In *ST, SF*.

Murray, Capt. John Coy comd. in
1/95th during Brit. invasion of Denmark
1807. Took part in the action at Køge
and Siege of Copenhagen. In *SP*.

Naig 'Nasty' Indian 'entrepreneur' who
ran officers' brothel of Brit. Army
during advance on, and siege of, Seringapatam, 1799. In *ST*.

Nana Rao Indian merchant in Bombay
from whom passengers sailing to and
from England bought or sold furniture
and equipment. Tried to cheat Sharpe
and others by burning his store down,
having removed the goods beforehand
with intention of selling them from an
accomplice's store. Sharpe discovered
his deceit and was able to secure com-
pensation by holding a pistol to his
head. In *STraf.*

Newgate Gaol Notorious main gaol in
London 1188–1902. Destroyed in the
Gordon Riots and rebuilt. Located
where Old Bailey now stands in Newgate Street, it was also the site of
public executions from 1783 until 1868,
after which they took place inside.

Nils [surname unknown], Capt. Merchant ship captain, deceased husband
of *Astrid*, who bore a striking resemblance to Sharpe – something that
helped her recover more quickly from
his death. He had been lost at sea in a
storm while carrying sugar from the
West Indies. In *SP*.

Nyboder (MAP 15) Poor area of Copenhagen where *Astrid Skovgaard*'s orphan-
age/hospital was located. The
orphanage was burnt down during
Brit. bombardment in Sept. 1807.

orlop deck The deck immediately
above the hold on a ship of the line;

included the cockpit, where the surgeon operated on the wounded during action.

Orrock, Lt-Col William EIC officer who commanded 1/8th Madras Native Infantry. At Assaye he led composite bn made up of picquets of the day (half a company from each bn). Instead of attacking as ordered with rest of Wellesley's army, he mistakenly advanced on well-defended village of Assaye and suffered devastating losses as a result. Despite his costly blunder, Wellesley kept him as commander of 1/8th Madras.

palanquin Royal carriage carried by servants/slaves – used by Indian rulers including Tippoo Sultan.

Panjit Lashti Indian merchant in Bombay who was in league with *Nana Rao* in cheating passengers sailing to and from England. He came off second best in a confrontation with Sharpe in June 1805. In *STraf.*

paymaster Officer of capt. rank responsible for the regiment's pay. Paymaster's commission could be purchased but the regtl col. had to approve.

Peel, Lt RN 1st lt of *HMS Pucelle* at Trafalgar in Oct. 1805. He was present at Copenhagen in 1807. In *STraf, SP.*

Peymann, Lt-Gen. Ernst C-in-C of Danish forces in Copenhagen in Aug.–Sept. 1807. A 72-year-old general who had never before commanded regular troops, he found himself besieged in the city by Brit. army and navy. He made a gallant attempt at defence (personally led one sortie and was wounded but continued in command). He several times refused to surrender

but was finally forced to do so after Brit. bombardment had set the city on fire and killed hundreds of civilians.

Pickering Surgeon on *HMS Pucelle* during the Battle of Trafalgar. In *STraf.*

picket or picquet Infantry outpost or sentry.

Pierce, Mr Dan Boyhood friend of Sharpe from his foundling-home days. They met again watching a dogfight in *Malone's Tavern* in July 1807. In *SP.*

Pinckney, Capt. EIC officer who commanded the engineers responsible for building the road through the jungle and hills for the breaching battery at Gawilghur in December 1803. In *SF.*

Plummer, Maj. Artillery officer commanding breaching battery at Gawilghur in Dec. 1803. In *SF.*

Pohlmann, Colonel Anthony Ex-Hanoverian sgt in EIC army who joined the forces of Scindia. At Battle of Assaye Sept. 1803 he was a colonel and de facto commander of the Indian Army opposed to Wellesley. A capable commander, but one who liked the trappings of power – he travelled mounted on an elephant surrounded by a gaudily uniformed escort. After the Mahratta Wars he returned to EIC service – this time as an officer. Shortly before Assaye he met Sharpe (in *STr*) and offered him a commission. He reappeared in *STraf* disguised as *Baron von Dornberg*, travelling back to Europe with Sharpe on merchant ship *Calliope*. After transferring to the French warship *Revenant, Baron von Dornberg* (Pohlmann) killed by a cannonball at Battle of Trafalgar Oct. 1805.

Prince of Wales, HMS 98-gun, three-decker, 1st rate ship. Launched at Portsmouth 1794; 1807 Channel Fleet and flagship of Adm. Gambier in the Baltic. Took part in the Danish campaign of that year. Out of commission 1815.

Prithviraj *Jetti* to whom *Jama* gave the task of killing Sharpe in Dec. 1803 after his kidnapping. Sharpe killed him with a spear. In *SF*.

Pucelle, HMS British 74-gun warship commanded by *Capt. Chase*. Recaptured EIC merchantman *Calliope* after it had been surrendered to the French near Mauritius in July 1805. Sharpe transferred to her from the *Calliope* for remainder of voyage to England. She took part in Battle of Trafalgar 21 Oct. 1805 and captured the *Revenant*. Also took part in expedition to Copenhagen 1807 (still under *Captain Chase*) and brought Sharpe home after the city fell. In *STraf SP*.

puckalee Indian watercarrier whose duties included supplying drinking water to troops on battlefield. Most were brave, loyal individuals like Rudyard Kipling's famous Gunga Din. *Sgt Hakeswill* was put in charge of them in Wellesley's army just prior to Battle of Assaye in *STr*.

Pumphrey, Lord William Foreign Office official working as civilian aide to Lt-Gen. Baird during 1807 Denmark campaign. Educated at Eton with *Capt. Lavisser*; briefed Sharpe on what to do if things went wrong during his mission to Copenhagen. In *SP*.

purser 'Being the [warrant] officer entrusted to receive the provisions and victualling stores, to keep and distribute the same to the Ship's company . . .' Thus was the job defined in the *Regulations and Instructions Relating to His Majesty's Service at Sea* dated 1808. *Cowper* was purser on *HMS*

Pucelle. When Sharpe was made QM it was the very approximate army equivalent to a purser.

quartermaster (QM) Officer responsible for supplies, rations, ammunition, stores, uniforms and equipment, etc within a bn or regt. Usually a lieutenant, often an ex-ranker like Sharpe. Regarded as inferior by combatant officers.

Rao, Gen. Appah Hindu bde commander in Tippoo Sultan's army at Seringapatam in 1799. Secretly turned traitor and gave information to *Col McCandless* on defences of city. Responsible for defence of Mysore Gate during siege. In *ST*.

regiment (regt) In Brit. Army an administrative military unit that recruited soldiers and sent them to war, usually as bns. Most Brit. regts provided 1 or 2 bns during Nap. Wars. In other European armies a tactical battlefield unit of 2 or 3 bns usually commanded by col.

Revenant 74-gun French warship commanded by *Capt. Louis Montmorin*. Operated out of Mauritius (Île de France) to capture merchant prizes. Was chased from the Indian Ocean to Trafalgar by *HMS Pucelle* (with Sharpe on board). Joined Franco-Spanish fleet at the battle; fought against, and was captured by, *HMS Pucelle*. In *STraf*.

Roberts, Capt. EIC officer 2IC at *Chasalgaon*, India, in 1803 when the garrison was wiped out by Mahrattas. In *STr*.

St Giles Rookery (MAP 12) Notorious slum area of London where Sharpe lived with *Maggie Joyce* from age 12–15. It was centred on what is now Tottenham Court Road tube station.

Saleur, Col French officer who commanded one of Scindia's larger regiments at the Battle of Assaye 23 Sept. 1803.

Samuels, Capt. RN Commanded HMS Cleopatra taking Sharpe to Denmark in Aug. 1807. In *SP*.

Sanjit Pandee Killadar (commander) of Indian garrison of Ahmednuggur in Aug. 1803. His authority was ignored by *Maj.* Dodd during defence of fort. Shot and killed when fort was stormed. In *STr*.

Sanjit Second clerk of *Capt. Torrance*, corrupt officer in charge of Wellesley's supplies in 1803 campaign against Mahrattas. *Sanjit* led Sharpe to his kidnapping, which almost resulted in his death. Sharpe killed him with his own penknife shortly before he shot *Torrance* on 9 Dec. 1803. In *SF*.

Scindia, Dowlat Rao A powerful Mahratta prince of Gwalior who was the main opponent of Wellesley in his summer 1803 campaign against the Mahrattas. His troops (plus allies) – although not under his command, as he had little stomach for fighting – fought Wellesley at Ahmednuggur, Assaye and Argaum. He employed many European officers to train and lead his native infantry and artillery. One of these, Col. Pohlmann, commanded in his absence at Battle of Assaye on 23 Sept. 1803.

Sedaseer Indian town in Western Ghats, scene of Brit. victory (under Lt-Gen. James Stuart) over Tippoo Sultan's forces 6 Mar. 1799.

sergeant-major Senior sgt in battalion

(one to each bn). Regimental sergeant-majors were not introduced until just prior to WWI.

Seringapatam, Siege of (MAPS 1 and 2) 30,000 of Tippoo Sultan's forces were besieged in the city Apr–May 1799. The 33rd played a prominent part in the storming, during which Sharpe killed the Tippoo.

Sevajee, Syud Leader of band of silladars who provided *Col. McCandless's* escort in 1803 campaign against Mahrattas. He was himself Mahratta, but had allied with Wellesley in order to avenge his father's poisoning by Beny Singh. He was present at the Battle of Argaum and the Siege of Gawilghur in December 1803. In *STr, SF*.

Seven Dials (MAP 12) Name for the area of London then known as the Rookery – a slum where Sharpe spent his early teens living with *Maggie Joyce* and learning to survive on his wits. Today's Tottenham Court Road tube station marks its centre.

shako Peaked, cylindrical head-dress usually made of felt, often black.

Shee, Maj. John Irish officer, overfond of the bottle, who became CO of 33rd after Wellesley took over general officer's responsibilities in 4th Mysore War against Tippoo Sultan. As Sharpe's CO he handed down 2,000 lashes (illegally) for striking *Sgt Hakeswill*. Died while having a fit in March 1802. In *ST*.

Sherbrooke, Lt-Col John Coape 2nd lt-col. of 33rd Foot 1794. As such he was Sharpe's commanding officer at Boxtel when 1st lt-col., Wesley, was acting as bde commander covering Brit. withdrawal.

Shipp, John Enlisted in 22nd Foot in

1797, became a sergeant, went to India and, like Sharpe, was commissioned without purchase for his exploits on the battlefield (at the Siege of Bhurtpore in 1805). Forced to sell his commission to pay off debts (he received special permission to do so). Re-enlisted into 24th Dragoons, rising to rank of sgt-maj. before again being commissioned, this time into 87th Foot. Court-martialled and put on half-pay in 1823. Later wrote an autobiography: *Paths of Glory*.

Shorncliffe, Kent Army camp 3 miles west of Folkestone on east Kent coast where Sir John Moore established famous training camp in 1802 for the Rifle Regiments, including the 95th Rifles. It no longer exists, but the present writer recalls it from the late 1950s.

silladars Mercenary Indian horsemen, often hired by the British, who were armed with an assortment of weapons including lances and bows and arrows. Effective for scouting, raids and providing information, but could seldom be used against a formed opposition on the battlefield. *Col McCandless* used a band of them as escort during summer 1803 campaign against Scindia in *STr*.

Sillière, Lt Young French officer serving in Dodd's compoo. He was in love with *Simone Joubert*, who was married to his much older captain. He was killed defending *Simone* during the storming of Ahmednuggur on 8 Aug. 1803. In *STr*.

Sita Ram Served 48 years in Bengal army, only becoming a subadar at the age of 65. Fought in the Nepalese War (1814–15), the war against the Pindarris (1817–18); he was at the second Siege of Bhurtpore (1825), marched into Kabul in 1839 and took part in the infamous retreat from that city 3 years later. Captured and sold as a slave to an Afghan merchant, but later escaped. Took part in the 1st Sikh War (1845–46) and the 2nd (1848–49). His final campaigning was during the Indian Mutiny of 1857. His memoirs, published in India in 1873 (English edition published 1970), constitute the only first-hand evidence of life as a sepoy. They make for a fascinating read – although some critics have questioned their veracity.

Skipton Yorkshire town where Sharpe got a job at a coaching tavern after running away from London. Here he fought and killed the tavern keeper over *Elsie*, which led to his enlisting to escape the law.

Skovgaard, Miss Astrid Beautiful daughter of *Ole Skovgaard*, recently widowed. Fell in love with Sharpe (and he with her) in Copenhagen, Aug. 1807. She worked at a children's hospital/ orphanage in the city. Sharpe slept with her on 3 Sept. 1807. He donated most of the British government gold that he recovered to the rebuilding of *Astrid*'s hospital after it was destroyed in the fire caused by Brit. bombardment. In *SP*.

Skovgaard, Mr Ole Danish gentleman acting as agent for Britain against France in 1807. He received intelligence from a number of business contacts in Germany. Sharpe fell in love with his daughter, *Astrid. Skovgaard* owned a house at Vester Fælled where Sharpe was briefly imprisoned before escaping through the chimney. *Skovgaard* was tortured to reveal his informant and rescued by Sharpe. In *SP*.

Smith, John 'Half-Hanged' Survived a hanging in 1709, hence his nickname. *Sgt Hakeswill*, too, was cut down alive after being hanged as a youth convicted of theft.

Sowerby Bridge Small town in the West Riding of Yorkshire where Sharpe enlisted into 33rd Foot in 1793.

Standfast, Sgt Matthew Landlord of the *French Horn (Frog Prick)* tavern in London. In *SP*.

standing rigging Rigging that supported the masts. It consisted of shrouds, stays and back stays.

stay Part of the rigging that supports mast.

Stevenson, Col. James Elderly but competent EIC officer who was Wellesley's trusted 2IC and friend during summer 1803 campaign against Mahrattas. Wellesley's strategy was that Stevenson's force should march separately from his own but combine on the battlefield. This intention was not fulfilled at Assaye, but they fought a combined battle at Argaum on 29 Nov. Stevenson exercised command from the back of an elephant rather than a horse due to an illness which eventually forced him to leave India. He died on the voyage home, probably without knowing he had been promoted majgen. on 1 Jan. 1805.

Stokes, Maj. John Somewhat eccentric, easy-going engineer officer in charge of armoury at Seringapatam, India. Sgt Sharpe worked for him from 1800–03. In charge of supervising construction of road to Gawilghur for siege battery. Took part in attack on Gawilghur Dec. 1803. In *ST, STr, SF*.

subadar Indian inf. rank equivalent to captain.

Sultanpetah (MAP 1) Village near Seringapatam. Scene of Wellington's (Wellesley's) only military defeat, when 33rd were repulsed in night attack on nearby woods. Sharpe had 'deserted' to the Tippoo's side and was shouting orders in English to confuse the attackers.

Surtees, William b. 1781, enlisted 1798 at 17 in Northumberland Militia, transferred to 56th Foot and saw service in Holland. Transferred to 95th in 1802 and served in Rifle Bde for 25 years. Was QMS of 2/95th in Denmark 1807, later became QM and served in Pen. War but missed Waterloo. Retired due to ill health in 1826, died 1830 aged 48. In many ways his early career resembled Sharpe's – similar age, rose up through ranks, served in Holland at same time, both in 95th, both QM, both in Pen. War. Surtees wrote a fascinating account of his experiences in *Twenty-Five Years in the Rifle Brigade*.

Sutherland, Col Former lt cashiered from 73rd Foot. Commanded largest of Scindia's compoos before it was taken over by Col. Pohlmann.

Swallow, Lt RM officer and 2IC to *Maj. Llewellyn* on *HMS Pucelle* at Trafalgar. In *STraf*.

Swinton, Maj. Samuel Acting commander of 74th Foot at storming of Ahmednuggur and Battle of Assaye in 1803 – the substantive CO, Lt-Col. Wallace, was acting as bde commander. At Assaye he mistakenly followed the picquets under Lt-Col. Orrock and suffered heavy losses in consequence.

tacking Process of working ship to windward by zigzagging into wind. A ship was said to be sailing on a specific tack – if the wind was coming from her larboard side she was on the larboard tack, if from the starboard then the starboard tack. All ships of both fleets started Battle of Trafalgar on port tack.

Tilsit, Treaty of Peace treaty between France and Russia (signed 7 July 1807) and France and Prussia (9 July 1807). Russia lost little, but Prussian territory was carved up by Napoleon. There were secret clauses, the most critical being that France would get the Danish Fleet and European ports would be closed to British ships. Britain was warned of these clauses, which prompted her invasion of Zealand and subsequent bombardment of Copenhagen and capture of the Danish Fleet.

Tippoo Sultan b. 1753. Became Muslim sultan of Mysore on death of his father (Hyder Ali) in 1782. Fought in Mahratta and Mysore Wars against Brit. Exceedingly cruel; favoured executing prisoners by having *jettis* drive 9-inch nails into their skulls or break their necks by twisting their heads. Courageous and competent soldier with a fixation for tigers. Killed at Seringapatam by Sharpe on 4 May 1799.

tops Broad, flat D-shaped platforms situated where masts were joined: maintops, foretops and mizzentops. Used by seamen working in rigging or as positions for sharpshooters in battle. Nelson was shot from the mizzentop of *Redoutable*.

Torrance, Capt. EIC officer detached from 7th Native Cavalry to command Wellesley's supply train after death of Capt. Mackay at Assaye. A useless and corrupt officer involved in theft of army stores. To conceal his involve-

ment he had his Indian clerk hanged. Plotted with *Sgt Hakeswill* to have Sharpe killed by a *jetti*. *Torrance* was killed by Sharpe (shot with his own pistol) and the death made to look like suicide on 9 Dec. 1803. In *SF*.

Tufnell, Lt Merchant marine officer in EIC service. First officer to *Capt. Cromwell* on the *Calliope* on her voyage from Bombay in the summer of 1805. Later took the ship to Cape Town after *Cromwell's* treachery led to ship being captured by French and then recaptured. In *STraf*.

tulwar Curved Indian sword.

Tyburn, London Now Marble Arch. Infamous place of public execution 1138–1783.

Ulfedt's Plads (MAP 15) Business area of Copenhagen in 1807 where *Skovgaard* had a house and warehouse. It was burnt down during the bombardment of the city and the area is now called Graadbodretorv. It was in *Skovgaard's* house that Sharpe imprisoned *Aksel Bang* and slept with *Astrid* in *SP*.

Urquhart, Capt. Sharpe's company commander in 74th Foot at Battle of Argaum 29 Nov. 1803. After the battle he was instrumental in getting Sharpe transferred from bn to supply column because as an ex-ranker he did not 'fit in' with the other officers. In *SF*.

Vaillard, Michel German-speaking Frenchman who pretended to be Swiss. Was on board the *Calliope* as 'servant' of *Baron von Dornberg* (Pohlmann). In fact he was a senior official who had concluded a secret agreement by which French would covertly re-arm Mahratta leader Holkar, and was en route to

Paris with the agreement. He was killed by Sharpe, who threw him overboard from the *Revenant* at the end of the Battle of Trafalgar. In *STraf.*

Vedbæk (MAP 13) Danish fishing village on coast midway between Helsingør and Copenhagen. It was here that the British troops began their landings on 16 Aug. 1807 prior to marching on Copenhagen.

Venables, Ensign Roderick 16-year-old officer in No. 7 Coy, 74th Foot. Until Sharpe's arrival he was the battalion's most junior officer. Only officer to offer Sharpe friendship. Fought at Argaum. In *SF.*

Vester Fælled (MAP 15) Area in northern suburbs of Copenhagen where *Ole Skovgaard* had a house in 1807.

Victoria Cross Highest Brit. battlefield decoration for gallantry instituted by Queen Victoria in 1856 after Crimean War.

Vielder, Dr Swiss doctor serving with Col. Pohlmann in Scindia's army 1803. He removed the pistol ball from *Col McCandless's* thigh. In *STr.*

Vinegar Street Actual street in Wapping, location of *Malone's Tavern* where Sharpe killed *Jem Hocking*. In *SP.*

Visser, Madame French agent working with *Capt. Lavisser* in Copenhagen in 1807. Sharpe had a confrontation with her in a house near Herfølge while searching for hidden gold. In *SP.*

Vygârd (MAP 13) Hamlet 3 miles SW of Køge, Zealand, Denmark. Residence of *Count of Vygârd,* grandfather of *Capt. Lavisser.* Sharpe went there on 31 Aug. 1807 to search for the missing gold. He had a confrontation with *Madame Visser,* a French agent, and

was briefly arrested for looting. Released when he discovered *Visser* was using a secret code, thus confirming her as an agent. In *SP.*

Wade, Lt-Col Hamlet Irishman. One of original members of 95th Rifles, having transferred as maj. from 25th Foot. Given command of 2/95th as lt-col. on formation in 1805. Fanatical shooting enthusiast and crack shot. Commanded the 5 companies of 2/95th at Copenhagen and at Køge in 1807.

Wall, Mrs Clare (nicknamed 'Brick') Good-looking European woman, dressed as an Indian, who was the servant of *Capt. Torrance* in India 1803. Her husband had died and she was working off her debt to *Torrance* as he had paid her husband's passage to India. *Sgt Hakeswill* cast his lustful eye over her. Sharpe managed to have one night with her on 11 Dec. 1803 shortly before assault on Gawilghur. *Torrance* suggested Sharpe marry her, but in the end she married *Sgt Eli Lockhart* of 19th Dragoons. In *SF.*

Wallace, Lt-Col William CO 74th Foot when Sharpe was commissioned into the regt in 1803. He was acting bde comd. at battles at Ahmednuggur, Assaye, Argaum and the taking of Gawilghur in that year.

wearing With tacking the ship's bows were put through the wind, with wearing it was the ship's stern. Tacking was only possible if the ship had sufficient speed to carry her head through the wind. Wearing (or veering) was possible in virtually any wind or sea conditions, but it needed much more time and space than tacking. Villeneuve wore his entire fleet before Trafalgar and it cost him his formation and over two hours – but tacking was impossible as the wind was so light.

weather *or* **windward** Side of ship from which wind is blowing. The top deck, being exposed to the weather, was often called the 'weather deck'. To have the weather gauge was to have your ship upwind of your enemy. Nelson had the weather gauge at Trafalgar, Villeneuve the lee gauge.

Wellesley, Arthur See Wellington.

Wellesley, Henry Youngest of three brothers; private secretary to Richard when he was governor-general of India 1797–1805.

Wellesley, Richard b. 1760. Elder brother of Arthur. As Lord Mornington was appointed governor-general of India in 1797. Found EIC a trading body; left it an imperial power. Ambassador to Spain 1809. Lord Lieutenant of Ireland 1821. Died 1842.

Wellington (Wesley, then Wellesley), Sir Arthur, Duke of Brit. and later allied C-in-C throughout Pen. War. Born Dublin 1769, educated at Eton and Military Academy at Angers, France. Purchased rapid promotion from ensign to lt-col. in 6 years, by which time he was only 24 and had been on the strength of 4 infantry and 2 cav. regts. As CO of 33rd Foot (later to become Duke of Wellington's Regt) handled his bn well in Flanders. Was acting bde comd. at Boxtel 1794. Sharpe fought as a young pte in the 33rd in this action. Arrived India with 33rd (and Sharpe) in 1797. Napoleon was to call him, contemptuously, the 'Sepoy General' after his victories at Assaye (where Sharpe saved his life and received a battlefield commission), Argaum and Gawilghur. Left India in 1805, shortly before Sharpe. By 33 he was maj-gen. In 1807 commanded reserve force in Danish campaign and won the action at Køge (in which Sharpe participated). Sept. 1809 created Viscount Wellington of Talavera; became Earl of Wellington Feb. 1812; marquess in Oct., promoted f-m. in Jul. 1813 after triumph at Vitória, made Duke of Wellington in 1814. Defeated Napoleon at Waterloo in 1815. Hit by musket balls on 3 occasions (Talavera, Salamanca and Orthez) but never seriously injured. Became C-in-C of Brit. Army on death of Duke of York in 1827 and Prime Minister following year. Retired from public life in 1846. Died 1852 aged 83; buried in St Paul's Cathedral.

West, Capt. Francis Commanded gren. coy 33rd Foot at Seringapatam, 1799.

Willsen, Capt. Henry Formerly of 50th Foot. Tasked with accompanying *Capt. Lavisser* on his mission in Denmark in 1807 but was murdered in London on orders of *Lavisser*. Sharpe replaced *Willsen* as 'minder' to *Lavisser*. In *SP*.

yards Spars from which square sails were hung. A man hung from the yard-arm was hanging from an extension to a yard.

Bibliography

London is the place of publication, unless otherwise specified

Brett-James, Anthony, *Life in Wellington's Army*, Allen & Unwin Ltd, 1972

Cope, Sir William H., *The History of the Rifle Brigade*, Chatto and Windus, 1887

Fortescue, Sir John W., *A History of the British Army*, Macmillan and Co., 1910–30

Glover, Michael, *Wellington's Army*, Douglas David and Charles Ltd, Canada, 1977

Hathaway, Eileen (ed.), *A Dorset Rifleman*, Shinglepicker Publications, 1995

Hibbert, Christopher (ed.), *The Recollections of Rifleman Harris*, Leo Cooper, 1970

Holmes, Richard, *Redcoat*, HarperCollins, 2001

Maxwell, Herbert, *The Life of Wellington*, Sampson Low, Marston and Co., 1907

Myatt, Frederick, *The Soldier's Trade*, Macdonald and Janes, 1974

Oatts, Lt-Col L. B., *Proud Heritage*, Thomas Nelson and Sons, 1959

Oman, Sir Charles W. C., *Wellington's Army*, Edward Arnold, 1912

Reid, Stuart, *Redcoat Officer*, Osprey, 2002

Surtees, William, *Twenty-Five Years in the Rifle Brigade*, Greenhill Books, 1996

Weller, Jac, *Wellington in India*, Longman, 1972

THE RICHARD SHARPE SERIES
by Bernard Cornwell

SHARPE'S TIGER

*Richard Sharpe and the Siege of
Seringapatam, 1799*
ISBN 0-06-093230-9 (trade paperback)
ISBN 0-06-101269-6 (mass market paperback)

The first of Richard Sharpe's India trilogy, in
which young Private Sharpe must battle both
man and beast behind enemy lines as the
British army fights its way through India.

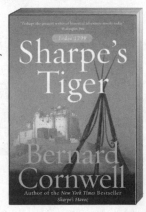

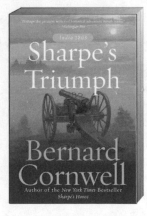

SHARPE'S TRIUMPH

*Richard Sharpe and the Battle of Assaye,
September 1803*
ISBN 0-06-095197-4 (trade paperback)
ISBN 0-06-074804-4 (mass market paperback)

Richard Sharpe must defeat the plans of a British
traitor and a native Indian mercenary army in this
second volume of the India trilogy.

SHARPE'S FORTRESS

*Richard Sharpe and the Siege of Gawilghur,
December 1803*
ISBN 0-06-109863-9 (trade paperback)
ISBN 0-06-101271-8 (mass market paperback)

In this explosive conclusion to the India trilogy,
Sharpe and Sir Arthur Wellesley's army try to
conquer an impregnable fort in a battle with
stakes both personal and professional.

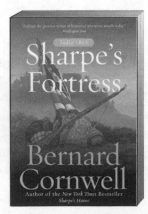

SHARPE'S TRAFALGAR

Richard Sharpe and the Battle of Trafalgar, 21 October 1805

ISBN 0-06-109862-0 (trade paperback)

Having secured a reputation as a fighting soldier in India, Ensign Richard Sharpe returns to England and gets caught up in one of the most spectacular naval battles in history.

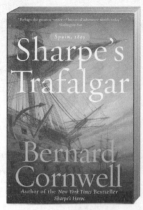

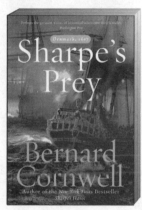

SHARPE'S PREY

Richard Sharpe and the Expedition to Denmark, 1807

ISBN 0-06-008453-7 (trade paperback)

Cornwell continues his popular series with Richard Sharpe's dangerous forays into Denmark, as he is fighting once again to keep the treacherous French troops at bay.

SHARPE'S HAVOC

Richard Sharpe and the Campaign in Northern Portugal, Spring 1809

ISBN 0-06-056670-1 (trade paperback)

It is 1809, and Sharpe finds himself once again in Portugal, fighting the savage armies of Napoléon Bonaparte, as they try to bring the Iberian Peninsula under their control.

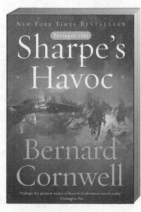

SHARPE'S ESCAPE

Richard Sharpe and the Bussaco Campaign, 1810
ISBN 0-06-056095-9 (mass market paperback)
ISBN 0-06-059172-2 (unabridged audio)

Sharpe has made enemies among the Portuguese,
and when the British army falls back through
Coimbra, he and Sergeant Harper are lured into a
trap designed to kill them.

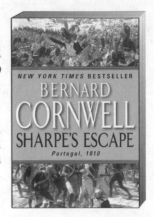

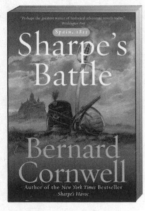

SHARPE'S BATTLE

Richard Sharpe and the Battle of
Fuentes de Oñoro, May 1811
ISBN 0-06-093228-7 (trade paperback)

As Napoléon threatens to crush Britain on the
battlefield, Lt. Col. Richard Sharpe leads a ragtag
army to exact personal revenge.

SHARPE'S DEVIL

Richard Sharpe and the Emperor, 1820–21
ISBN 0-06-093229-5 (trade paperback)

An honored veteran of the Napoleonic Wars,
Lt. Col. Richard Sharpe is drawn into a deadly
battle, both on land and on the high seas.

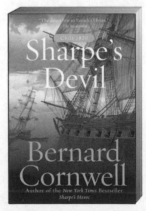